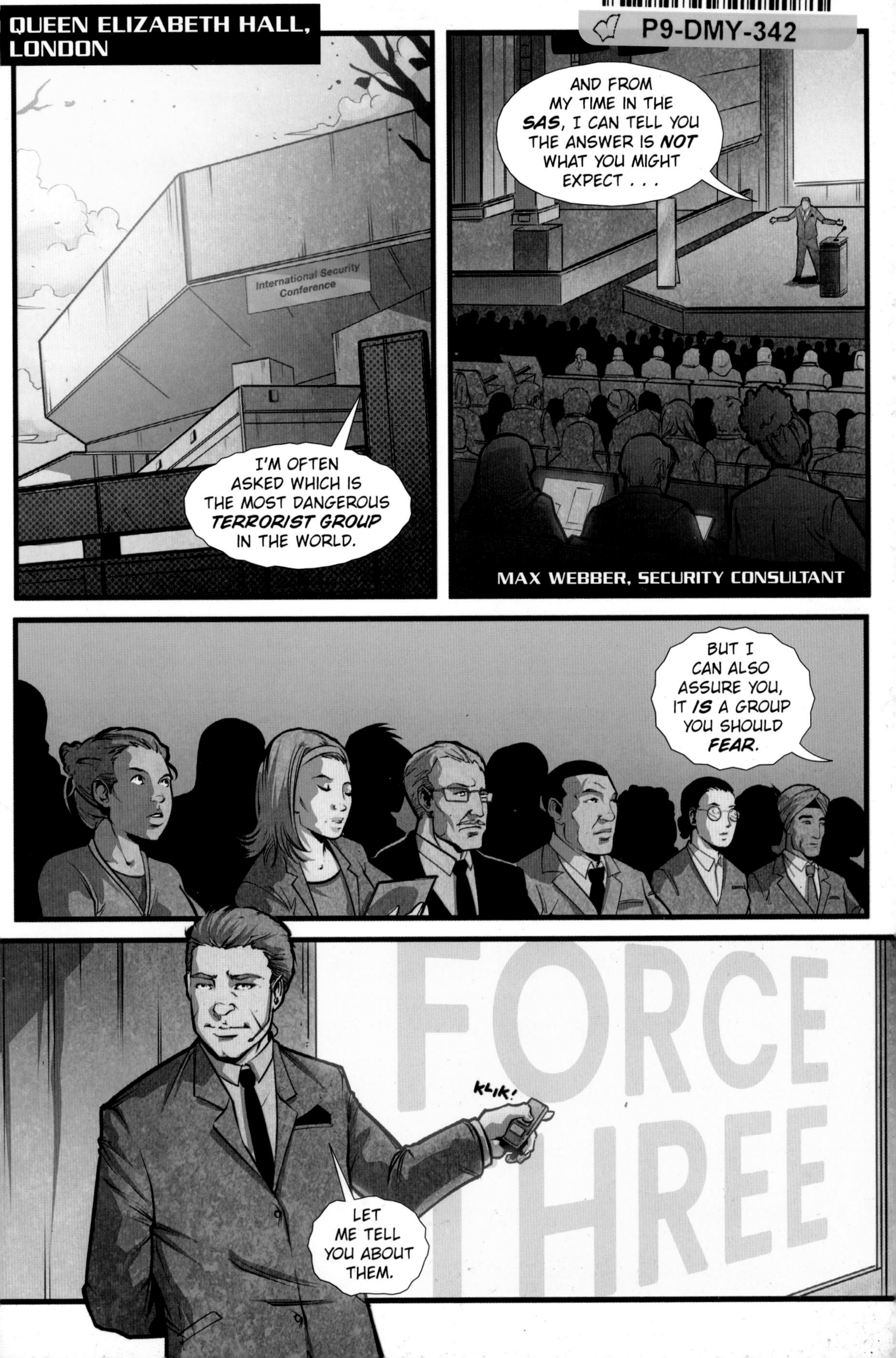

QUEEN ELIZABETH HALL, LONDON
International Security Conference
I'M OFTEN ASKED WHICH IS THE MOST DANGEROUS TERRORIST GROUP IN THE WORLD.
AND FROM MY TIME IN THE SAS, I CAN TELL YOU THE ANSWER IS NOT WHAT YOU MIGHT EXPECT . . .
MAX WEBBER, SECURITY CONSULTANT
BUT I CAN ALSO ASSURE YOU, IT IS A GROUP YOU SHOULD FEAR.
FORCE THREE
KLIK!
LET ME TELL YOU ABOUT THEM.

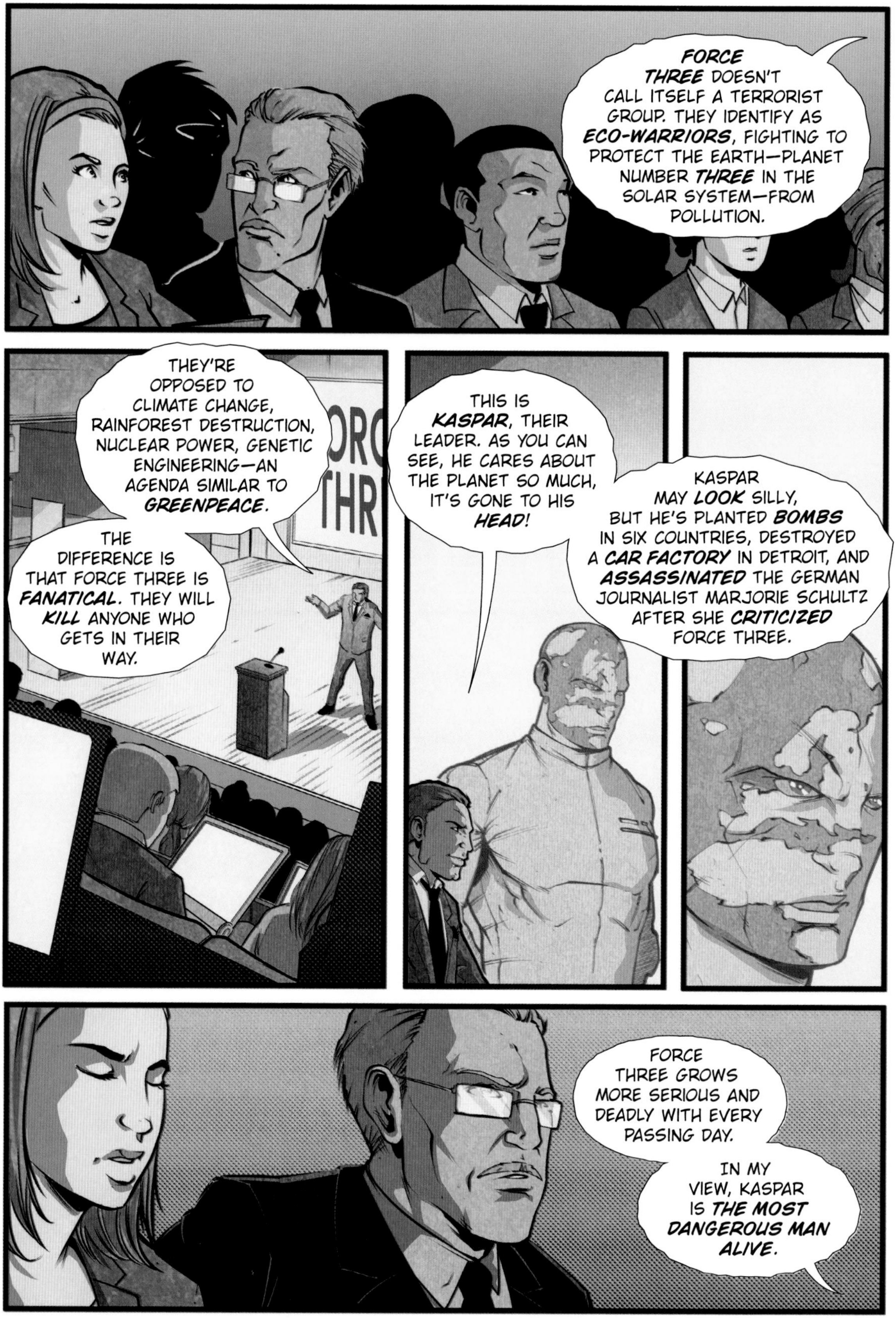
FORCE THREE DOESN'T CALL ITSELF A TERRORIST GROUP. THEY IDENTIFY AS ECO-WARRIORS, FIGHTING TO PROTECT THE EARTH—PLANET NUMBER THREE IN THE SOLAR SYSTEM—FROM POLLUTION.
THEY'RE OPPOSED TO CLIMATE CHANGE, RAINFOREST DESTRUCTION, NUCLEAR POWER, GENETIC ENGINEERING—AN AGENDA SIMILAR TO GREENPEACE.
THE DIFFERENCE IS THAT FORCE THREE IS FANATICAL. THEY WILL KILL ANYONE WHO GETS IN THEIR WAY.
THIS IS KASPAR, THEIR LEADER. AS YOU CAN SEE, HE CARES ABOUT THE PLANET SO MUCH, IT'S GONE TO HIS HEAD!
KASPAR MAY LOOK SILLY, BUT HE'S PLANTED BOMBS IN SIX COUNTRIES, DESTROYED A CAR FACTORY IN DETROIT, AND ASSASSINATED THE GERMAN JOURNALIST MARJORIE SCHULTZ AFTER SHE CRITICIZED FORCE THREE.
FORCE THREE GROWS MORE SERIOUS AND DEADLY WITH EVERY PASSING DAY.
IN MY VIEW, KASPAR IS THE MOST DANGEROUS MAN ALIVE.

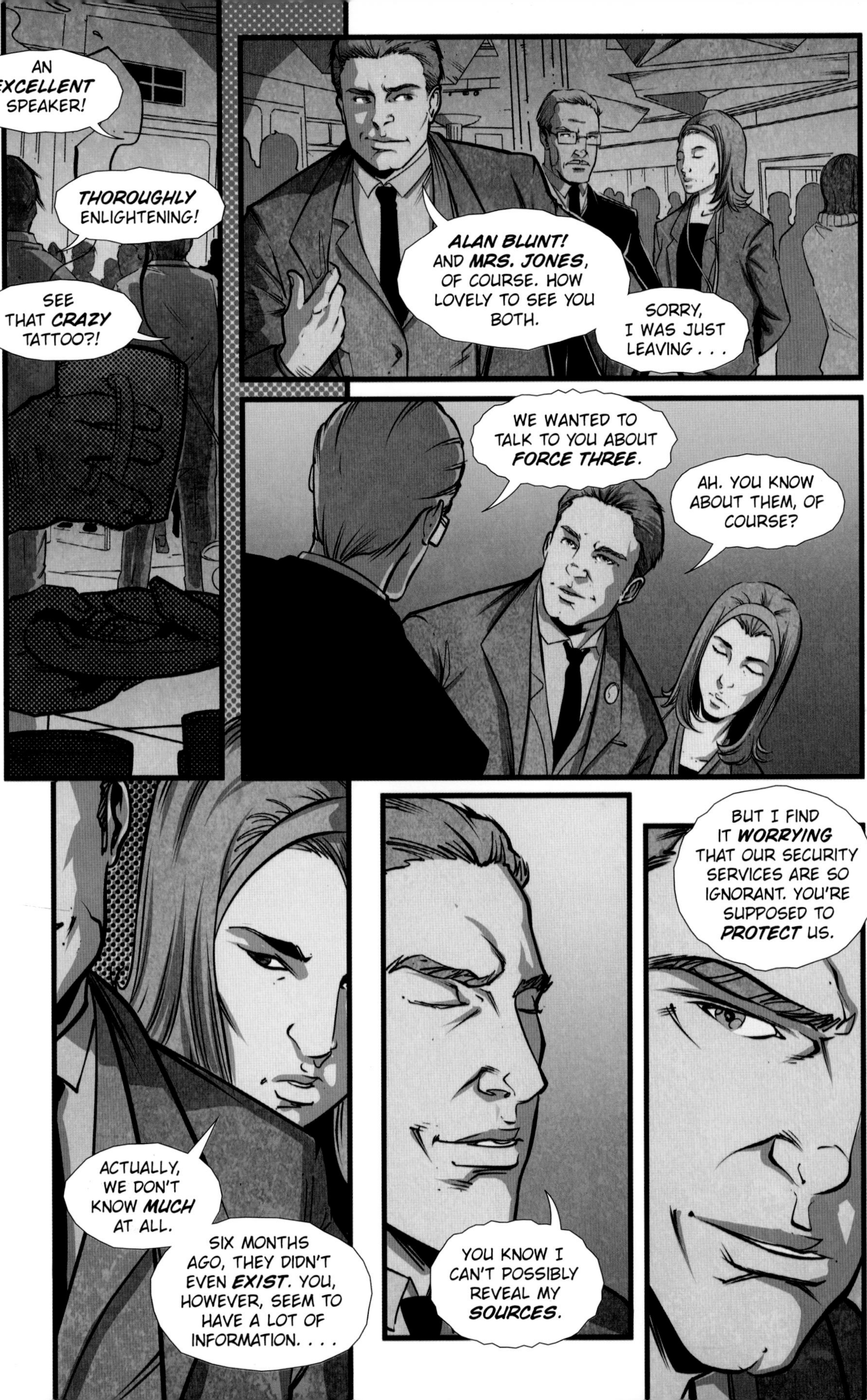

AN EXCELLENT SPEAKER!
THOROUGHLY ENLIGHTENING!
SEE THAT CRAZY TATTOO?!
ALAN BLUNT! AND MRS. JONES, OF COURSE. HOW LOVELY TO SEE YOU BOTH.
SORRY, I WAS JUST LEAVING . . .
WE WANTED TO TALK TO YOU ABOUT FORCE THREE.
AH. YOU KNOW ABOUT THEM, OF COURSE?
ACTUALLY, WE DON'T KNOW MUCH AT ALL.
SIX MONTHS AGO, THEY DIDN'T EVEN EXIST. YOU, HOWEVER, SEEM TO HAVE A LOT OF INFORMATION. . . .
YOU KNOW I CAN'T POSSIBLY REVEAL MY SOURCES.
BUT I FIND IT WORRYING THAT OUR SECURITY SERVICES ARE SO IGNORANT. YOU'RE SUPPOSED TO PROTECT US.

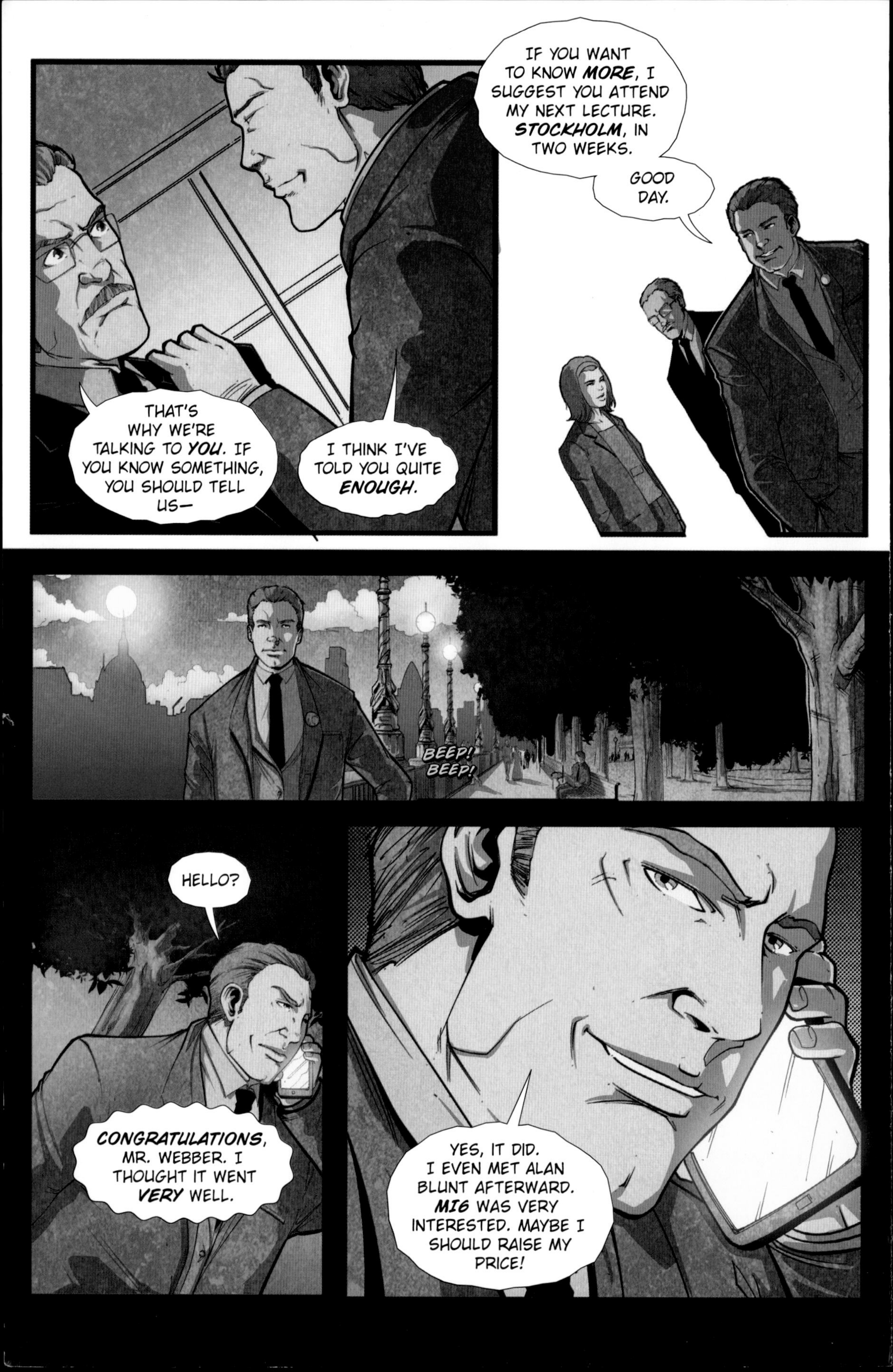
THAT'S WHY WE'RE TALKING TO *YOU*. IF YOU KNOW SOMETHING, YOU SHOULD TELL US—
I THINK I'VE TOLD YOU QUITE *ENOUGH*.
IF YOU WANT TO KNOW *MORE*, I SUGGEST YOU ATTEND MY NEXT LECTURE. *STOCKHOLM*, IN TWO WEEKS.
GOOD DAY.
BEEP! BEEP!
HELLO?
CONGRATULATIONS, MR. WEBBER. I THOUGHT IT WENT *VERY* WELL.
YES, IT DID. I EVEN MET ALAN BLUNT AFTERWARD. *MI6* WAS VERY INTERESTED. MAYBE I SHOULD RAISE MY PRICE!

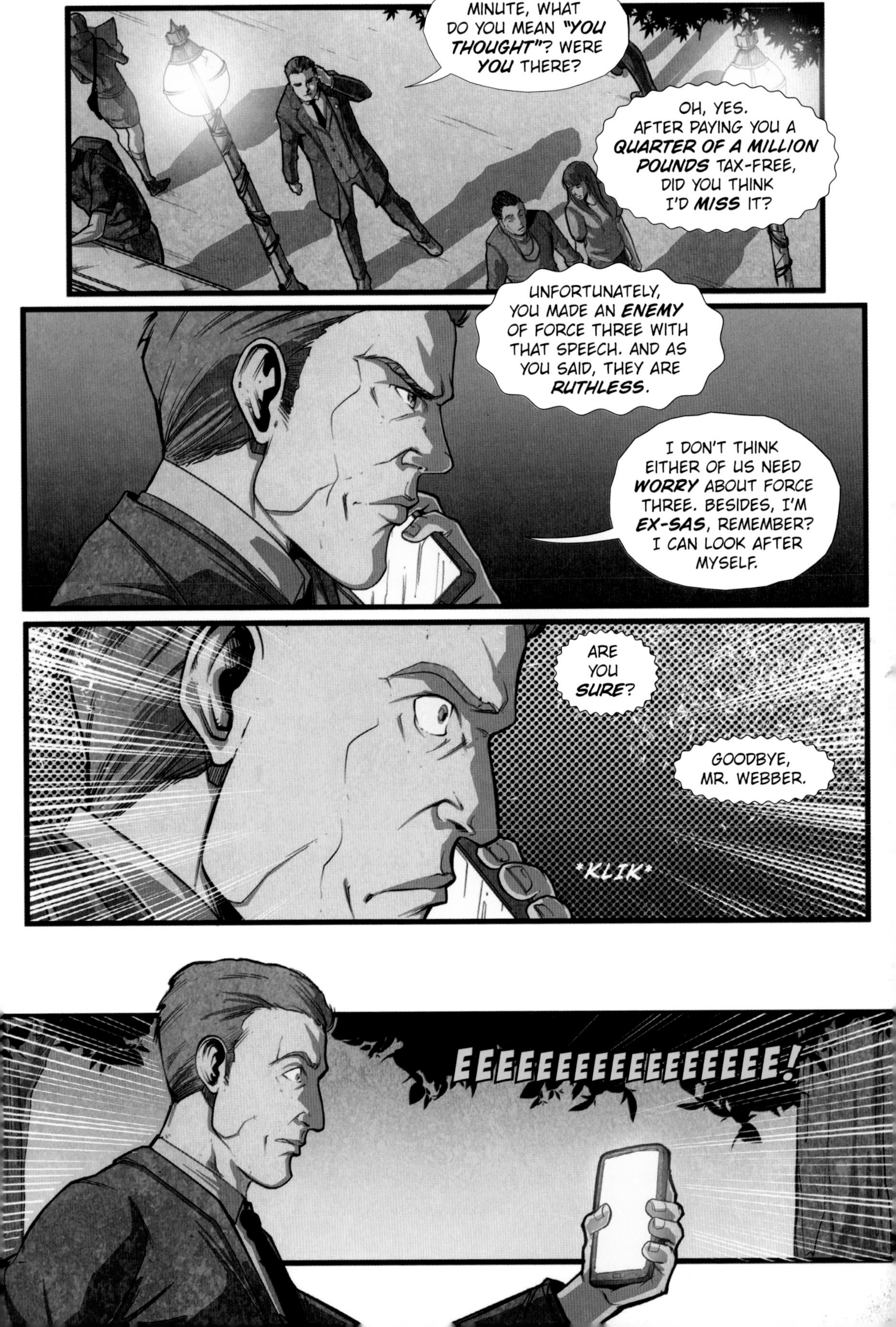
WAIT A MINUTE, WHAT DO YOU MEAN "YOU THOUGHT"? WERE YOU THERE?
OH, YES. AFTER PAYING YOU A QUARTER OF A MILLION POUNDS TAX-FREE, DID YOU THINK I'D MISS IT?
UNFORTUNATELY, YOU MADE AN ENEMY OF FORCE THREE WITH THAT SPEECH. AND AS YOU SAID, THEY ARE RUTHLESS.
I DON'T THINK EITHER OF US NEED WORRY ABOUT FORCE THREE. BESIDES, I'M EX-SAS, REMEMBER? I CAN LOOK AFTER MYSELF.
ARE YOU SURE?
GOODBYE, MR. WEBBER.
KLIK
EEEEEEEEEEEEEEEE!

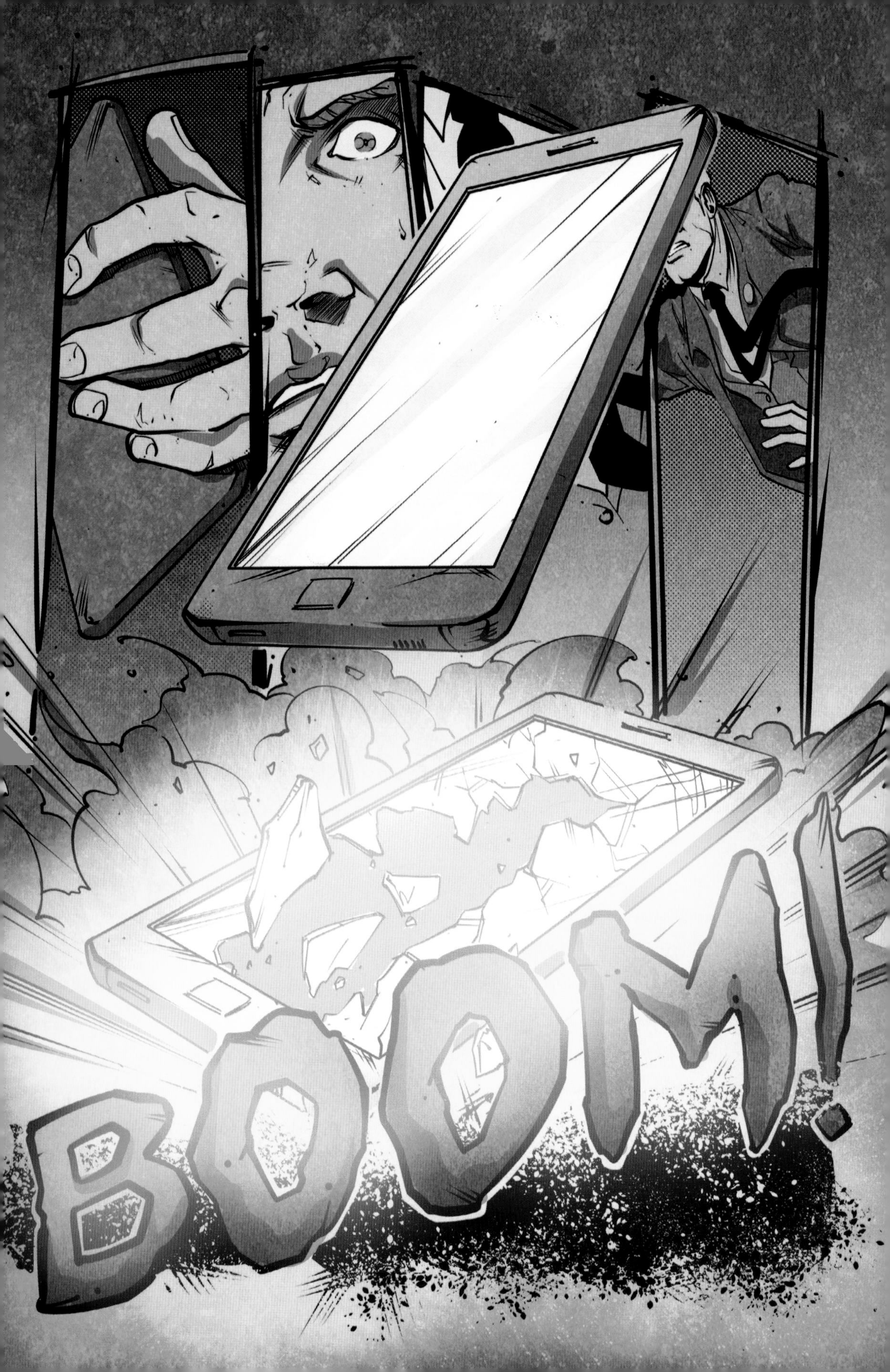
BOOM!

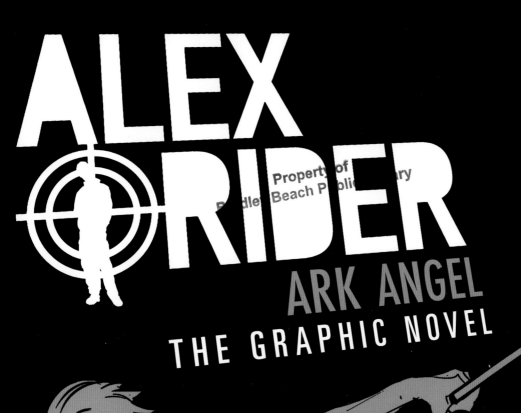

ALEX RIDER

ARK ANGEL

THE GRAPHIC NOVEL

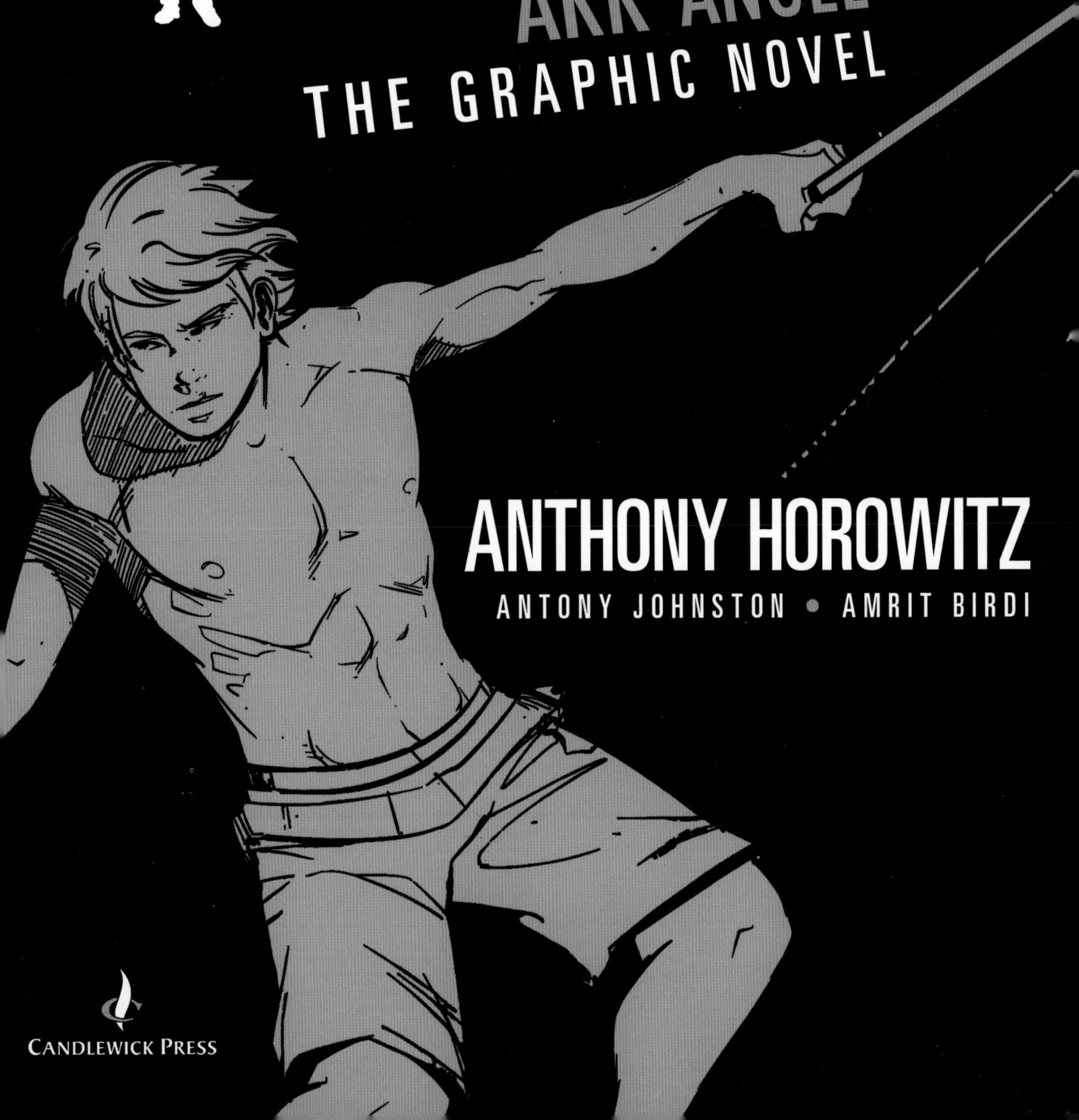

ANTHONY HOROWITZ

ANTONY JOHNSTON • AMRIT BIRDI

CANDLEWICK PRESS

Copyright © 2020 by Walker Books Ltd.
Based on the original novel *Ark Angel* copyright © 2005
Stormbreaker Productions Ltd.
Trademarks © 2003 Stormbreaker Productions Ltd.
Alex Rider™, Boy with Torch Logo™, AR Logo™

Adapted by Antony Johnston
Illustrations by Amrit Birdi & Co. Ltd

First US edition 2020

Library of Congress Catalog Card Number pending
ISBN 978-1-5362-0733-0

20 21 22 23 24 25 APS 10 9 8 7 6 5 4 3 2 1

Printed in Humen, Dongguan, China

This book was typeset in Wild Words and Serpentine Bold.

Candlewick Press
99 Dover Street
Somerville, Massachusetts 02144

www.candlewick.com

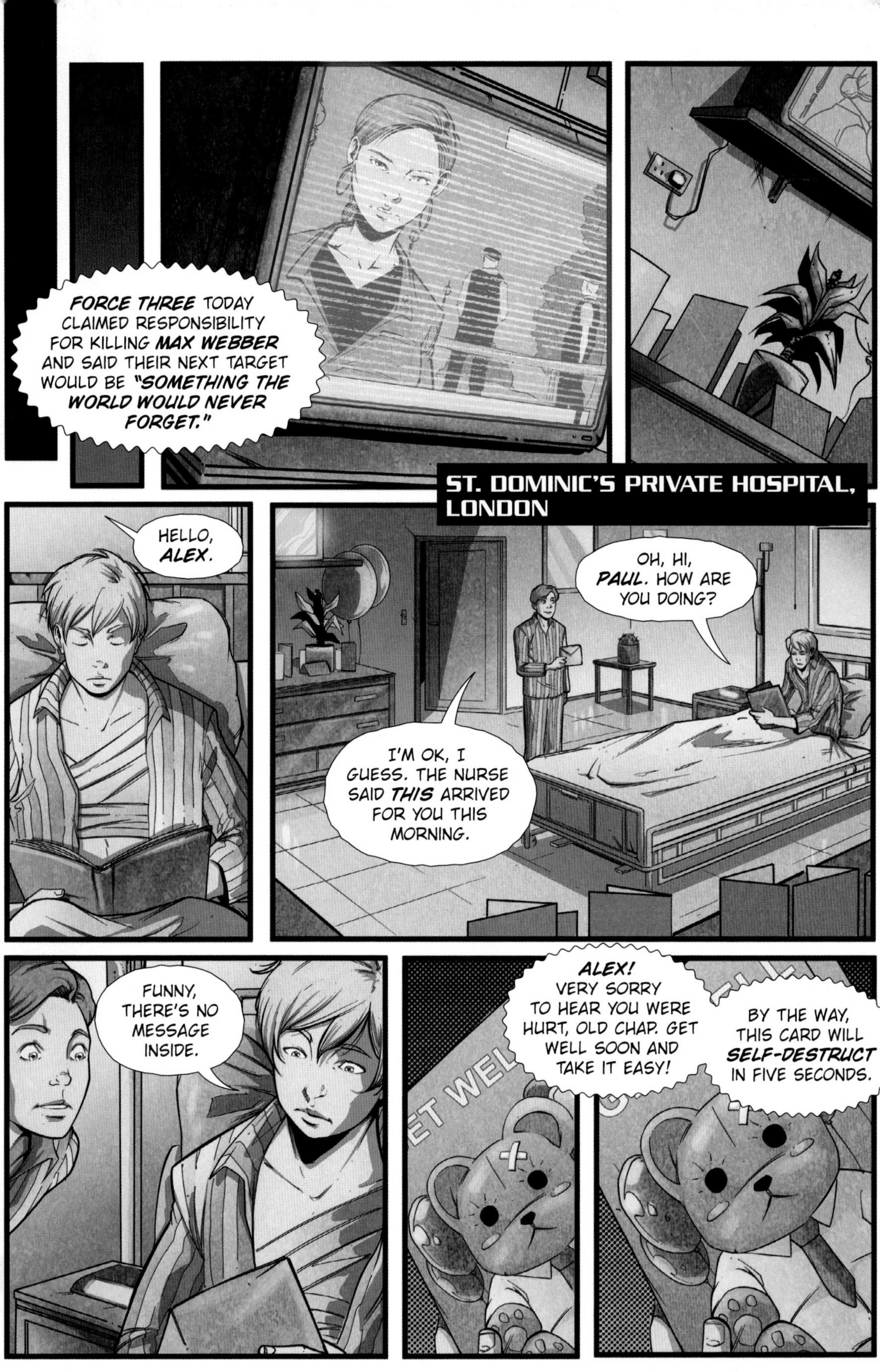
FORCE THREE TODAY CLAIMED RESPONSIBILITY FOR KILLING MAX WEBBER AND SAID THEIR NEXT TARGET WOULD BE "SOMETHING THE WORLD WOULD NEVER FORGET."
ST. DOMINIC'S PRIVATE HOSPITAL, LONDON
HELLO, ALEX.
OH, HI, PAUL. HOW ARE YOU DOING?
I'M OK, I GUESS. THE NURSE SAID THIS ARRIVED FOR YOU THIS MORNING.
FUNNY, THERE'S NO MESSAGE INSIDE.
ALEX! VERY SORRY TO HEAR YOU WERE HURT, OLD CHAP. GET WELL SOON AND TAKE IT EASY!
BY THE WAY, THIS CARD WILL SELF-DESTRUCT IN FIVE SECONDS.

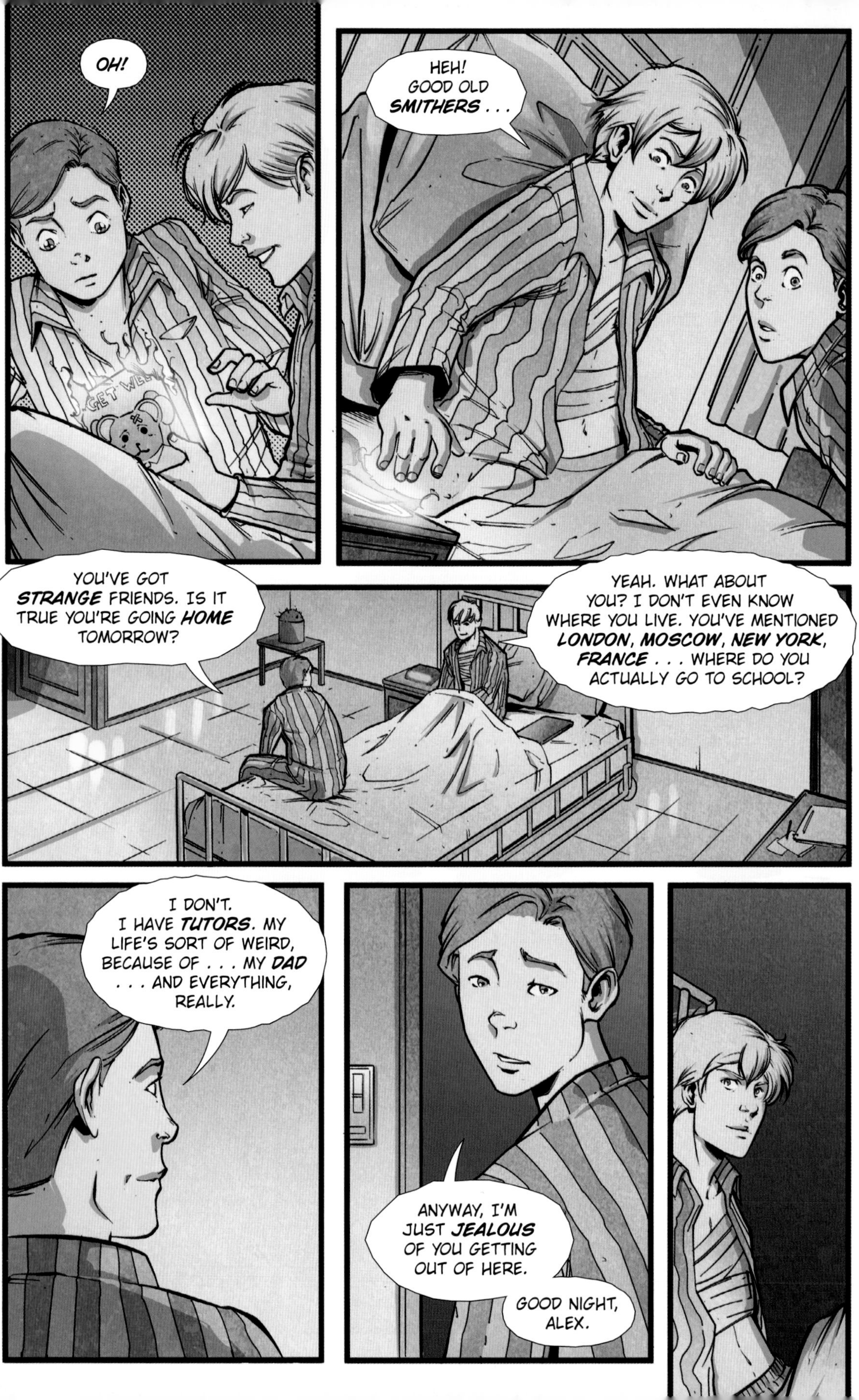
OH!
GET WELL
HEH! GOOD OLD SMITHERS . . .
YOU'VE GOT STRANGE FRIENDS. IS IT TRUE YOU'RE GOING HOME TOMORROW?
YEAH. WHAT ABOUT YOU? I DON'T EVEN KNOW WHERE YOU LIVE. YOU'VE MENTIONED LONDON, MOSCOW, NEW YORK, FRANCE . . . WHERE DO YOU ACTUALLY GO TO SCHOOL?
I DON'T. I HAVE TUTORS. MY LIFE'S SORT OF WEIRD, BECAUSE OF . . . MY DAD . . . AND EVERYTHING, REALLY.
ANYWAY, I'M JUST JEALOUS OF YOU GETTING OUT OF HERE.
GOOD NIGHT, ALEX.

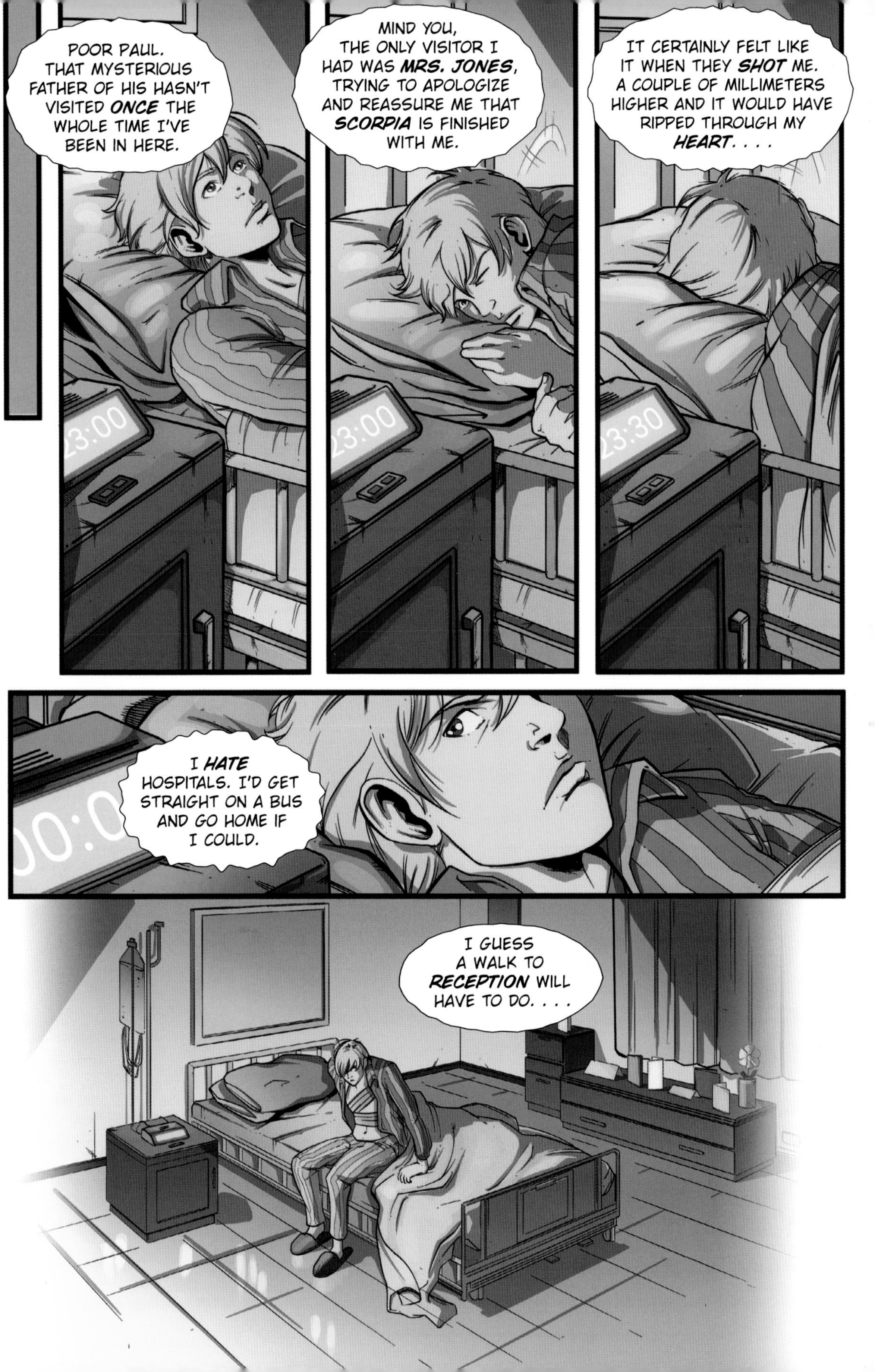
POOR PAUL. THAT MYSTERIOUS FATHER OF HIS HASN'T VISITED **ONCE** THE WHOLE TIME I'VE BEEN IN HERE.
MIND YOU, THE ONLY VISITOR I HAD WAS **MRS. JONES**, TRYING TO APOLOGIZE AND REASSURE ME THAT **SCORPIA** IS FINISHED WITH ME.
IT CERTAINLY FELT LIKE IT WHEN THEY **SHOT** ME. A COUPLE OF MILLIMETERS HIGHER AND IT WOULD HAVE RIPPED THROUGH MY **HEART**. . . .
23:00
23:00
23:30
I **HATE** HOSPITALS. I'D GET STRAIGHT ON A BUS AND GO HOME IF I COULD.
I GUESS A WALK TO **RECEPTION** WILL HAVE TO DO. . . .

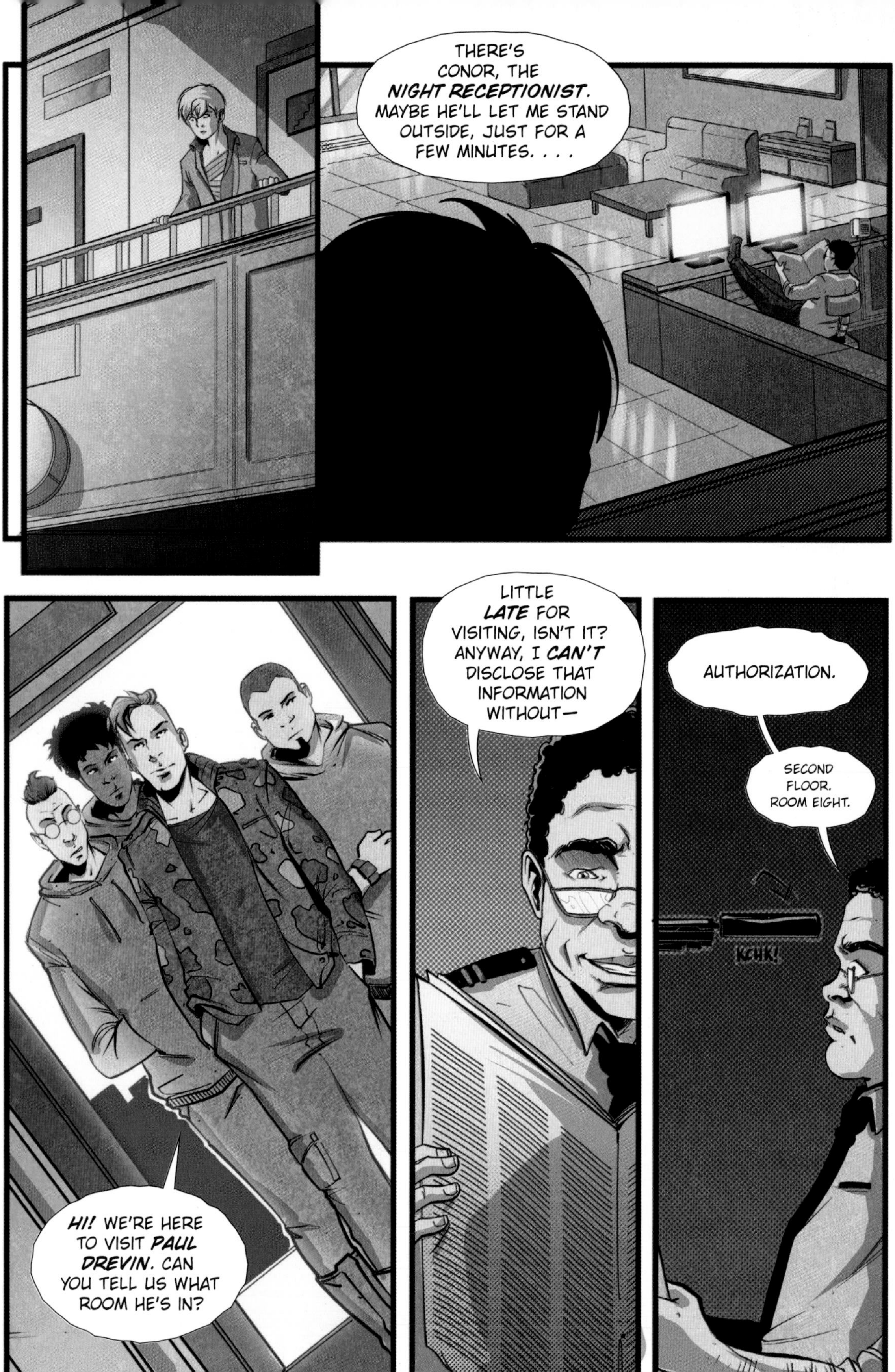
THERE'S CONOR, THE NIGHT RECEPTIONIST. MAYBE HE'LL LET ME STAND OUTSIDE, JUST FOR A FEW MINUTES. . . .
HI! WE'RE HERE TO VISIT PAUL DREVIN. CAN YOU TELL US WHAT ROOM HE'S IN?
LITTLE LATE FOR VISITING, ISN'T IT? ANYWAY, I CAN'T DISCLOSE THAT INFORMATION WITHOUT—
AUTHORIZATION.
SECOND FLOOR. ROOM EIGHT.
KCHK!

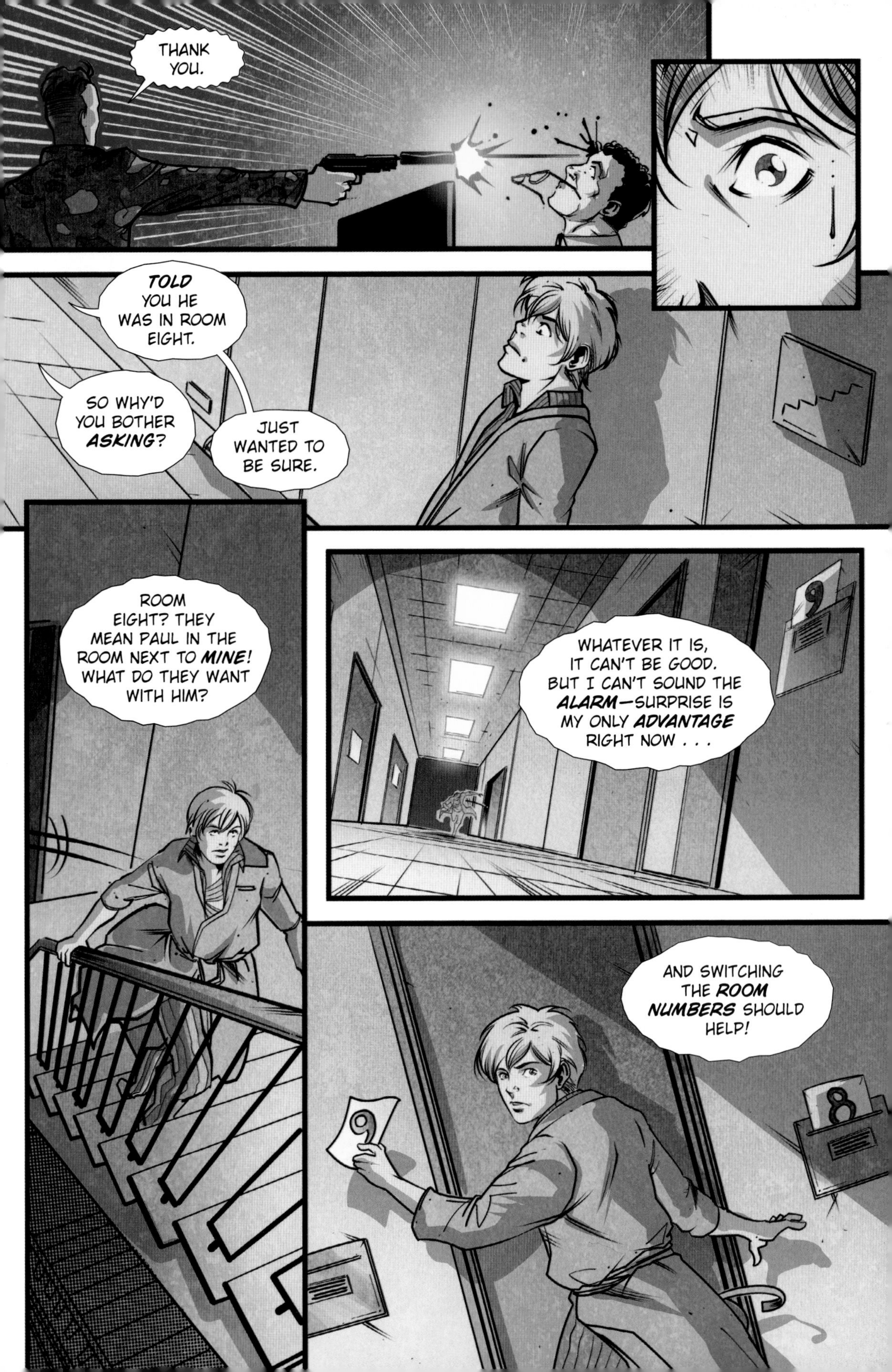
THANK YOU.
TOLD YOU HE WAS IN ROOM EIGHT.
SO WHY'D YOU BOTHER ASKING?
JUST WANTED TO BE SURE.
ROOM EIGHT? THEY MEAN PAUL IN THE ROOM NEXT TO MINE! WHAT DO THEY WANT WITH HIM?
WHATEVER IT IS, IT CAN'T BE GOOD. BUT I CAN'T SOUND THE ALARM—SURPRISE IS MY ONLY ADVANTAGE RIGHT NOW . . .
9
AND SWITCHING THE ROOM NUMBERS SHOULD HELP!
9
8

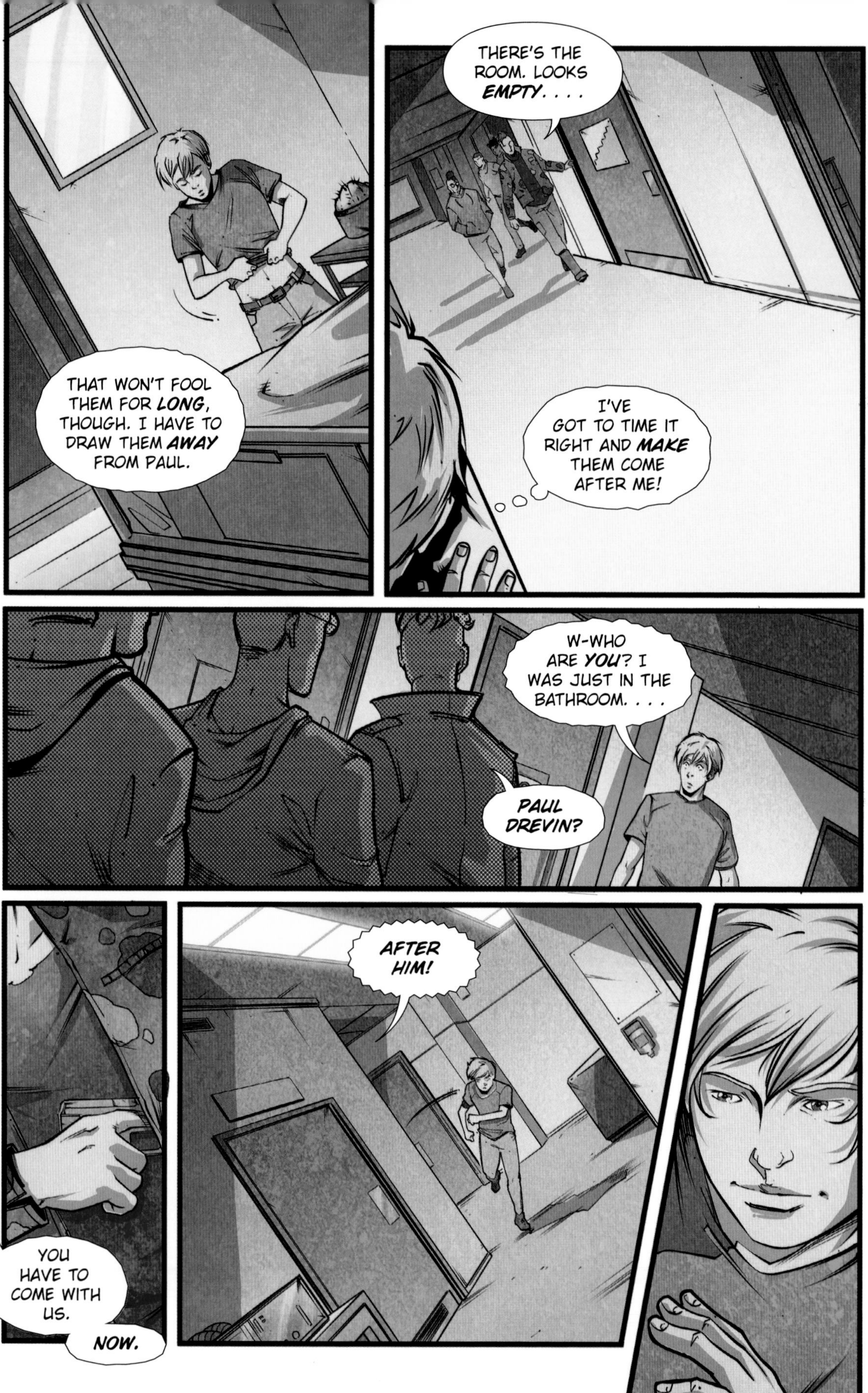
THAT WON'T FOOL THEM FOR LONG, THOUGH. I HAVE TO DRAW THEM AWAY FROM PAUL.
THERE'S THE ROOM. LOOKS EMPTY. . . .
I'VE GOT TO TIME IT RIGHT AND MAKE THEM COME AFTER ME!
W-WHO ARE YOU? I WAS JUST IN THE BATHROOM. . . .
PAUL DREVIN?
YOU HAVE TO COME WITH US.
NOW.
AFTER HIM!

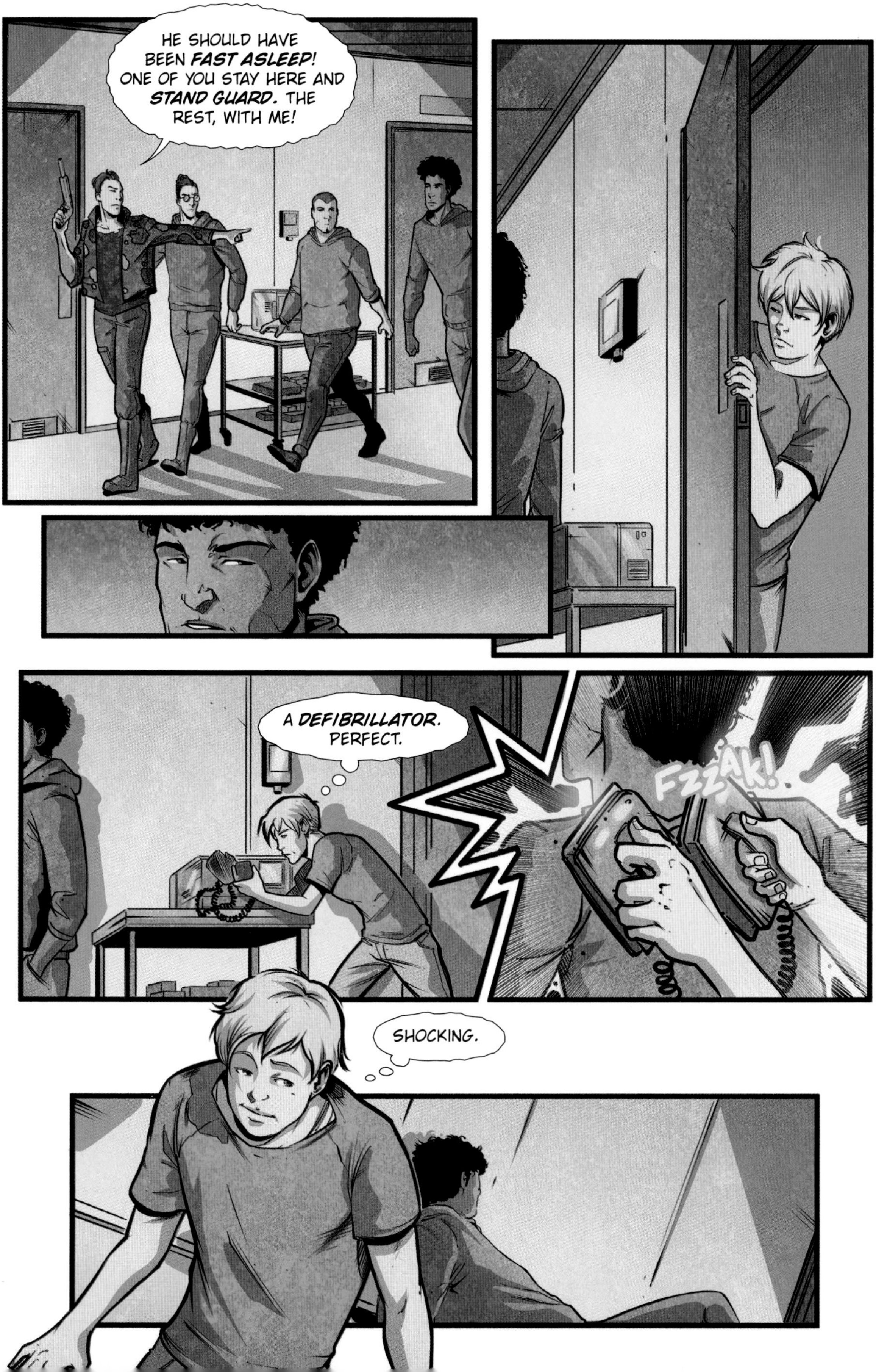
HE SHOULD HAVE BEEN FAST ASLEEP! ONE OF YOU STAY HERE AND STAND GUARD. THE REST, WITH ME!
A DEFIBRILLATOR. PERFECT.
FZZAK!
SHOCKING.

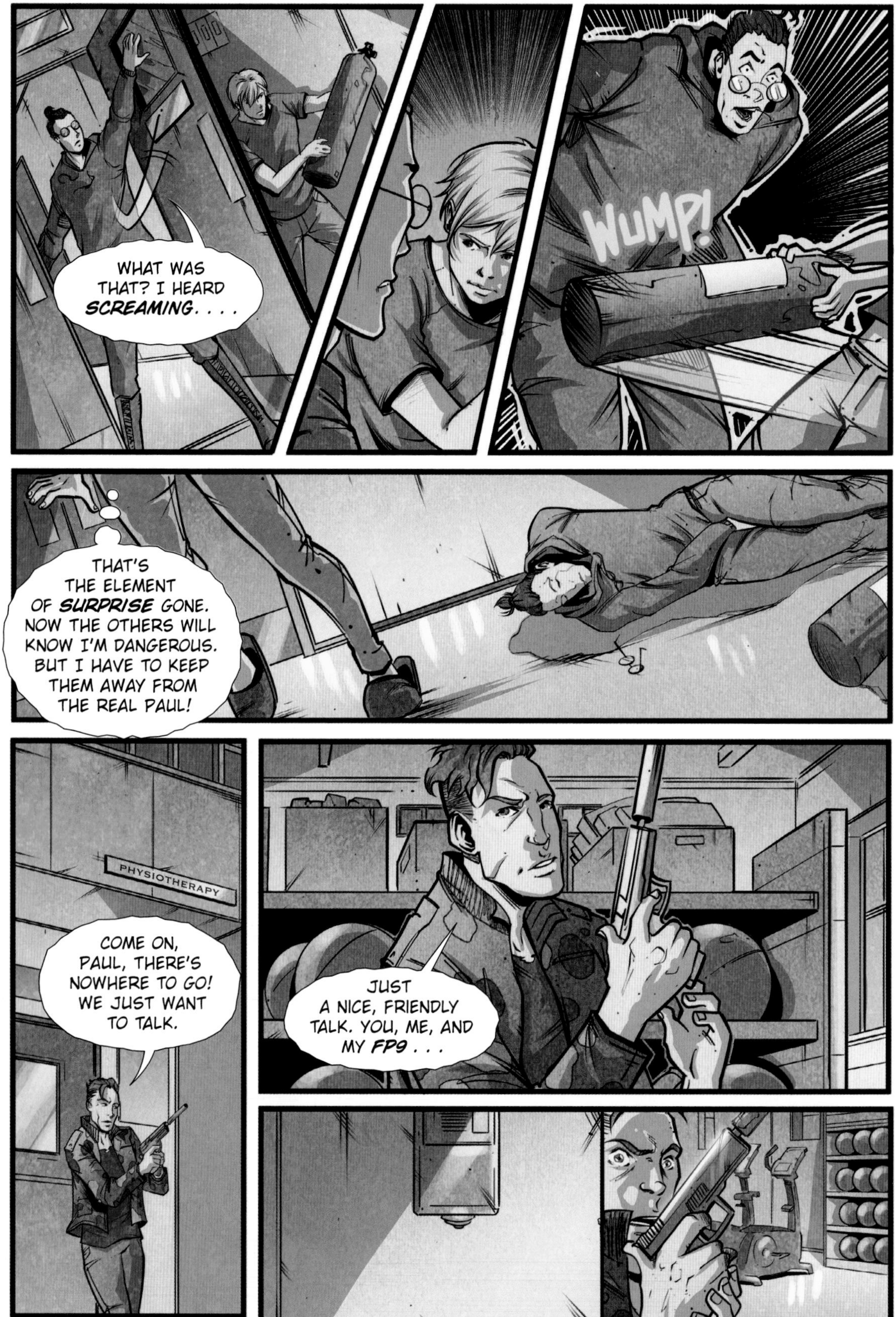
WHAT WAS THAT? I HEARD SCREAMING. . . .
WUMP!
THAT'S THE ELEMENT OF SURPRISE GONE. NOW THE OTHERS WILL KNOW I'M DANGEROUS. BUT I HAVE TO KEEP THEM AWAY FROM THE REAL PAUL!
PHYSIOTHERAPY
COME ON, PAUL, THERE'S NOWHERE TO GO! WE JUST WANT TO TALK.
JUST A NICE, FRIENDLY TALK. YOU, ME, AND MY FP9 . . .

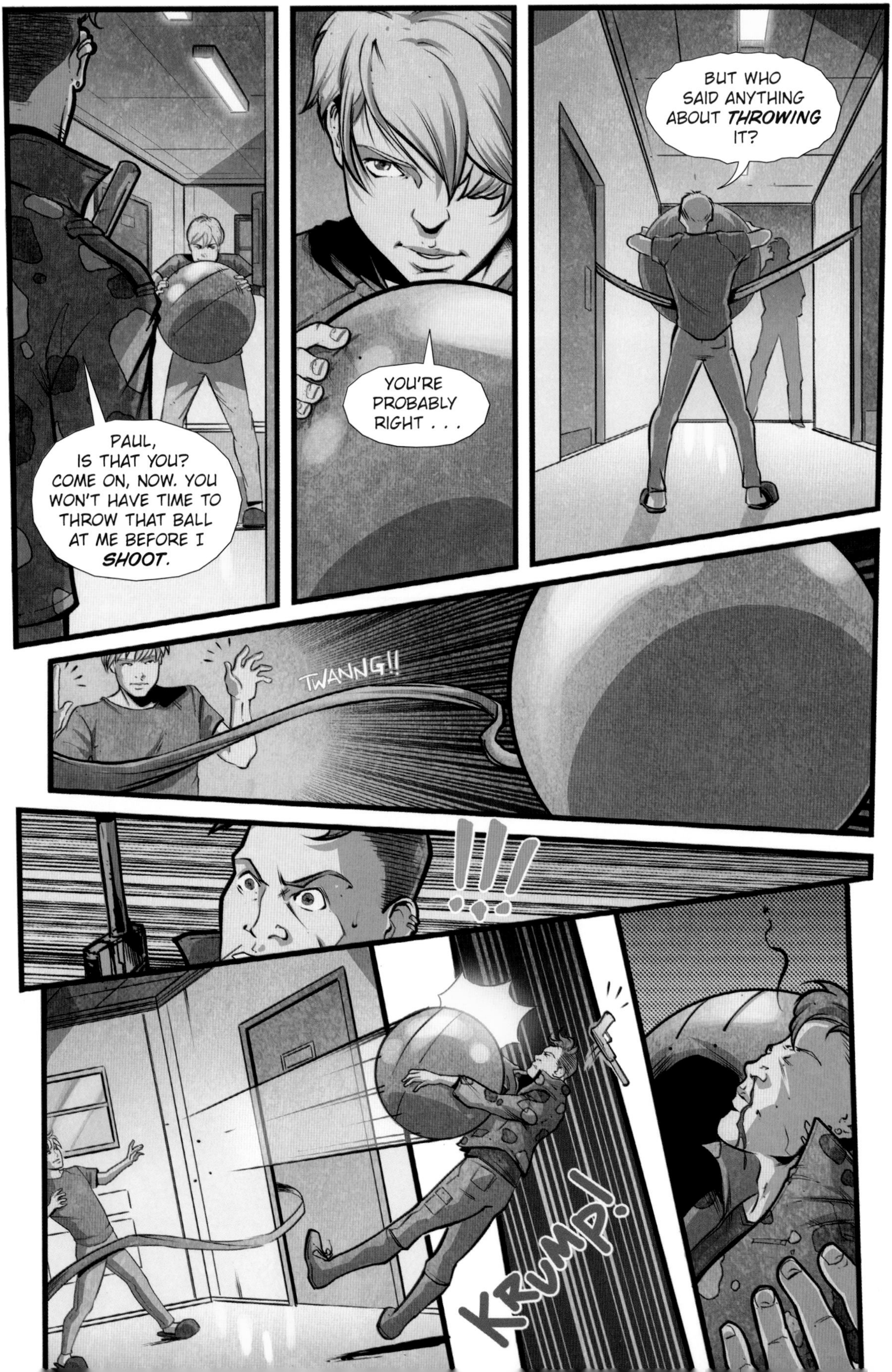
PAUL, IS THAT YOU? COME ON, NOW. YOU WON'T HAVE TIME TO THROW THAT BALL AT ME BEFORE I **SHOOT**.
YOU'RE PROBABLY RIGHT . . .
BUT WHO SAID ANYTHING ABOUT ***THROWING*** IT?
TWANNG!!
!!!
KRUMP!

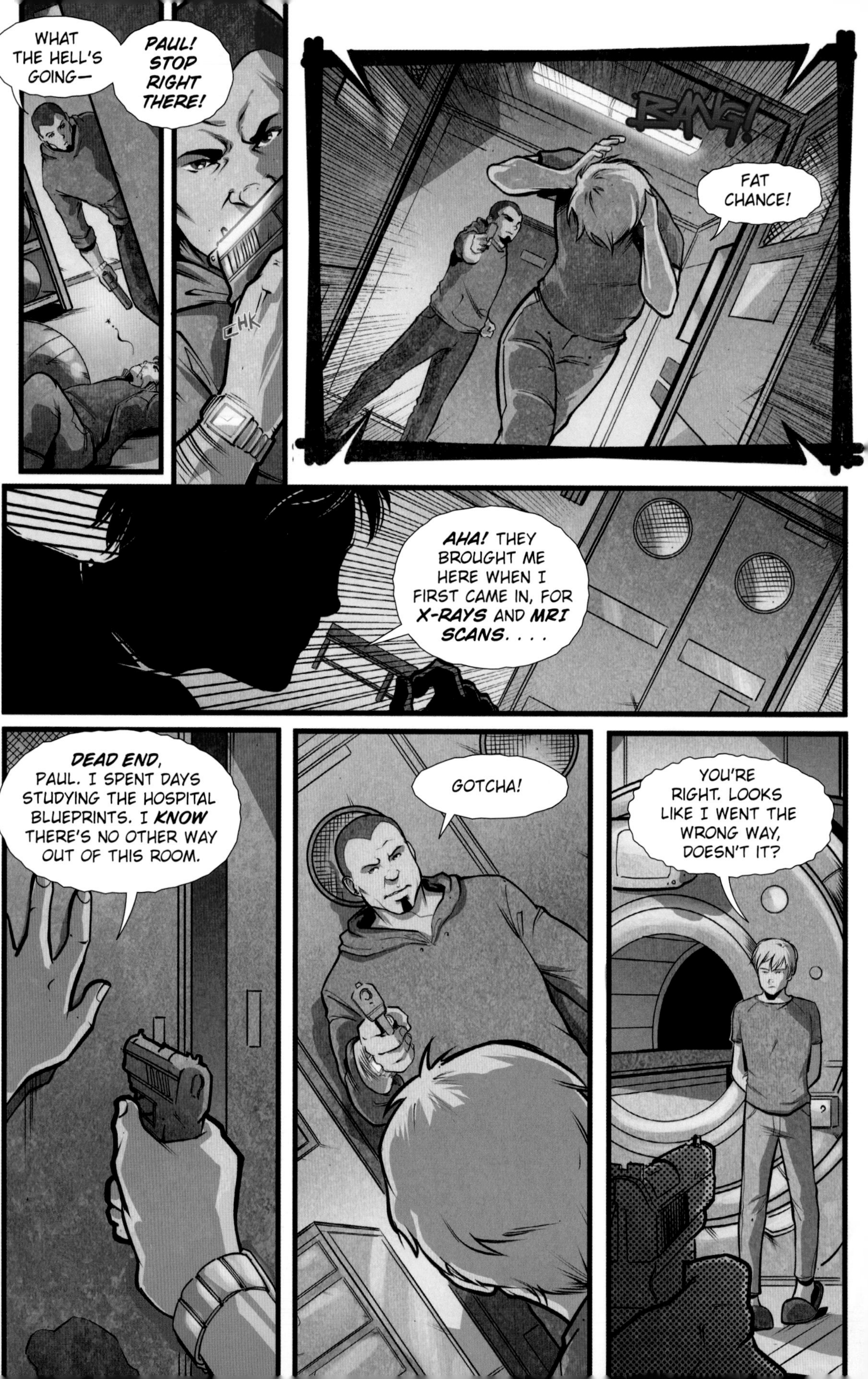
WHAT THE HELL'S GOING—
PAUL! STOP RIGHT THERE!
CHK
BANG!
FAT CHANCE!
AHA! THEY BROUGHT ME HERE WHEN I FIRST CAME IN, FOR X-RAYS AND MRI SCANS. . . .
DEAD END, PAUL. I SPENT DAYS STUDYING THE HOSPITAL BLUEPRINTS. I KNOW THERE'S NO OTHER WAY OUT OF THIS ROOM.
GOTCHA!
YOU'RE RIGHT. LOOKS LIKE I WENT THE WRONG WAY, DOESN'T IT?

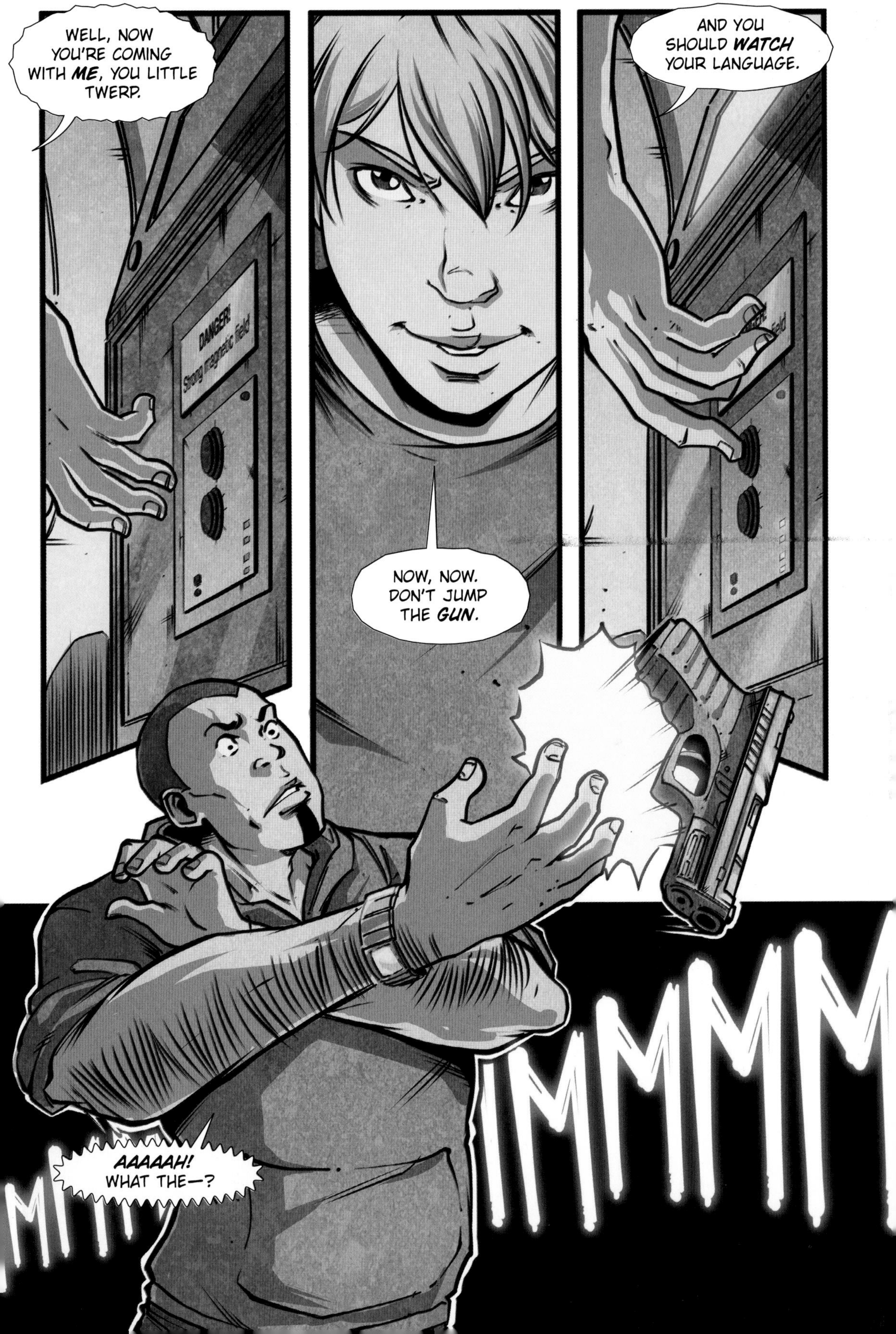
WELL, NOW YOU'RE COMING WITH ***ME***, YOU LITTLE TWERP.
DANGER! Strong magnetic field
NOW, NOW. DON'T JUMP THE ***GUN***.
AND YOU SHOULD ***WATCH*** YOUR LANGUAGE.
AAAAAH! WHAT THE—?

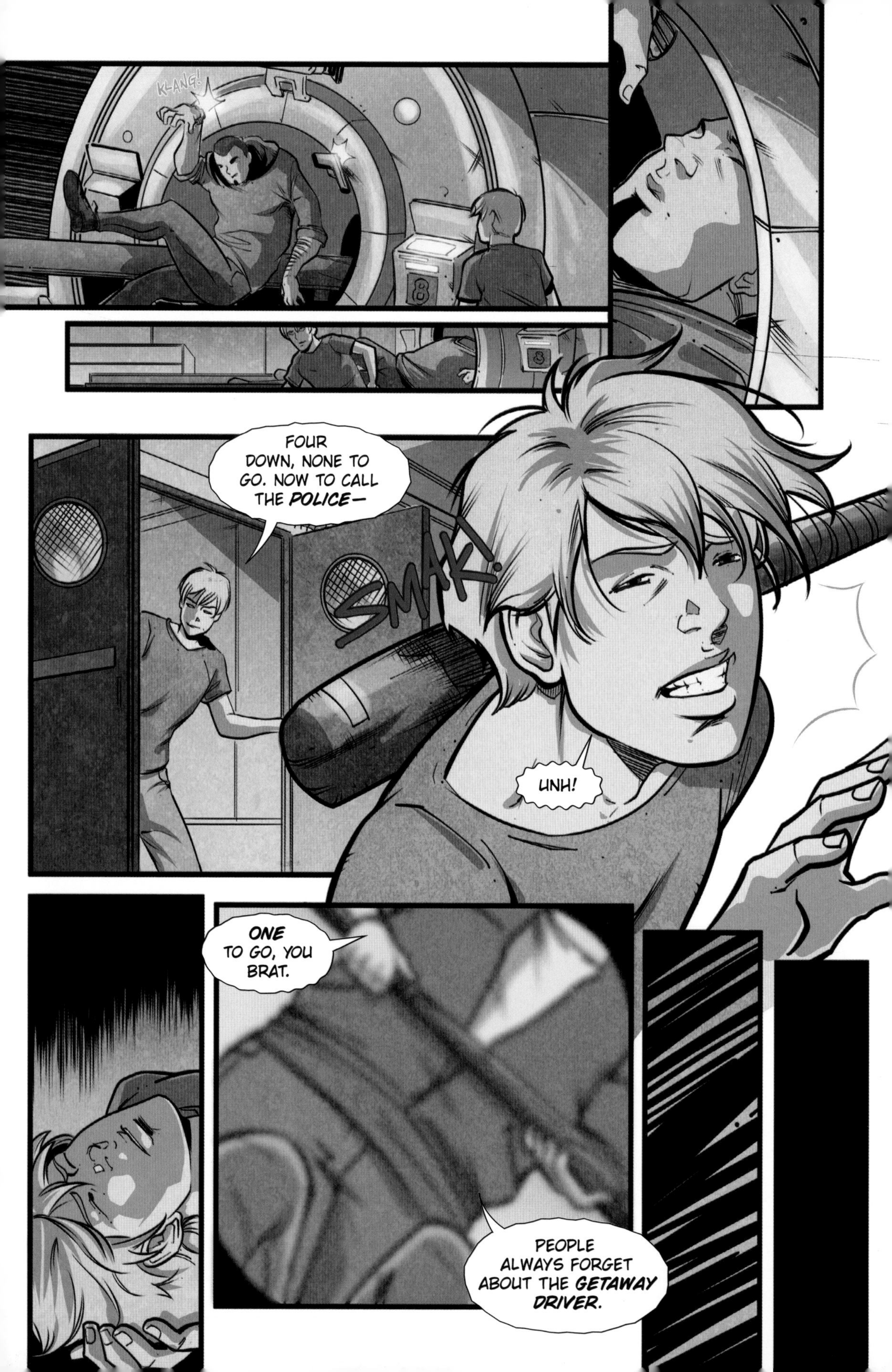
KLANG!
FOUR DOWN, NONE TO GO. NOW TO CALL THE POLICE—
SMAK!
UNH!
ONE TO GO, YOU BRAT.
PEOPLE ALWAYS FORGET ABOUT THE GETAWAY DRIVER.

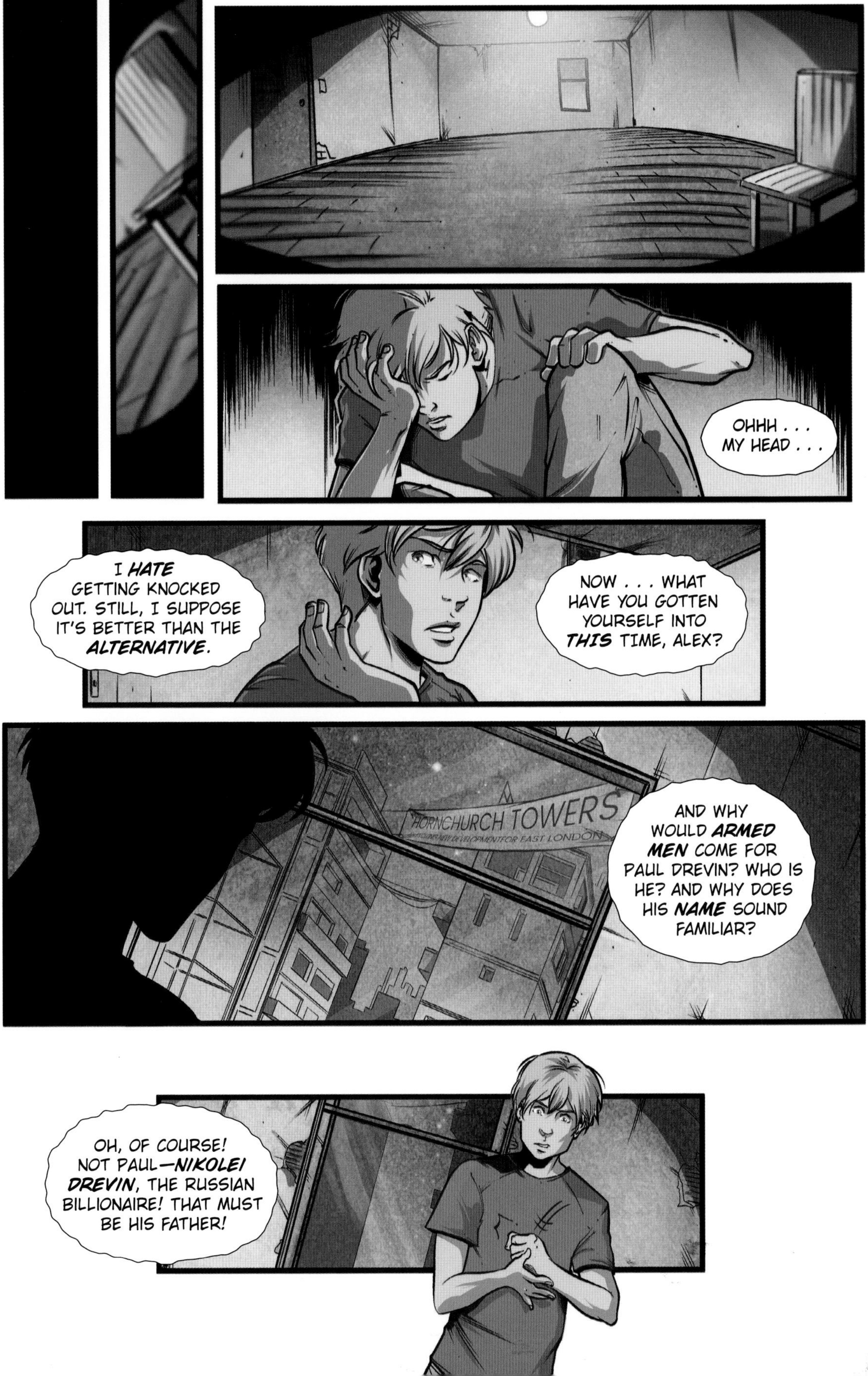
OHHH . . . MY HEAD . . .
I HATE GETTING KNOCKED OUT. STILL, I SUPPOSE IT'S BETTER THAN THE ALTERNATIVE.
NOW . . . WHAT HAVE YOU GOTTEN YOURSELF INTO THIS TIME, ALEX?
HORNCHURCH TOWERS
AND WHY WOULD ARMED MEN COME FOR PAUL DREVIN? WHO IS HE? AND WHY DOES HIS NAME SOUND FAMILIAR?
OH, OF COURSE! NOT PAUL—NIKOLEI DREVIN, THE RUSSIAN BILLIONAIRE! THAT MUST BE HIS FATHER!

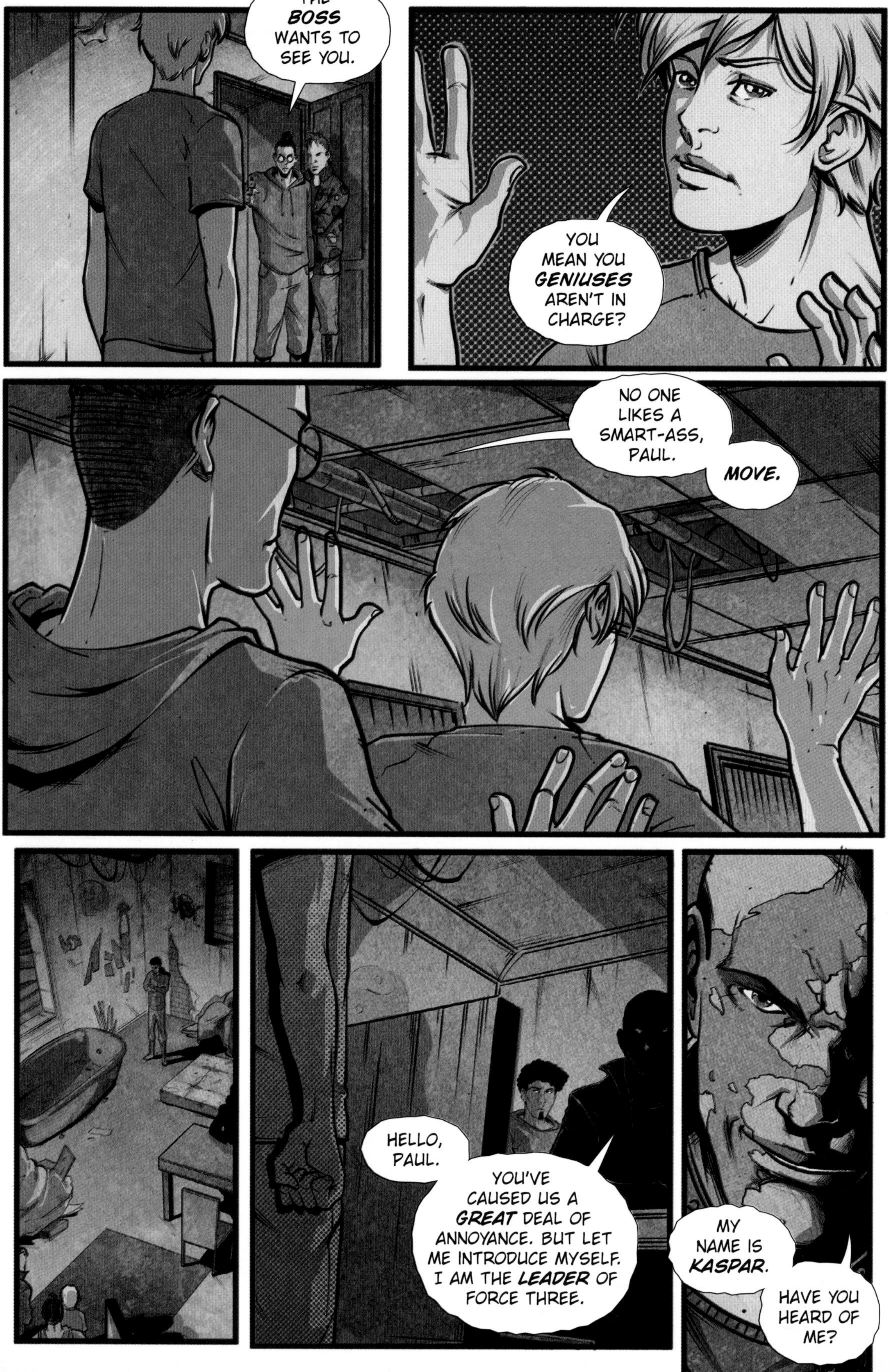
THE BOSS WANTS TO SEE YOU.
YOU MEAN YOU GENIUSES AREN'T IN CHARGE?
NO ONE LIKES A SMART-ASS, PAUL.
MOVE.
HELLO, PAUL.
YOU'VE CAUSED US A GREAT DEAL OF ANNOYANCE. BUT LET ME INTRODUCE MYSELF. I AM THE LEADER OF FORCE THREE.
MY NAME IS KASPAR.
HAVE YOU HEARD OF ME?

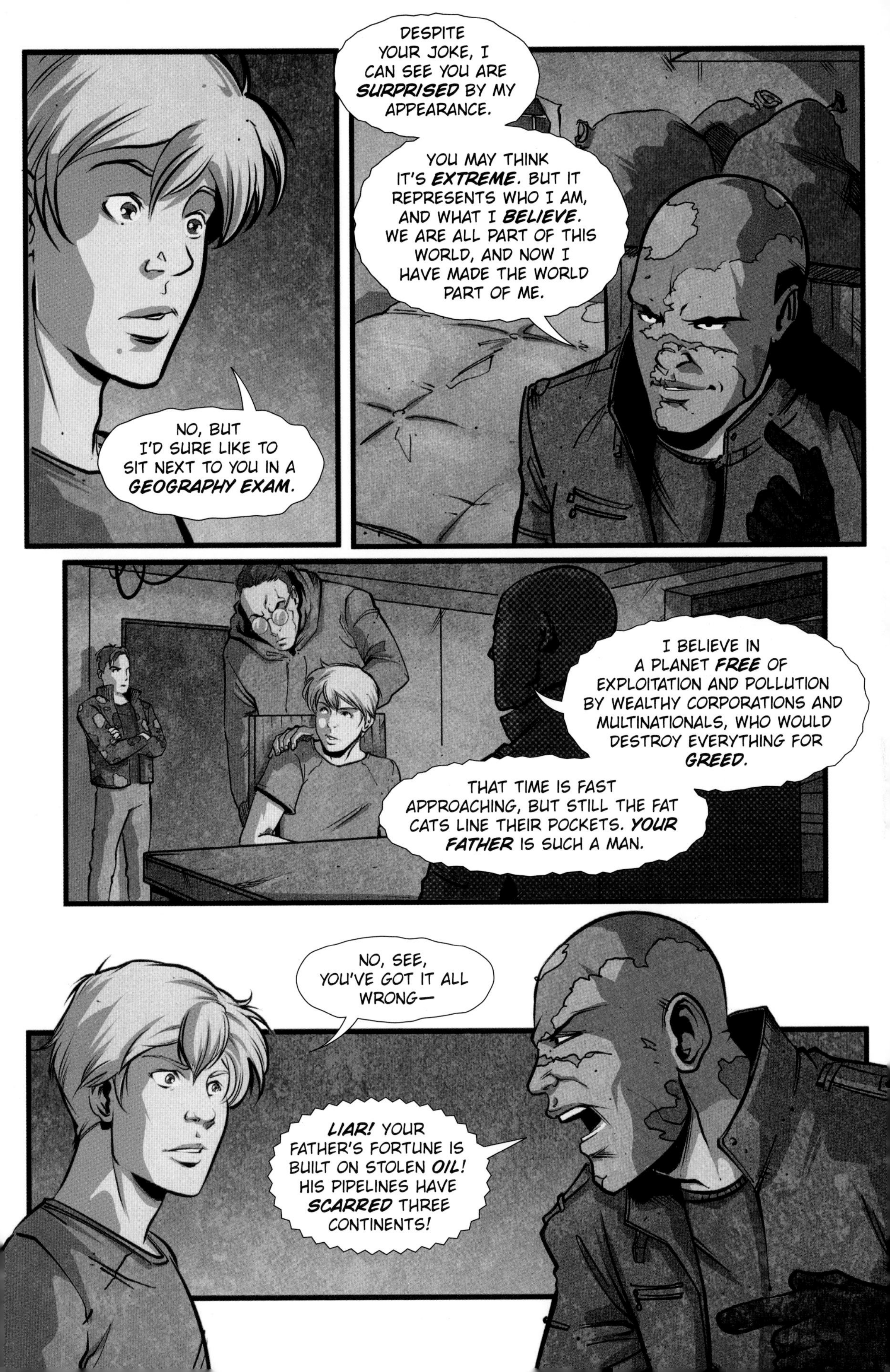
DESPITE YOUR JOKE, I CAN SEE YOU ARE SURPRISED BY MY APPEARANCE.
YOU MAY THINK IT'S EXTREME. BUT IT REPRESENTS WHO I AM, AND WHAT I BELIEVE. WE ARE ALL PART OF THIS WORLD, AND NOW I HAVE MADE THE WORLD PART OF ME.
NO, BUT I'D SURE LIKE TO SIT NEXT TO YOU IN A GEOGRAPHY EXAM.
I BELIEVE IN A PLANET FREE OF EXPLOITATION AND POLLUTION BY WEALTHY CORPORATIONS AND MULTINATIONALS, WHO WOULD DESTROY EVERYTHING FOR GREED.
THAT TIME IS FAST APPROACHING, BUT STILL THE FAT CATS LINE THEIR POCKETS. YOUR FATHER IS SUCH A MAN.
NO, SEE, YOU'VE GOT IT ALL WRONG—
LIAR! YOUR FATHER'S FORTUNE IS BUILT ON STOLEN OIL! HIS PIPELINES HAVE SCARRED THREE CONTINENTS!

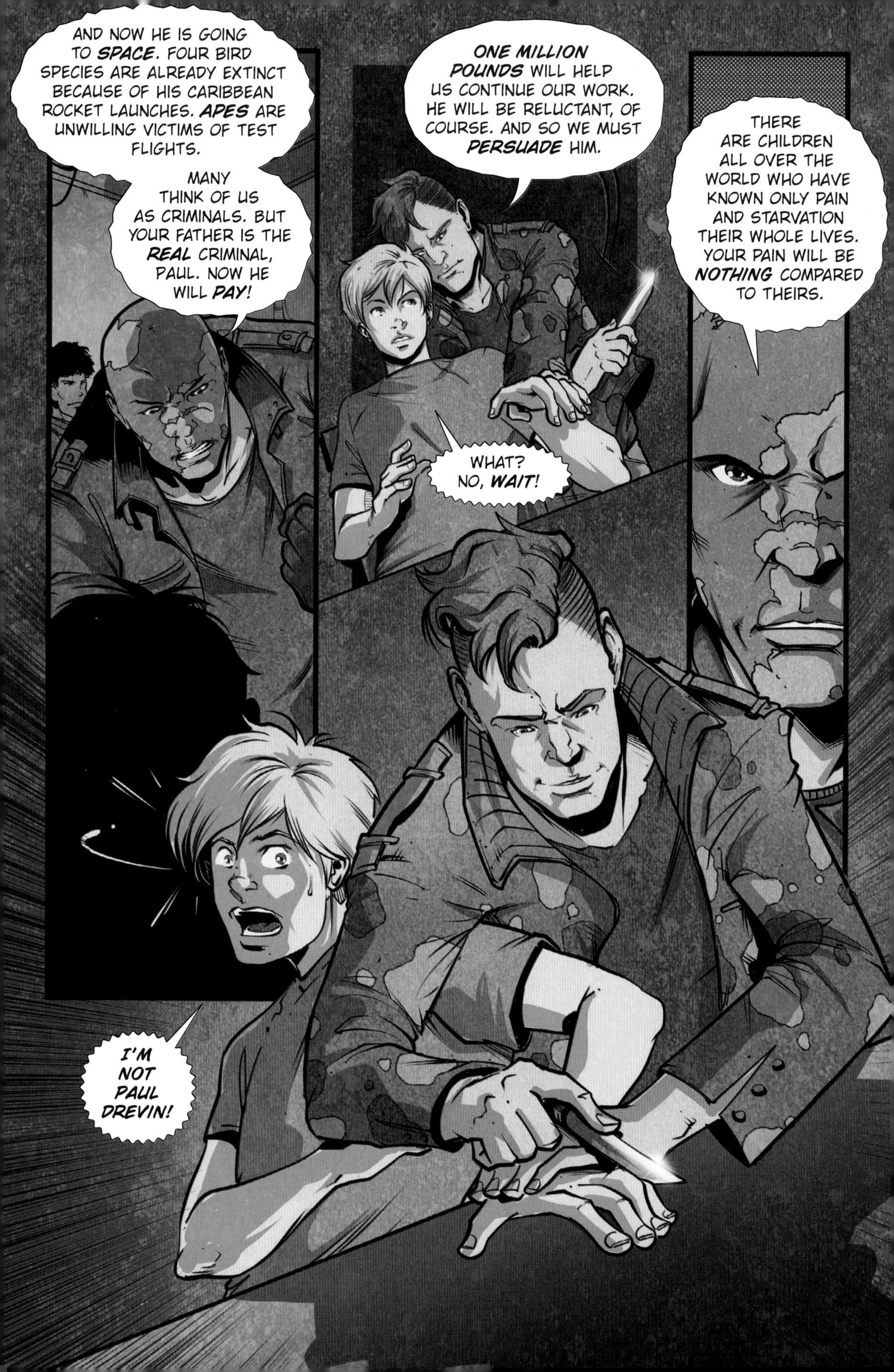
AND NOW HE IS GOING TO SPACE. FOUR BIRD SPECIES ARE ALREADY EXTINCT BECAUSE OF HIS CARIBBEAN ROCKET LAUNCHES. APES ARE UNWILLING VICTIMS OF TEST FLIGHTS.
MANY THINK OF US AS CRIMINALS. BUT YOUR FATHER IS THE REAL CRIMINAL, PAUL. NOW HE WILL PAY!
ONE MILLION POUNDS WILL HELP US CONTINUE OUR WORK. HE WILL BE RELUCTANT, OF COURSE. AND SO WE MUST PERSUADE HIM.
WHAT? NO, WAIT!
THERE ARE CHILDREN ALL OVER THE WORLD WHO HAVE KNOWN ONLY PAIN AND STARVATION THEIR WHOLE LIVES. YOUR PAIN WILL BE NOTHING COMPARED TO THEIRS.
I'M NOT PAUL DREVIN!

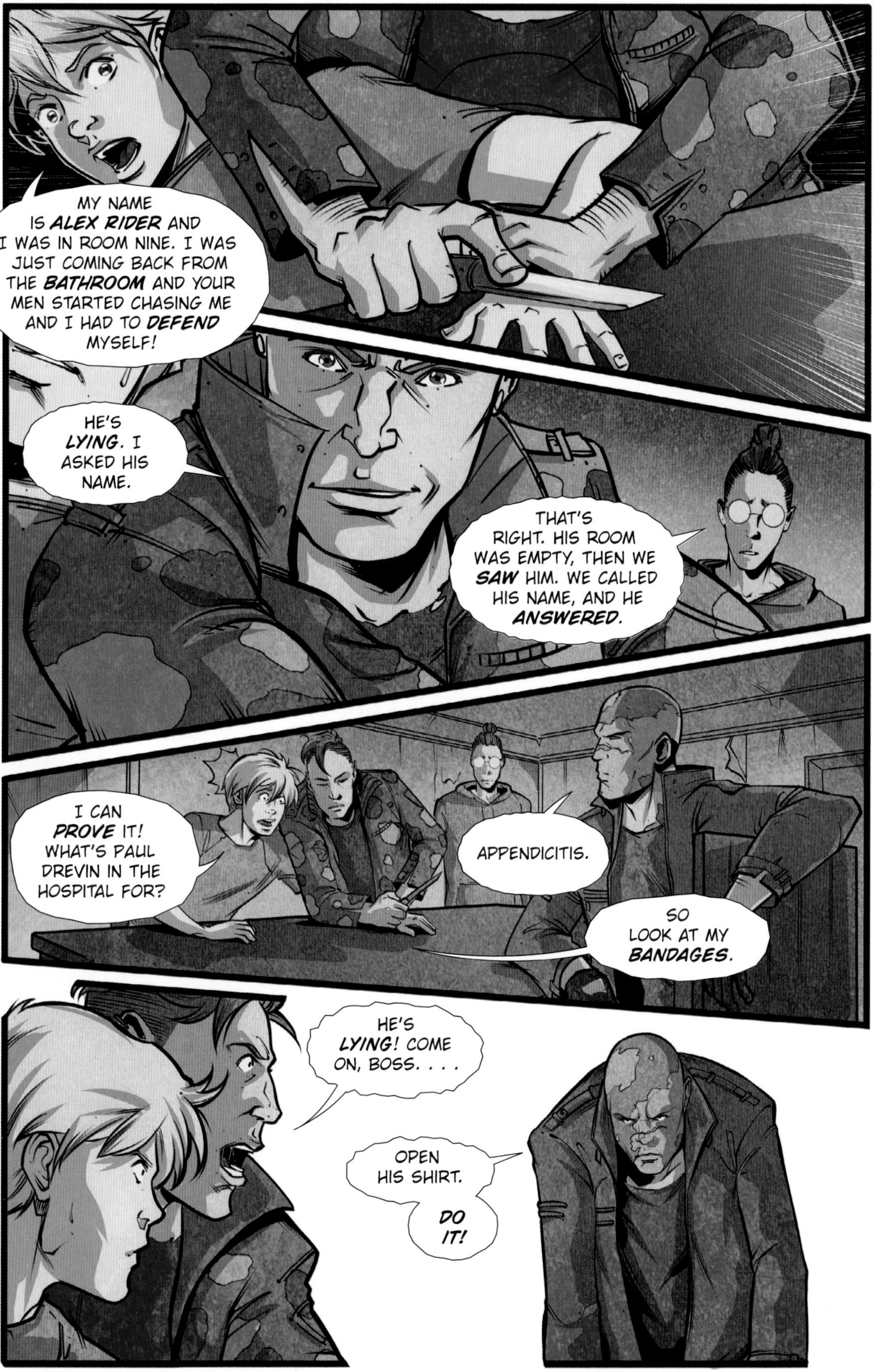
MY NAME IS ALEX RIDER AND I WAS IN ROOM NINE. I WAS JUST COMING BACK FROM THE BATHROOM AND YOUR MEN STARTED CHASING ME AND I HAD TO DEFEND MYSELF!
HE'S LYING. I ASKED HIS NAME.
THAT'S RIGHT. HIS ROOM WAS EMPTY, THEN WE SAW HIM. WE CALLED HIS NAME, AND HE ANSWERED.
I CAN PROVE IT! WHAT'S PAUL DREVIN IN THE HOSPITAL FOR?
APPENDICITIS.
SO LOOK AT MY BANDAGES.
HE'S LYING! COME ON, BOSS. . . .
OPEN HIS SHIRT.
DO IT!

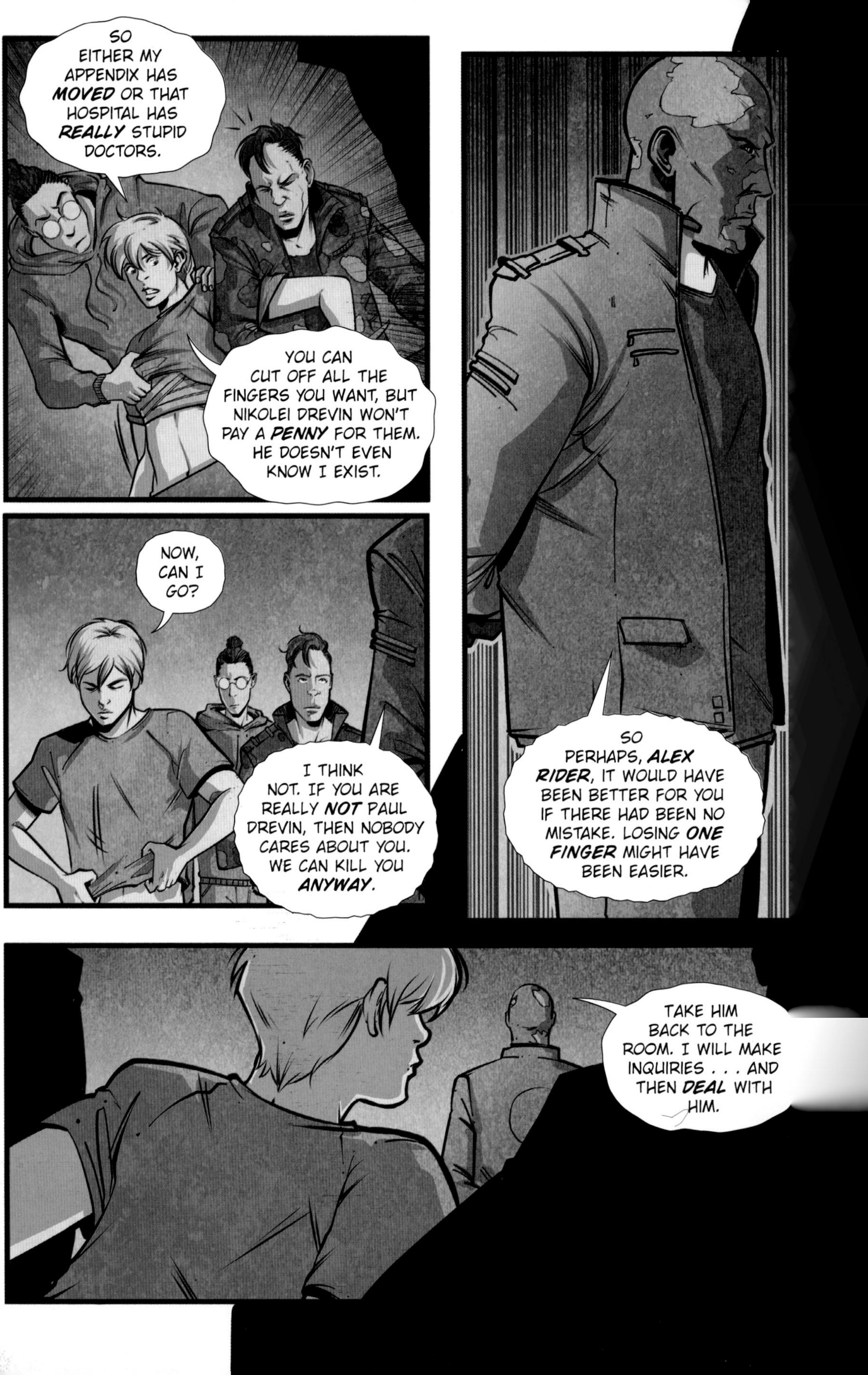
SO EITHER MY APPENDIX HAS MOVED OR THAT HOSPITAL HAS REALLY STUPID DOCTORS.
YOU CAN CUT OFF ALL THE FINGERS YOU WANT, BUT NIKOLEI DREVIN WON'T PAY A PENNY FOR THEM. HE DOESN'T EVEN KNOW I EXIST.
NOW, CAN I GO?
I THINK NOT. IF YOU ARE REALLY NOT PAUL DREVIN, THEN NOBODY CARES ABOUT YOU. WE CAN KILL YOU ANYWAY.
SO PERHAPS, ALEX RIDER, IT WOULD HAVE BEEN BETTER FOR YOU IF THERE HAD BEEN NO MISTAKE. LOSING ONE FINGER MIGHT HAVE BEEN EASIER.
TAKE HIM BACK TO THE ROOM. I WILL MAKE INQUIRIES . . . AND THEN DEAL WITH HIM.

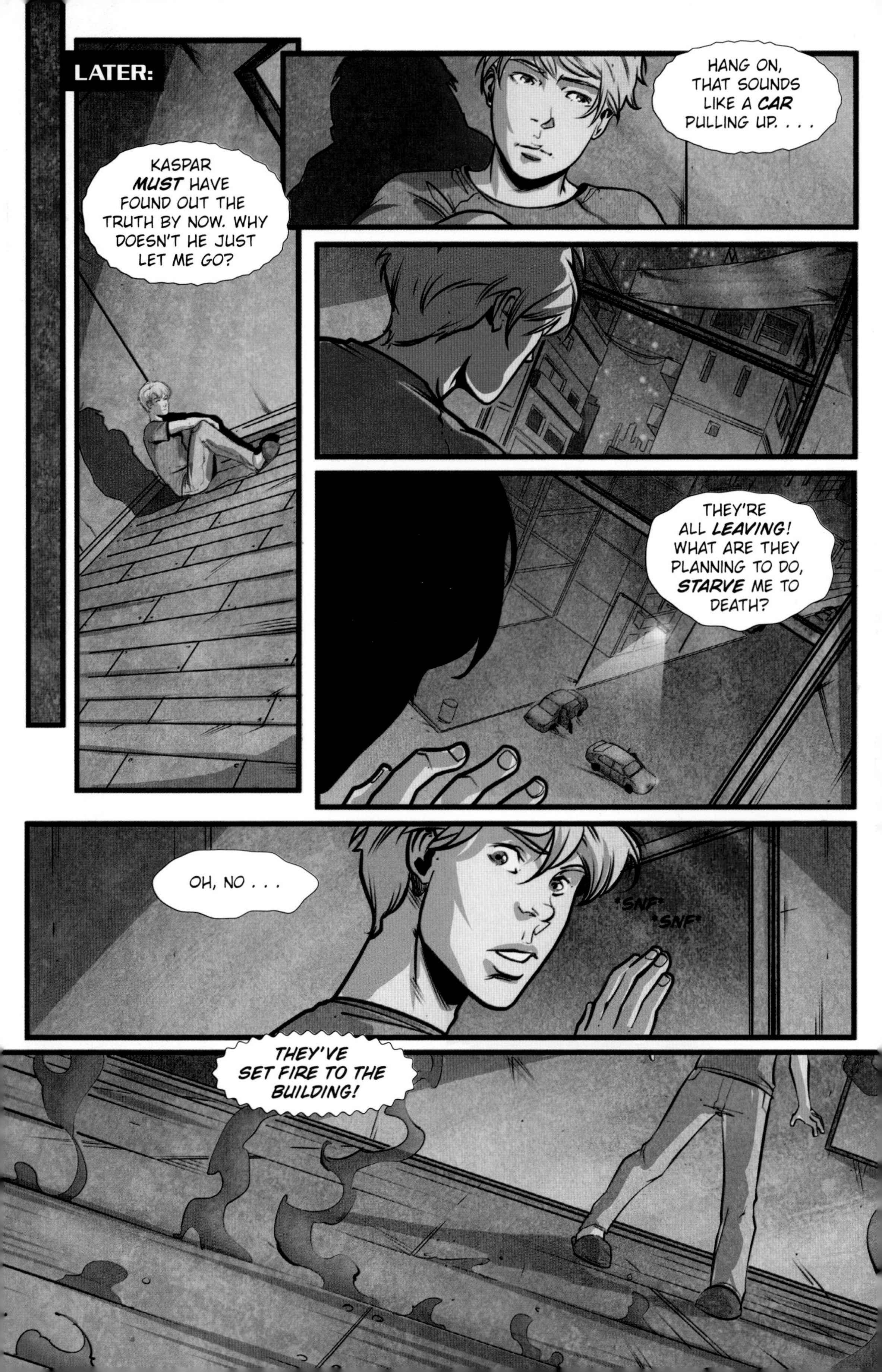
LATER:
KASPAR MUST HAVE FOUND OUT THE TRUTH BY NOW. WHY DOESN'T HE JUST LET ME GO?
HANG ON, THAT SOUNDS LIKE A CAR PULLING UP. . . .
THEY'RE ALL LEAVING! WHAT ARE THEY PLANNING TO DO, STARVE ME TO DEATH?
OH, NO . . .
SNF
SNF
THEY'VE SET FIRE TO THE BUILDING!

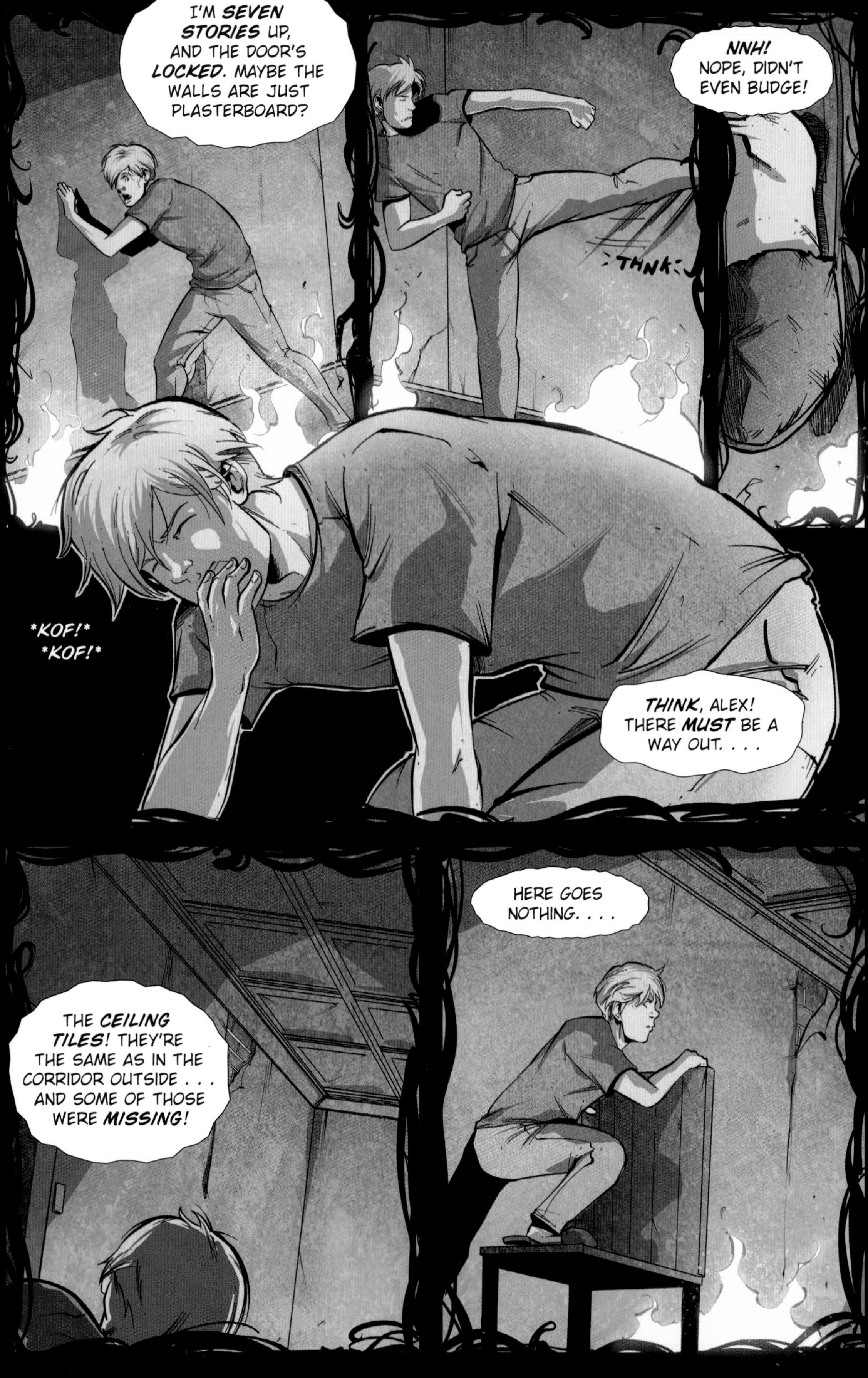
I'M SEVEN STORIES UP, AND THE DOOR'S LOCKED. MAYBE THE WALLS ARE JUST PLASTERBOARD?
THNK
NNH! NOPE, DIDN'T EVEN BUDGE!
KOF! *KOF!*
THINK, ALEX! THERE MUST BE A WAY OUT. . . .
THE CEILING TILES! THEY'RE THE SAME AS IN THE CORRIDOR OUTSIDE . . . AND SOME OF THOSE WERE MISSING!
HERE GOES NOTHING. . . .

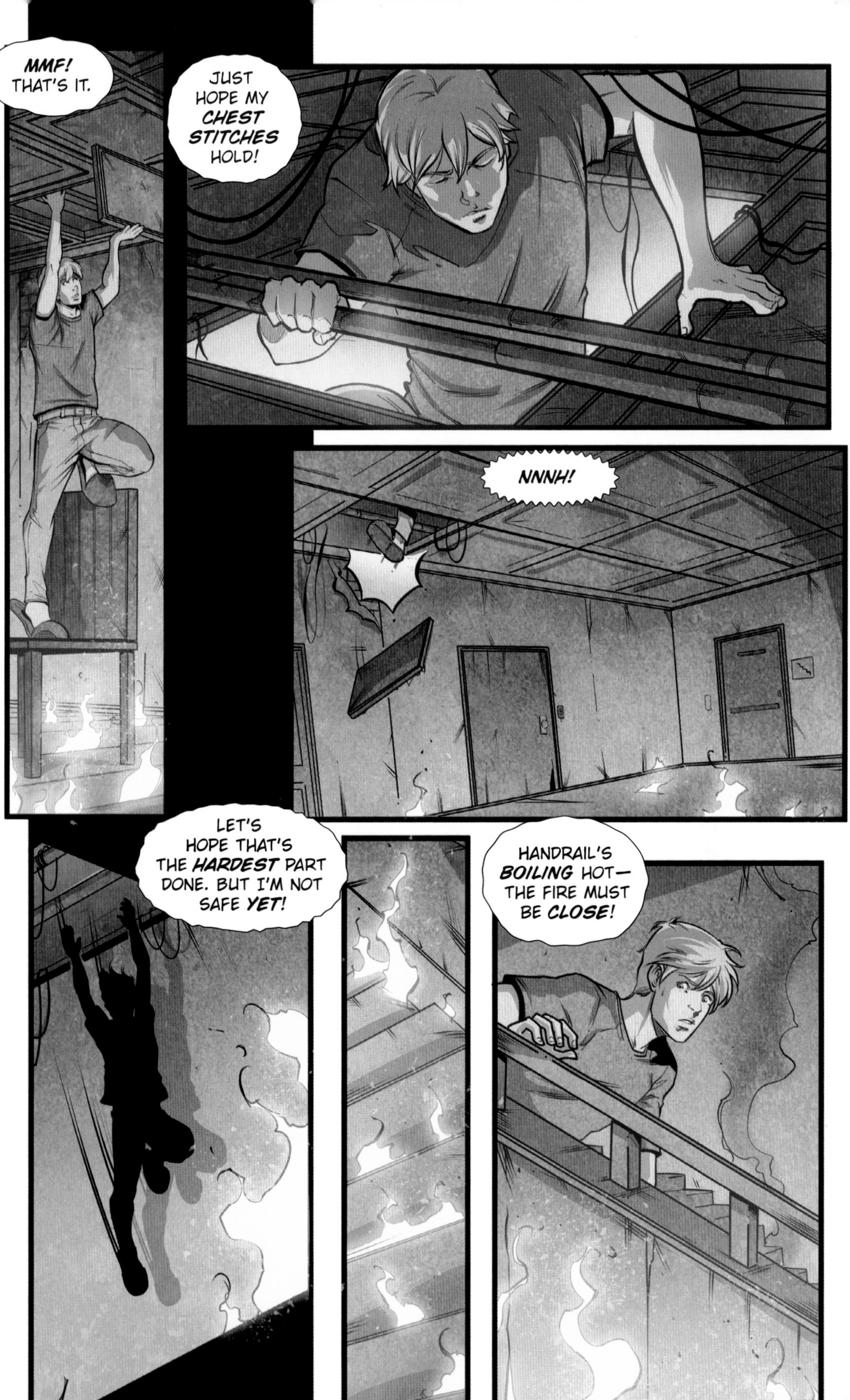
MMF! THAT'S IT.
JUST HOPE MY CHEST STITCHES HOLD!
NNNH!
LET'S HOPE THAT'S THE HARDEST PART DONE. BUT I'M NOT SAFE YET!
HANDRAIL'S BOILING HOT— THE FIRE MUST BE CLOSE!

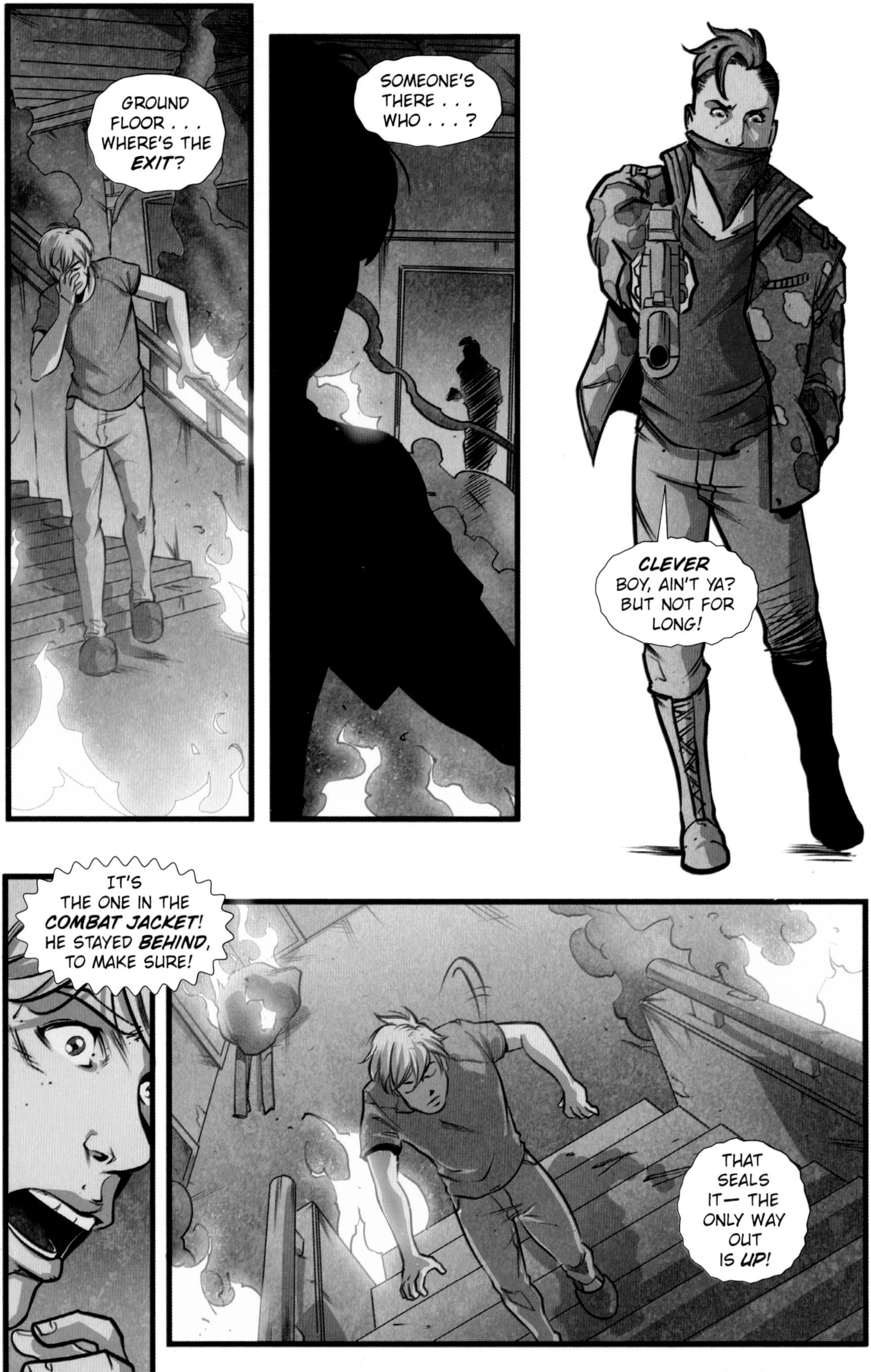
GROUND FLOOR . . . WHERE'S THE EXIT?
SOMEONE'S THERE . . . WHO . . . ?
CLEVER BOY, AIN'T YA? BUT NOT FOR LONG!
IT'S THE ONE IN THE COMBAT JACKET! HE STAYED BEHIND, TO MAKE SURE!
THAT SEALS IT— THE ONLY WAY OUT IS UP!

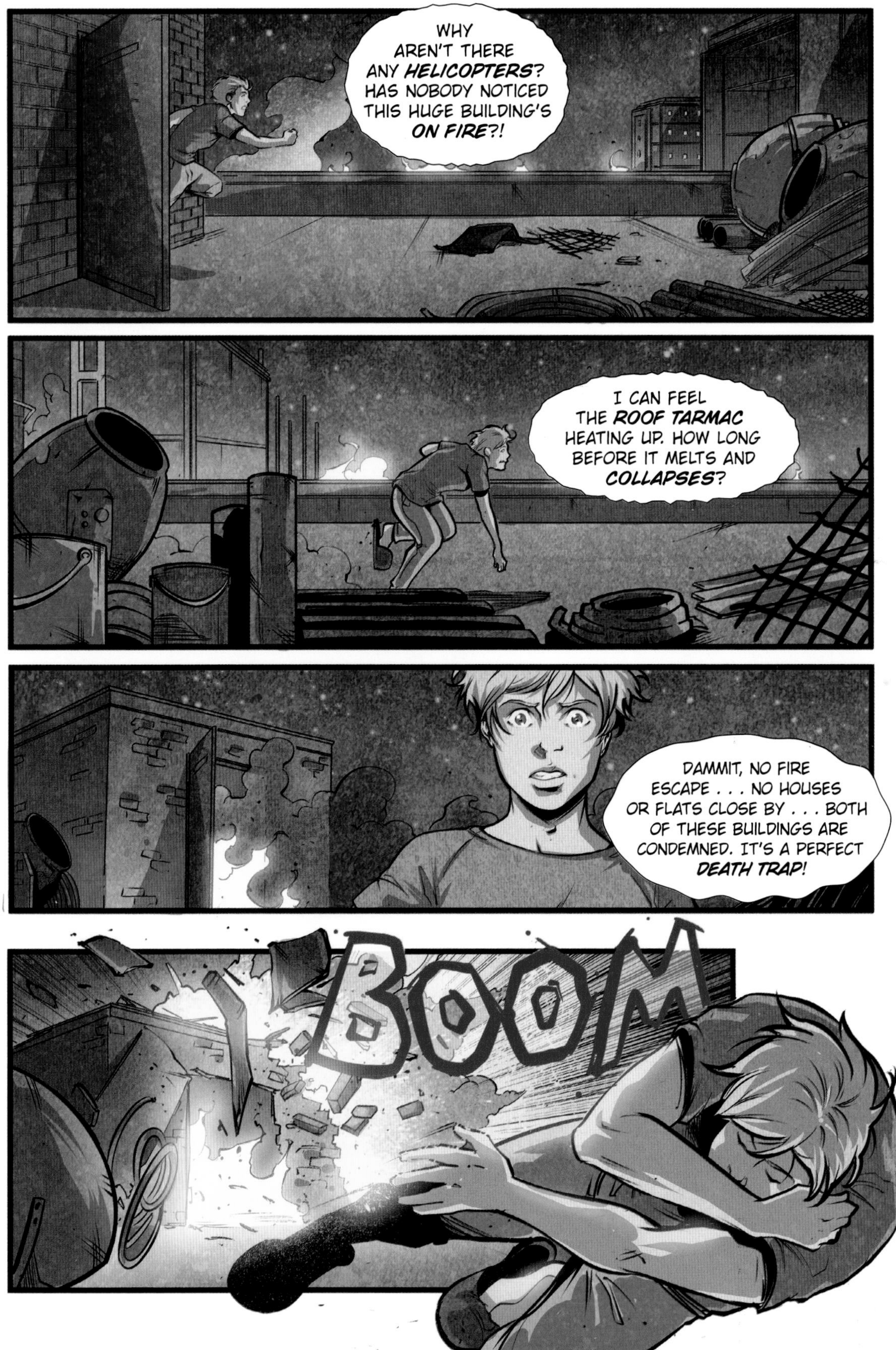
WHY AREN'T THERE ANY HELICOPTERS? HAS NOBODY NOTICED THIS HUGE BUILDING'S ON FIRE?!
I CAN FEEL THE ROOF TARMAC HEATING UP. HOW LONG BEFORE IT MELTS AND COLLAPSES?
DAMMIT, NO FIRE ESCAPE . . . NO HOUSES OR FLATS CLOSE BY . . . BOTH OF THESE BUILDINGS ARE CONDEMNED. IT'S A PERFECT DEATH TRAP!
BOOM

NNH! NO TIME . . . AND NO WAY DOWN . . .

I'LL NEVER *CRAWL* ACROSS THAT BANNER. BUT *UNCLE IAN* ONCE TOLD ME THAT TIGHTROPE WALKING IS ALL ABOUT *LOWERING* YOUR CENTER OF GRAVITY. . . .

HORNCHURCH TOWERS

EXCITING NEW DEVELOPMENT FOR EAST LONDON

BUT MAYBE THERE'S A WAY *ACROSS!*

AND THIS *GARBAGE* THE BUILDERS LEFT BEHIND WILL DO EXACTLY THAT!

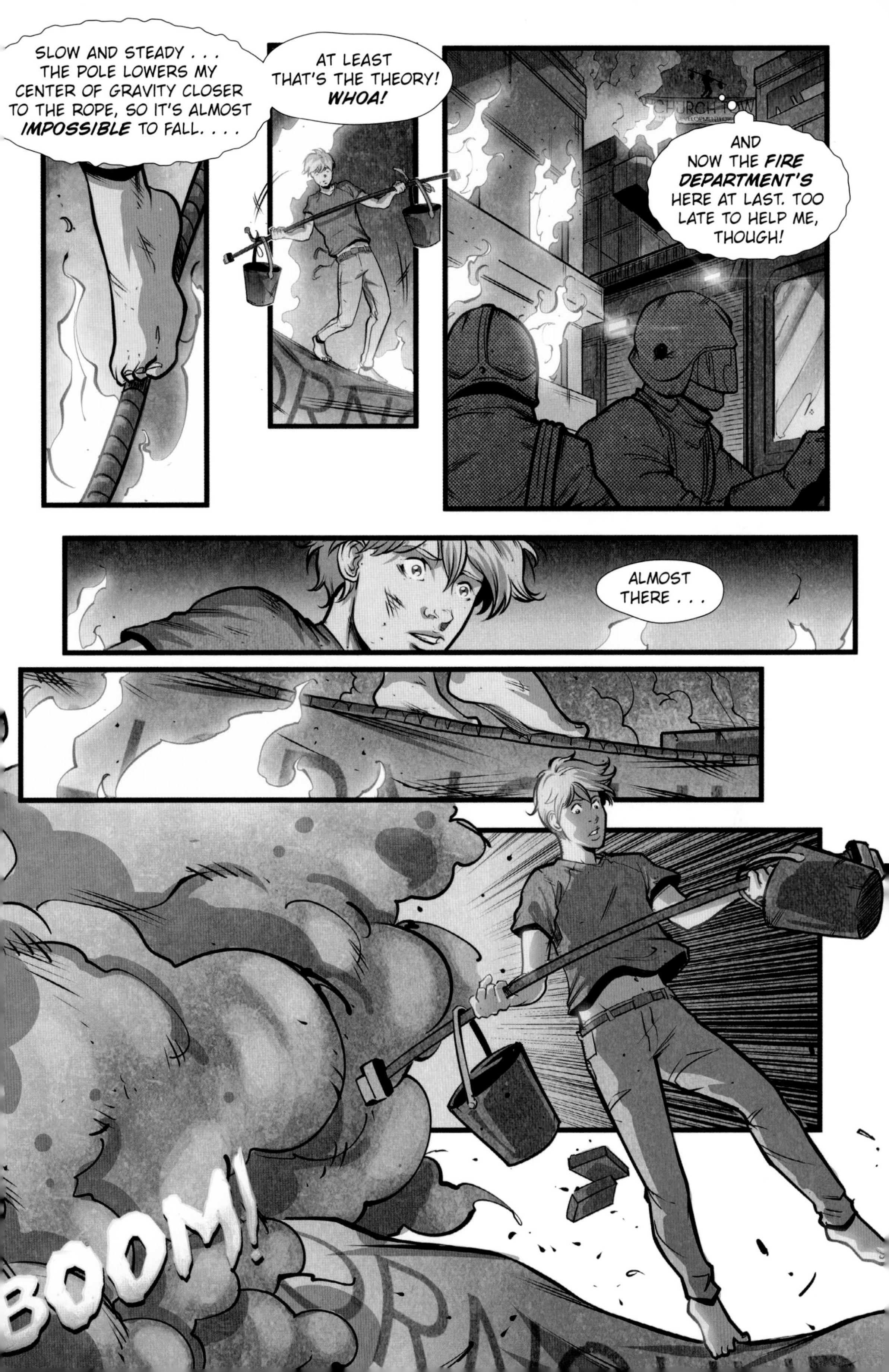
SLOW AND STEADY . . . THE POLE LOWERS MY CENTER OF GRAVITY CLOSER TO THE ROPE, SO IT'S ALMOST *IMPOSSIBLE* TO FALL. . . .
AT LEAST THAT'S THE THEORY! *WHOA!*
CHURCH TOW
AND NOW THE *FIRE DEPARTMENT'S* HERE AT LAST. TOO LATE TO HELP ME, THOUGH!
ALMOST THERE . . .
BOOM!

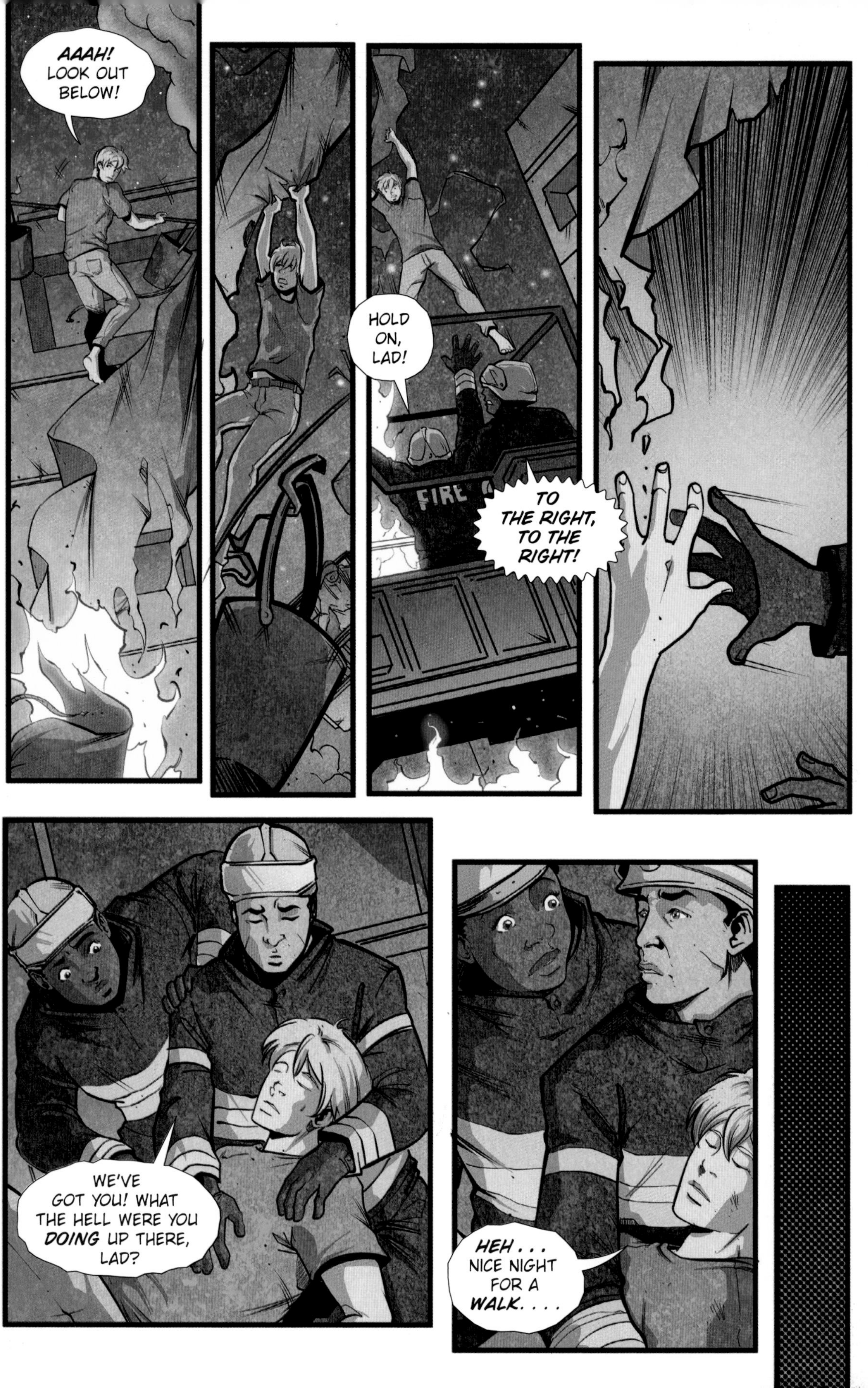
AAAH! LOOK OUT BELOW!
HOLD ON, LAD!
FIRE
TO THE RIGHT, TO THE RIGHT!
WE'VE GOT YOU! WHAT THE HELL WERE YOU DOING UP THERE, LAD?
HEH . . . NICE NIGHT FOR A WALK. . . .

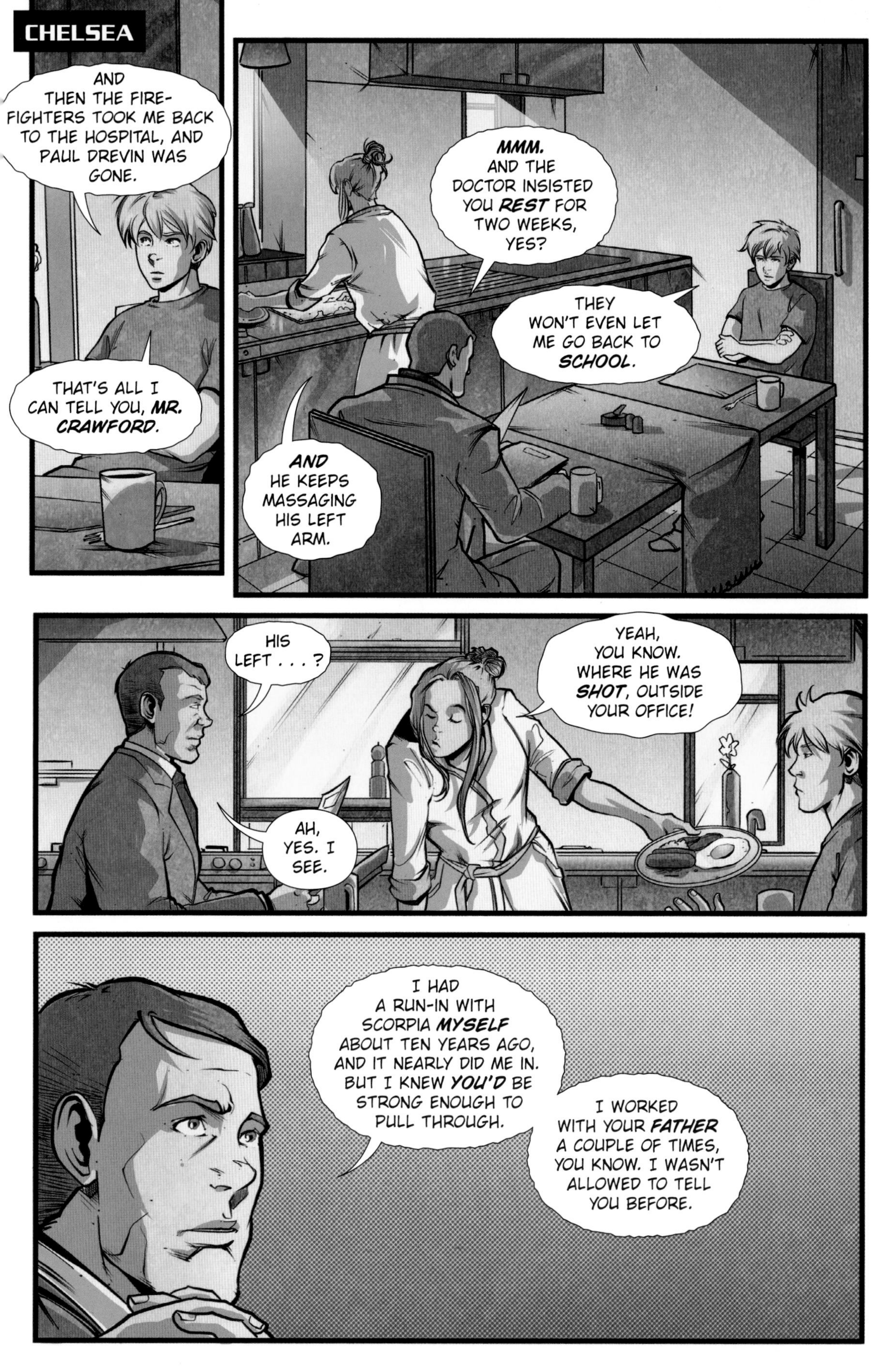
CHELSEA
AND THEN THE FIRE-FIGHTERS TOOK ME BACK TO THE HOSPITAL, AND PAUL DREVIN WAS GONE.
THAT'S ALL I CAN TELL YOU, MR. CRAWFORD.
MMM. AND THE DOCTOR INSISTED YOU REST FOR TWO WEEKS, YES?
THEY WON'T EVEN LET ME GO BACK TO SCHOOL.
AND HE KEEPS MASSAGING HIS LEFT ARM.
HIS LEFT . . . ?
YEAH, YOU KNOW. WHERE HE WAS SHOT, OUTSIDE YOUR OFFICE!
AH, YES. I SEE.
I HAD A RUN-IN WITH SCORPIA MYSELF ABOUT TEN YEARS AGO, AND IT NEARLY DID ME IN. BUT I KNEW YOU'D BE STRONG ENOUGH TO PULL THROUGH.
I WORKED WITH YOUR FATHER A COUPLE OF TIMES, YOU KNOW. I WASN'T ALLOWED TO TELL YOU BEFORE.

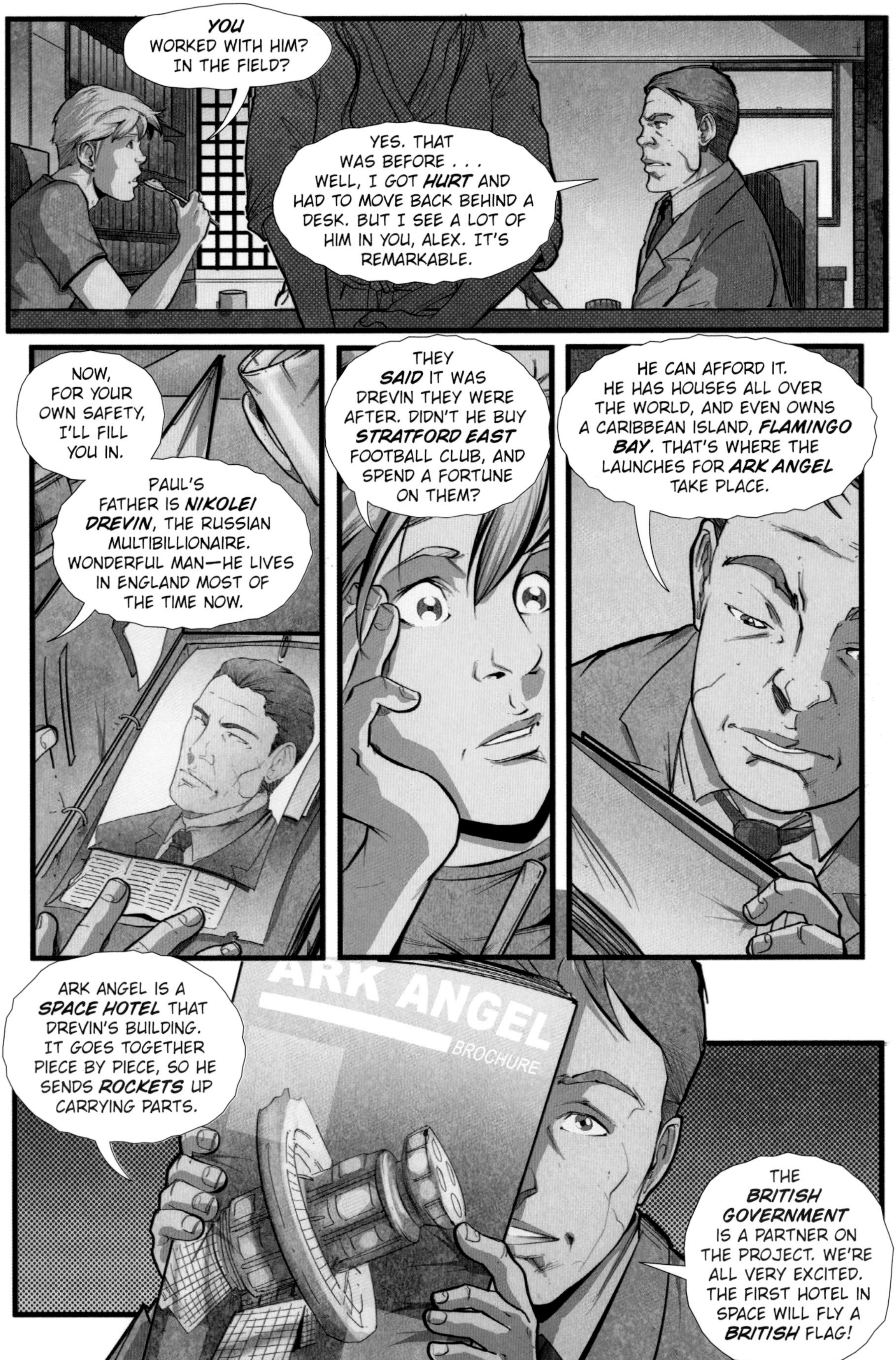
YOU WORKED WITH HIM? IN THE FIELD?
YES. THAT WAS BEFORE . . . WELL, I GOT HURT AND HAD TO MOVE BACK BEHIND A DESK. BUT I SEE A LOT OF HIM IN YOU, ALEX. IT'S REMARKABLE.
NOW, FOR YOUR OWN SAFETY, I'LL FILL YOU IN.
PAUL'S FATHER IS NIKOLEI DREVIN, THE RUSSIAN MULTIBILLIONAIRE. WONDERFUL MAN—HE LIVES IN ENGLAND MOST OF THE TIME NOW.
THEY SAID IT WAS DREVIN THEY WERE AFTER. DIDN'T HE BUY STRATFORD EAST FOOTBALL CLUB, AND SPEND A FORTUNE ON THEM?
HE CAN AFFORD IT. HE HAS HOUSES ALL OVER THE WORLD, AND EVEN OWNS A CARIBBEAN ISLAND, FLAMINGO BAY. THAT'S WHERE THE LAUNCHES FOR ARK ANGEL TAKE PLACE.
ARK ANGEL IS A SPACE HOTEL THAT DREVIN'S BUILDING. IT GOES TOGETHER PIECE BY PIECE, SO HE SENDS ROCKETS UP CARRYING PARTS.
ARK ANGEL
BROCHURE
THE BRITISH GOVERNMENT IS A PARTNER ON THE PROJECT. WE'RE ALL VERY EXCITED. THE FIRST HOTEL IN SPACE WILL FLY A BRITISH FLAG!

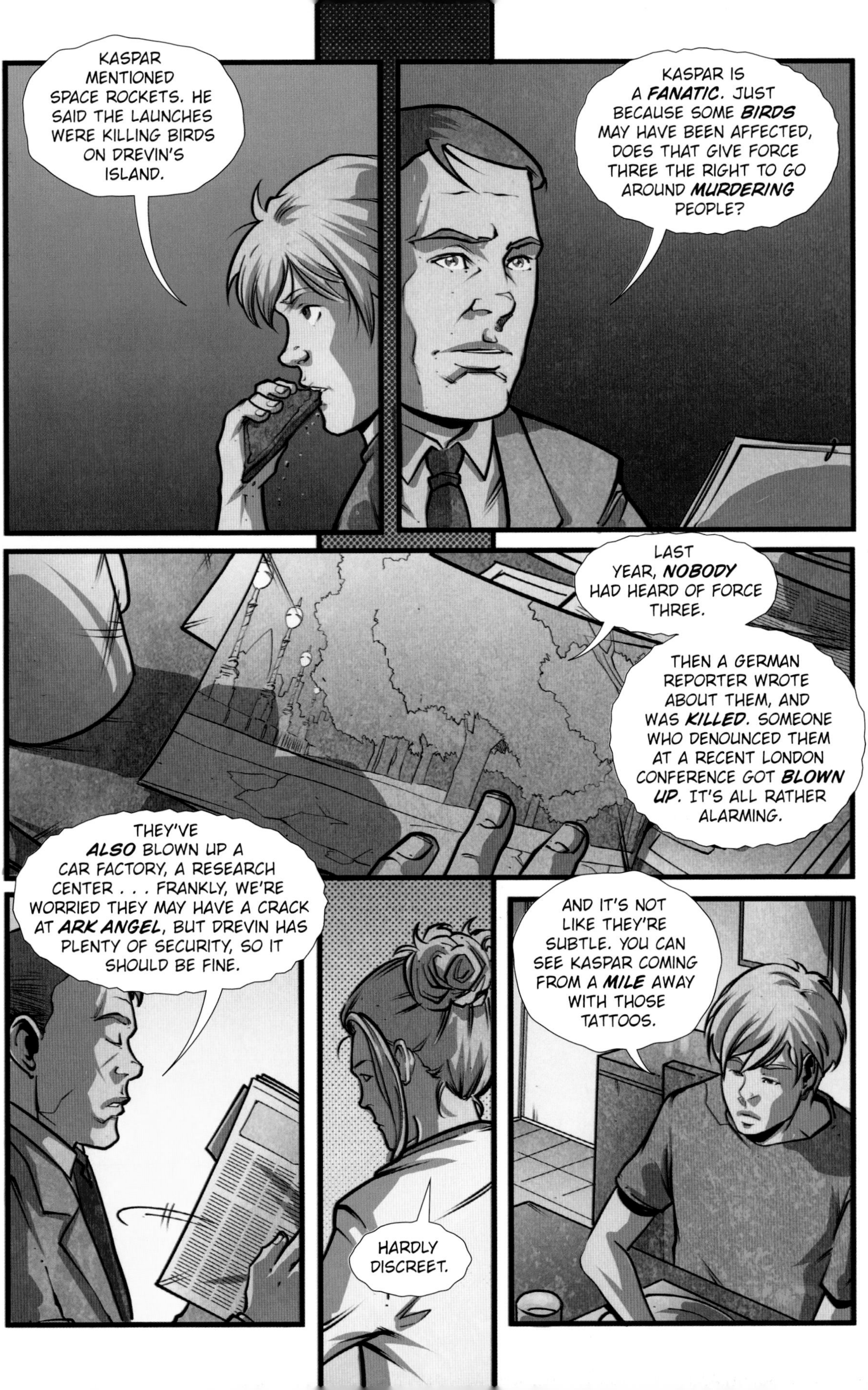
KASPAR MENTIONED SPACE ROCKETS. HE SAID THE LAUNCHES WERE KILLING BIRDS ON DREVIN'S ISLAND.
KASPAR IS A FANATIC. JUST BECAUSE SOME BIRDS MAY HAVE BEEN AFFECTED, DOES THAT GIVE FORCE THREE THE RIGHT TO GO AROUND MURDERING PEOPLE?
LAST YEAR, NOBODY HAD HEARD OF FORCE THREE.
THEN A GERMAN REPORTER WROTE ABOUT THEM, AND WAS KILLED. SOMEONE WHO DENOUNCED THEM AT A RECENT LONDON CONFERENCE GOT BLOWN UP. IT'S ALL RATHER ALARMING.
THEY'VE ALSO BLOWN UP A CAR FACTORY, A RESEARCH CENTER . . . FRANKLY, WE'RE WORRIED THEY MAY HAVE A CRACK AT ARK ANGEL, BUT DREVIN HAS PLENTY OF SECURITY, SO IT SHOULD BE FINE.
HARDLY DISCREET.
AND IT'S NOT LIKE THEY'RE SUBTLE. YOU CAN SEE KASPAR COMING FROM A MILE AWAY WITH THOSE TATTOOS.

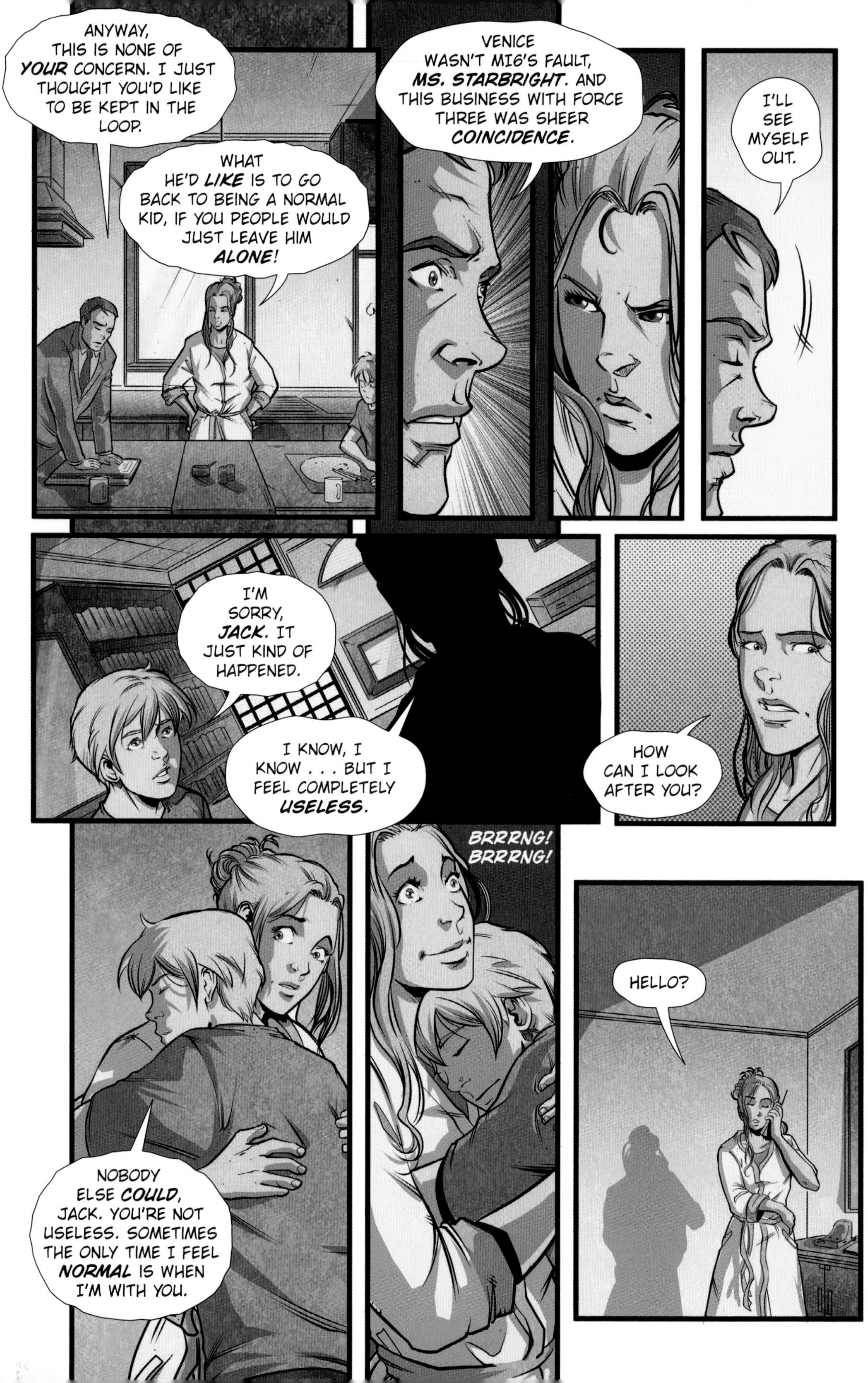
ANYWAY, THIS IS NONE OF YOUR CONCERN. I JUST THOUGHT YOU'D LIKE TO BE KEPT IN THE LOOP.
WHAT HE'D LIKE IS TO GO BACK TO BEING A NORMAL KID, IF YOU PEOPLE WOULD JUST LEAVE HIM ALONE!
VENICE WASN'T MI6'S FAULT, MS. STARBRIGHT. AND THIS BUSINESS WITH FORCE THREE WAS SHEER COINCIDENCE.
I'LL SEE MYSELF OUT.
I'M SORRY, JACK. IT JUST KIND OF HAPPENED.
I KNOW, I KNOW . . . BUT I FEEL COMPLETELY USELESS.
HOW CAN I LOOK AFTER YOU?
NOBODY ELSE COULD, JACK. YOU'RE NOT USELESS. SOMETIMES THE ONLY TIME I FEEL NORMAL IS WHEN I'M WITH YOU.
BRRRNG! BRRRNG!
HELLO?

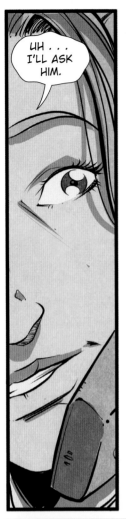

UH . . . I'LL ASK HIM.

I DON'T BELIEVE IT! *NIKOLEI DREVIN'S* ON THE PHONE! HE WANTS US TO HAVE TEA WITH HIM THIS AFTERNOON AT THE *WATERFRONT HOTEL*!

DO YOU THINK WE SHOULD? I MEAN, THE *LAST* TIME I MET A MULTIMILLIONAIRE WAS *DAMIAN CRAY*. THAT DIDN'T END WELL. . . .

MILLION, SHMILLION. DREVIN'S A MULTI*BILLION*AIRE! AND YOU SAVED HIM A LOT OF MONEY. HE MIGHT BE *VERY* GRATEFUL. . . .

HAHA! PLUS, I SUPPOSE THIS TIME THE ENEMY IS KASPAR, NOT *DREVIN*. . . .

OK, TELL HIM WE'LL BE THERE. LET'S HAVE SOME FUN.

YAY!

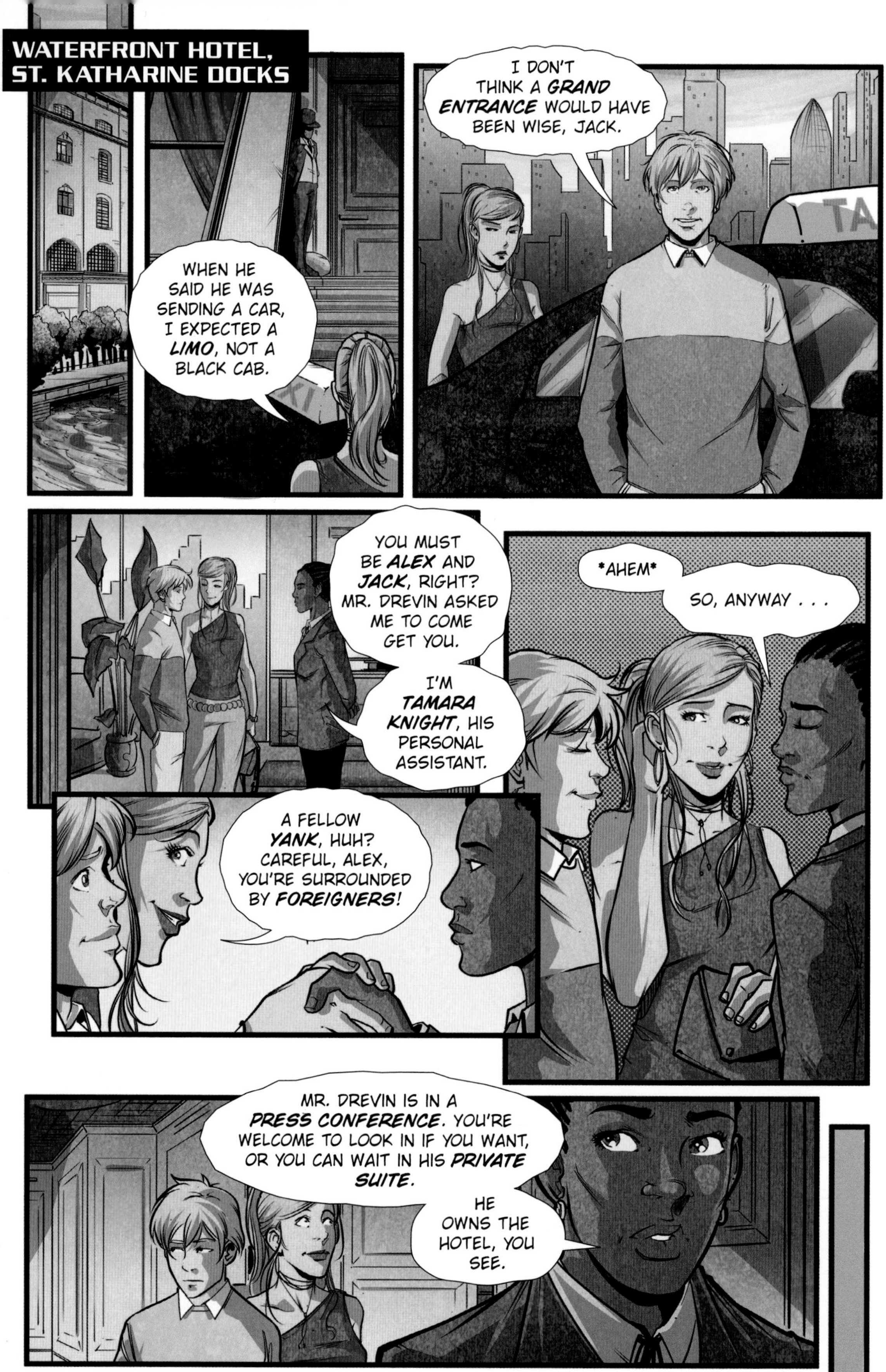
WATERFRONT HOTEL, ST. KATHARINE DOCKS
WHEN HE SAID HE WAS SENDING A CAR, I EXPECTED A LIMO, NOT A BLACK CAB.
I DON'T THINK A GRAND ENTRANCE WOULD HAVE BEEN WISE, JACK.
YOU MUST BE ALEX AND JACK, RIGHT? MR. DREVIN ASKED ME TO COME GET YOU.
I'M TAMARA KNIGHT, HIS PERSONAL ASSISTANT.
A FELLOW YANK, HUH? CAREFUL, ALEX, YOU'RE SURROUNDED BY FOREIGNERS!
AHEM
SO, ANYWAY . . .
MR. DREVIN IS IN A PRESS CONFERENCE. YOU'RE WELCOME TO LOOK IN IF YOU WANT, OR YOU CAN WAIT IN HIS PRIVATE SUITE.
HE OWNS THE HOTEL, YOU SEE.

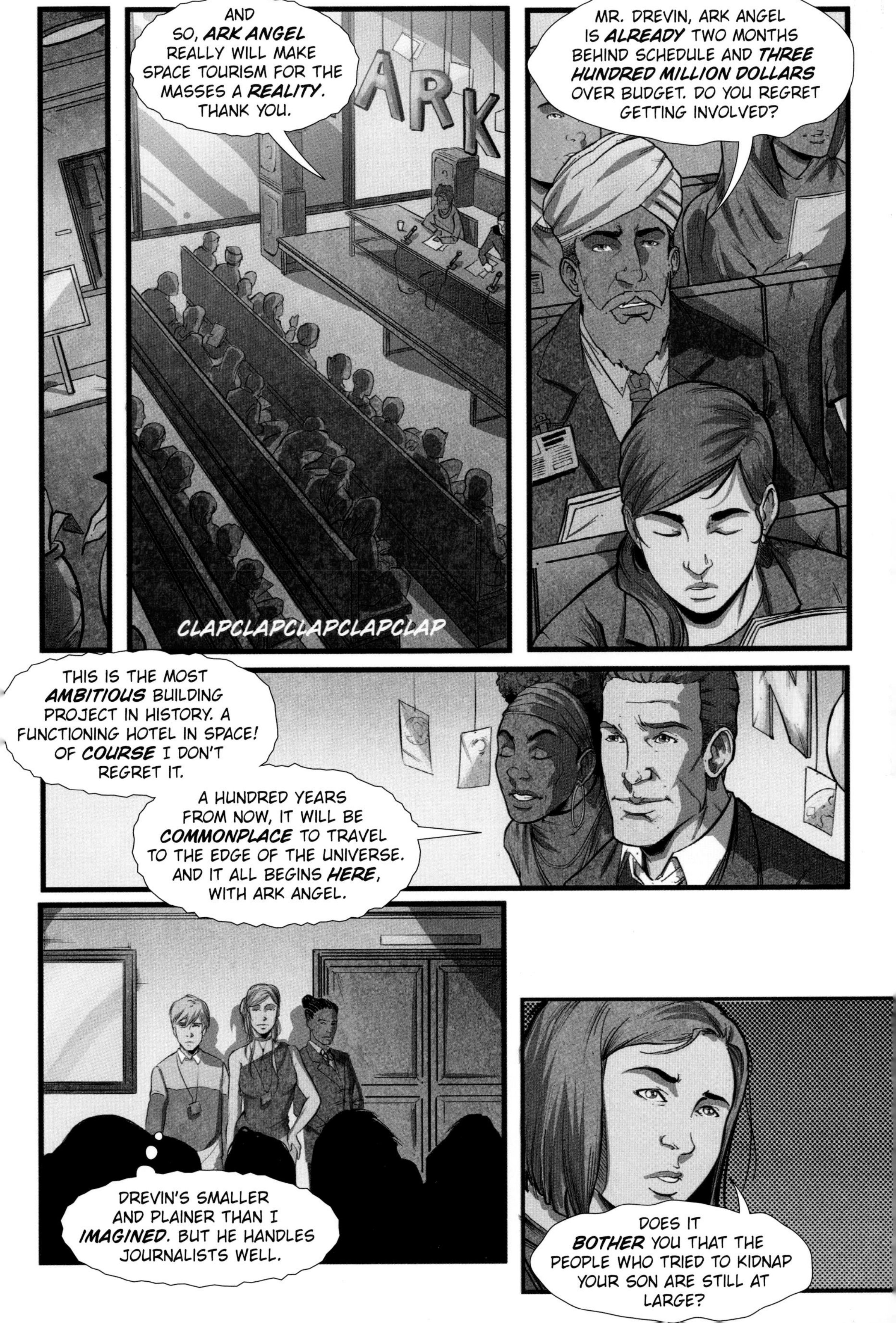
AND SO, ARK ANGEL REALLY WILL MAKE SPACE TOURISM FOR THE MASSES A REALITY. THANK YOU.
ARK
CLAPCLAPCLAPCLAPCLAP
MR. DREVIN, ARK ANGEL IS ALREADY TWO MONTHS BEHIND SCHEDULE AND THREE HUNDRED MILLION DOLLARS OVER BUDGET. DO YOU REGRET GETTING INVOLVED?
THIS IS THE MOST AMBITIOUS BUILDING PROJECT IN HISTORY. A FUNCTIONING HOTEL IN SPACE! OF COURSE I DON'T REGRET IT.
A HUNDRED YEARS FROM NOW, IT WILL BE COMMONPLACE TO TRAVEL TO THE EDGE OF THE UNIVERSE. AND IT ALL BEGINS HERE, WITH ARK ANGEL.
DREVIN'S SMALLER AND PLAINER THAN I IMAGINED. BUT HE HANDLES JOURNALISTS WELL.
DOES IT BOTHER YOU THAT THE PEOPLE WHO TRIED TO KIDNAP YOUR SON ARE STILL AT LARGE?

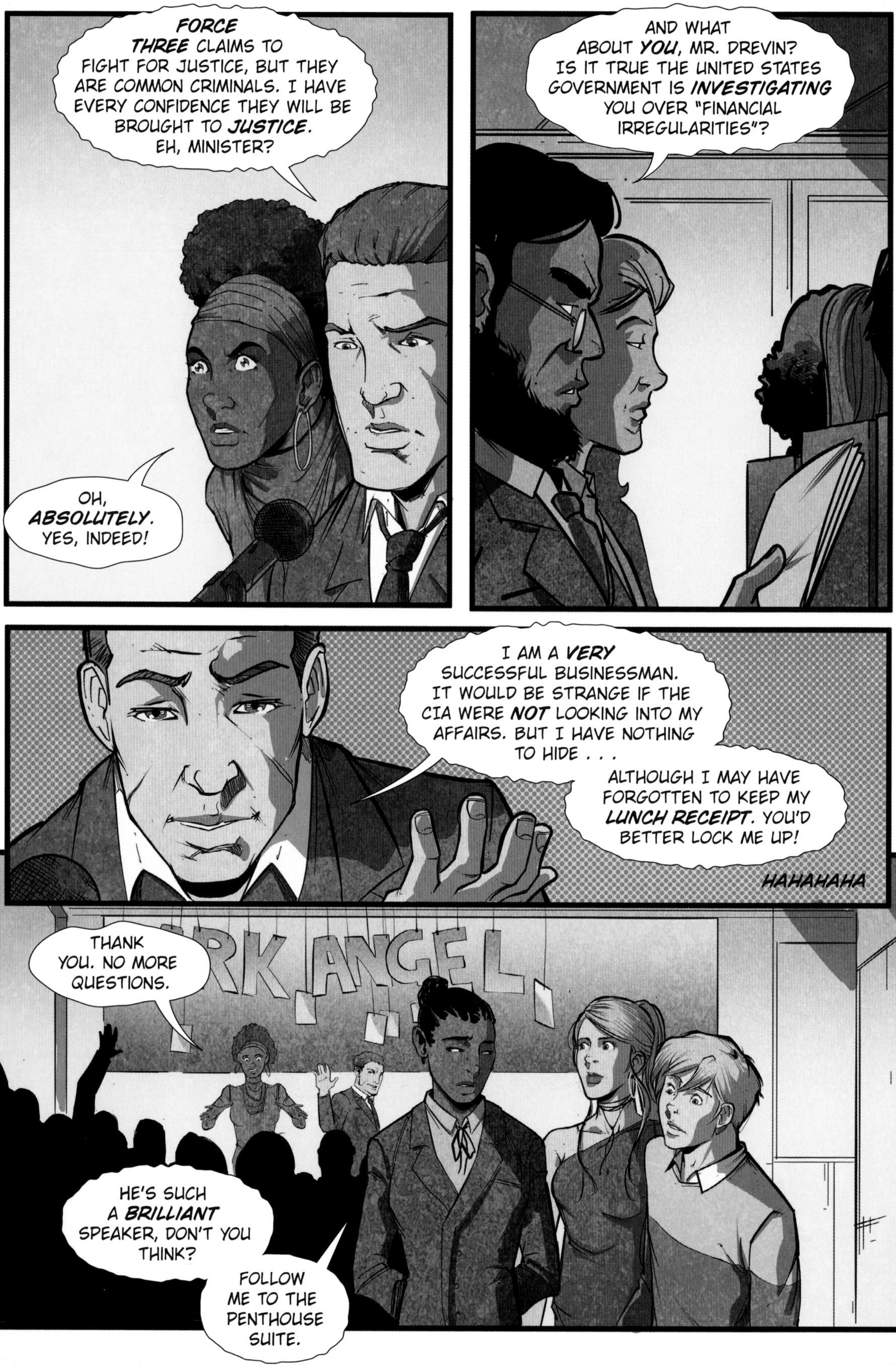
FORCE THREE CLAIMS TO FIGHT FOR JUSTICE, BUT THEY ARE COMMON CRIMINALS. I HAVE EVERY CONFIDENCE THEY WILL BE BROUGHT TO JUSTICE. EH, MINISTER?
OH, ABSOLUTELY. YES, INDEED!
AND WHAT ABOUT YOU, MR. DREVIN? IS IT TRUE THE UNITED STATES GOVERNMENT IS INVESTIGATING YOU OVER "FINANCIAL IRREGULARITIES"?
I AM A VERY SUCCESSFUL BUSINESSMAN. IT WOULD BE STRANGE IF THE CIA WERE NOT LOOKING INTO MY AFFAIRS. BUT I HAVE NOTHING TO HIDE . . .
ALTHOUGH I MAY HAVE FORGOTTEN TO KEEP MY LUNCH RECEIPT. YOU'D BETTER LOCK ME UP!
HAHAHAHA
THANK YOU. NO MORE QUESTIONS.
RK ANGEL
HE'S SUCH A BRILLIANT SPEAKER, DON'T YOU THINK?
FOLLOW ME TO THE PENTHOUSE SUITE.

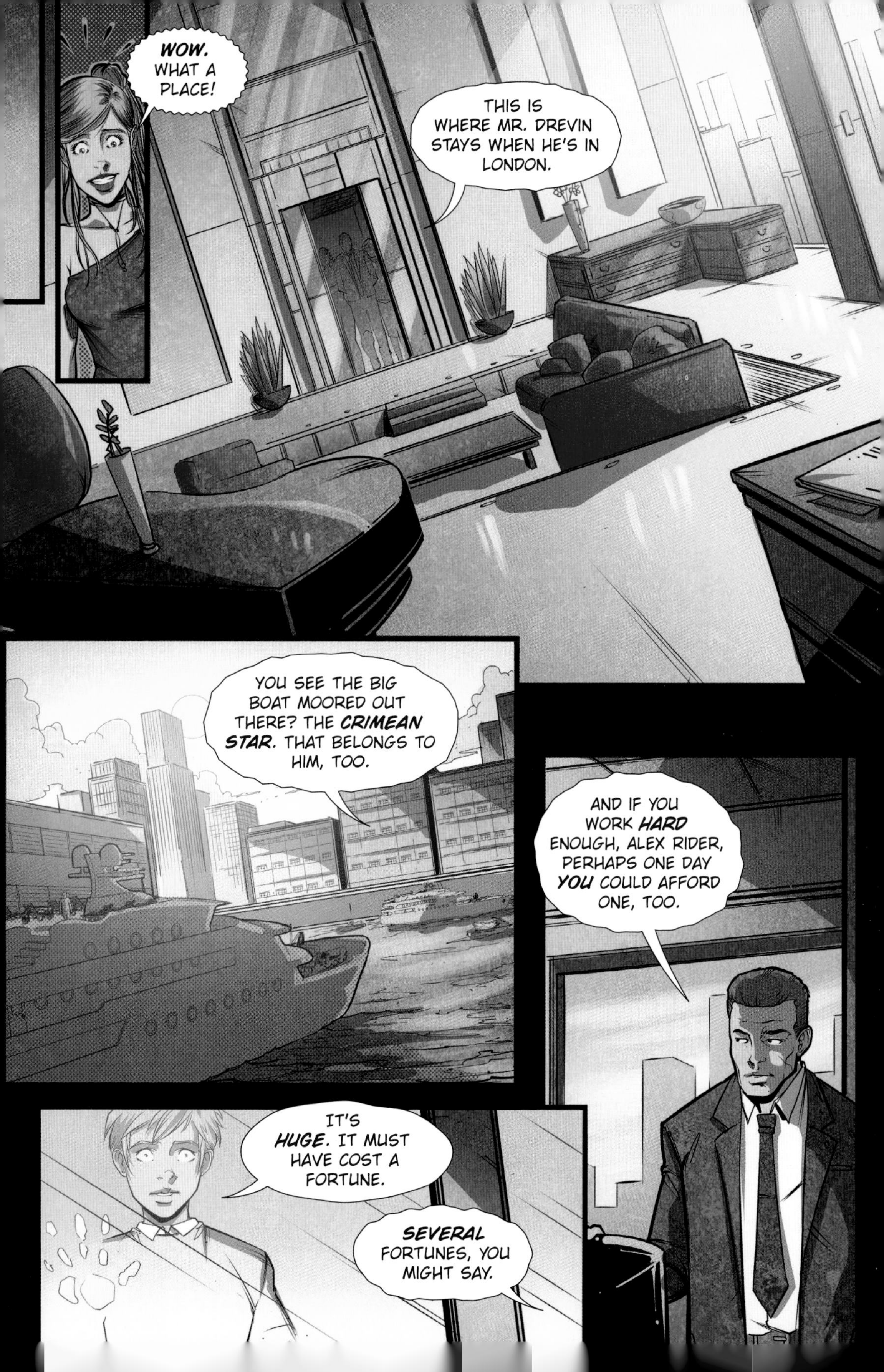
WOW. WHAT A PLACE!
THIS IS WHERE MR. DREVIN STAYS WHEN HE'S IN LONDON.
YOU SEE THE BIG BOAT MOORED OUT THERE? THE CRIMEAN STAR. THAT BELONGS TO HIM, TOO.
AND IF YOU WORK HARD ENOUGH, ALEX RIDER, PERHAPS ONE DAY YOU COULD AFFORD ONE, TOO.
IT'S HUGE. IT MUST HAVE COST A FORTUNE.
SEVERAL FORTUNES, YOU MIGHT SAY.

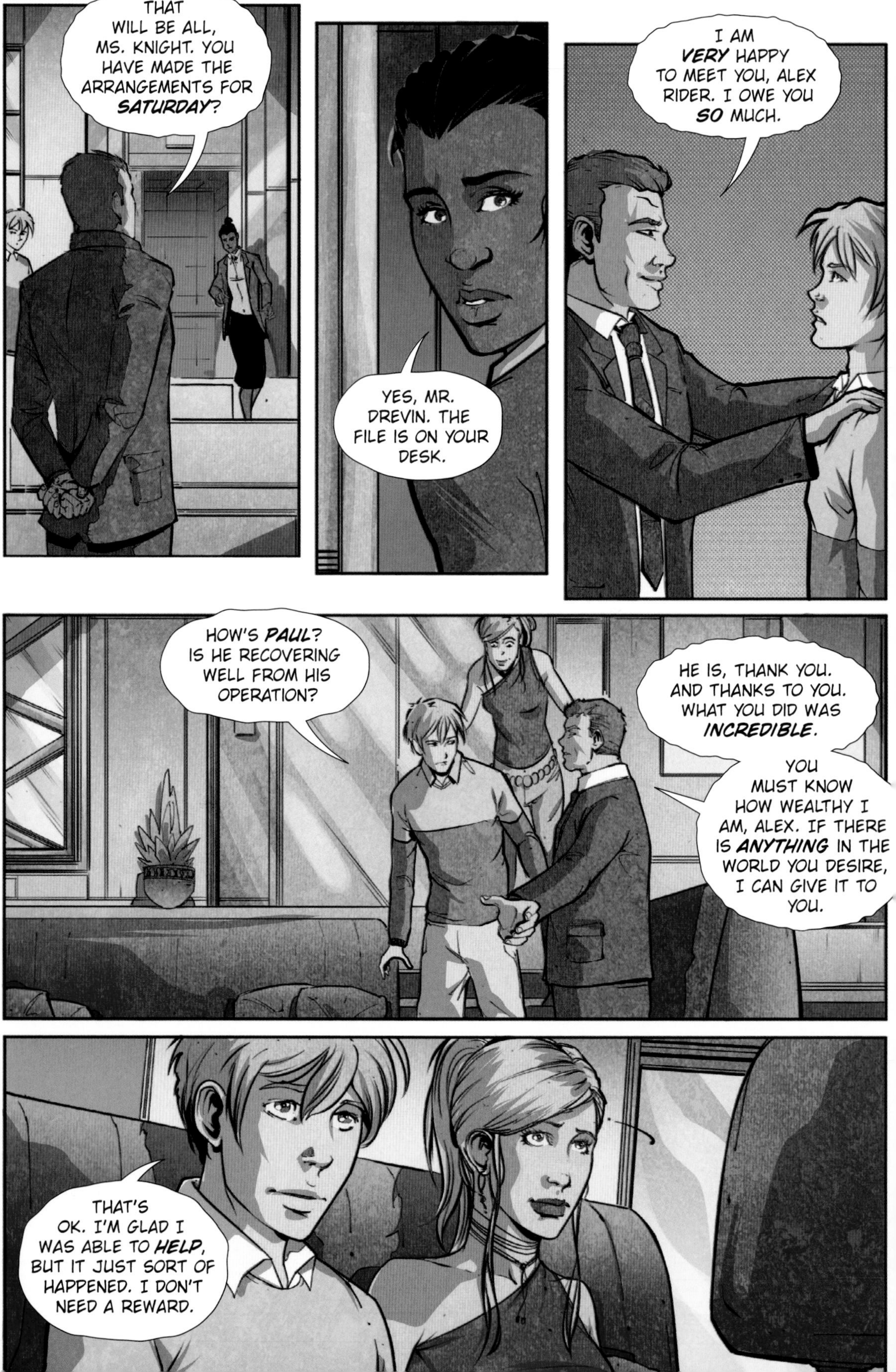
THAT WILL BE ALL, MS. KNIGHT. YOU HAVE MADE THE ARRANGEMENTS FOR SATURDAY?
YES, MR. DREVIN. THE FILE IS ON YOUR DESK.
I AM VERY HAPPY TO MEET YOU, ALEX RIDER. I OWE YOU SO MUCH.
HOW'S PAUL? IS HE RECOVERING WELL FROM HIS OPERATION?
HE IS, THANK YOU. AND THANKS TO YOU. WHAT YOU DID WAS INCREDIBLE.
YOU MUST KNOW HOW WEALTHY I AM, ALEX. IF THERE IS ANYTHING IN THE WORLD YOU DESIRE, I CAN GIVE IT TO YOU.
THAT'S OK. I'M GLAD I WAS ABLE TO HELP, BUT IT JUST SORT OF HAPPENED. I DON'T NEED A REWARD.

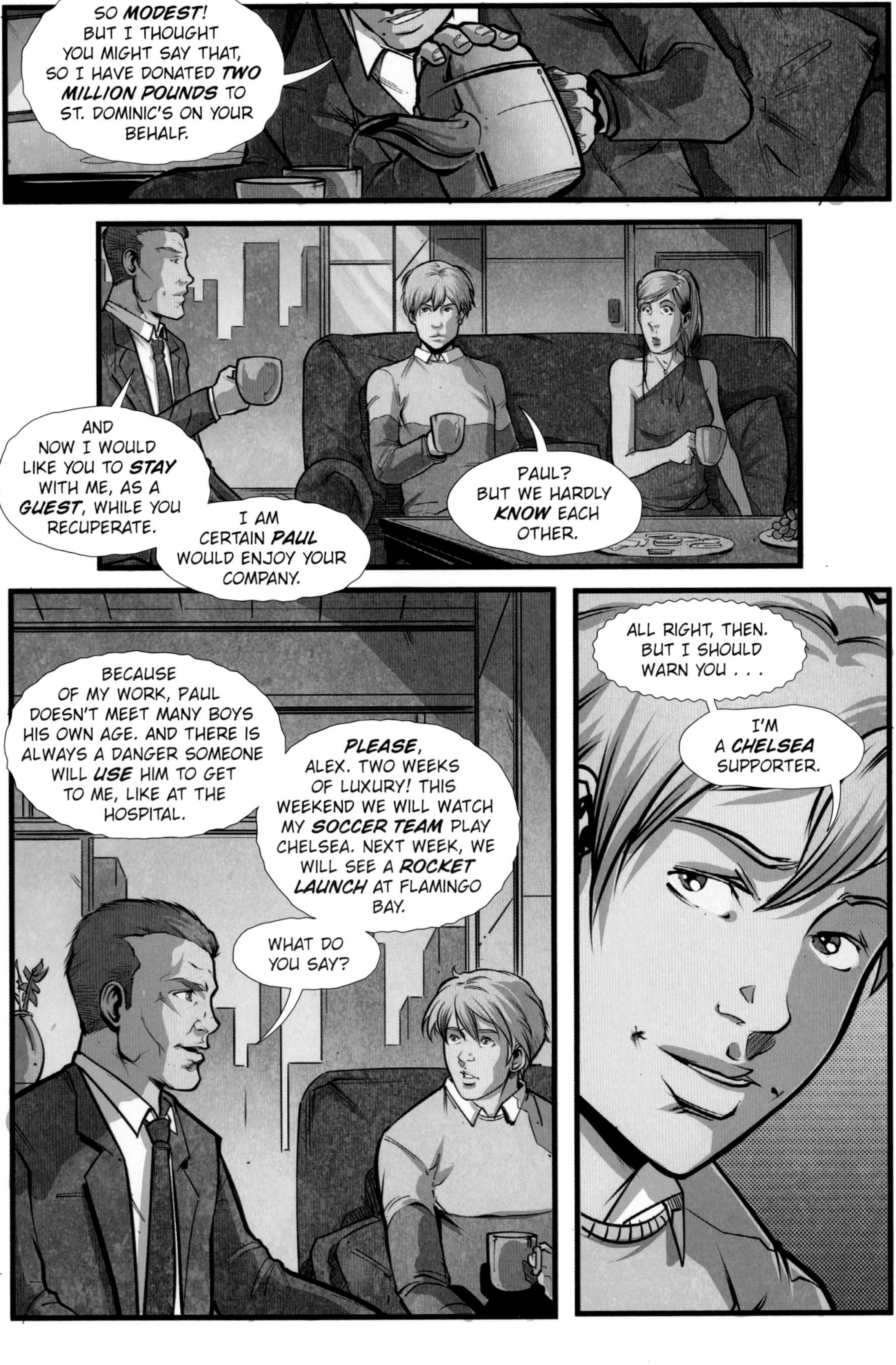
SO **MODEST**! BUT I THOUGHT YOU MIGHT SAY THAT, SO I HAVE DONATED **TWO MILLION POUNDS** TO ST. DOMINIC'S ON YOUR BEHALF.
AND NOW I WOULD LIKE YOU TO **STAY** WITH ME, AS A **GUEST**, WHILE YOU RECUPERATE.
I AM CERTAIN **PAUL** WOULD ENJOY YOUR COMPANY.
PAUL? BUT WE HARDLY **KNOW** EACH OTHER.
BECAUSE OF MY WORK, PAUL DOESN'T MEET MANY BOYS HIS OWN AGE. AND THERE IS ALWAYS A DANGER SOMEONE WILL **USE** HIM TO GET TO ME, LIKE AT THE HOSPITAL.
PLEASE, ALEX. TWO WEEKS OF LUXURY! THIS WEEKEND WE WILL WATCH MY **SOCCER TEAM** PLAY CHELSEA. NEXT WEEK, WE WILL SEE A **ROCKET LAUNCH** AT FLAMINGO BAY.
WHAT DO YOU SAY?
ALL RIGHT, THEN. BUT I SHOULD WARN YOU . . .
I'M A **CHELSEA** SUPPORTER.

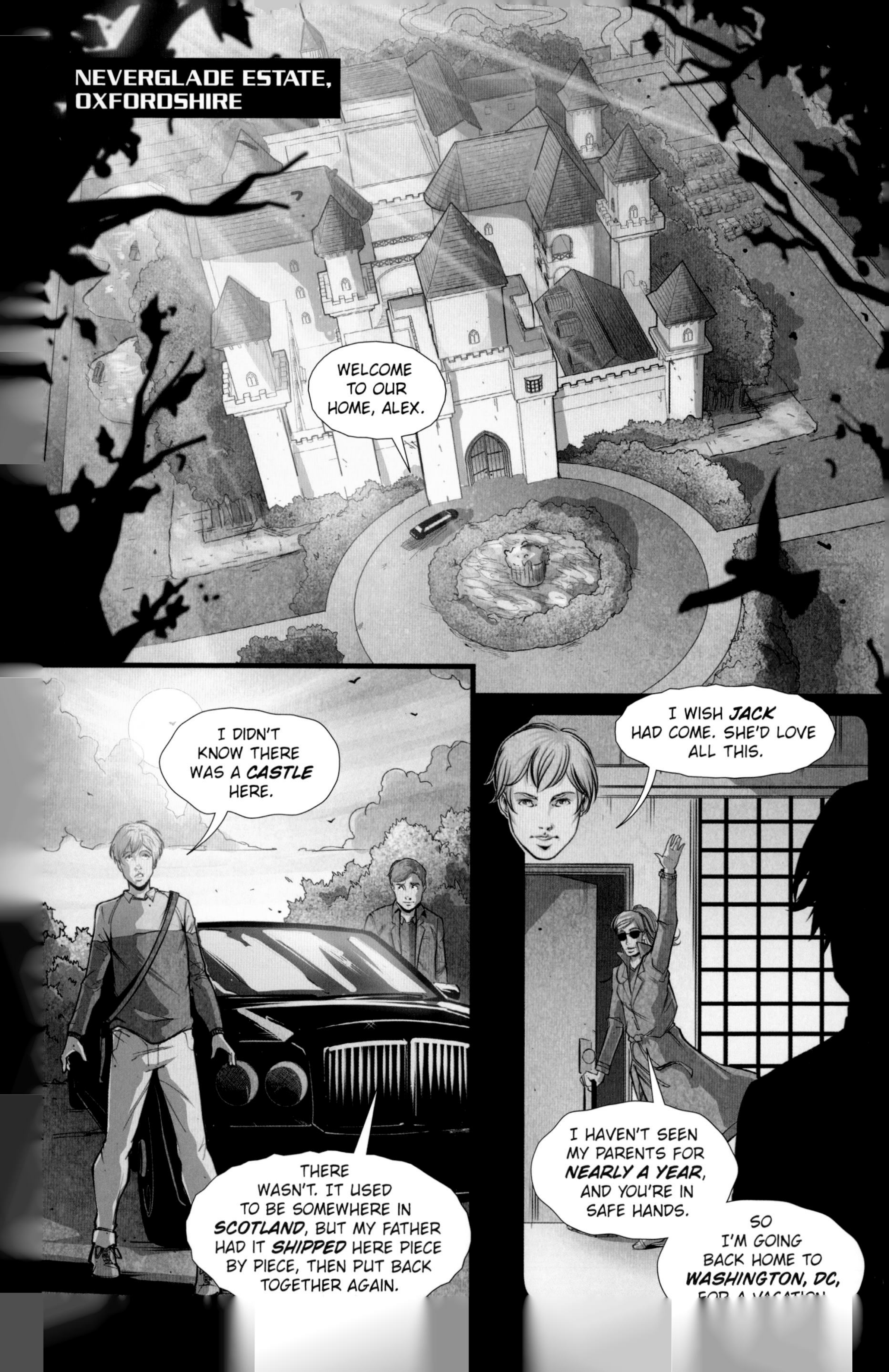
NEVERGLADE ESTATE, OXFORDSHIRE
WELCOME TO OUR HOME, ALEX.
I DIDN'T KNOW THERE WAS A CASTLE HERE.
THERE WASN'T. IT USED TO BE SOMEWHERE IN SCOTLAND, BUT MY FATHER HAD IT SHIPPED HERE PIECE BY PIECE, THEN PUT BACK TOGETHER AGAIN.
I WISH JACK HAD COME. SHE'D LOVE ALL THIS.
I HAVEN'T SEEN MY PARENTS FOR NEARLY A YEAR, AND YOU'RE IN SAFE HANDS.
SO I'M GOING BACK HOME TO WASHINGTON, DC,

WHAT YOU DID WAS AMAZING, ALEX. THOSE MEN NEARLY KILLED YOU BECAUSE OF ME! I'M GLAD YOU AGREED TO COME.
YOUR FATHER MADE IT HARD TO REFUSE.
YEAH, HE'S LIKE THAT.
HHHHH
SORRY, JUST A MINUTE. I HAVE ASTHMA.
HHHHH
WE'VE GOT THIRTY BEDROOMS AND THEY'RE NEVER FULL, SO THIS IS YOURS.
YOU'VE GOT A 100-INCH PLASMA TV, BLU-RAY, ALL THE LATEST CONSOLES, A BUTLER ON SPEED DIAL . . . ANYTHING YOU WANT, JUST PICK UP THE PHONE.
I'M SORRY, THIS MUST BE WEIRD. YOU DON'T EVEN KNOW ME. YOU PROBABLY THINK I'M A SPOILED BRAT . . .
BUT MONEY CAN'T BUY FRIENDS. I'LL UNDERSTAND IF YOU WANT TO TURN AROUND AND GO. SOMETIMES I FEEL LIKE THAT.
NO . . . I CAN'T GO BACK TO SCHOOL, AND I'M MEANT TO BE RESTING, SO WHY NOT LET YOUR DAD TREAT ME LIKE A MILLIONAIRE FOR A WHILE?
COOL! THEN I'LL SEE YOU AT DINNER.

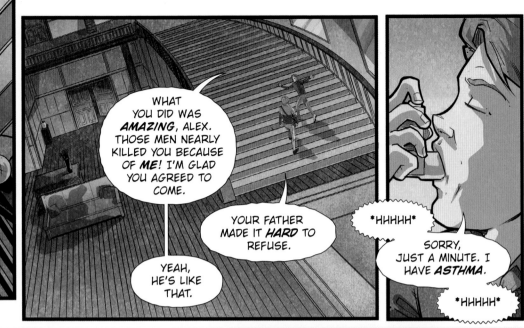

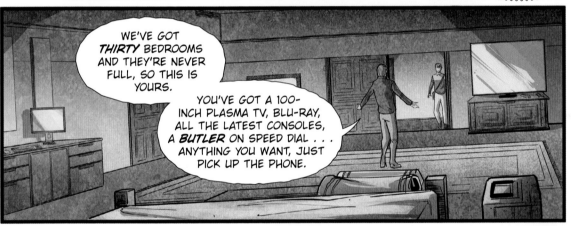

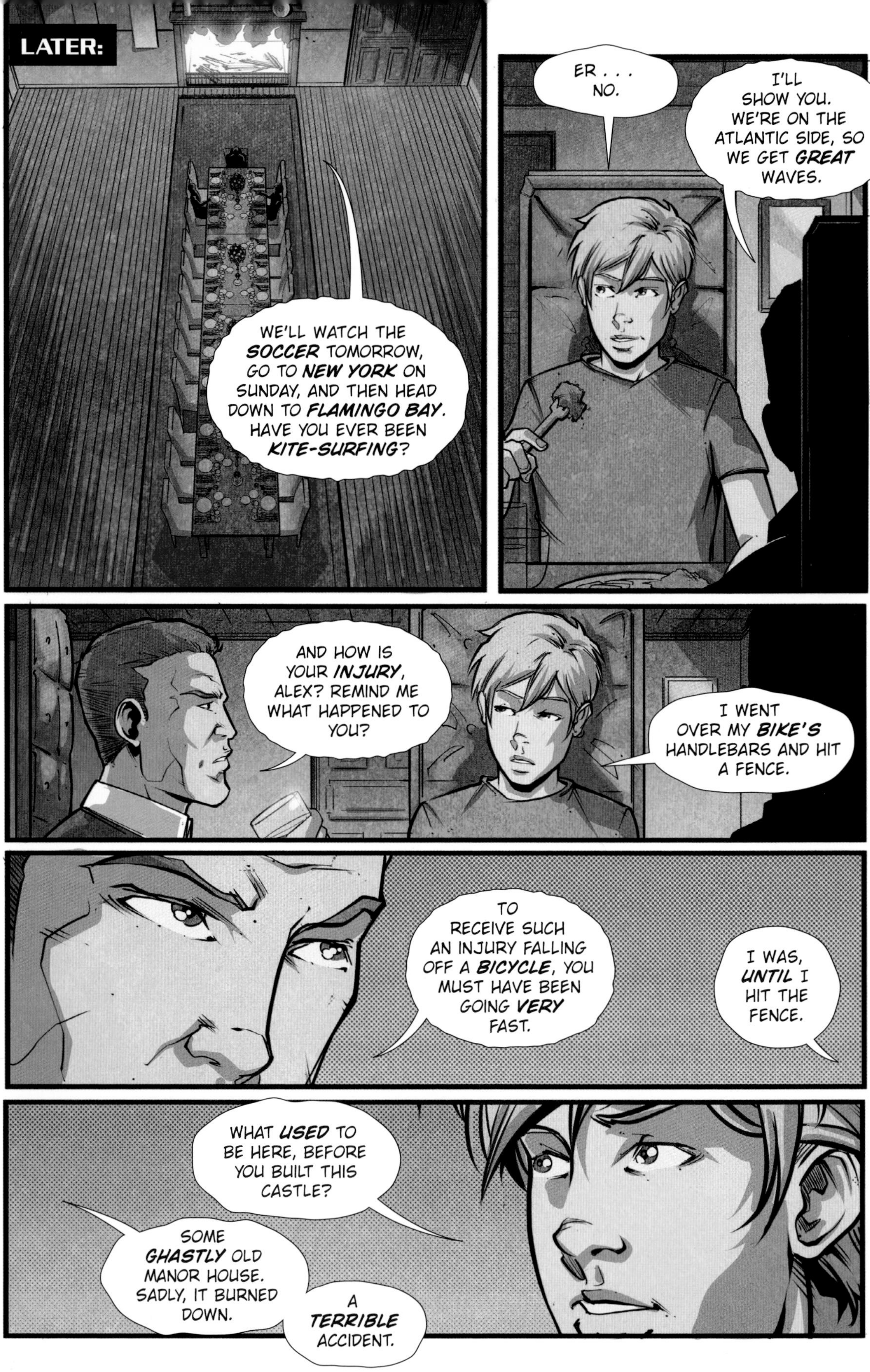
LATER:
WE'LL WATCH THE SOCCER TOMORROW, GO TO NEW YORK ON SUNDAY, AND THEN HEAD DOWN TO FLAMINGO BAY. HAVE YOU EVER BEEN KITE-SURFING?
ER . . . NO.
I'LL SHOW YOU. WE'RE ON THE ATLANTIC SIDE, SO WE GET GREAT WAVES.
AND HOW IS YOUR INJURY, ALEX? REMIND ME WHAT HAPPENED TO YOU?
I WENT OVER MY BIKE'S HANDLEBARS AND HIT A FENCE.
TO RECEIVE SUCH AN INJURY FALLING OFF A BICYCLE, YOU MUST HAVE BEEN GOING VERY FAST.
I WAS, UNTIL I HIT THE FENCE.
WHAT USED TO BE HERE, BEFORE YOU BUILT THIS CASTLE?
SOME GHASTLY OLD MANOR HOUSE. SADLY, IT BURNED DOWN.
A TERRIBLE ACCIDENT.

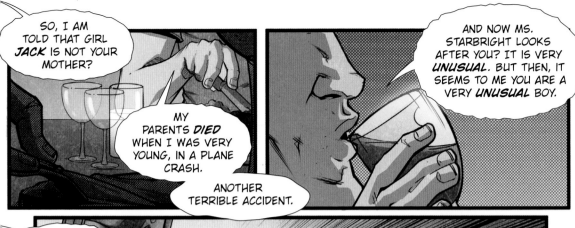

SO, I AM TOLD THAT GIRL *JACK* IS NOT YOUR MOTHER?

MY PARENTS *DIED* WHEN I WAS VERY YOUNG, IN A PLANE CRASH.

ANOTHER TERRIBLE ACCIDENT.

AND NOW MS. STARBRIGHT LOOKS AFTER YOU? IT IS VERY *UNUSUAL*. BUT THEN, IT SEEMS TO ME YOU ARE A VERY *UNUSUAL* BOY.

IT WOULD BE INTERESTING, I THINK, TO HAVE A *SON* LIKE YOU.

KOF!

KOF!

HHHNNNNN!

FOR GOD'S SAKE, PAUL, USE YOUR *INHALER!*

LEFT FRONT POCKET, PAUL.

HHHHH

THANKS, ALEX.

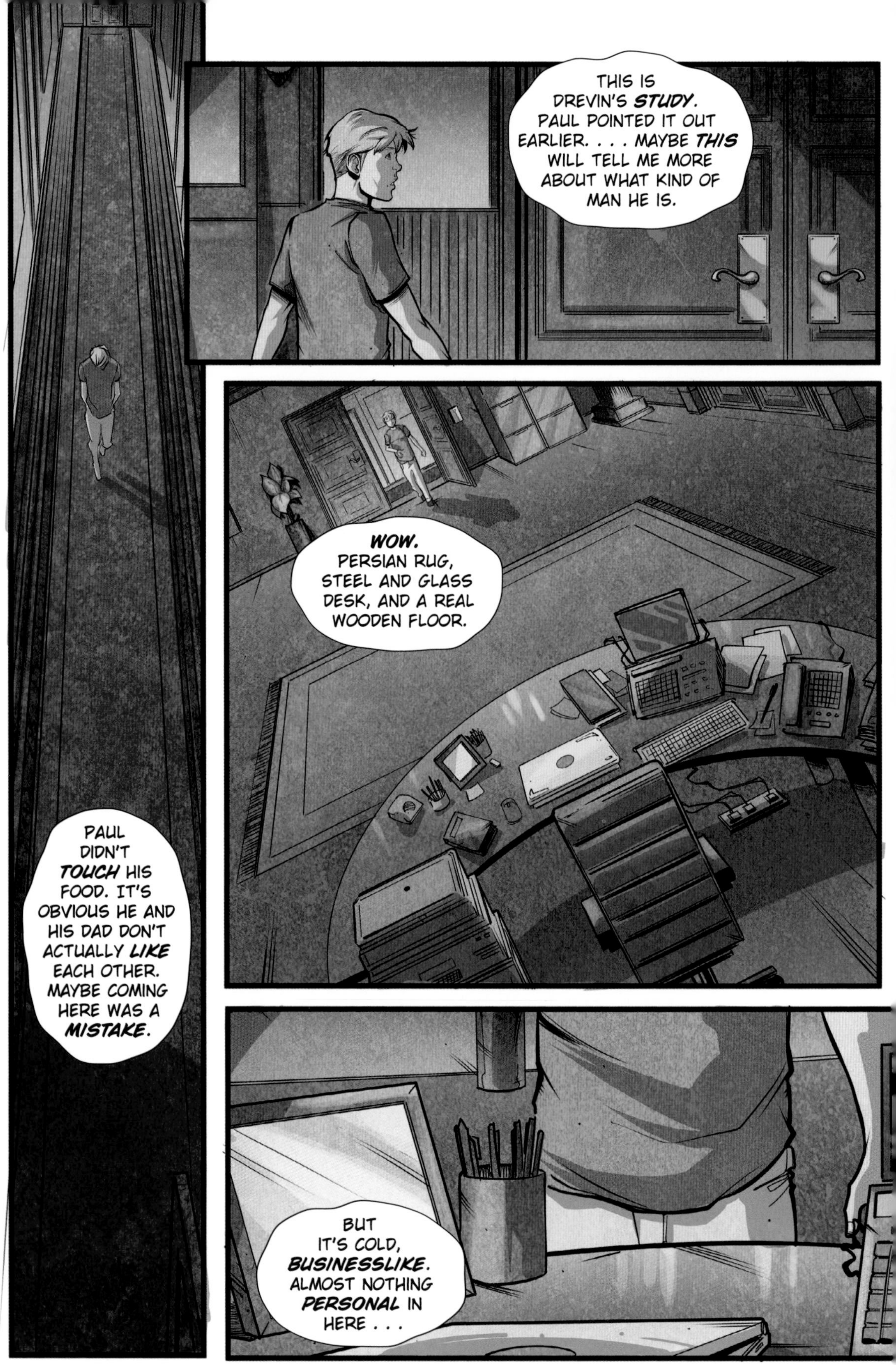
THIS IS DREVIN'S STUDY. PAUL POINTED IT OUT EARLIER. . . . MAYBE THIS WILL TELL ME MORE ABOUT WHAT KIND OF MAN HE IS.
WOW. PERSIAN RUG, STEEL AND GLASS DESK, AND A REAL WOODEN FLOOR.
PAUL DIDN'T TOUCH HIS FOOD. IT'S OBVIOUS HE AND HIS DAD DON'T ACTUALLY LIKE EACH OTHER. MAYBE COMING HERE WAS A MISTAKE.
BUT IT'S COLD, BUSINESSLIKE. ALMOST NOTHING PERSONAL IN HERE . . .

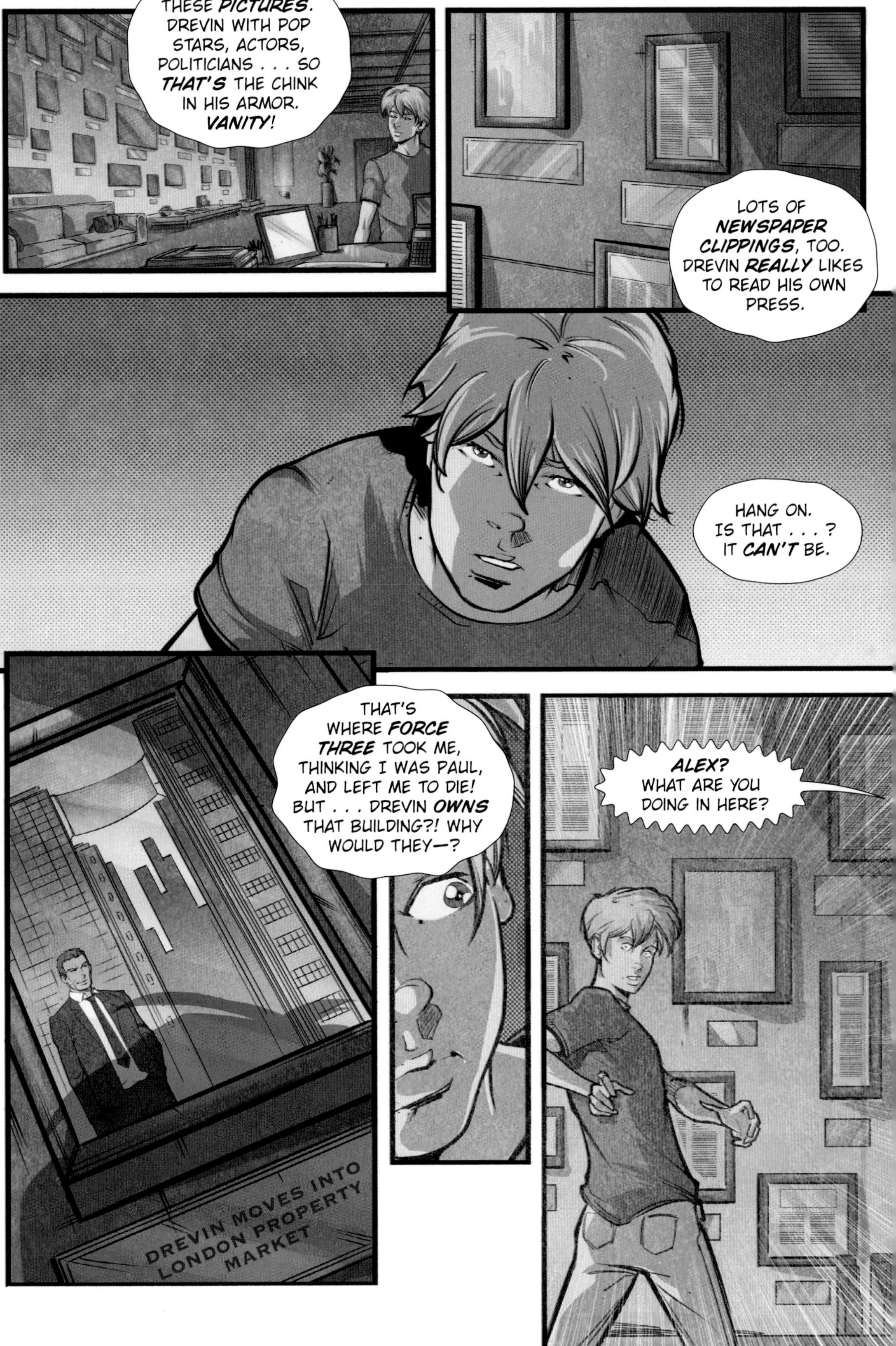
EXCEPT THESE **PICTURES**. DREVIN WITH POP STARS, ACTORS, POLITICIANS . . . SO **THAT'S** THE CHINK IN HIS ARMOR. **VANITY**!
LOTS OF **NEWSPAPER CLIPPINGS**, TOO. DREVIN **REALLY** LIKES TO READ HIS OWN PRESS.
HANG ON. IS THAT . . . ? IT **CAN'T** BE.
DREVIN MOVES INTO LONDON PROPERTY MARKET
THAT'S WHERE **FORCE THREE** TOOK ME, THINKING I WAS PAUL, AND LEFT ME TO DIE! BUT . . . DREVIN **OWNS** THAT BUILDING?! WHY WOULD THEY—?
ALEX? WHAT ARE YOU DOING IN HERE?

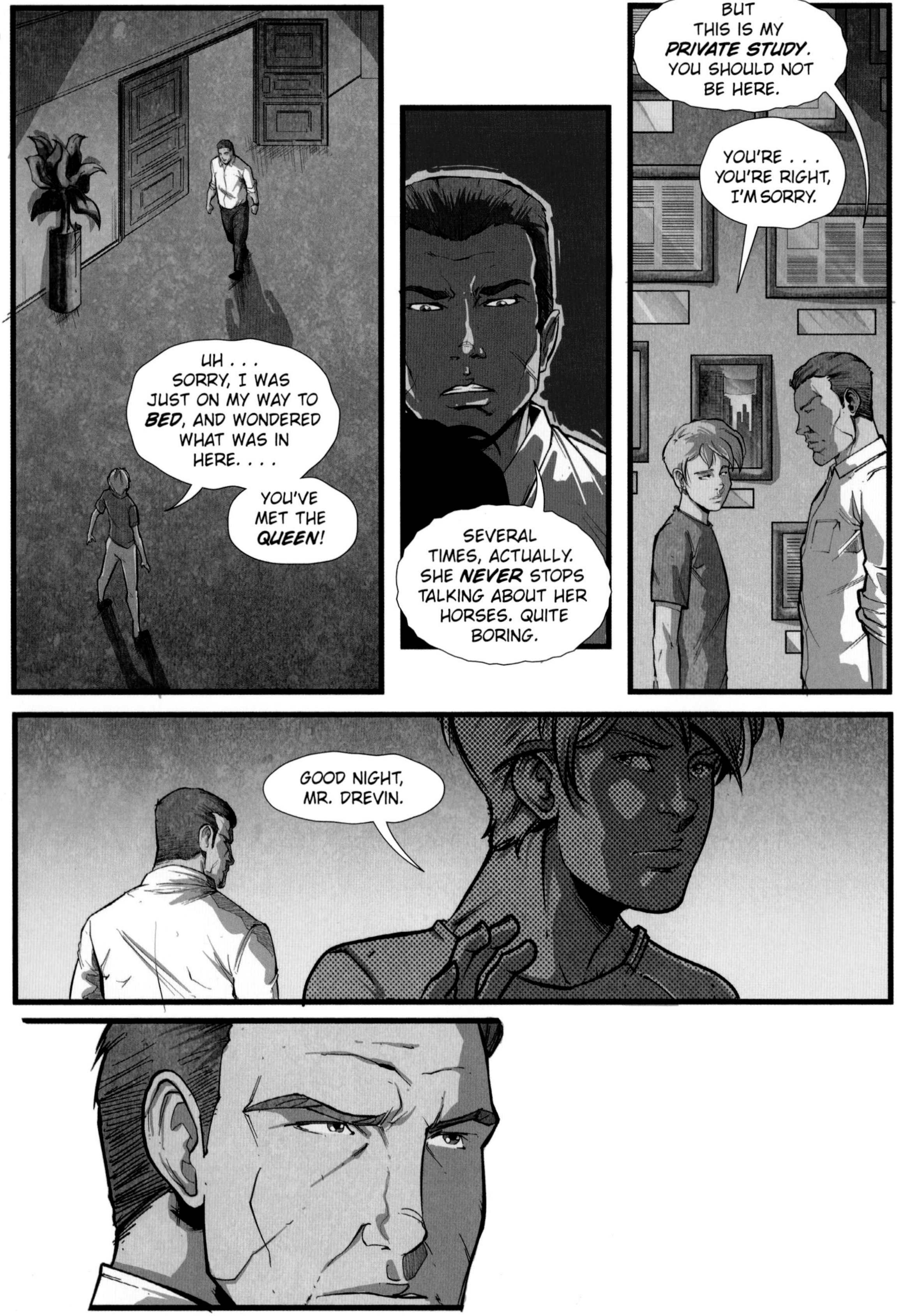
UH . . . SORRY, I WAS JUST ON MY WAY TO BED, AND WONDERED WHAT WAS IN HERE. . . .
YOU'VE MET THE QUEEN!
SEVERAL TIMES, ACTUALLY. SHE NEVER STOPS TALKING ABOUT HER HORSES. QUITE BORING.
BUT THIS IS MY PRIVATE STUDY. YOU SHOULD NOT BE HERE.
YOU'RE . . . YOU'RE RIGHT, I'M SORRY.
GOOD NIGHT, MR. DREVIN.

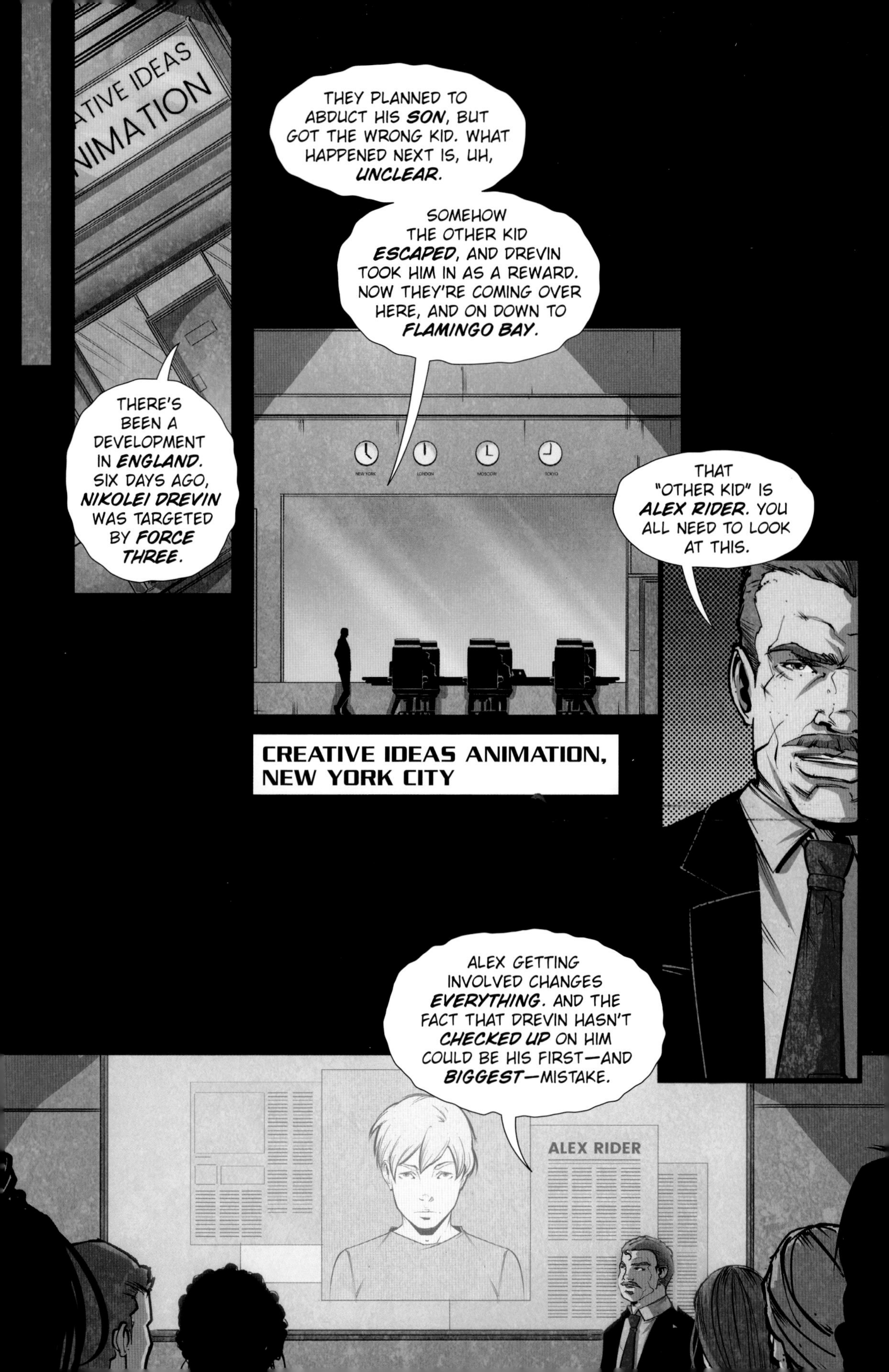

ATIVE IDEAS
NIMATION
THERE'S BEEN A DEVELOPMENT IN ENGLAND. SIX DAYS AGO, NIKOLEI DREVIN WAS TARGETED BY FORCE THREE.
THEY PLANNED TO ABDUCT HIS SON, BUT GOT THE WRONG KID. WHAT HAPPENED NEXT IS, UH, UNCLEAR.
SOMEHOW THE OTHER KID ESCAPED, AND DREVIN TOOK HIM IN AS A REWARD. NOW THEY'RE COMING OVER HERE, AND ON DOWN TO FLAMINGO BAY.
NEW YORK
LONDON
MOSCOW
TOKYO
CREATIVE IDEAS ANIMATION, NEW YORK CITY
THAT "OTHER KID" IS ALEX RIDER. YOU ALL NEED TO LOOK AT THIS.
ALEX GETTING INVOLVED CHANGES EVERYTHING. AND THE FACT THAT DREVIN HASN'T CHECKED UP ON HIM COULD BE HIS FIRST—AND BIGGEST—MISTAKE.
ALEX RIDER

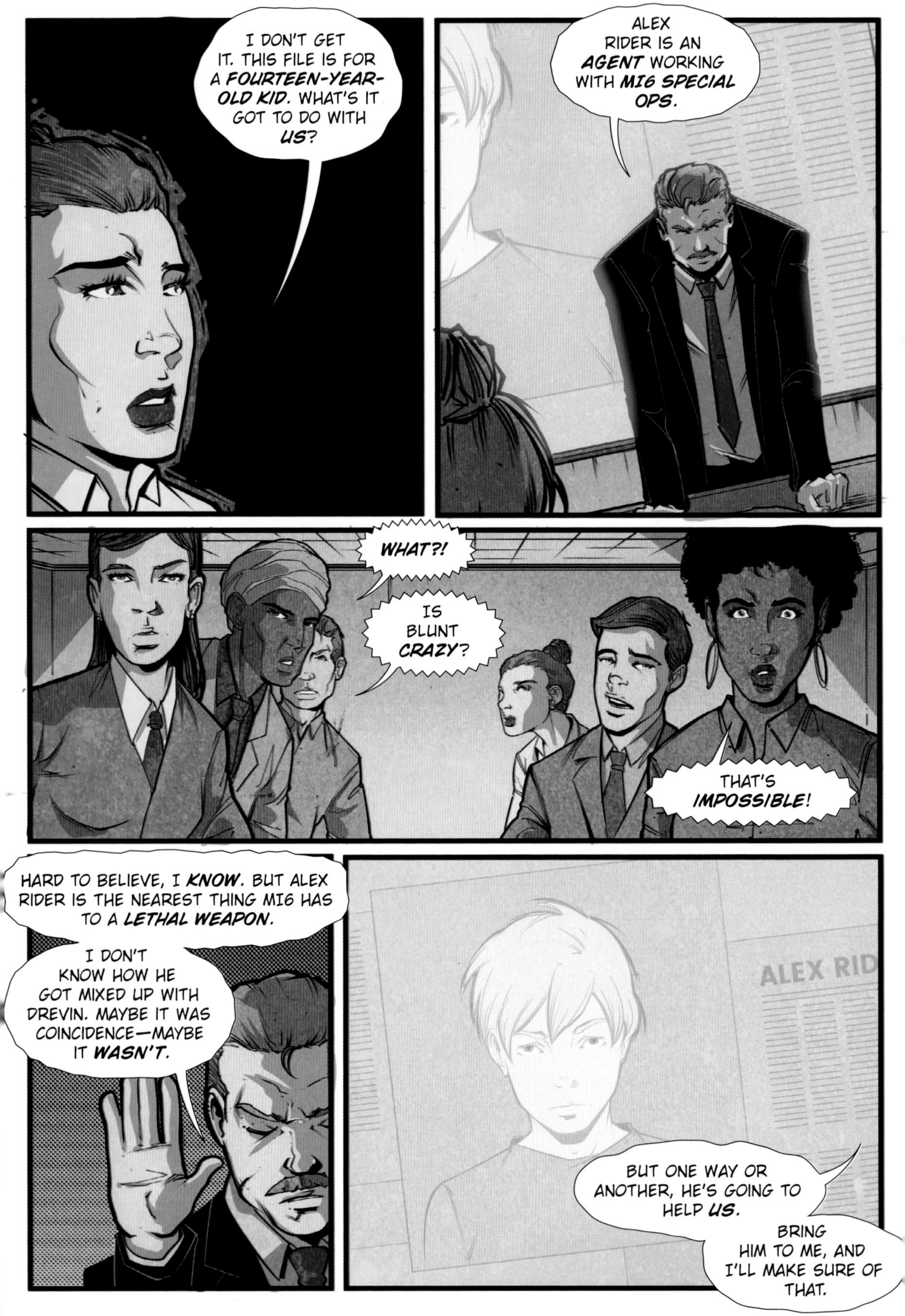

I DON'T GET IT. THIS FILE IS FOR A FOURTEEN-YEAR-OLD KID. WHAT'S IT GOT TO DO WITH US?
ALEX RIDER IS AN AGENT WORKING WITH MI6 SPECIAL OPS.
WHAT?!
IS BLUNT CRAZY?
THAT'S IMPOSSIBLE!
HARD TO BELIEVE, I KNOW. BUT ALEX RIDER IS THE NEAREST THING MI6 HAS TO A LETHAL WEAPON.
I DON'T KNOW HOW HE GOT MIXED UP WITH DREVIN. MAYBE IT WAS COINCIDENCE—MAYBE IT WASN'T.
ALEX RID
BUT ONE WAY OR ANOTHER, HE'S GOING TO HELP US.
BRING HIM TO ME, AND I'LL MAKE SURE OF THAT.

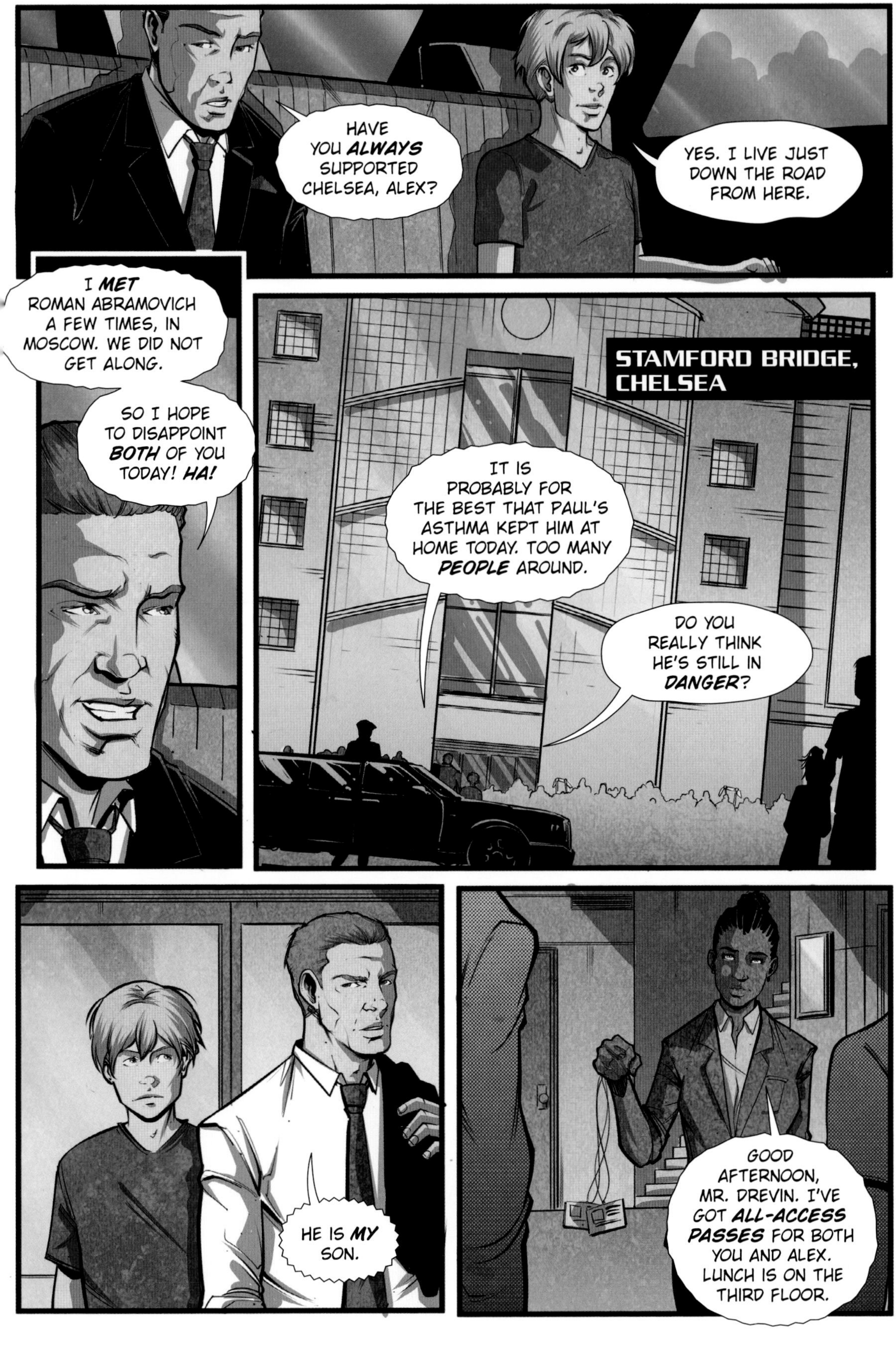

HAVE YOU **ALWAYS** SUPPORTED CHELSEA, ALEX?
YES. I LIVE JUST DOWN THE ROAD FROM HERE.
I **MET** ROMAN ABRAMOVICH A FEW TIMES, IN MOSCOW. WE DID NOT GET ALONG.
SO I HOPE TO DISAPPOINT **BOTH** OF YOU TODAY! **HA!**
STAMFORD BRIDGE, CHELSEA
IT IS PROBABLY FOR THE BEST THAT PAUL'S ASTHMA KEPT HIM AT HOME TODAY. TOO MANY **PEOPLE** AROUND.
DO YOU REALLY THINK HE'S STILL IN **DANGER**?
HE IS **MY** SON.
GOOD AFTERNOON, MR. DREVIN. I'VE GOT **ALL-ACCESS PASSES** FOR BOTH YOU AND ALEX. LUNCH IS ON THE THIRD FLOOR.

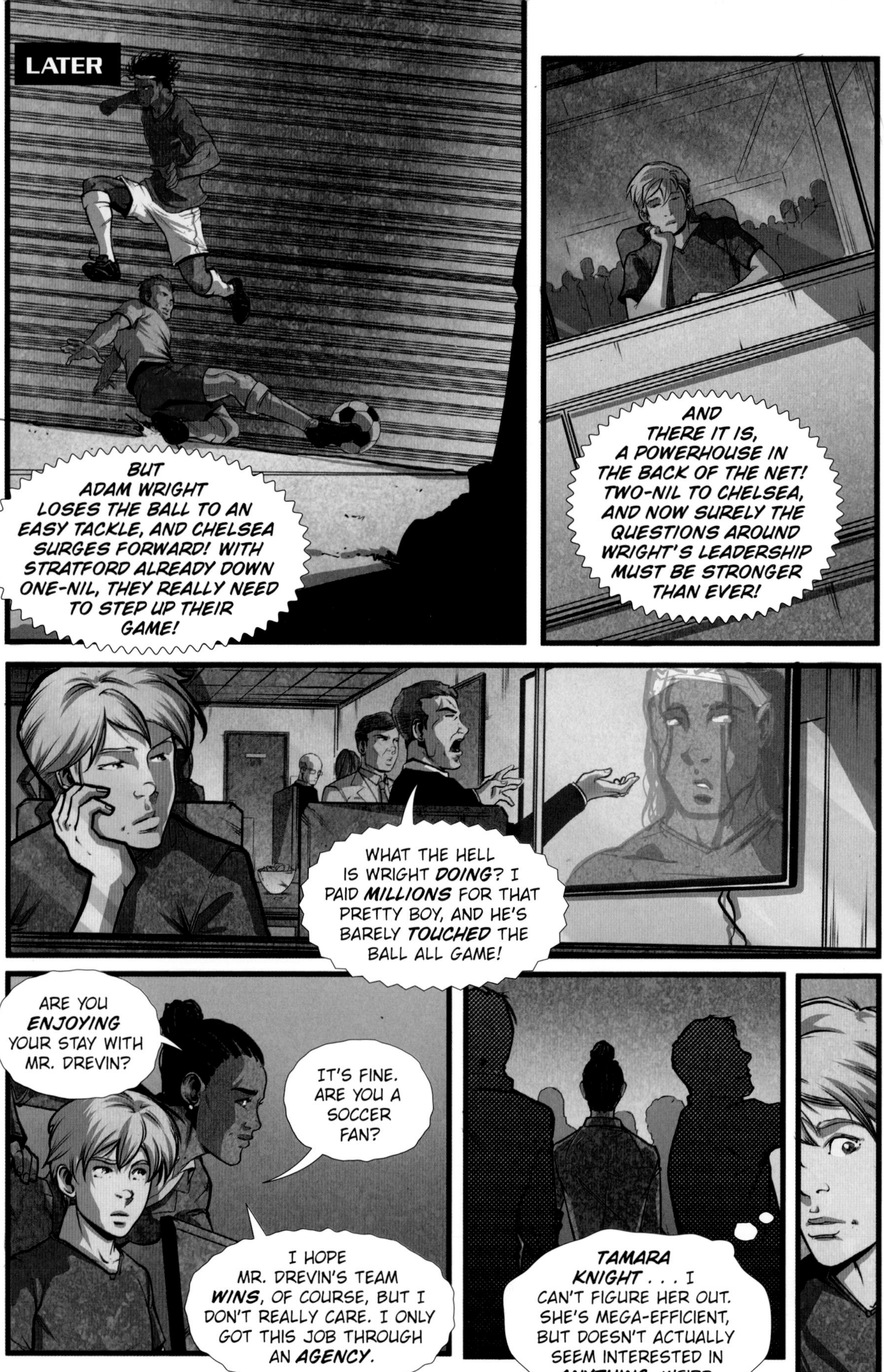
LATER
BUT ADAM WRIGHT LOSES THE BALL TO AN EASY TACKLE, AND CHELSEA SURGES FORWARD! WITH STRATFORD ALREADY DOWN ONE-NIL, THEY REALLY NEED TO STEP UP THEIR GAME!
AND THERE IT IS, A POWERHOUSE IN THE BACK OF THE NET! TWO-NIL TO CHELSEA, AND NOW SURELY THE QUESTIONS AROUND WRIGHT'S LEADERSHIP MUST BE STRONGER THAN EVER!
WHAT THE HELL IS WRIGHT DOING? I PAID MILLIONS FOR THAT PRETTY BOY, AND HE'S BARELY TOUCHED THE BALL ALL GAME!
ARE YOU ENJOYING YOUR STAY WITH MR. DREVIN?
IT'S FINE. ARE YOU A SOCCER FAN?
I HOPE MR. DREVIN'S TEAM WINS, OF COURSE, BUT I DON'T REALLY CARE. I ONLY GOT THIS JOB THROUGH AN AGENCY.
TAMARA KNIGHT . . . I CAN'T FIGURE HER OUT. SHE'S MEGA-EFFICIENT, BUT DOESN'T ACTUALLY SEEM INTERESTED IN ANYTHING. WEIRD.

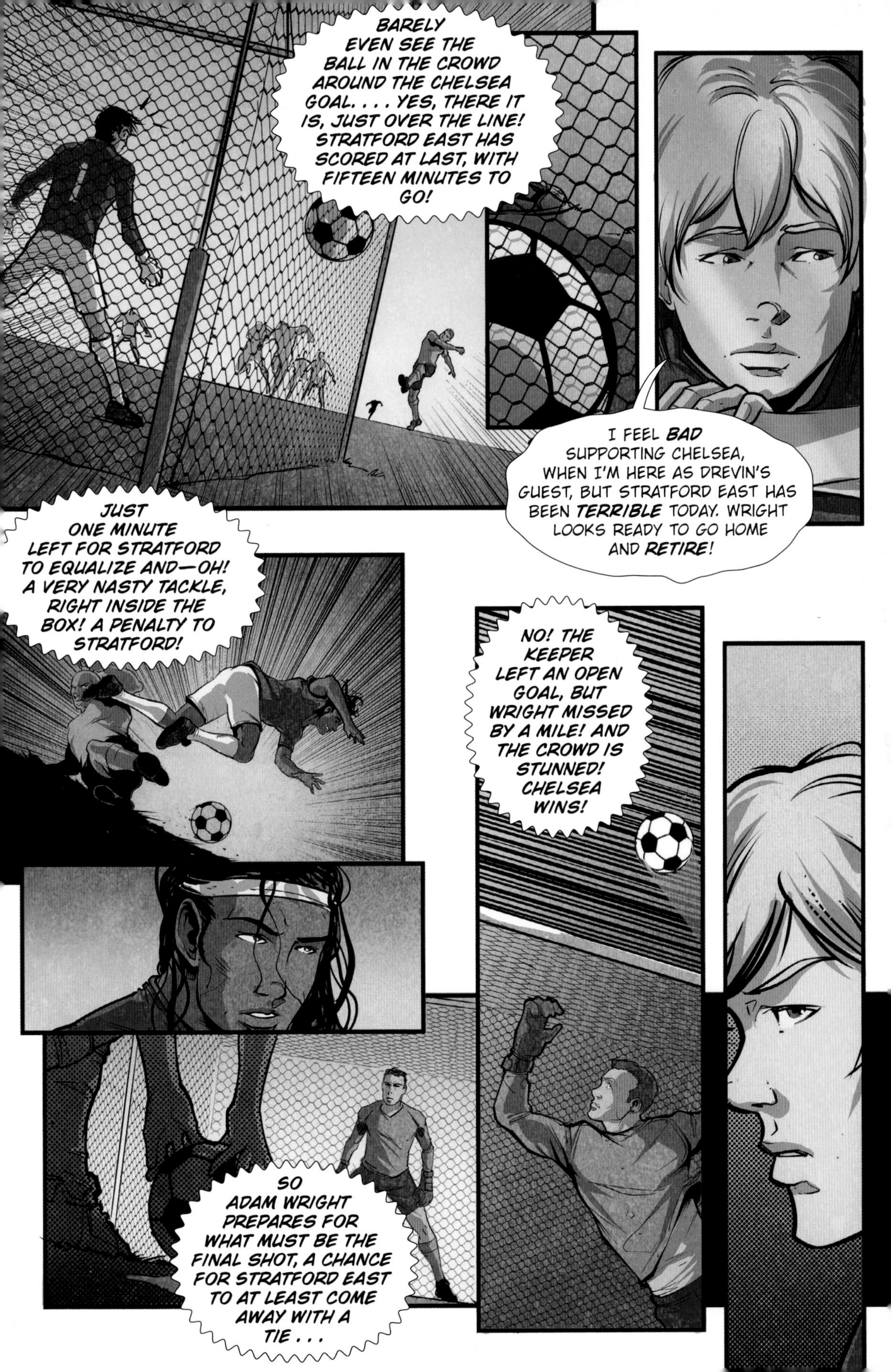
BARELY EVEN SEE THE BALL IN THE CROWD AROUND THE CHELSEA GOAL. . . . YES, THERE IT IS, JUST OVER THE LINE! STRATFORD EAST HAS SCORED AT LAST, WITH FIFTEEN MINUTES TO GO!
I FEEL BAD SUPPORTING CHELSEA, WHEN I'M HERE AS DREVIN'S GUEST, BUT STRATFORD EAST HAS BEEN TERRIBLE TODAY. WRIGHT LOOKS READY TO GO HOME AND RETIRE!
JUST ONE MINUTE LEFT FOR STRATFORD TO EQUALIZE AND—OH! A VERY NASTY TACKLE, RIGHT INSIDE THE BOX! A PENALTY TO STRATFORD!
SO ADAM WRIGHT PREPARES FOR WHAT MUST BE THE FINAL SHOT, A CHANCE FOR STRATFORD EAST TO AT LEAST COME AWAY WITH A TIE . . .
NO! THE KEEPER LEFT AN OPEN GOAL, BUT WRIGHT MISSED BY A MILE! AND THE CROWD IS STUNNED! CHELSEA WINS!

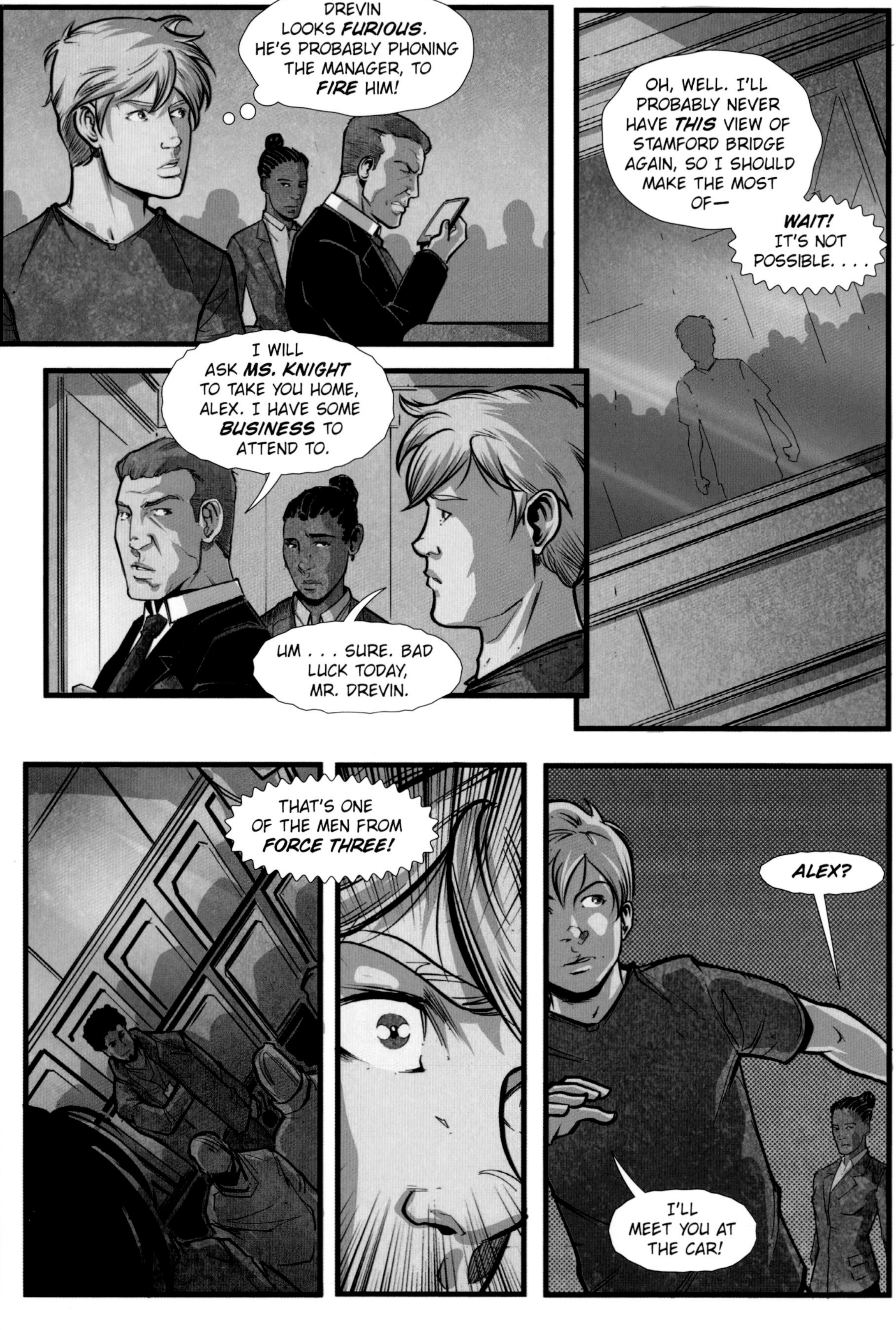
DREVIN LOOKS FURIOUS. HE'S PROBABLY PHONING THE MANAGER, TO FIRE HIM!
OH, WELL. I'LL PROBABLY NEVER HAVE THIS VIEW OF STAMFORD BRIDGE AGAIN, SO I SHOULD MAKE THE MOST OF—
WAIT! IT'S NOT POSSIBLE. . . .
I WILL ASK MS. KNIGHT TO TAKE YOU HOME, ALEX. I HAVE SOME BUSINESS TO ATTEND TO.
UM . . . SURE. BAD LUCK TODAY, MR. DREVIN.
THAT'S ONE OF THE MEN FROM FORCE THREE!
ALEX?
I'LL MEET YOU AT THE CAR!

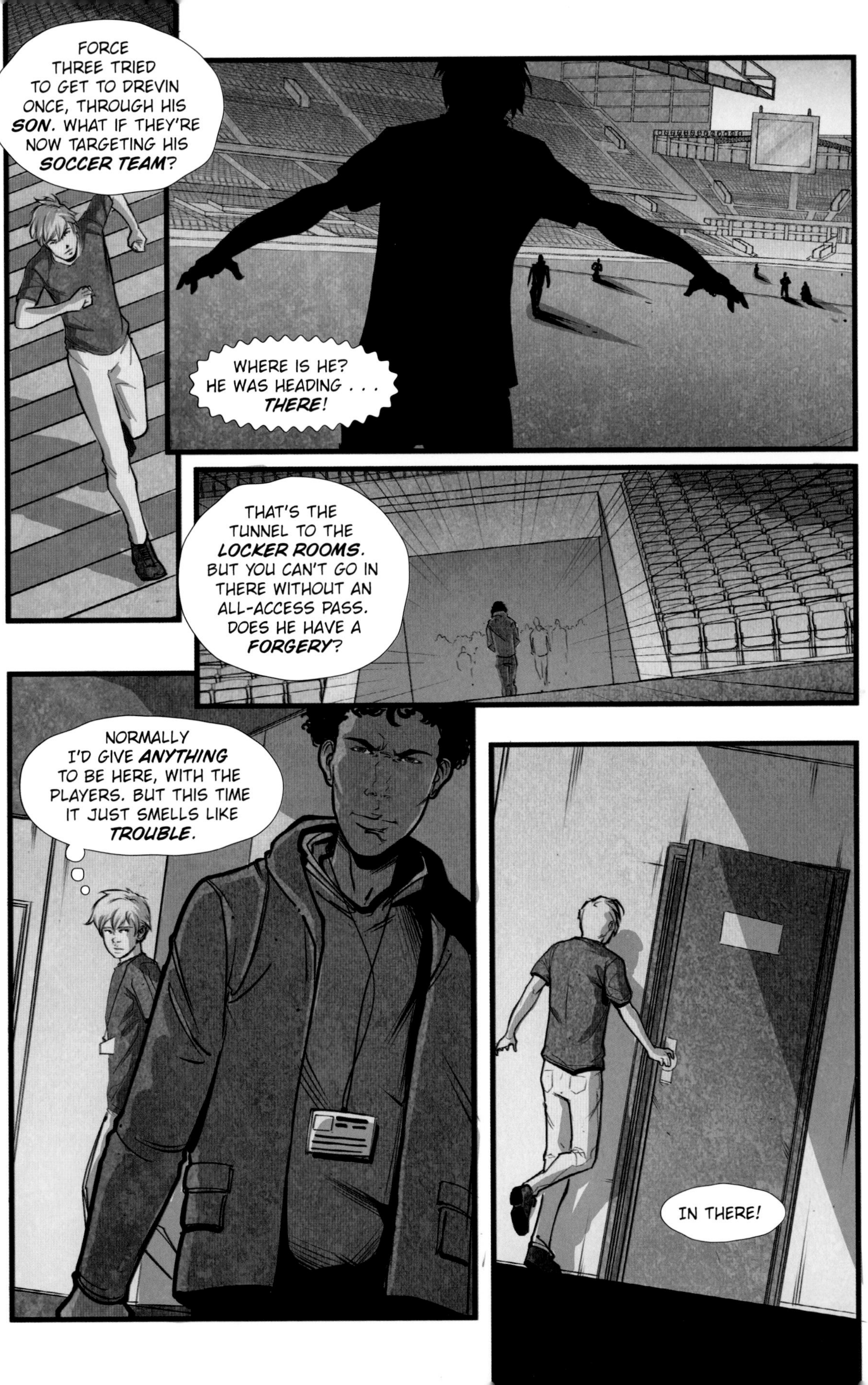
FORCE THREE TRIED TO GET TO DREVIN ONCE, THROUGH HIS SON. WHAT IF THEY'RE NOW TARGETING HIS SOCCER TEAM?
WHERE IS HE? HE WAS HEADING . . . THERE!
THAT'S THE TUNNEL TO THE LOCKER ROOMS. BUT YOU CAN'T GO IN THERE WITHOUT AN ALL-ACCESS PASS. DOES HE HAVE A FORGERY?
NORMALLY I'D GIVE ANYTHING TO BE HERE, WITH THE PLAYERS. BUT THIS TIME IT JUST SMELLS LIKE TROUBLE.
IN THERE!

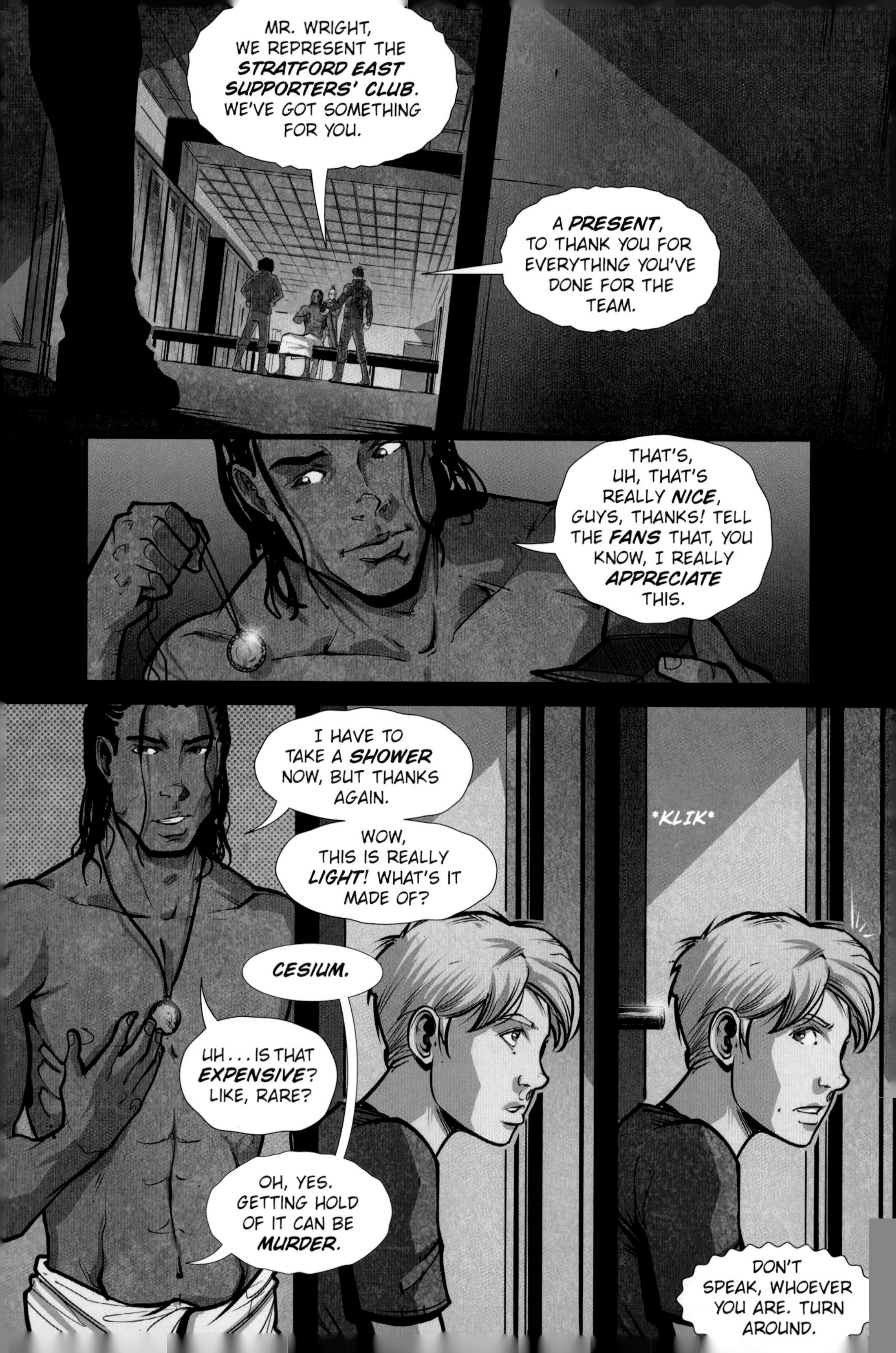
MR. WRIGHT, WE REPRESENT THE STRATFORD EAST SUPPORTERS' CLUB. WE'VE GOT SOMETHING FOR YOU.
A PRESENT, TO THANK YOU FOR EVERYTHING YOU'VE DONE FOR THE TEAM.
THAT'S, UH, THAT'S REALLY NICE, GUYS, THANKS! TELL THE FANS THAT, YOU KNOW, I REALLY APPRECIATE THIS.
I HAVE TO TAKE A SHOWER NOW, BUT THANKS AGAIN.
WOW, THIS IS REALLY LIGHT! WHAT'S IT MADE OF?
CESIUM.
UH . . . IS THAT EXPENSIVE? LIKE, RARE?
OH, YES. GETTING HOLD OF IT CAN BE MURDER.
KLIK
DON'T SPEAK, WHOEVER YOU ARE. TURN AROUND.

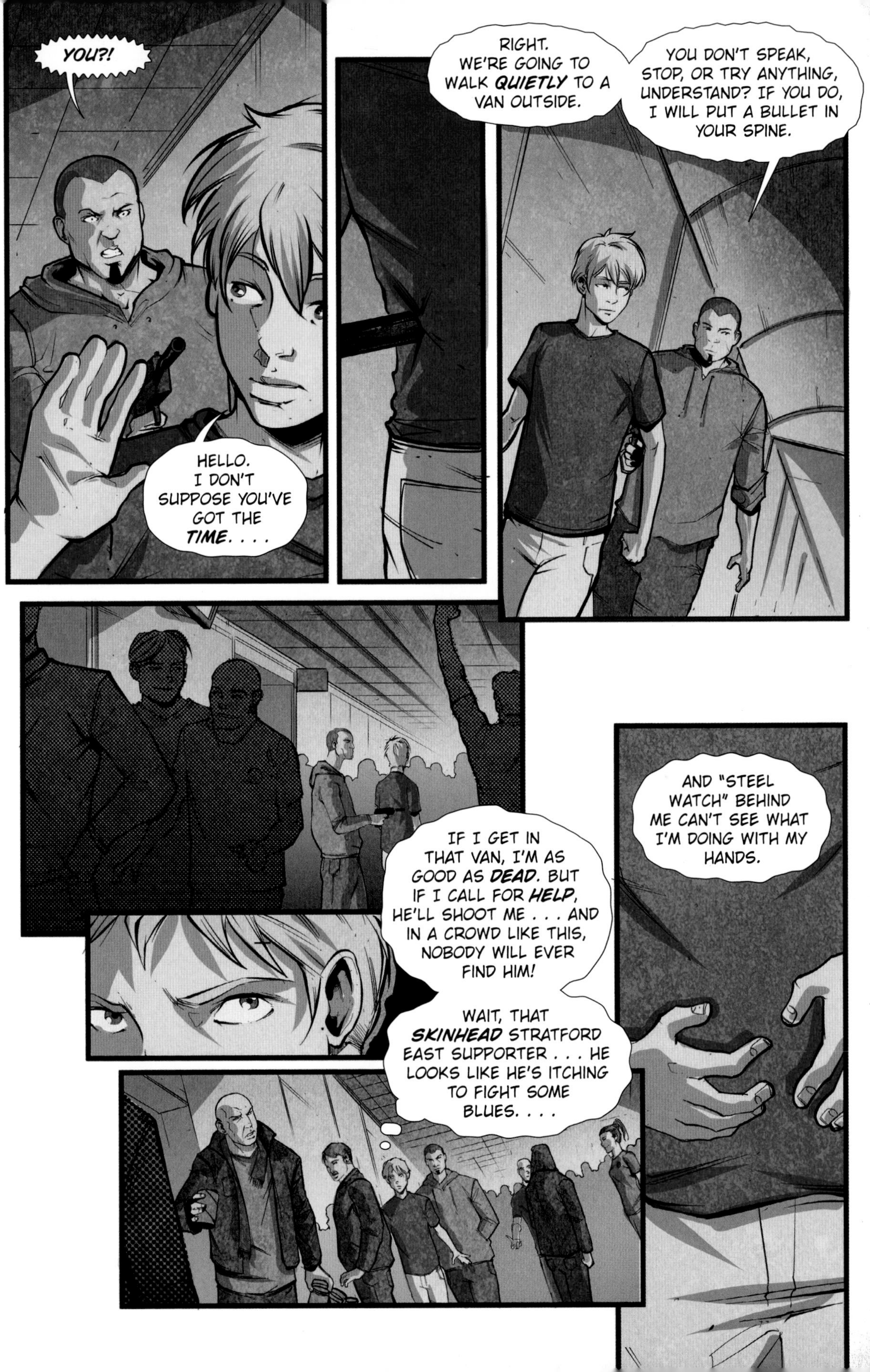
YOU?!
HELLO. I DON'T SUPPOSE YOU'VE GOT THE TIME. . . .
RIGHT. WE'RE GOING TO WALK QUIETLY TO A VAN OUTSIDE.
YOU DON'T SPEAK, STOP, OR TRY ANYTHING, UNDERSTAND? IF YOU DO, I WILL PUT A BULLET IN YOUR SPINE.
IF I GET IN THAT VAN, I'M AS GOOD AS DEAD. BUT IF I CALL FOR HELP, HE'LL SHOOT ME . . . AND IN A CROWD LIKE THIS, NOBODY WILL EVER FIND HIM!
AND "STEEL WATCH" BEHIND ME CAN'T SEE WHAT I'M DOING WITH MY HANDS.
WAIT, THAT SKINHEAD STRATFORD EAST SUPPORTER . . . HE LOOKS LIKE HE'S ITCHING TO FIGHT SOME BLUES. . . .

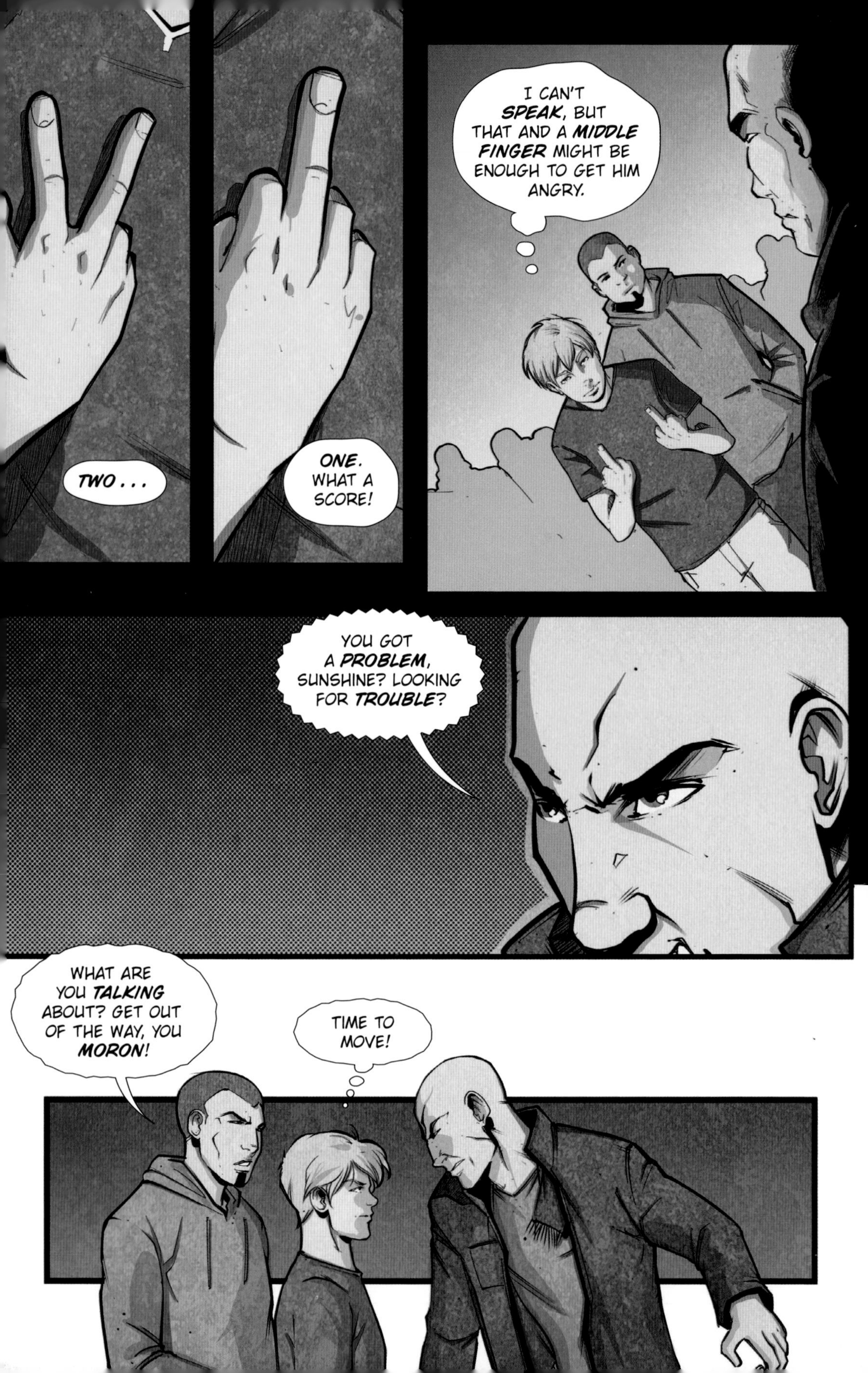
TWO . . .
ONE. WHAT A SCORE!
I CAN'T SPEAK, BUT THAT AND A MIDDLE FINGER MIGHT BE ENOUGH TO GET HIM ANGRY.
YOU GOT A PROBLEM, SUNSHINE? LOOKING FOR TROUBLE?
WHAT ARE YOU TALKING ABOUT? GET OUT OF THE WAY, YOU MORON!
TIME TO MOVE!

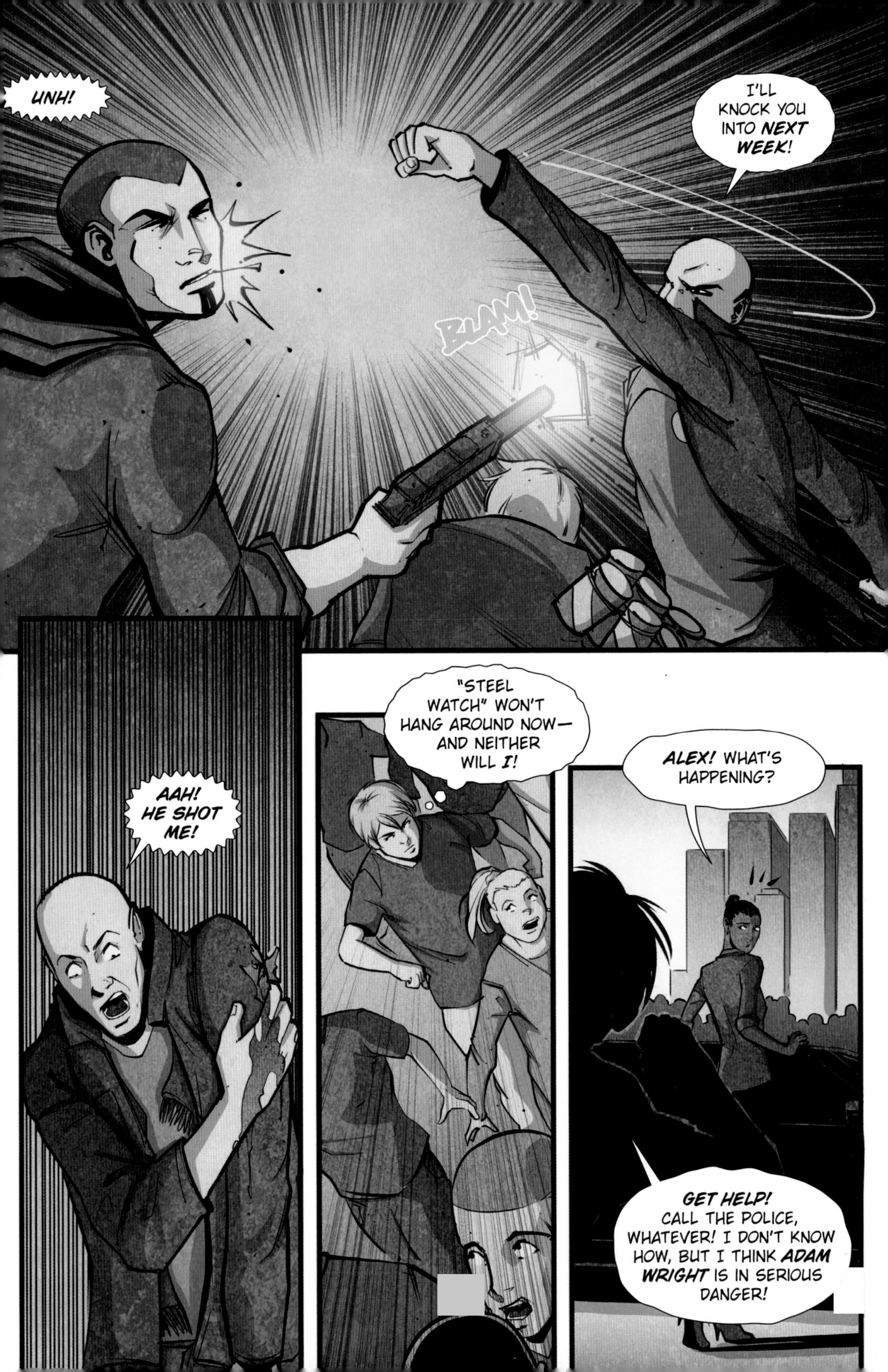
UNH!
I'LL KNOCK YOU INTO NEXT WEEK!
BLAM!
AAH! HE SHOT ME!
"STEEL WATCH" WON'T HANG AROUND NOW— AND NEITHER WILL I!
ALEX! WHAT'S HAPPENING?
GET HELP! CALL THE POLICE, WHATEVER! I DON'T KNOW HOW, BUT I THINK ADAM WRIGHT IS IN SERIOUS DANGER!

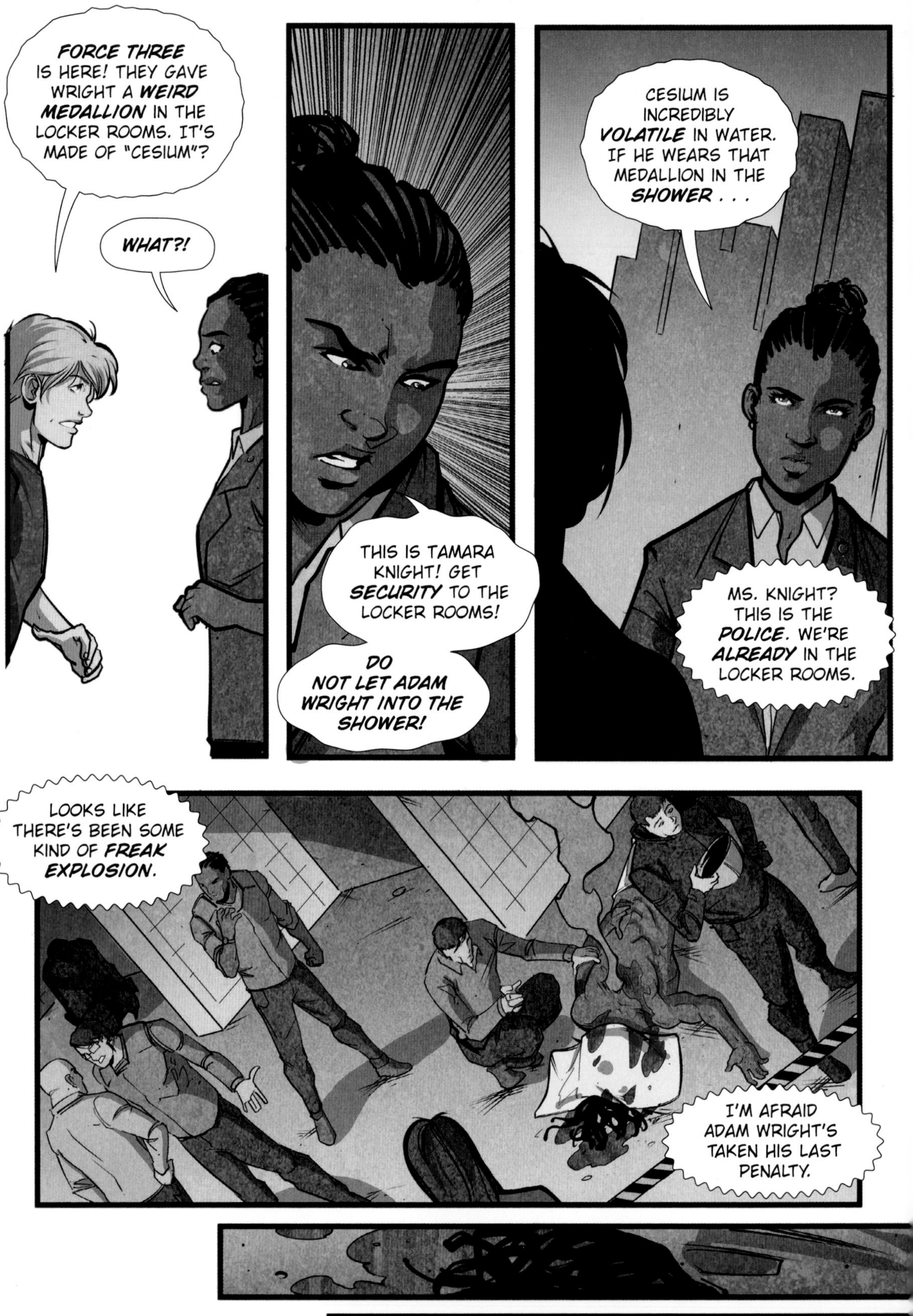
FORCE THREE IS HERE! THEY GAVE WRIGHT A WEIRD MEDALLION IN THE LOCKER ROOMS. IT'S MADE OF "CESIUM"?
WHAT?!
THIS IS TAMARA KNIGHT! GET SECURITY TO THE LOCKER ROOMS!
DO NOT LET ADAM WRIGHT INTO THE SHOWER!
CESIUM IS INCREDIBLY VOLATILE IN WATER. IF HE WEARS THAT MEDALLION IN THE SHOWER . . .
MS. KNIGHT? THIS IS THE POLICE. WE'RE ALREADY IN THE LOCKER ROOMS.
LOOKS LIKE THERE'S BEEN SOME KIND OF FREAK EXPLOSION.
I'M AFRAID ADAM WRIGHT'S TAKEN HIS LAST PENALTY.

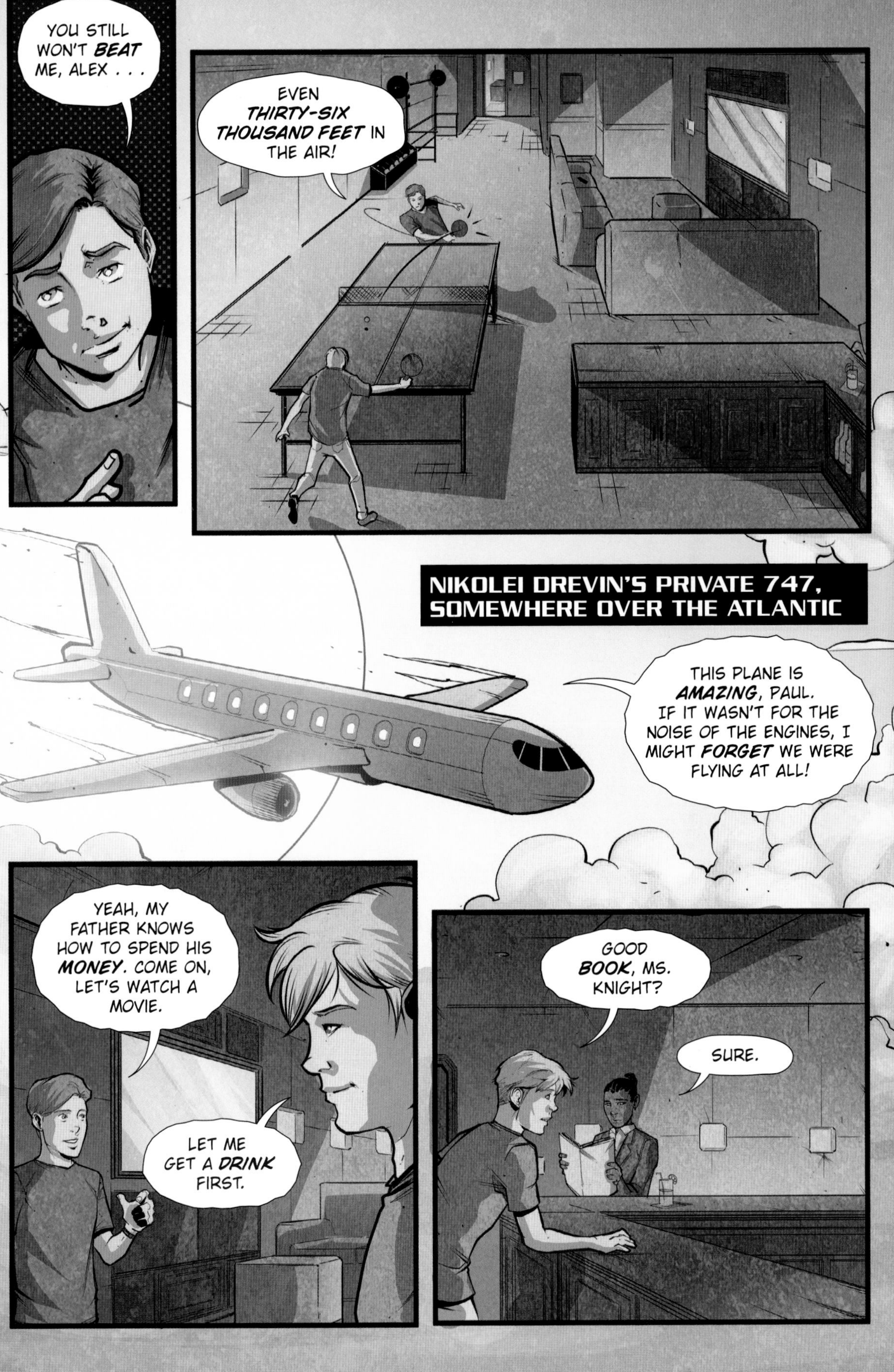
YOU STILL WON'T BEAT ME, ALEX . . .
EVEN THIRTY-SIX THOUSAND FEET IN THE AIR!
NIKOLEI DREVIN'S PRIVATE 747, SOMEWHERE OVER THE ATLANTIC
THIS PLANE IS AMAZING, PAUL. IF IT WASN'T FOR THE NOISE OF THE ENGINES, I MIGHT FORGET WE WERE FLYING AT ALL!
YEAH, MY FATHER KNOWS HOW TO SPEND HIS MONEY. COME ON, LET'S WATCH A MOVIE.
LET ME GET A DRINK FIRST.
GOOD BOOK, MS. KNIGHT?
SURE.

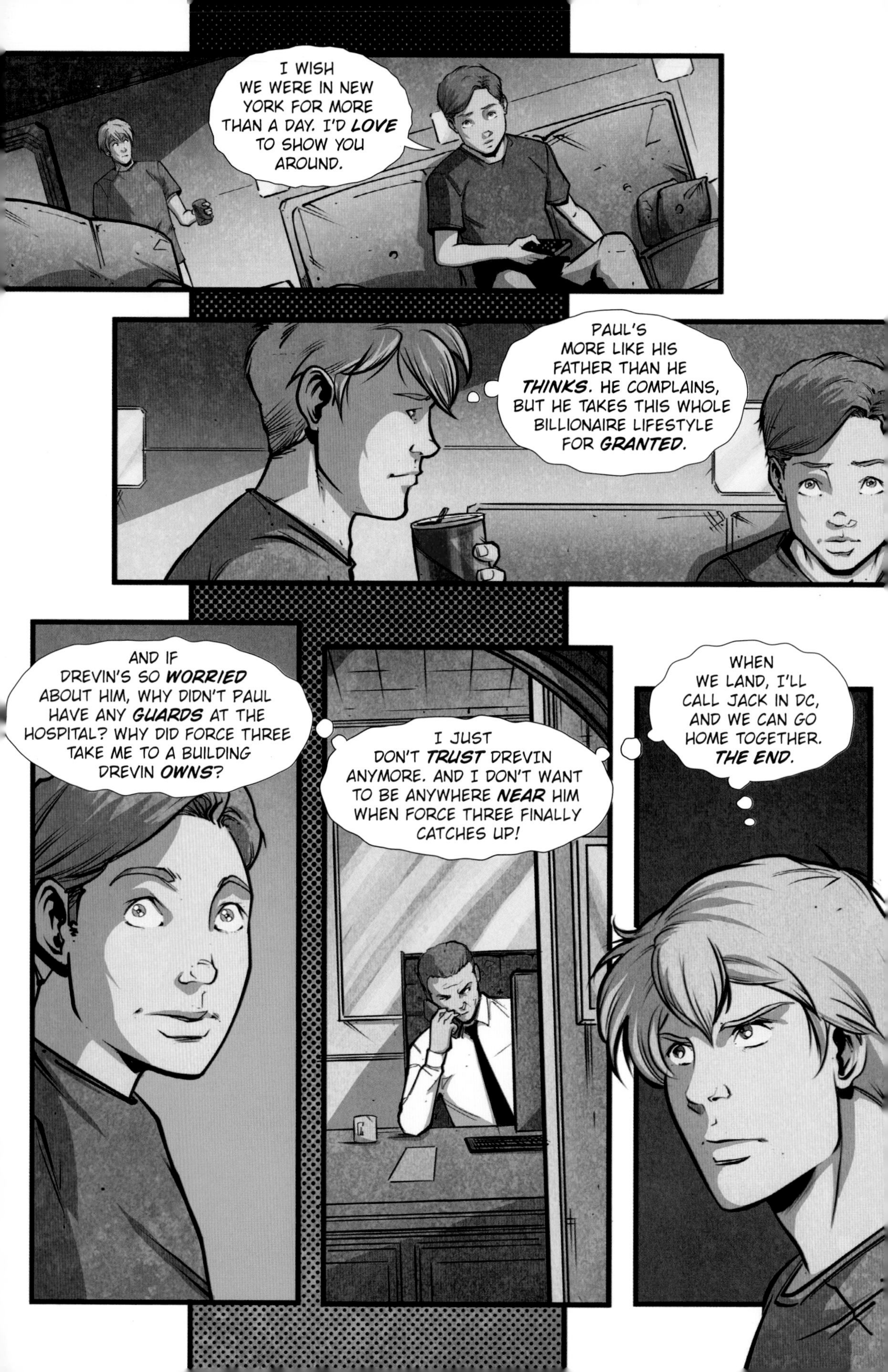
I WISH WE WERE IN NEW YORK FOR MORE THAN A DAY. I'D LOVE TO SHOW YOU AROUND.
PAUL'S MORE LIKE HIS FATHER THAN HE THINKS. HE COMPLAINS, BUT HE TAKES THIS WHOLE BILLIONAIRE LIFESTYLE FOR GRANTED.
AND IF DREVIN'S SO WORRIED ABOUT HIM, WHY DIDN'T PAUL HAVE ANY GUARDS AT THE HOSPITAL? WHY DID FORCE THREE TAKE ME TO A BUILDING DREVIN OWNS?
I JUST DON'T TRUST DREVIN ANYMORE. AND I DON'T WANT TO BE ANYWHERE NEAR HIM WHEN FORCE THREE FINALLY CATCHES UP!
WHEN WE LAND, I'LL CALL JACK IN DC, AND WE CAN GO HOME TOGETHER. THE END.

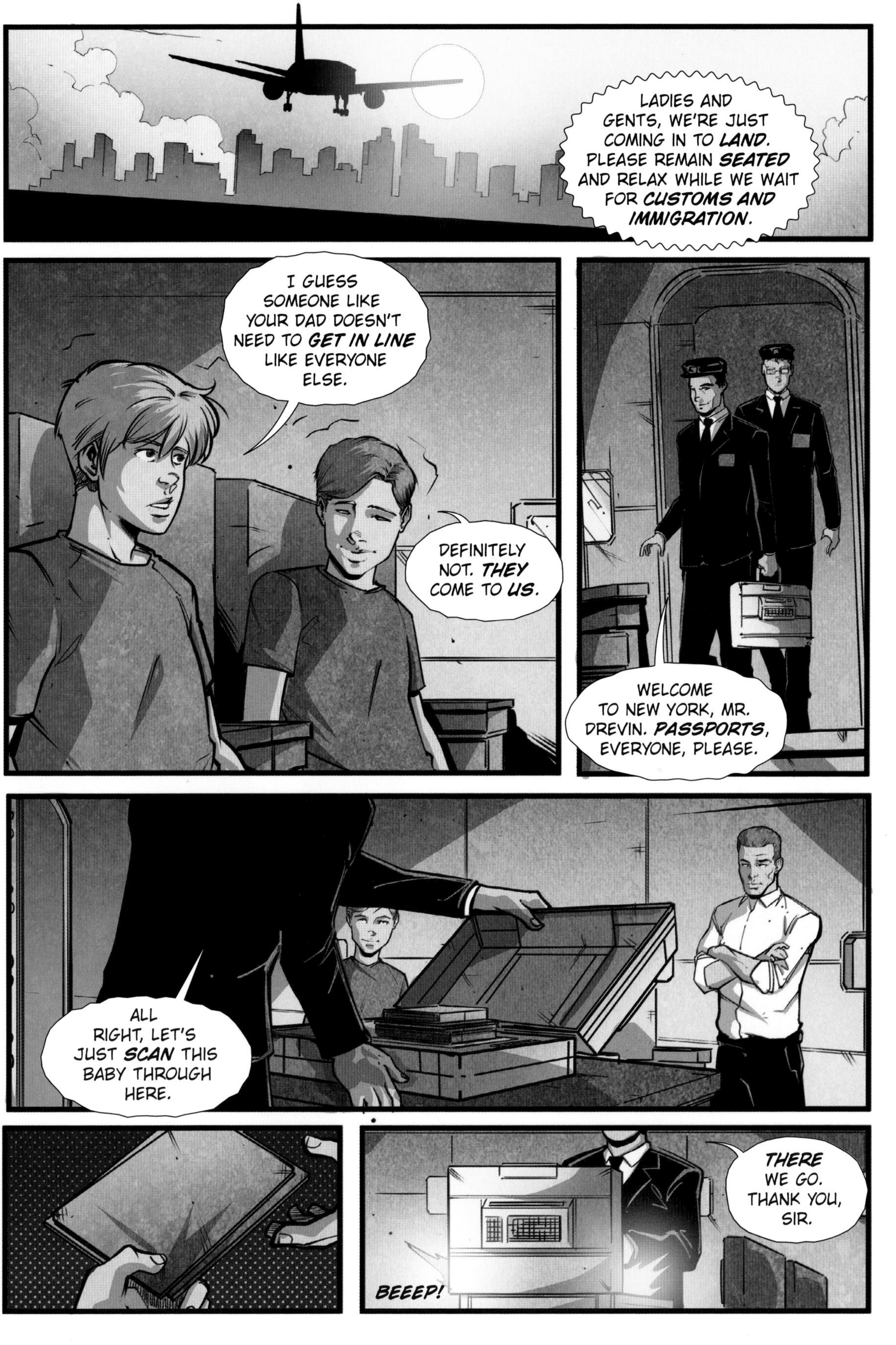
LADIES AND GENTS, WE'RE JUST COMING IN TO LAND. PLEASE REMAIN SEATED AND RELAX WHILE WE WAIT FOR CUSTOMS AND IMMIGRATION.
I GUESS SOMEONE LIKE YOUR DAD DOESN'T NEED TO GET IN LINE LIKE EVERYONE ELSE.
DEFINITELY NOT. THEY COME TO US.
WELCOME TO NEW YORK, MR. DREVIN. PASSPORTS, EVERYONE, PLEASE.
ALL RIGHT, LET'S JUST SCAN THIS BABY THROUGH HERE.
THERE WE GO. THANK YOU, SIR.
BEEEP!

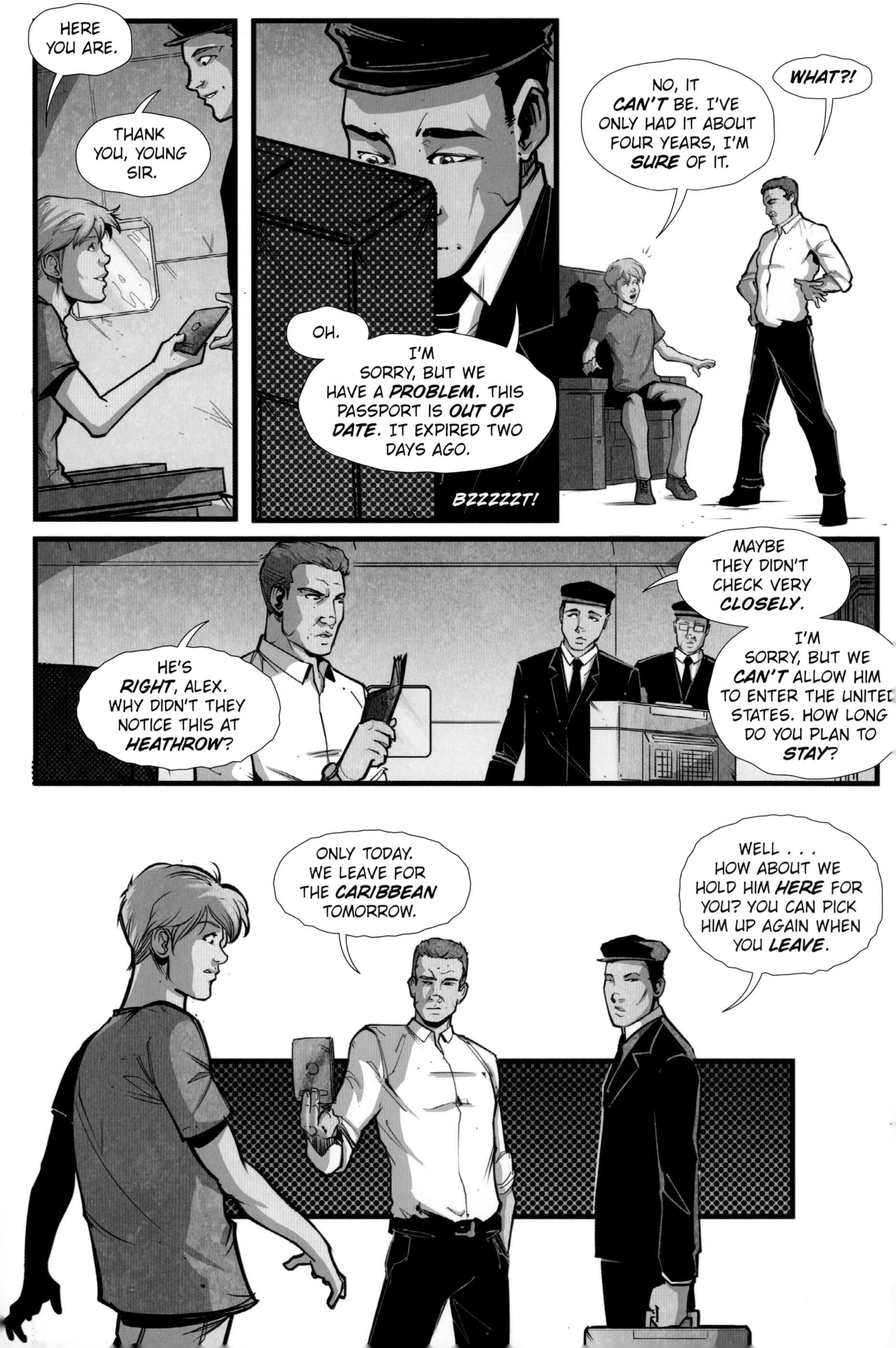
HERE YOU ARE.
THANK YOU, YOUNG SIR.
OH.
I'M SORRY, BUT WE HAVE A PROBLEM. THIS PASSPORT IS OUT OF DATE. IT EXPIRED TWO DAYS AGO.
BZZZZZT!
WHAT?!
NO, IT CAN'T BE. I'VE ONLY HAD IT ABOUT FOUR YEARS, I'M SURE OF IT.
HE'S RIGHT, ALEX. WHY DIDN'T THEY NOTICE THIS AT HEATHROW?
MAYBE THEY DIDN'T CHECK VERY CLOSELY.
I'M SORRY, BUT WE CAN'T ALLOW HIM TO ENTER THE UNITED STATES. HOW LONG DO YOU PLAN TO STAY?
ONLY TODAY. WE LEAVE FOR THE CARIBBEAN TOMORROW.
WELL . . . HOW ABOUT WE HOLD HIM HERE FOR YOU? YOU CAN PICK HIM UP AGAIN WHEN YOU LEAVE.

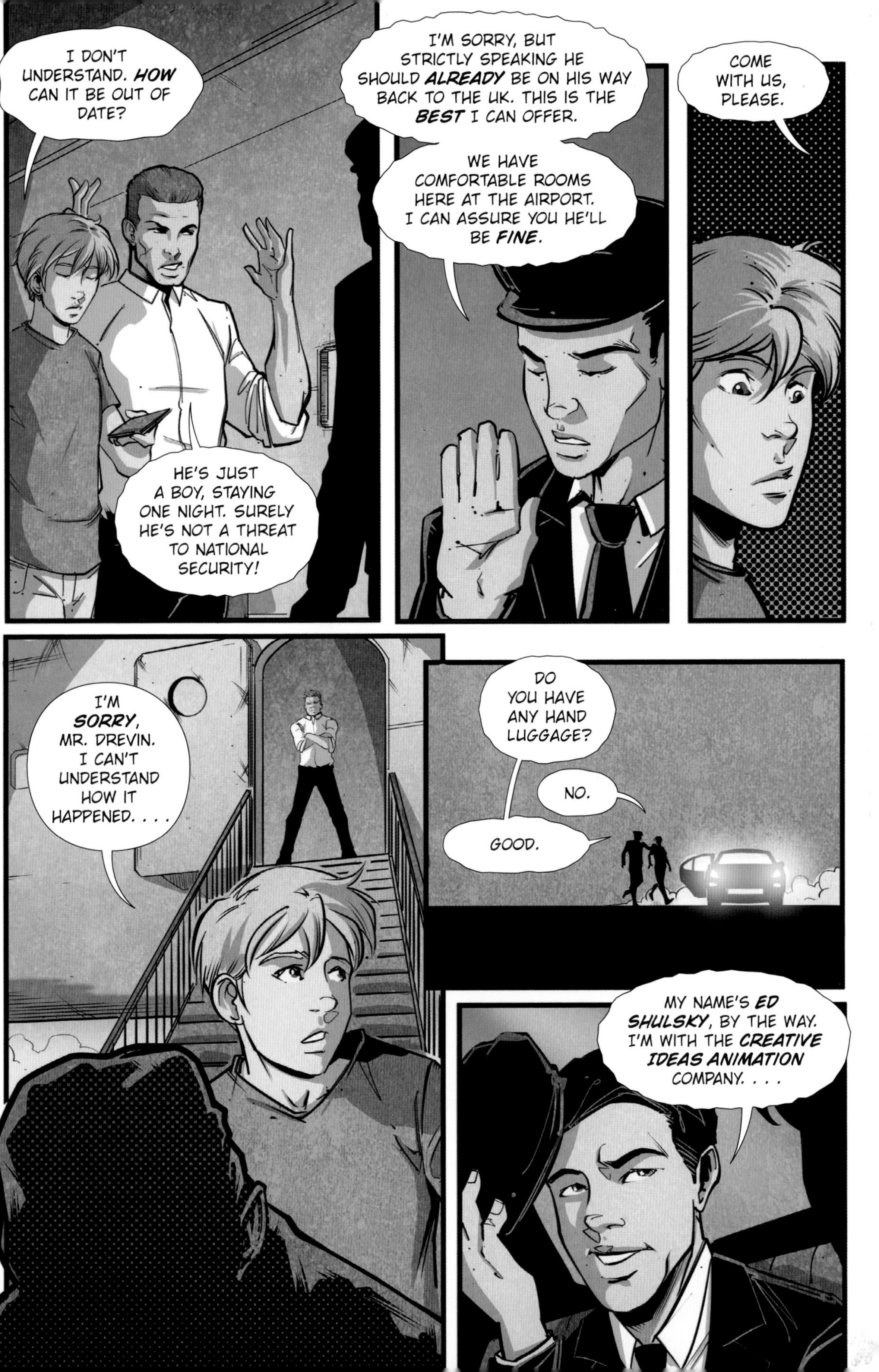
I DON'T UNDERSTAND. HOW CAN IT BE OUT OF DATE?
HE'S JUST A BOY, STAYING ONE NIGHT. SURELY HE'S NOT A THREAT TO NATIONAL SECURITY!
I'M SORRY, BUT STRICTLY SPEAKING HE SHOULD ALREADY BE ON HIS WAY BACK TO THE UK. THIS IS THE BEST I CAN OFFER.
WE HAVE COMFORTABLE ROOMS HERE AT THE AIRPORT. I CAN ASSURE YOU HE'LL BE FINE.
COME WITH US, PLEASE.
I'M SORRY, MR. DREVIN. I CAN'T UNDERSTAND HOW IT HAPPENED. . . .
DO YOU HAVE ANY HAND LUGGAGE?
NO.
GOOD.
MY NAME'S ED SHULSKY, BY THE WAY. I'M WITH THE CREATIVE IDEAS ANIMATION COMPANY. . . .

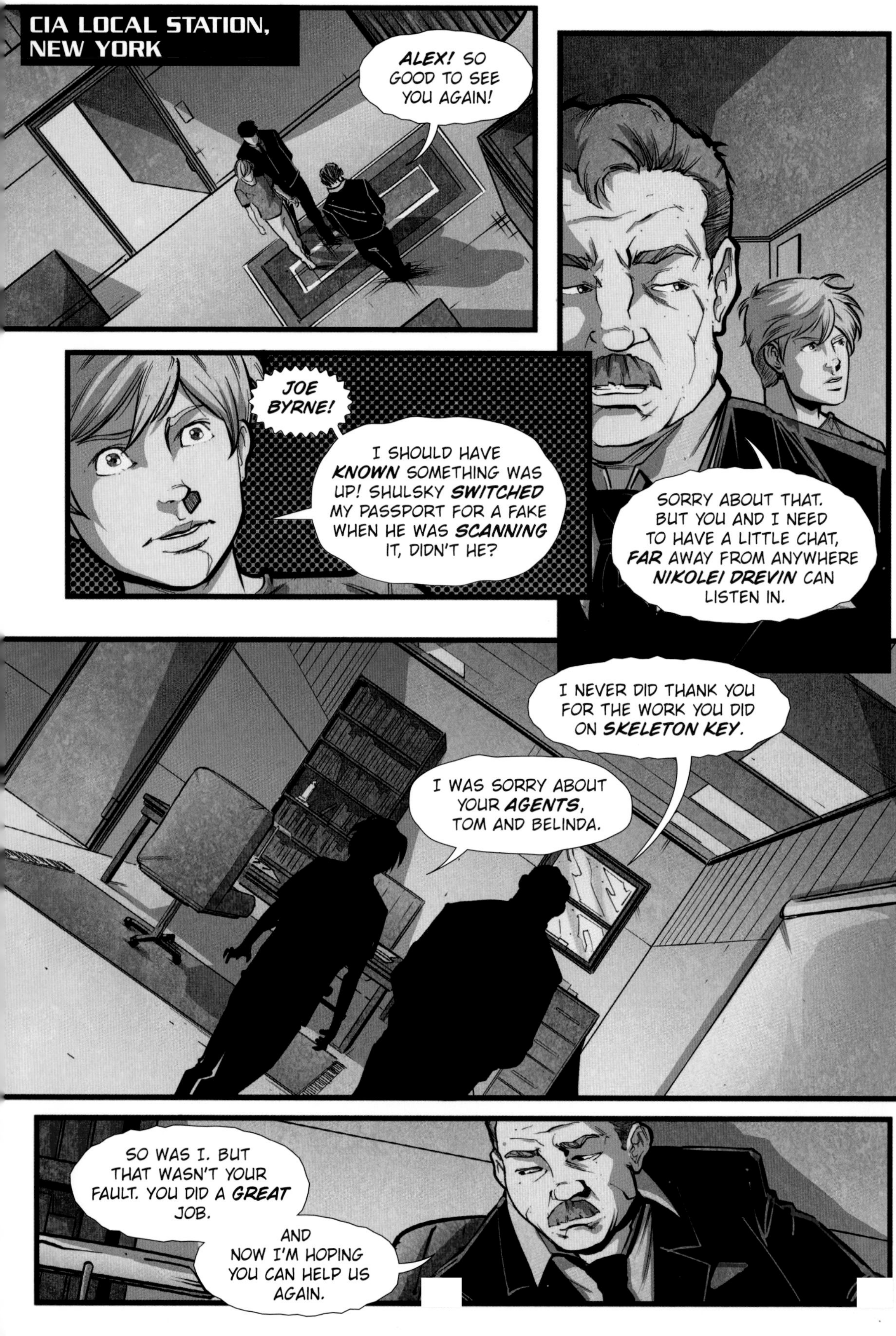
CIA LOCAL STATION, NEW YORK
ALEX! SO GOOD TO SEE YOU AGAIN!
JOE BYRNE!
I SHOULD HAVE KNOWN SOMETHING WAS UP! SHULSKY SWITCHED MY PASSPORT FOR A FAKE WHEN HE WAS SCANNING IT, DIDN'T HE?
SORRY ABOUT THAT. BUT YOU AND I NEED TO HAVE A LITTLE CHAT, FAR AWAY FROM ANYWHERE NIKOLEI DREVIN CAN LISTEN IN.
I NEVER DID THANK YOU FOR THE WORK YOU DID ON SKELETON KEY.
I WAS SORRY ABOUT YOUR AGENTS, TOM AND BELINDA.
SO WAS I. BUT THAT WASN'T YOUR FAULT. YOU DID A GREAT JOB.
AND NOW I'M HOPING YOU CAN HELP US AGAIN.

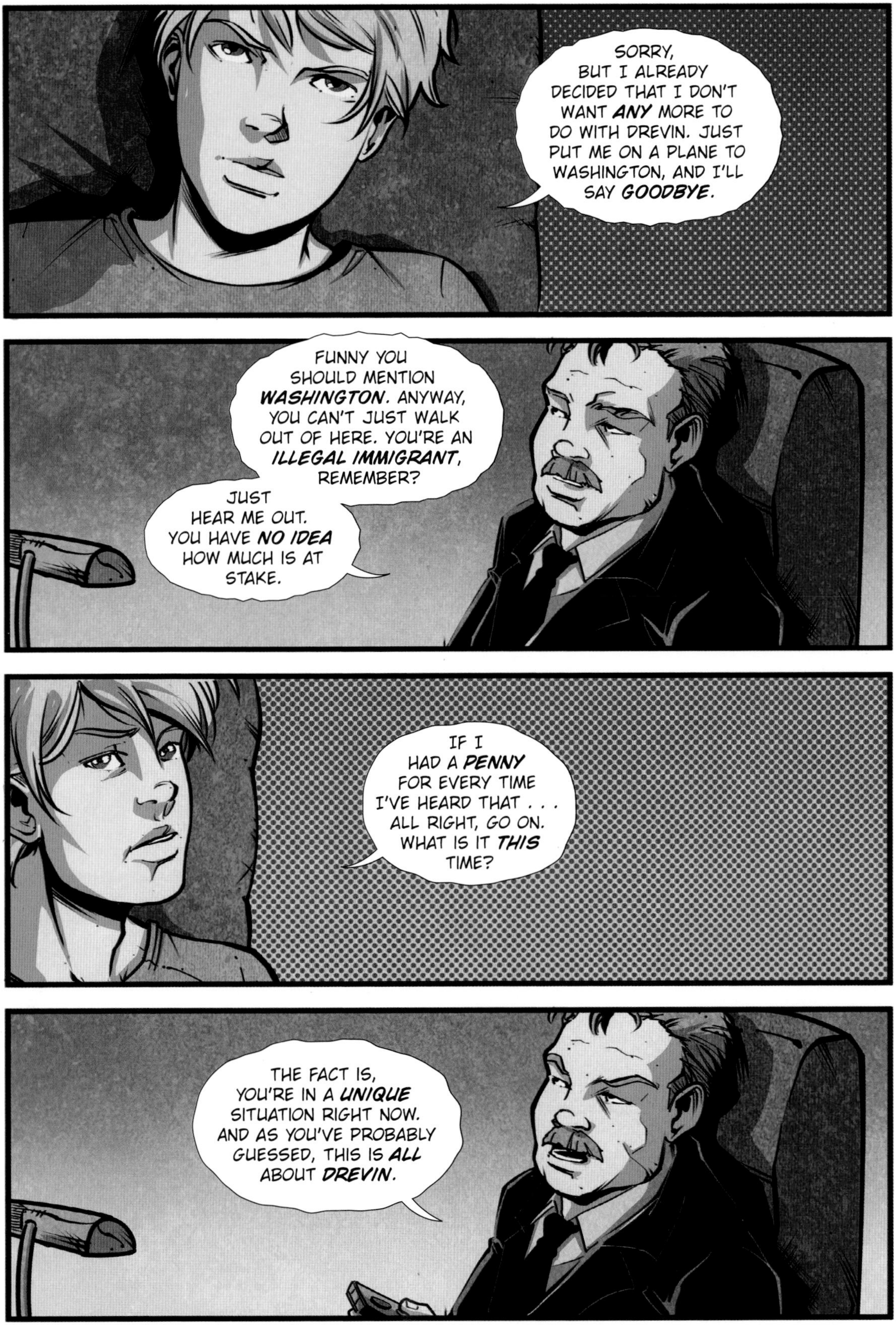
SORRY, BUT I ALREADY DECIDED THAT I DON'T WANT ANY MORE TO DO WITH DREVIN. JUST PUT ME ON A PLANE TO WASHINGTON, AND I'LL SAY GOODBYE.
FUNNY YOU SHOULD MENTION WASHINGTON. ANYWAY, YOU CAN'T JUST WALK OUT OF HERE. YOU'RE AN ILLEGAL IMMIGRANT, REMEMBER?
JUST HEAR ME OUT. YOU HAVE NO IDEA HOW MUCH IS AT STAKE.
IF I HAD A PENNY FOR EVERY TIME I'VE HEARD THAT . . . ALL RIGHT, GO ON. WHAT IS IT THIS TIME?
THE FACT IS, YOU'RE IN A UNIQUE SITUATION RIGHT NOW. AND AS YOU'VE PROBABLY GUESSED, THIS IS ALL ABOUT DREVIN.

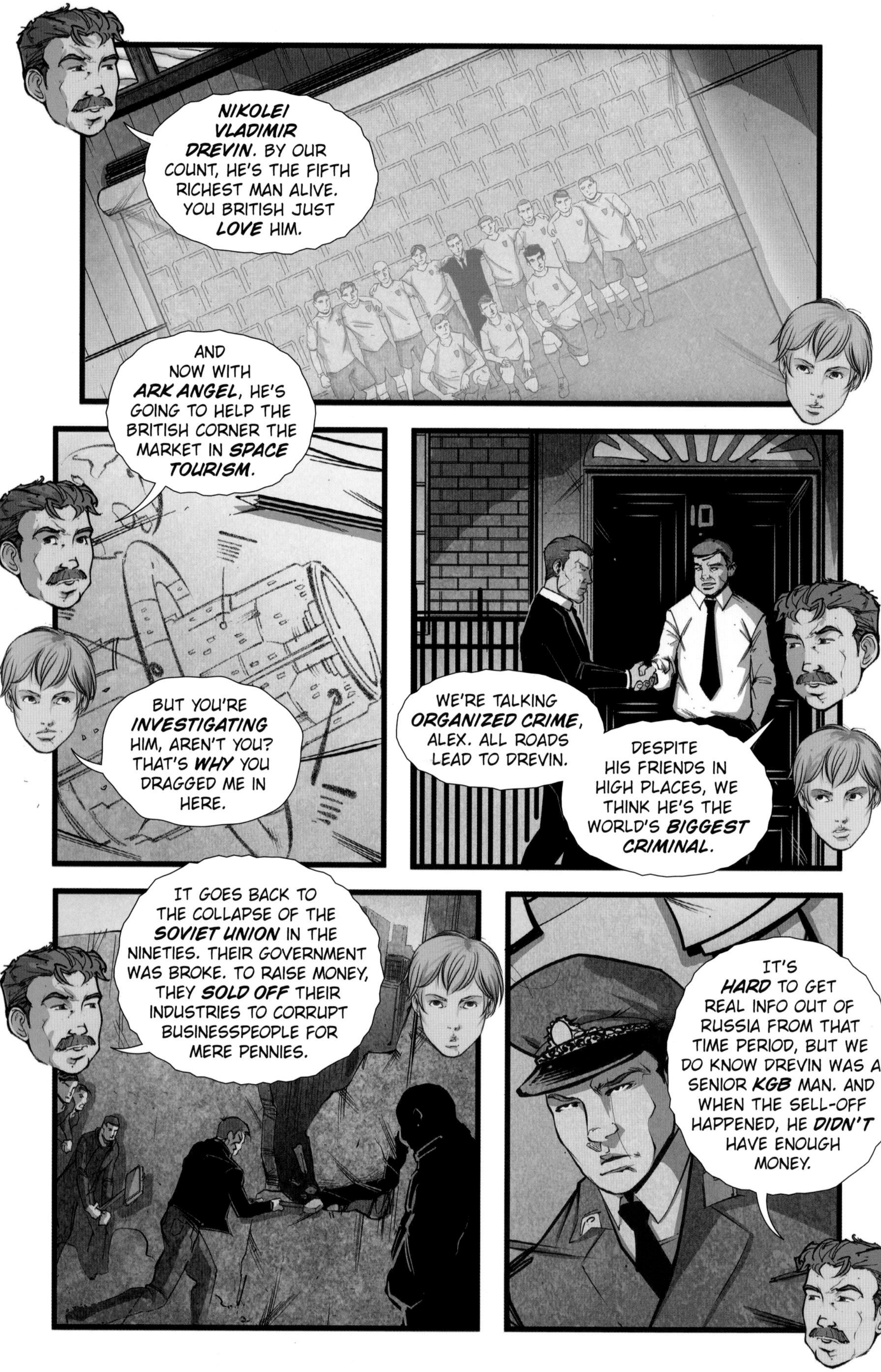
NIKOLEI VLADIMIR DREVIN. BY OUR COUNT, HE'S THE FIFTH RICHEST MAN ALIVE. YOU BRITISH JUST LOVE HIM.
AND NOW WITH ARK ANGEL, HE'S GOING TO HELP THE BRITISH CORNER THE MARKET IN SPACE TOURISM.
BUT YOU'RE INVESTIGATING HIM, AREN'T YOU? THAT'S WHY YOU DRAGGED ME IN HERE.
10
WE'RE TALKING ORGANIZED CRIME, ALEX. ALL ROADS LEAD TO DREVIN.
DESPITE HIS FRIENDS IN HIGH PLACES, WE THINK HE'S THE WORLD'S BIGGEST CRIMINAL.
IT GOES BACK TO THE COLLAPSE OF THE SOVIET UNION IN THE NINETIES. THEIR GOVERNMENT WAS BROKE. TO RAISE MONEY, THEY SOLD OFF THEIR INDUSTRIES TO CORRUPT BUSINESSPEOPLE FOR MERE PENNIES.
IT'S HARD TO GET REAL INFO OUT OF RUSSIA FROM THAT TIME PERIOD, BUT WE DO KNOW DREVIN WAS A SENIOR KGB MAN. AND WHEN THE SELL-OFF HAPPENED, HE DIDN'T HAVE ENOUGH MONEY.

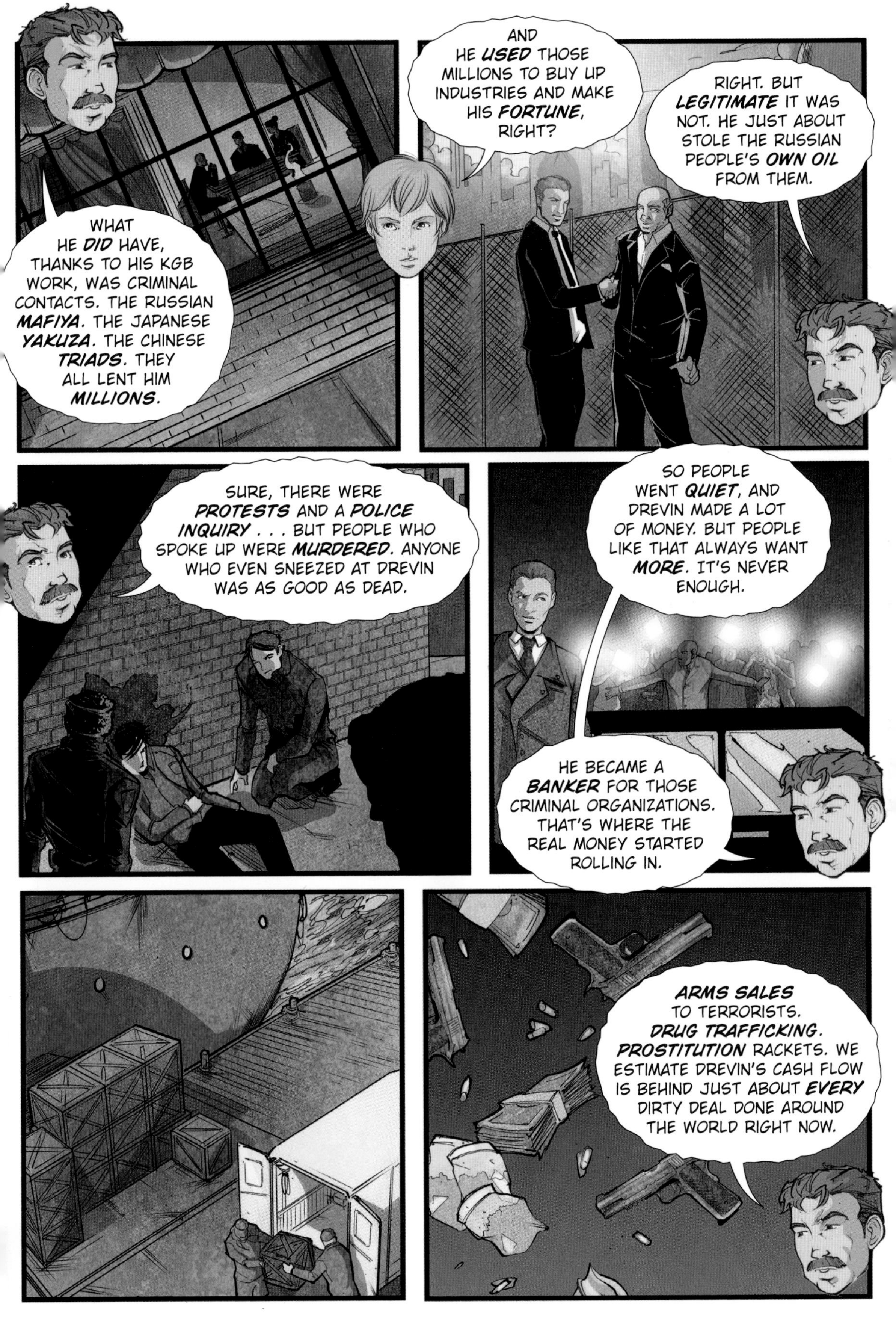
WHAT HE DID HAVE, THANKS TO HIS KGB WORK, WAS CRIMINAL CONTACTS. THE RUSSIAN MAFIYA. THE JAPANESE YAKUZA. THE CHINESE TRIADS. THEY ALL LENT HIM MILLIONS.
AND HE USED THOSE MILLIONS TO BUY UP INDUSTRIES AND MAKE HIS FORTUNE, RIGHT?
RIGHT. BUT LEGITIMATE IT WAS NOT. HE JUST ABOUT STOLE THE RUSSIAN PEOPLE'S OWN OIL FROM THEM.
SURE, THERE WERE PROTESTS AND A POLICE INQUIRY . . . BUT PEOPLE WHO SPOKE UP WERE MURDERED. ANYONE WHO EVEN SNEEZED AT DREVIN WAS AS GOOD AS DEAD.
SO PEOPLE WENT QUIET, AND DREVIN MADE A LOT OF MONEY. BUT PEOPLE LIKE THAT ALWAYS WANT MORE. IT'S NEVER ENOUGH.
HE BECAME A BANKER FOR THOSE CRIMINAL ORGANIZATIONS. THAT'S WHERE THE REAL MONEY STARTED ROLLING IN.
ARMS SALES TO TERRORISTS. DRUG TRAFFICKING. PROSTITUTION RACKETS. WE ESTIMATE DREVIN'S CASH FLOW IS BEHIND JUST ABOUT EVERY DIRTY DEAL DONE AROUND THE WORLD RIGHT NOW.

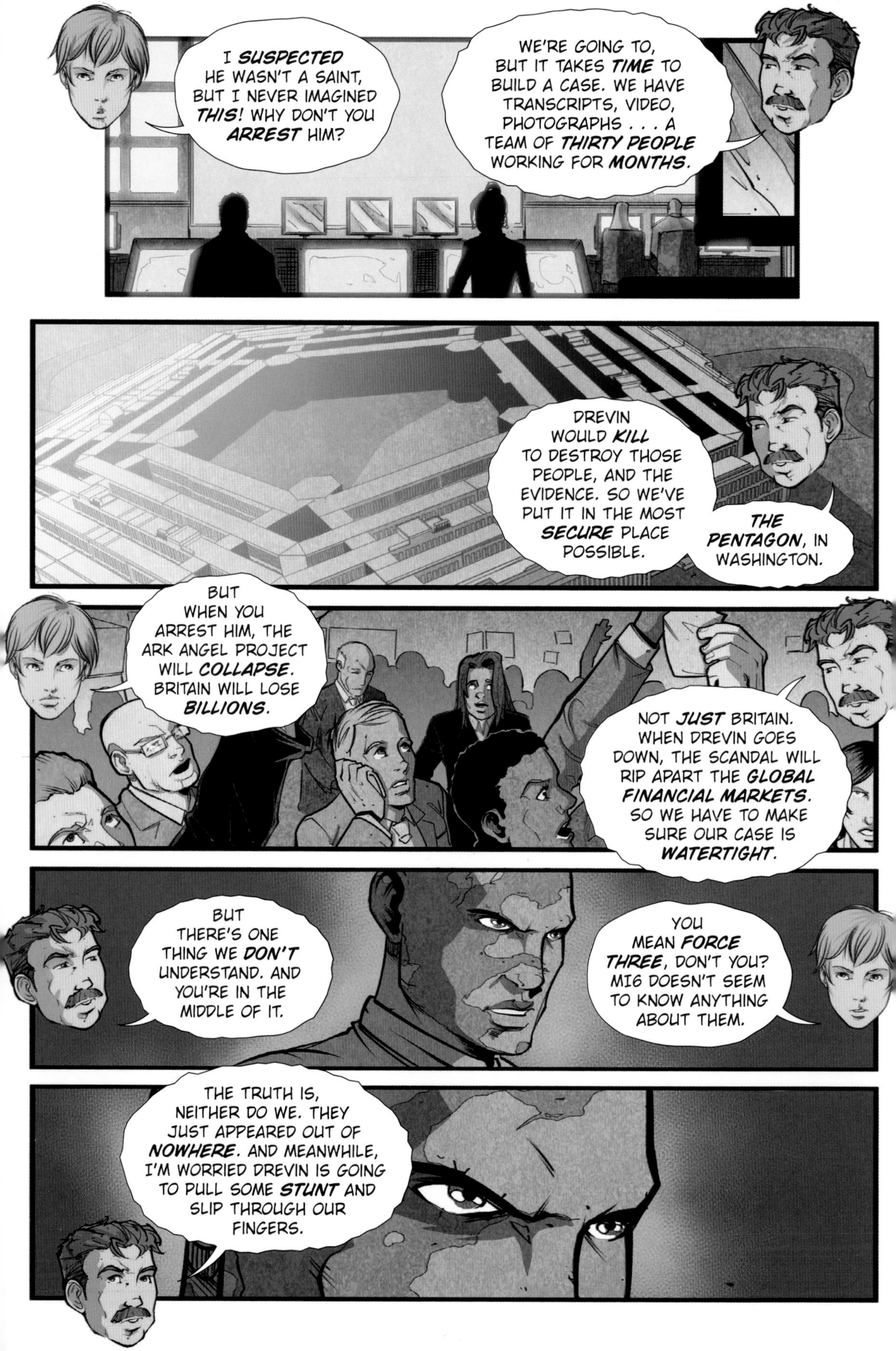
I SUSPECTED HE WASN'T A SAINT, BUT I NEVER IMAGINED THIS! WHY DON'T YOU ARREST HIM?
WE'RE GOING TO, BUT IT TAKES TIME TO BUILD A CASE. WE HAVE TRANSCRIPTS, VIDEO, PHOTOGRAPHS . . . A TEAM OF THIRTY PEOPLE WORKING FOR MONTHS.
DREVIN WOULD KILL TO DESTROY THOSE PEOPLE, AND THE EVIDENCE. SO WE'VE PUT IT IN THE MOST SECURE PLACE POSSIBLE.
THE PENTAGON, IN WASHINGTON.
BUT WHEN YOU ARREST HIM, THE ARK ANGEL PROJECT WILL COLLAPSE. BRITAIN WILL LOSE BILLIONS.
NOT JUST BRITAIN. WHEN DREVIN GOES DOWN, THE SCANDAL WILL RIP APART THE GLOBAL FINANCIAL MARKETS. SO WE HAVE TO MAKE SURE OUR CASE IS WATERTIGHT.
BUT THERE'S ONE THING WE DON'T UNDERSTAND. AND YOU'RE IN THE MIDDLE OF IT.
YOU MEAN FORCE THREE, DON'T YOU? MI6 DOESN'T SEEM TO KNOW ANYTHING ABOUT THEM.
THE TRUTH IS, NEITHER DO WE. THEY JUST APPEARED OUT OF NOWHERE. AND MEANWHILE, I'M WORRIED DREVIN IS GOING TO PULL SOME STUNT AND SLIP THROUGH OUR FINGERS.

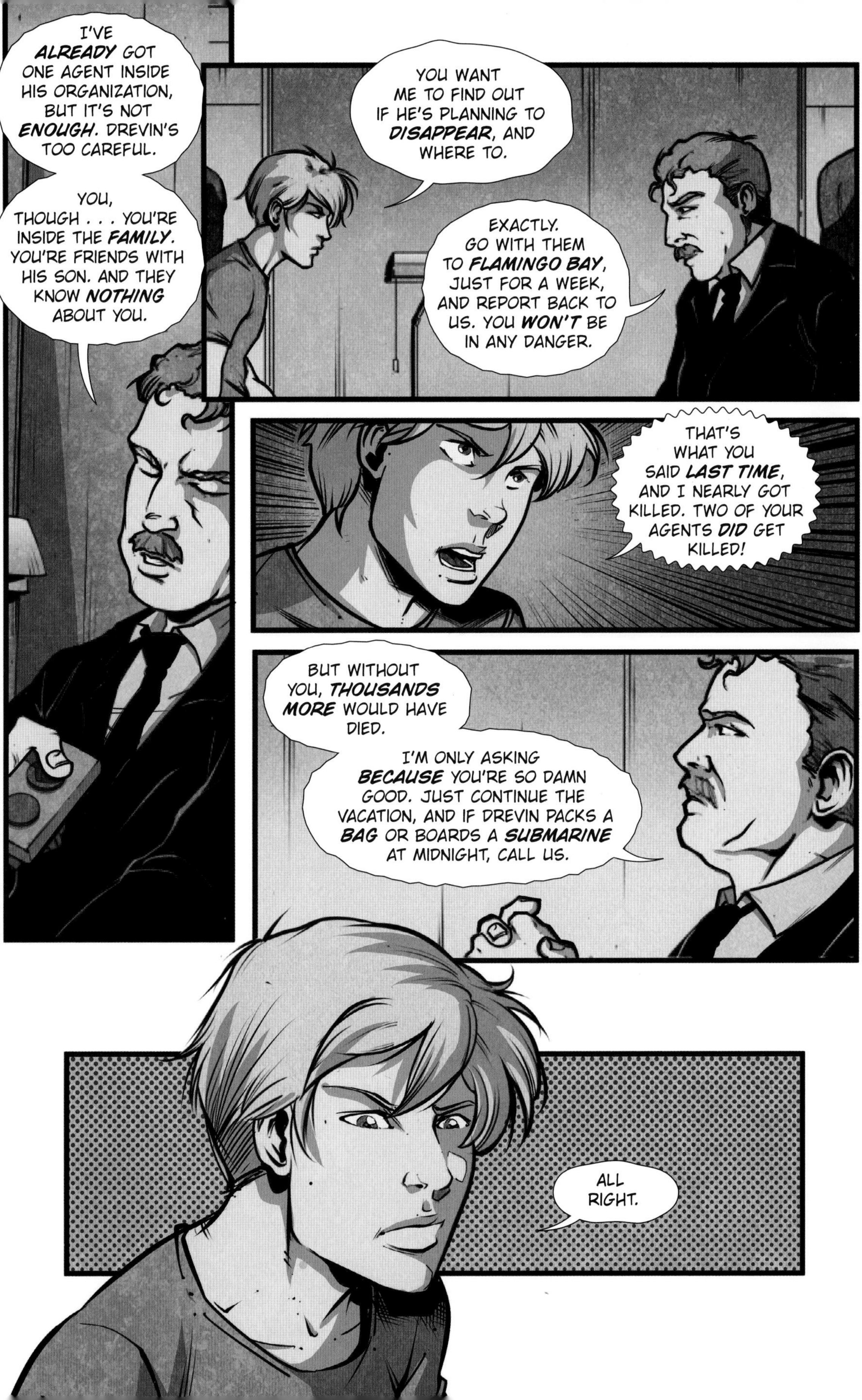
I'VE ALREADY GOT ONE AGENT INSIDE HIS ORGANIZATION, BUT IT'S NOT ENOUGH. DREVIN'S TOO CAREFUL.
YOU, THOUGH . . . YOU'RE INSIDE THE FAMILY. YOU'RE FRIENDS WITH HIS SON. AND THEY KNOW NOTHING ABOUT YOU.
YOU WANT ME TO FIND OUT IF HE'S PLANNING TO DISAPPEAR, AND WHERE TO.
EXACTLY. GO WITH THEM TO FLAMINGO BAY, JUST FOR A WEEK, AND REPORT BACK TO US. YOU WON'T BE IN ANY DANGER.
THAT'S WHAT YOU SAID LAST TIME, AND I NEARLY GOT KILLED. TWO OF YOUR AGENTS DID GET KILLED!
BUT WITHOUT YOU, THOUSANDS MORE WOULD HAVE DIED.
I'M ONLY ASKING BECAUSE YOU'RE SO DAMN GOOD. JUST CONTINUE THE VACATION, AND IF DREVIN PACKS A BAG OR BOARDS A SUBMARINE AT MIDNIGHT, CALL US.
ALL RIGHT.

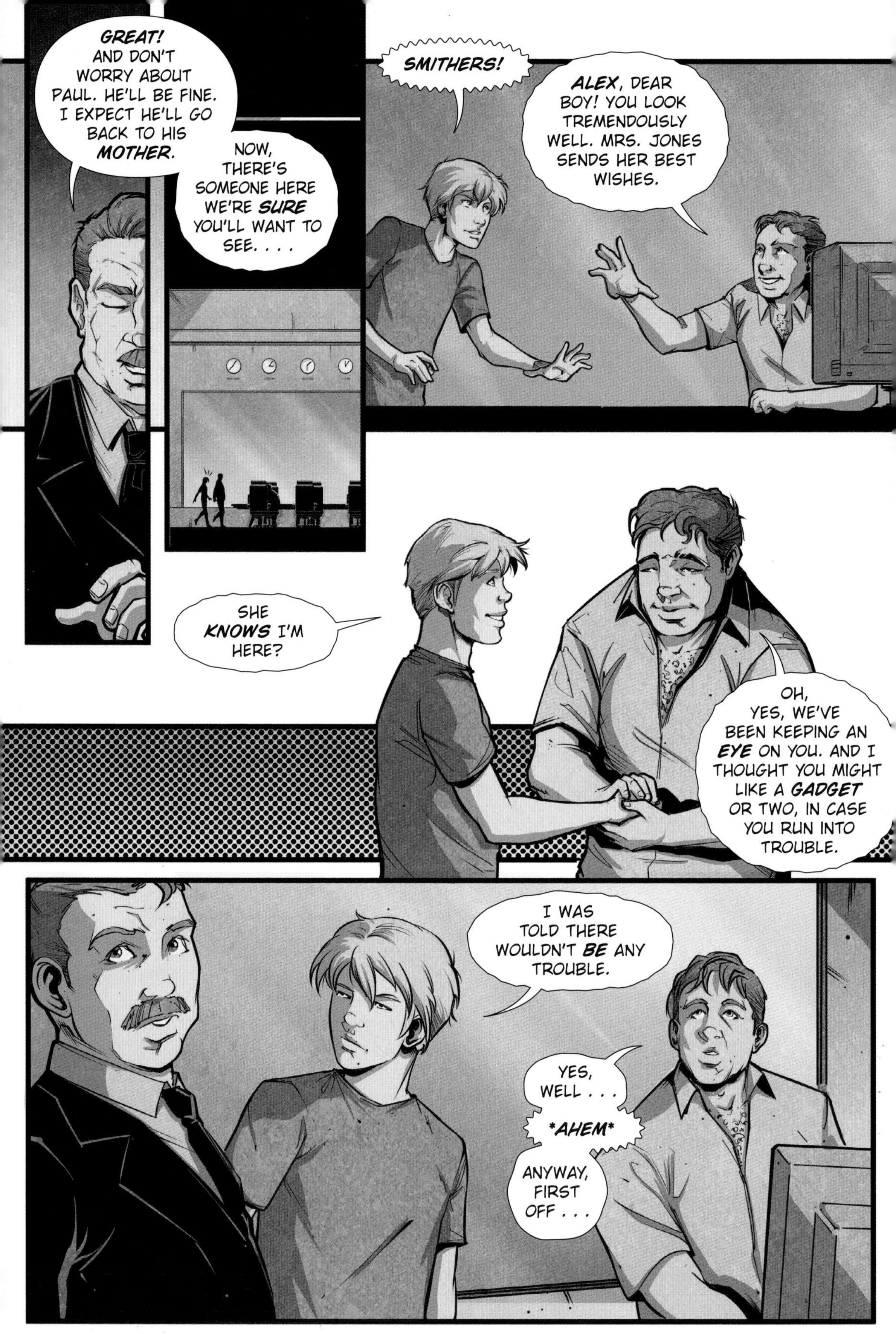
GREAT! AND DON'T WORRY ABOUT PAUL. HE'LL BE FINE. I EXPECT HE'LL GO BACK TO HIS MOTHER.
NOW, THERE'S SOMEONE HERE WE'RE SURE YOU'LL WANT TO SEE. . . .
SMITHERS!
ALEX, DEAR BOY! YOU LOOK TREMENDOUSLY WELL. MRS. JONES SENDS HER BEST WISHES.
SHE KNOWS I'M HERE?
OH, YES, WE'VE BEEN KEEPING AN EYE ON YOU. AND I THOUGHT YOU MIGHT LIKE A GADGET OR TWO, IN CASE YOU RUN INTO TROUBLE.
I WAS TOLD THERE WOULDN'T BE ANY TROUBLE.
YES, WELL . . .
AHEM
ANYWAY, FIRST OFF . . .

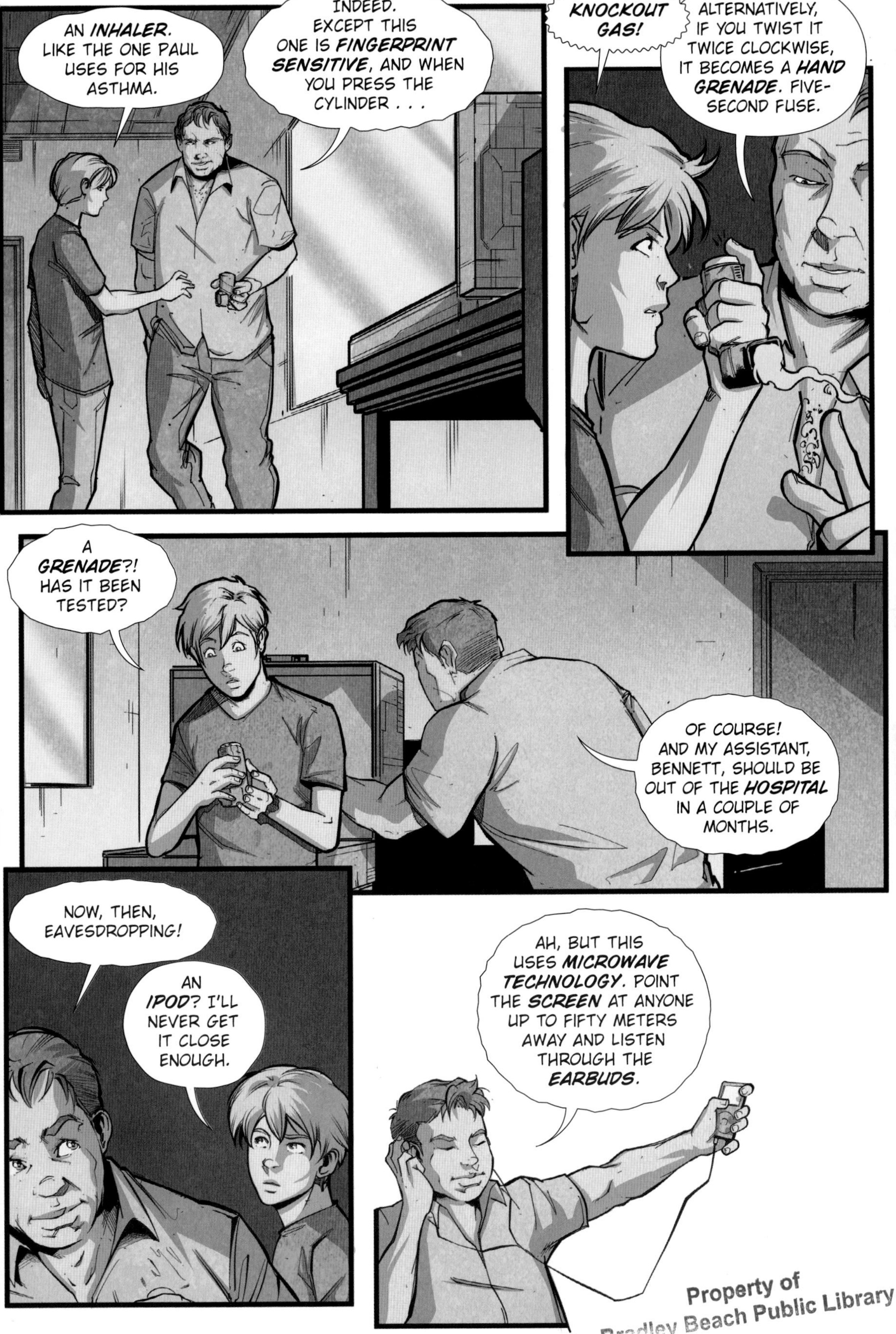
AN INHALER. LIKE THE ONE PAUL USES FOR HIS ASTHMA.
INDEED. EXCEPT THIS ONE IS FINGERPRINT SENSITIVE, AND WHEN YOU PRESS THE CYLINDER . . .
KNOCKOUT GAS!
ALTERNATIVELY, IF YOU TWIST IT TWICE CLOCKWISE, IT BECOMES A HAND GRENADE. FIVE-SECOND FUSE.
A GRENADE?! HAS IT BEEN TESTED?
OF COURSE! AND MY ASSISTANT, BENNETT, SHOULD BE OUT OF THE HOSPITAL IN A COUPLE OF MONTHS.
NOW, THEN, EAVESDROPPING!
AN IPOD? I'LL NEVER GET IT CLOSE ENOUGH.
AH, BUT THIS USES MICROWAVE TECHNOLOGY. POINT THE SCREEN AT ANYONE UP TO FIFTY METERS AWAY AND LISTEN THROUGH THE EARBUDS.

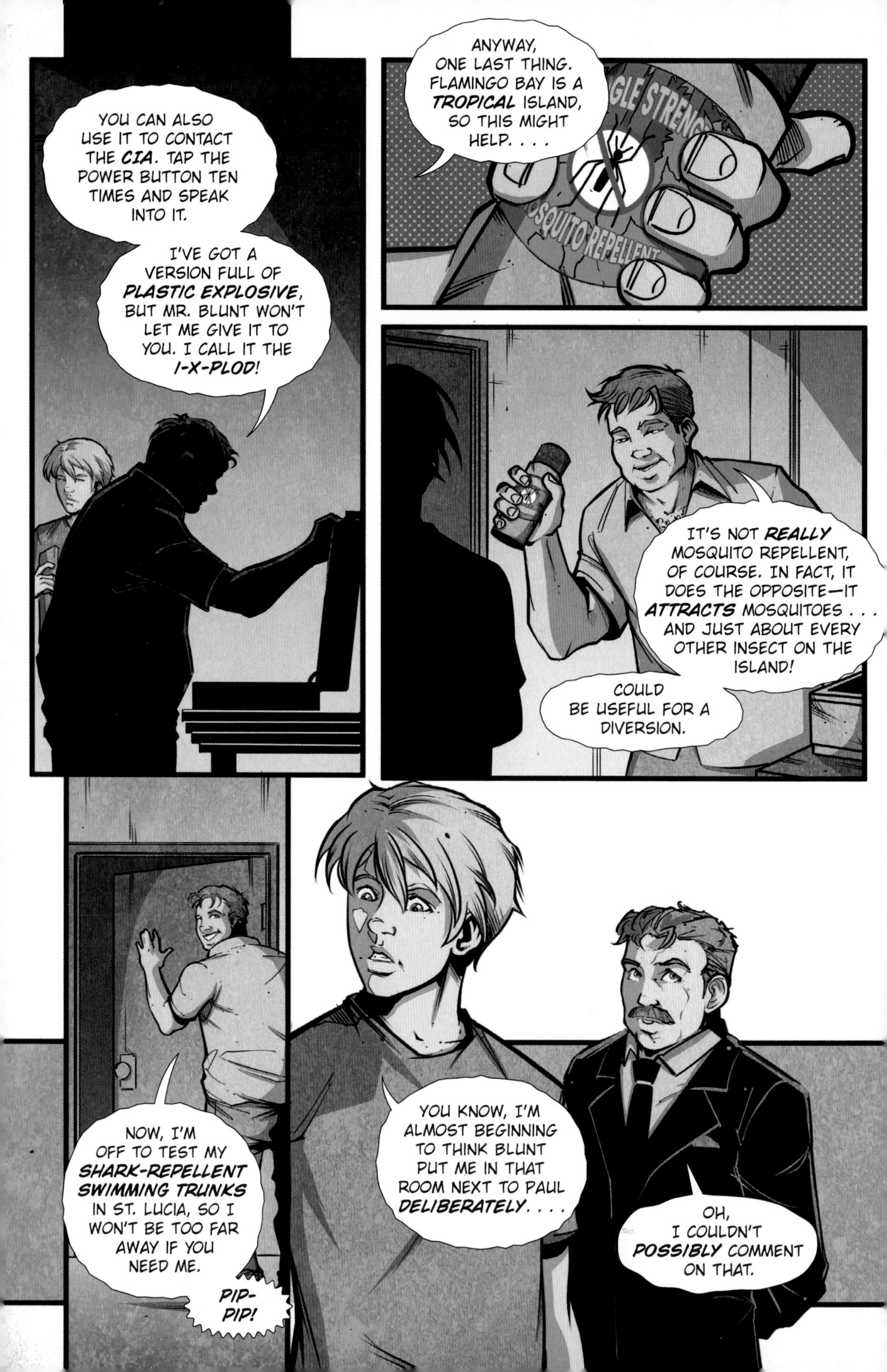
YOU CAN ALSO USE IT TO CONTACT THE CIA. TAP THE POWER BUTTON TEN TIMES AND SPEAK INTO IT.
I'VE GOT A VERSION FULL OF PLASTIC EXPLOSIVE, BUT MR. BLUNT WON'T LET ME GIVE IT TO YOU. I CALL IT THE I-X-PLOD!
ANYWAY, ONE LAST THING. FLAMINGO BAY IS A TROPICAL ISLAND, SO THIS MIGHT HELP. . . .
MOSQUITO REPELLENT
IT'S NOT REALLY MOSQUITO REPELLENT, OF COURSE. IN FACT, IT DOES THE OPPOSITE—IT ATTRACTS MOSQUITOES . . . AND JUST ABOUT EVERY OTHER INSECT ON THE ISLAND!
COULD BE USEFUL FOR A DIVERSION.
NOW, I'M OFF TO TEST MY SHARK-REPELLENT SWIMMING TRUNKS IN ST. LUCIA, SO I WON'T BE TOO FAR AWAY IF YOU NEED ME.
PIP-PIP!
YOU KNOW, I'M ALMOST BEGINNING TO THINK BLUNT PUT ME IN THAT ROOM NEXT TO PAUL DELIBERATELY. . . .
OH, I COULDN'T POSSIBLY COMMENT ON THAT.

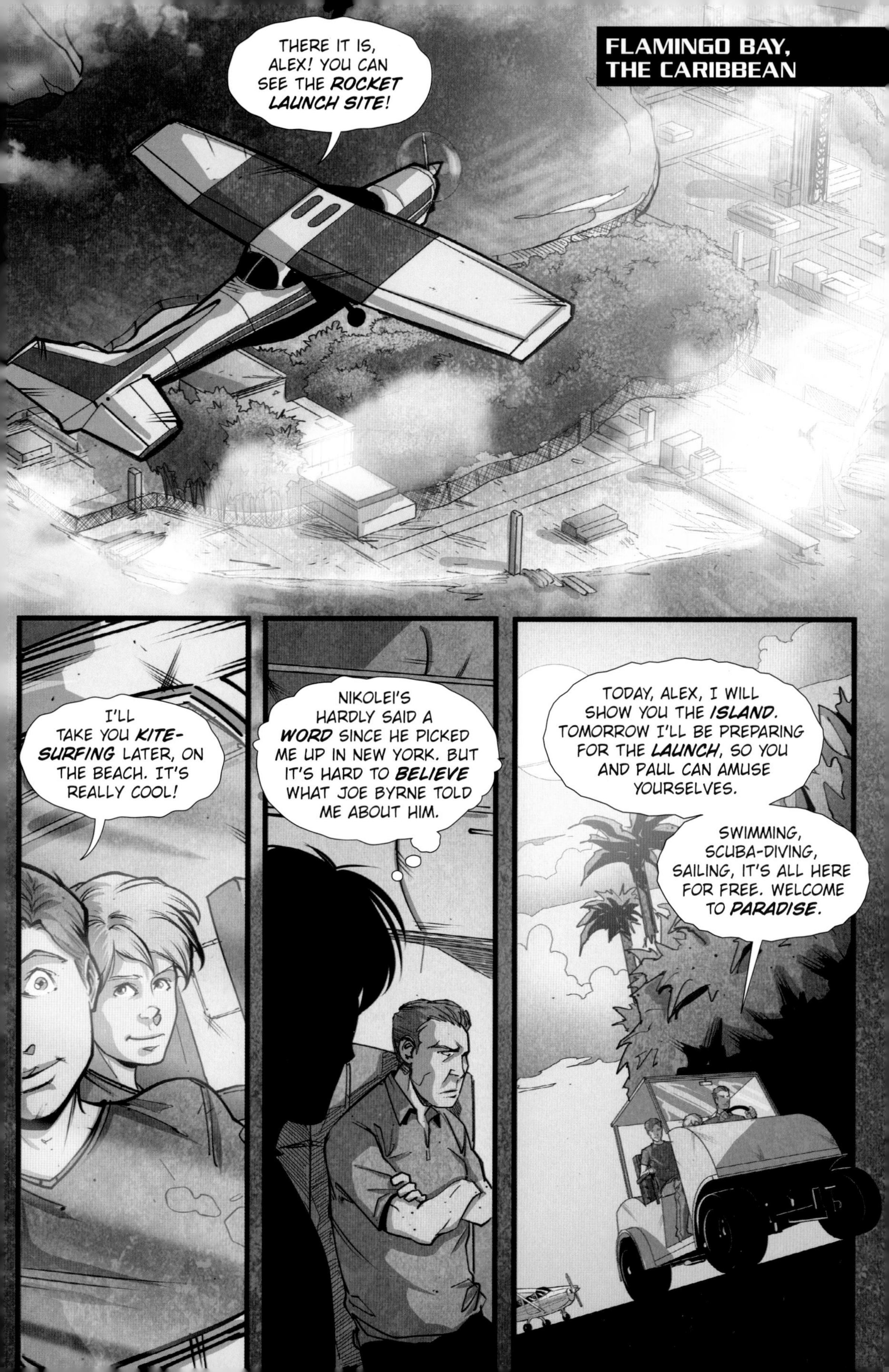
FLAMINGO BAY, THE CARIBBEAN
THERE IT IS, ALEX! YOU CAN SEE THE ROCKET LAUNCH SITE!
I'LL TAKE YOU KITE-SURFING LATER, ON THE BEACH. IT'S REALLY COOL!
NIKOLEI'S HARDLY SAID A WORD SINCE HE PICKED ME UP IN NEW YORK. BUT IT'S HARD TO BELIEVE WHAT JOE BYRNE TOLD ME ABOUT HIM.
TODAY, ALEX, I WILL SHOW YOU THE ISLAND. TOMORROW I'LL BE PREPARING FOR THE LAUNCH, SO YOU AND PAUL CAN AMUSE YOURSELVES.
SWIMMING, SCUBA-DIVING, SAILING, IT'S ALL HERE FOR FREE. WELCOME TO PARADISE.

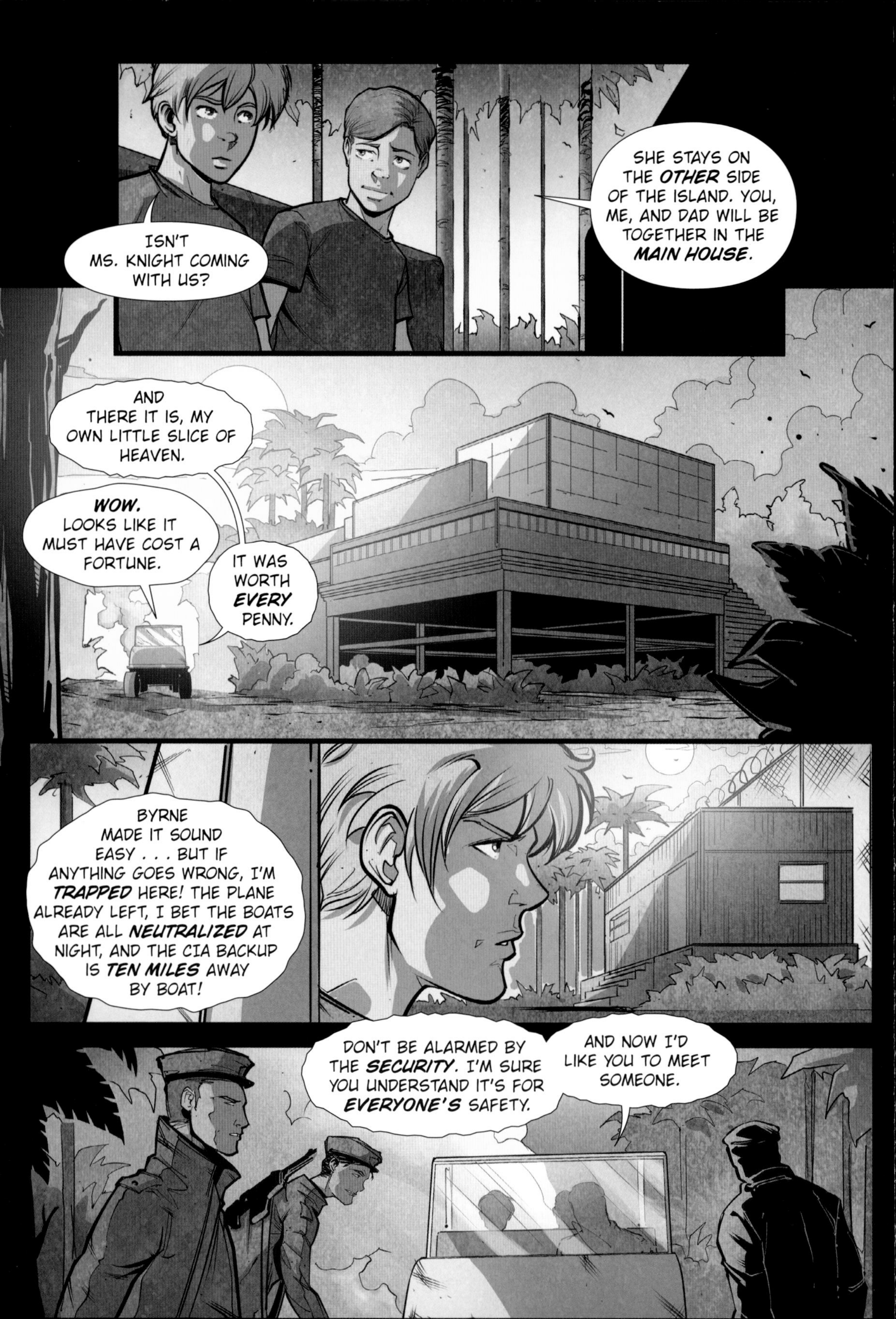
ISN'T MS. KNIGHT COMING WITH US?
SHE STAYS ON THE OTHER SIDE OF THE ISLAND. YOU, ME, AND DAD WILL BE TOGETHER IN THE MAIN HOUSE.
AND THERE IT IS, MY OWN LITTLE SLICE OF HEAVEN.
WOW. LOOKS LIKE IT MUST HAVE COST A FORTUNE.
IT WAS WORTH EVERY PENNY.
BYRNE MADE IT SOUND EASY . . . BUT IF ANYTHING GOES WRONG, I'M TRAPPED HERE! THE PLANE ALREADY LEFT, I BET THE BOATS ARE ALL NEUTRALIZED AT NIGHT, AND THE CIA BACKUP IS TEN MILES AWAY BY BOAT!
DON'T BE ALARMED BY THE SECURITY. I'M SURE YOU UNDERSTAND IT'S FOR EVERYONE'S SAFETY.
AND NOW I'D LIKE YOU TO MEET SOMEONE.

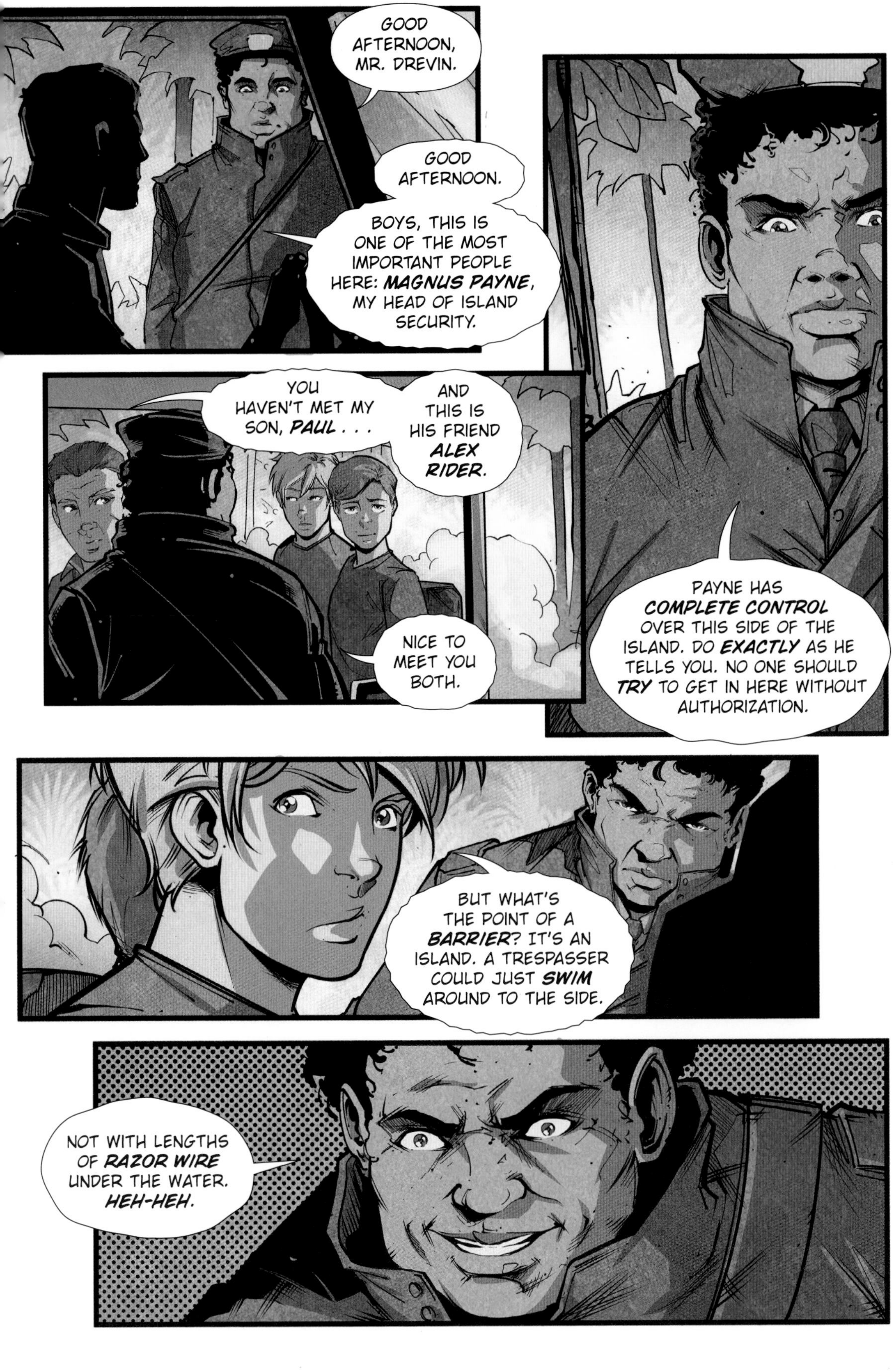
GOOD AFTERNOON, MR. DREVIN.
GOOD AFTERNOON.
BOYS, THIS IS ONE OF THE MOST IMPORTANT PEOPLE HERE: MAGNUS PAYNE, MY HEAD OF ISLAND SECURITY.
YOU HAVEN'T MET MY SON, PAUL . . .
AND THIS IS HIS FRIEND ALEX RIDER.
NICE TO MEET YOU BOTH.
PAYNE HAS COMPLETE CONTROL OVER THIS SIDE OF THE ISLAND. DO EXACTLY AS HE TELLS YOU. NO ONE SHOULD TRY TO GET IN HERE WITHOUT AUTHORIZATION.
BUT WHAT'S THE POINT OF A BARRIER? IT'S AN ISLAND. A TRESPASSER COULD JUST SWIM AROUND TO THE SIDE.
NOT WITH LENGTHS OF RAZOR WIRE UNDER THE WATER. HEH-HEH.

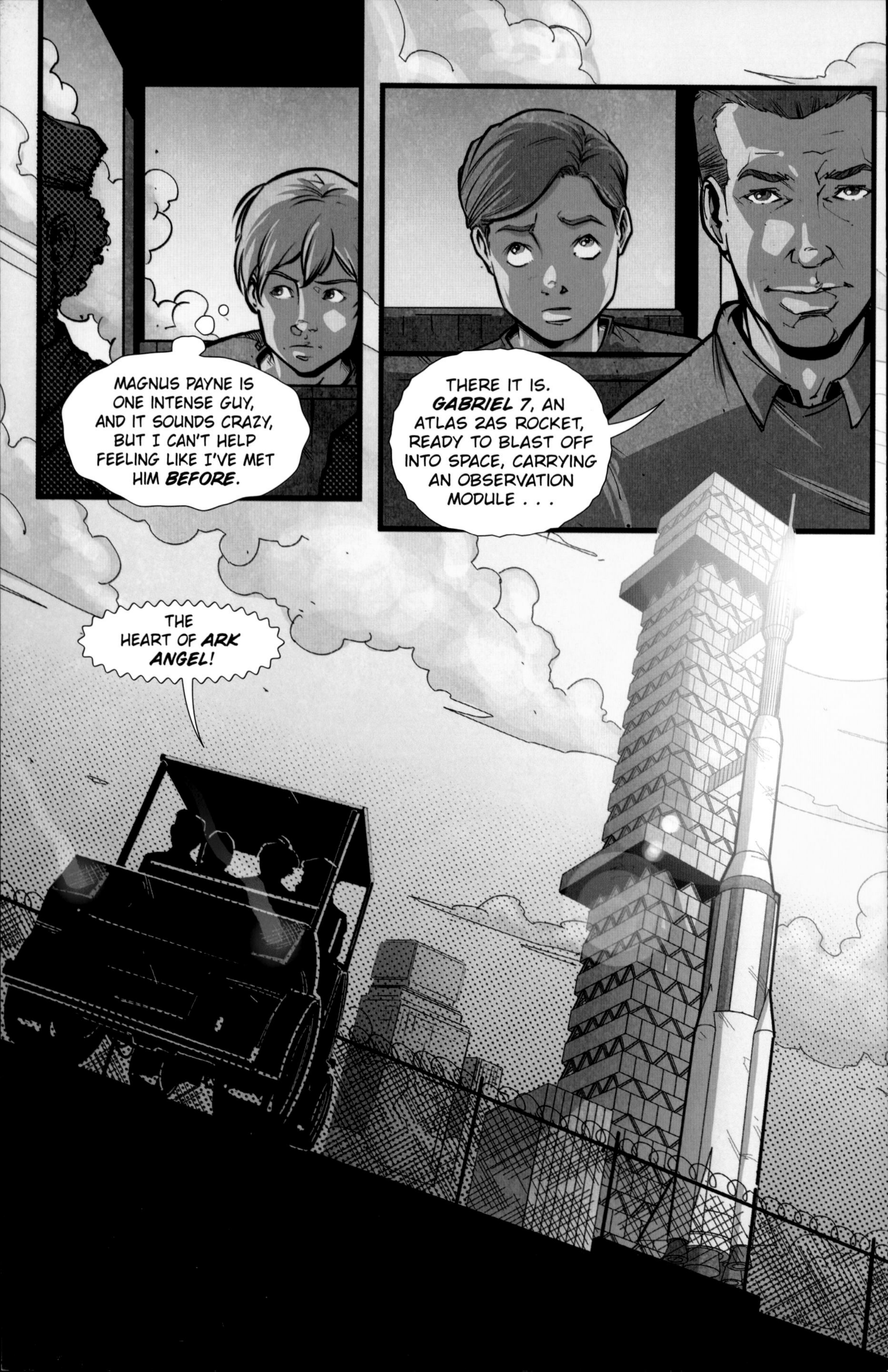
MAGNUS PAYNE IS ONE INTENSE GUY, AND IT SOUNDS CRAZY, BUT I CAN'T HELP FEELING LIKE I'VE MET HIM ***BEFORE***.
THERE IT IS. ***GABRIEL 7***, AN ATLAS 2AS ROCKET, READY TO BLAST OFF INTO SPACE, CARRYING AN OBSERVATION MODULE . . .
THE HEART OF ***ARK ANGEL***!

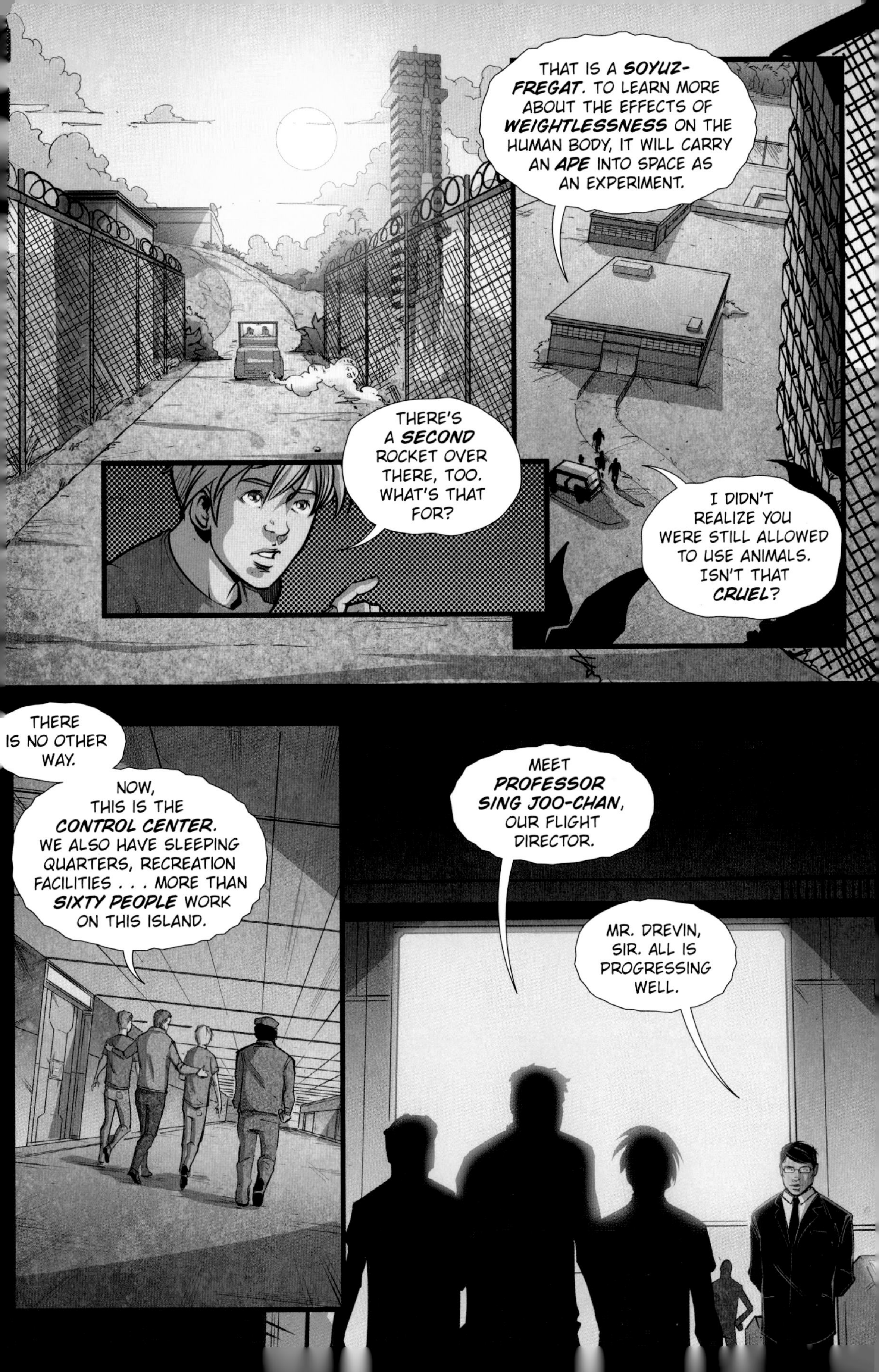
THAT IS A SOYUZ-FREGAT. TO LEARN MORE ABOUT THE EFFECTS OF WEIGHTLESSNESS ON THE HUMAN BODY, IT WILL CARRY AN APE INTO SPACE AS AN EXPERIMENT.
THERE'S A SECOND ROCKET OVER THERE, TOO. WHAT'S THAT FOR?
I DIDN'T REALIZE YOU WERE STILL ALLOWED TO USE ANIMALS. ISN'T THAT CRUEL?
THERE IS NO OTHER WAY.
NOW, THIS IS THE CONTROL CENTER. WE ALSO HAVE SLEEPING QUARTERS, RECREATION FACILITIES . . . MORE THAN SIXTY PEOPLE WORK ON THIS ISLAND.
MEET PROFESSOR SING JOO-CHAN, OUR FLIGHT DIRECTOR.
MR. DREVIN, SIR. ALL IS PROGRESSING WELL.

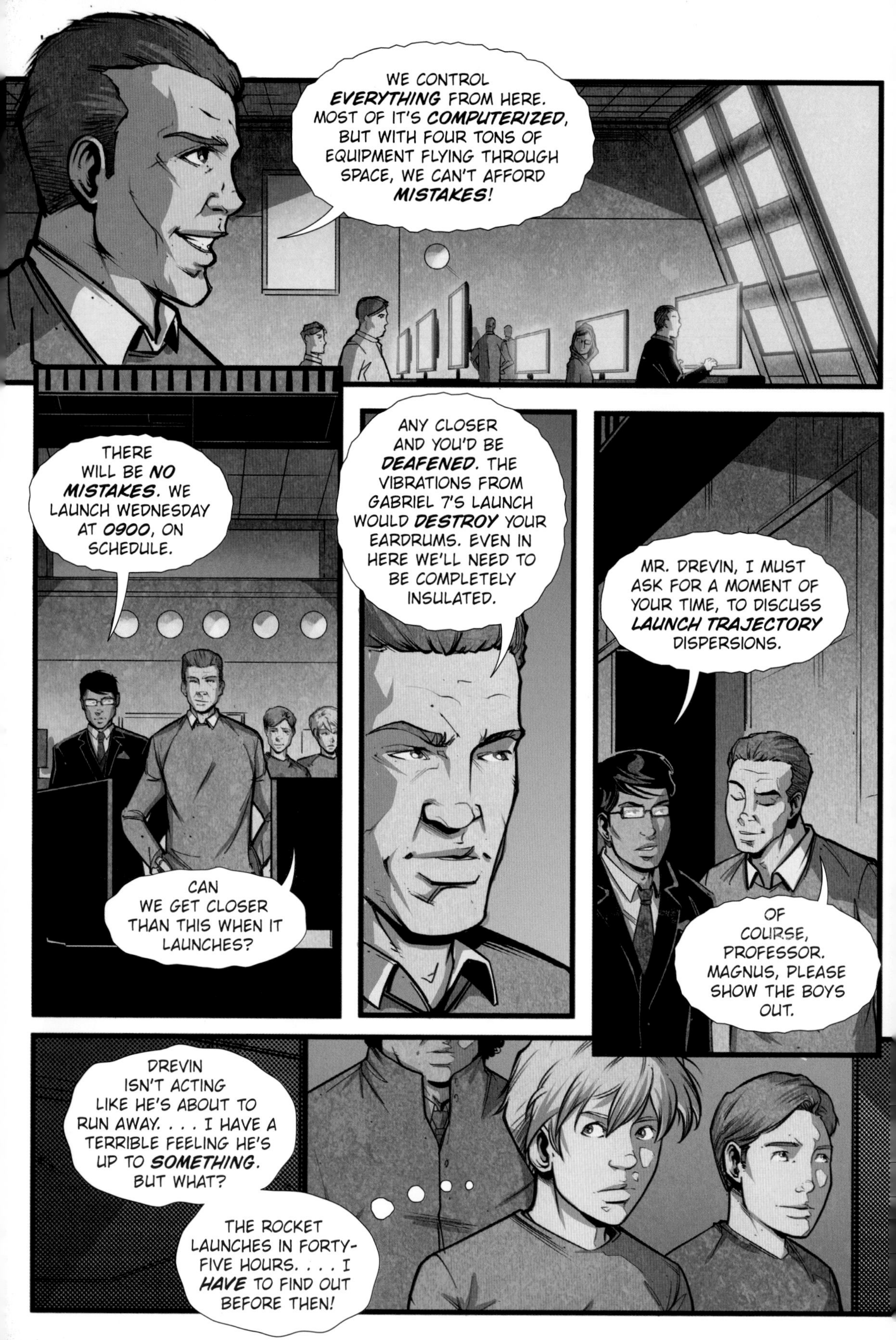
WE CONTROL EVERYTHING FROM HERE. MOST OF IT'S COMPUTERIZED, BUT WITH FOUR TONS OF EQUIPMENT FLYING THROUGH SPACE, WE CAN'T AFFORD MISTAKES!
THERE WILL BE NO MISTAKES. WE LAUNCH WEDNESDAY AT 0900, ON SCHEDULE.
CAN WE GET CLOSER THAN THIS WHEN IT LAUNCHES?
ANY CLOSER AND YOU'D BE DEAFENED. THE VIBRATIONS FROM GABRIEL 7'S LAUNCH WOULD DESTROY YOUR EARDRUMS. EVEN IN HERE WE'LL NEED TO BE COMPLETELY INSULATED.
MR. DREVIN, I MUST ASK FOR A MOMENT OF YOUR TIME, TO DISCUSS LAUNCH TRAJECTORY DISPERSIONS.
OF COURSE, PROFESSOR. MAGNUS, PLEASE SHOW THE BOYS OUT.
DREVIN ISN'T ACTING LIKE HE'S ABOUT TO RUN AWAY. . . . I HAVE A TERRIBLE FEELING HE'S UP TO SOMETHING. BUT WHAT?
THE ROCKET LAUNCHES IN FORTY-FIVE HOURS. . . . I HAVE TO FIND OUT BEFORE THEN!

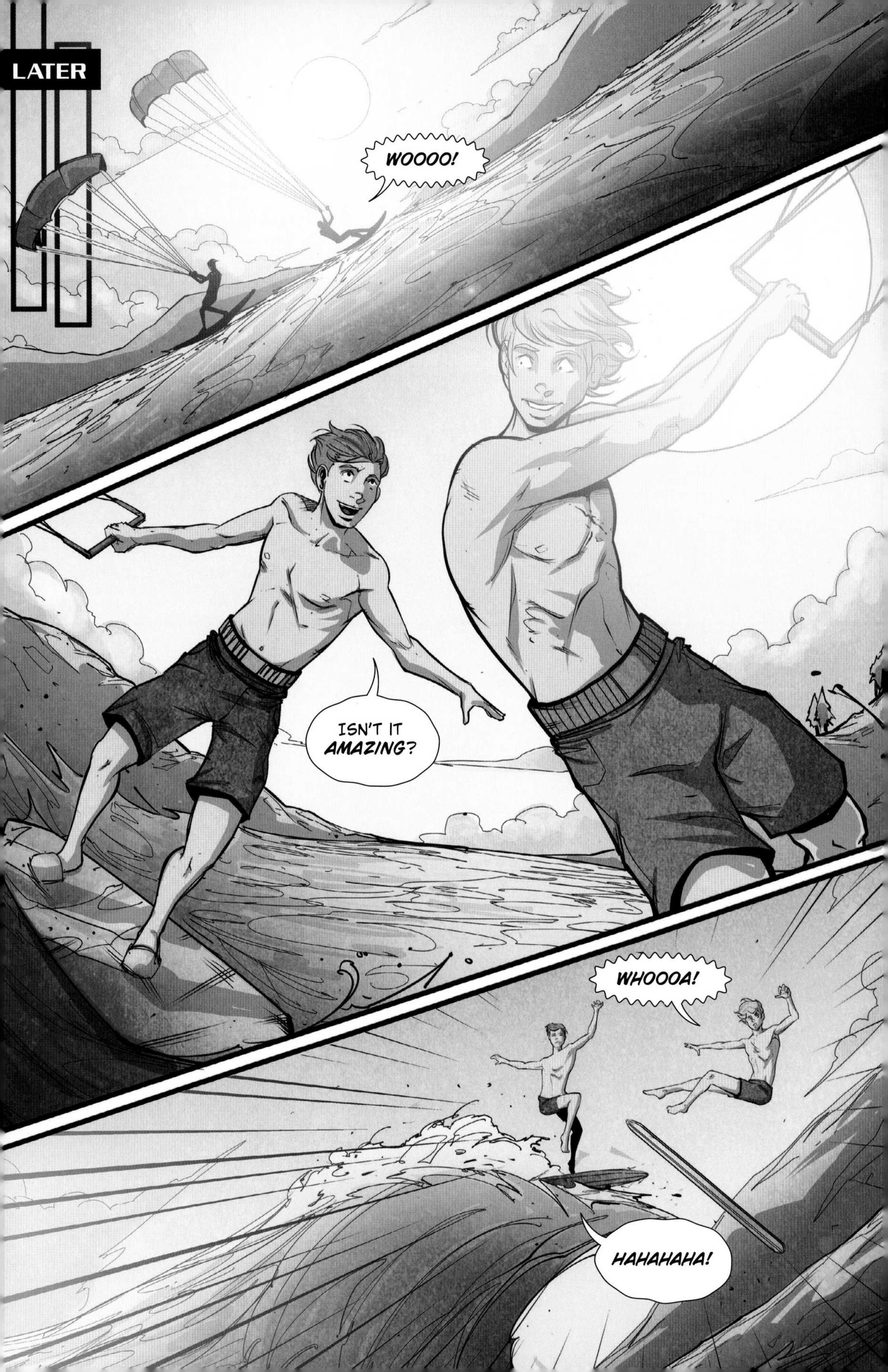
LATER
WOOOO!
ISN'T IT AMAZING?
WHOOOA!
HAHAHAHA!

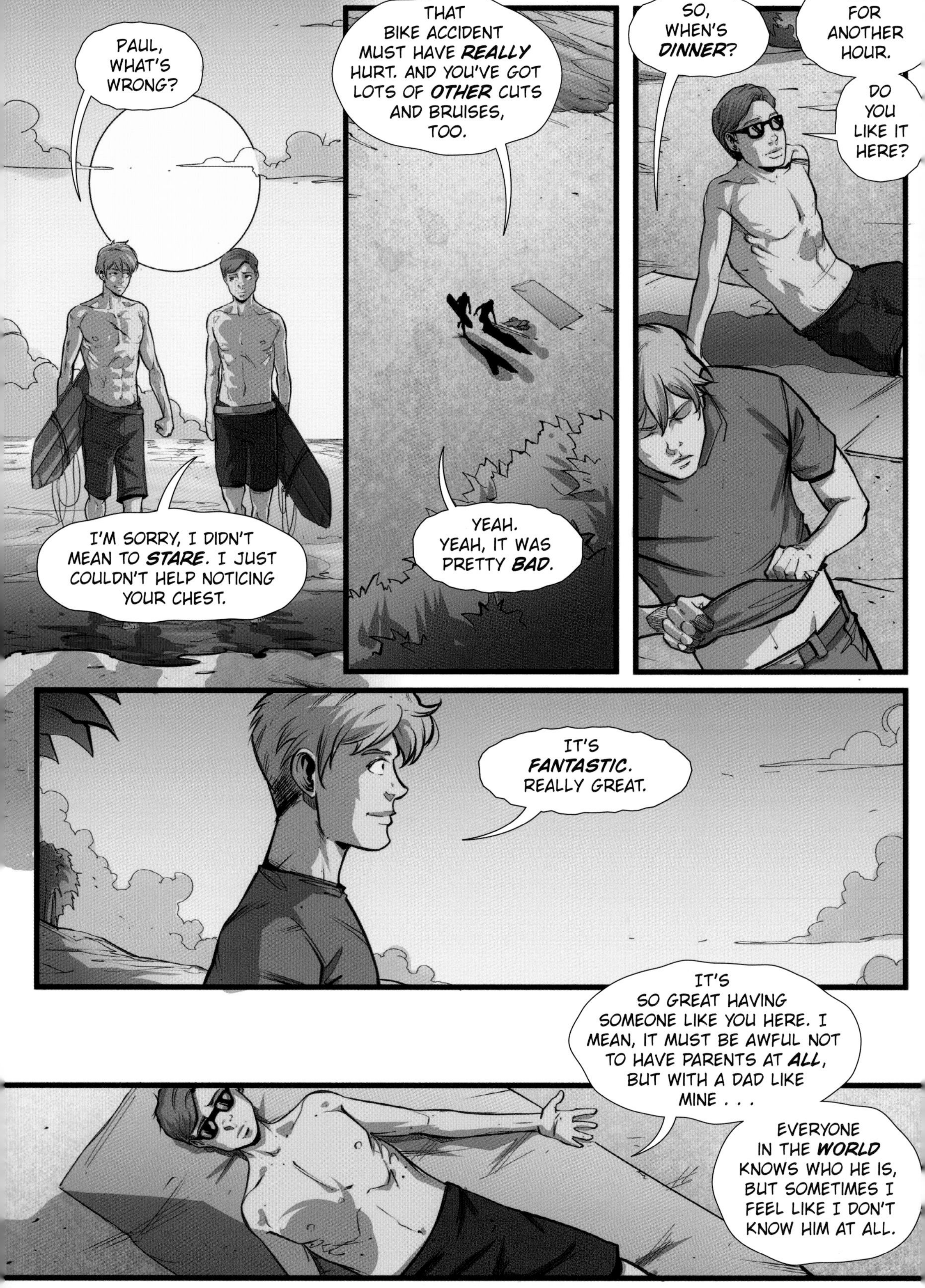

PAUL, WHAT'S WRONG?
I'M SORRY, I DIDN'T MEAN TO STARE. I JUST COULDN'T HELP NOTICING YOUR CHEST.
THAT BIKE ACCIDENT MUST HAVE REALLY HURT. AND YOU'VE GOT LOTS OF OTHER CUTS AND BRUISES, TOO.
YEAH. YEAH, IT WAS PRETTY BAD.
SO, WHEN'S DINNER?
NOT FOR ANOTHER HOUR.
DO YOU LIKE IT HERE?
IT'S FANTASTIC. REALLY GREAT.
IT'S SO GREAT HAVING SOMEONE LIKE YOU HERE. I MEAN, IT MUST BE AWFUL NOT TO HAVE PARENTS AT ALL, BUT WITH A DAD LIKE MINE . . .
EVERYONE IN THE WORLD KNOWS WHO HE IS, BUT SOMETIMES I FEEL LIKE I DON'T KNOW HIM AT ALL.

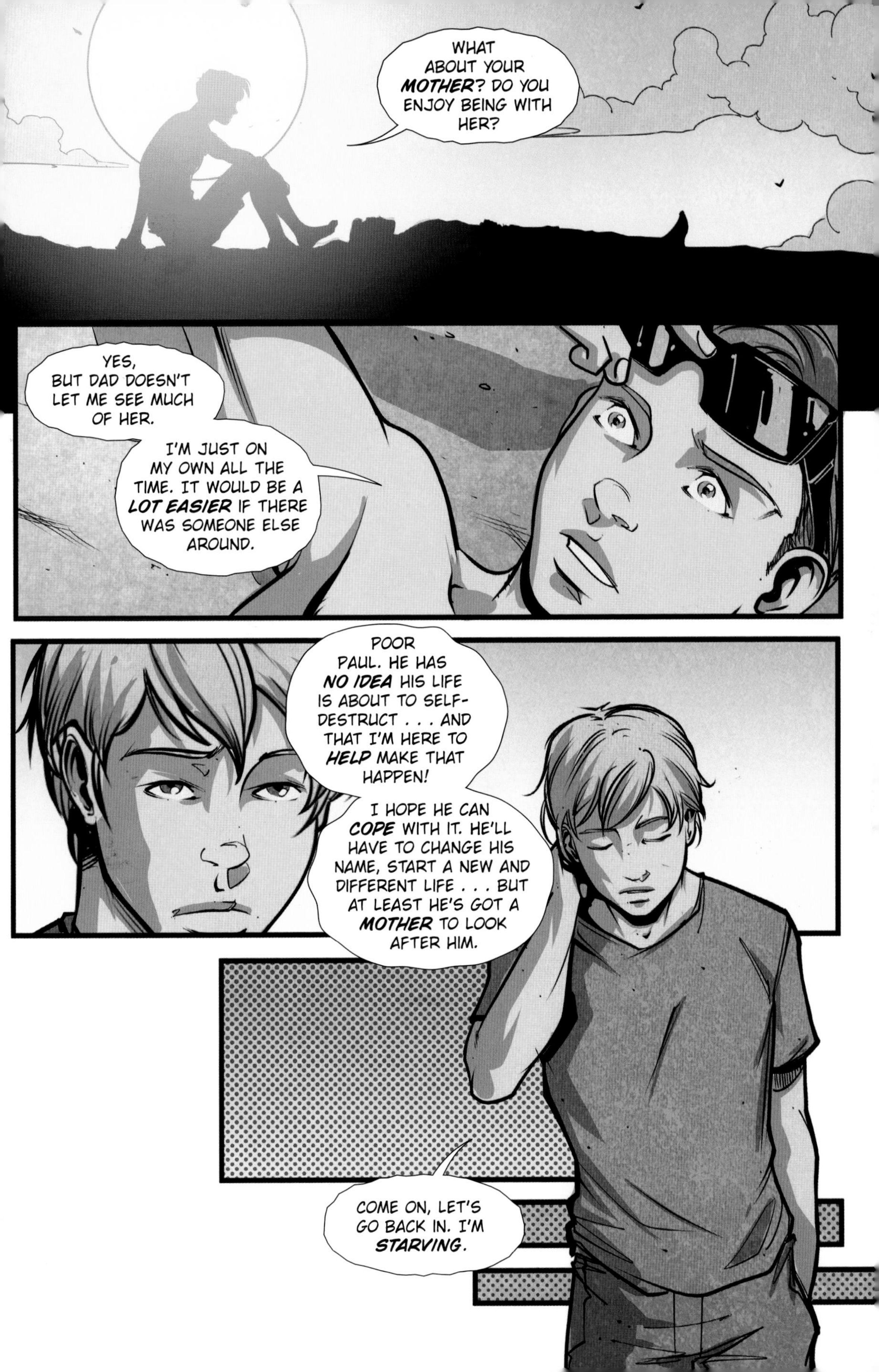
WHAT ABOUT YOUR MOTHER? DO YOU ENJOY BEING WITH HER?
YES, BUT DAD DOESN'T LET ME SEE MUCH OF HER.
I'M JUST ON MY OWN ALL THE TIME. IT WOULD BE A LOT EASIER IF THERE WAS SOMEONE ELSE AROUND.
POOR PAUL. HE HAS NO IDEA HIS LIFE IS ABOUT TO SELF-DESTRUCT . . . AND THAT I'M HERE TO HELP MAKE THAT HAPPEN!
I HOPE HE CAN COPE WITH IT. HE'LL HAVE TO CHANGE HIS NAME, START A NEW AND DIFFERENT LIFE . . . BUT AT LEAST HE'S GOT A MOTHER TO LOOK AFTER HIM.
COME ON, LET'S GO BACK IN. I'M STARVING.

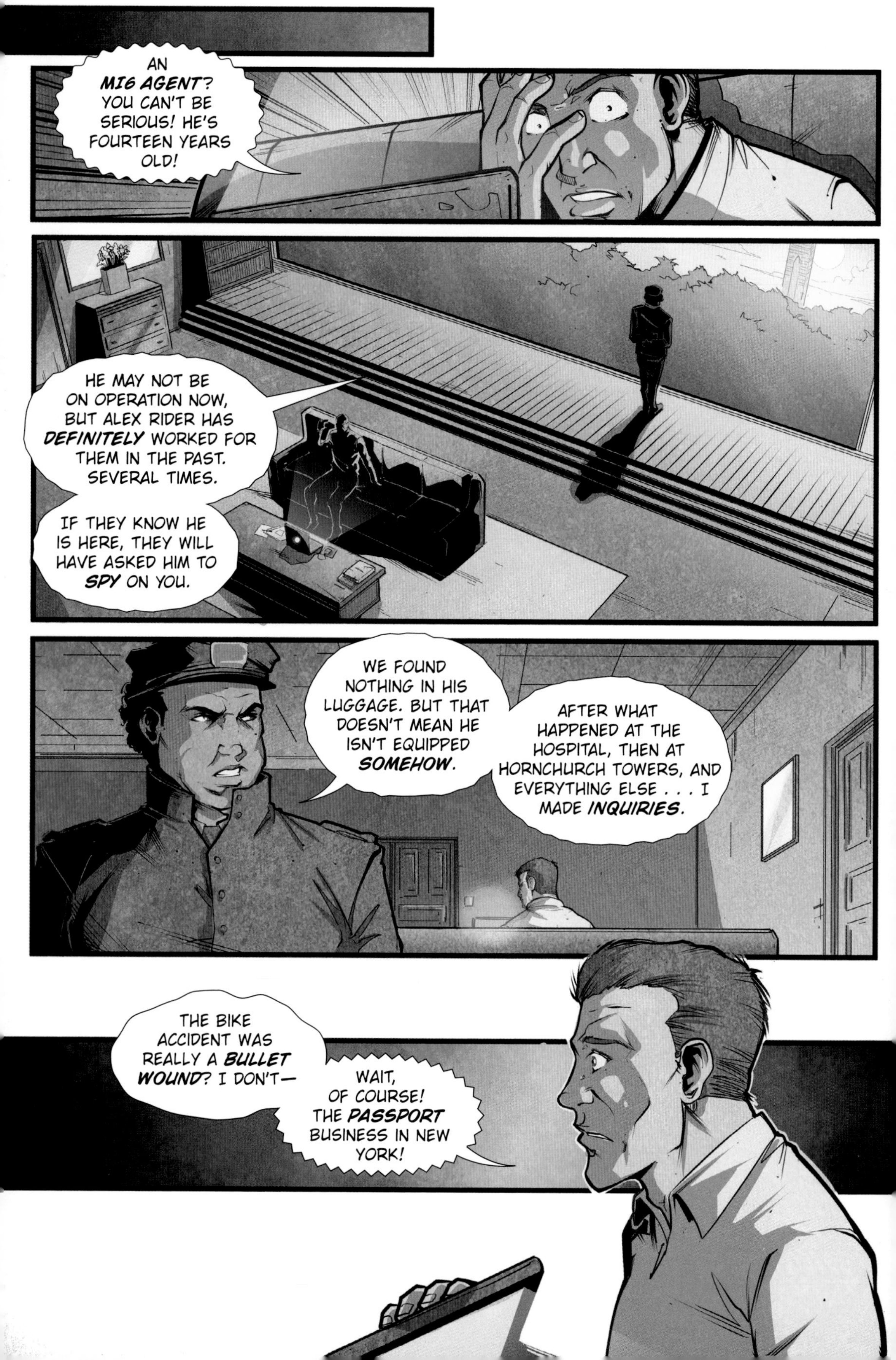
AN MI6 AGENT? YOU CAN'T BE SERIOUS! HE'S FOURTEEN YEARS OLD!
HE MAY NOT BE ON OPERATION NOW, BUT ALEX RIDER HAS DEFINITELY WORKED FOR THEM IN THE PAST. SEVERAL TIMES.
IF THEY KNOW HE IS HERE, THEY WILL HAVE ASKED HIM TO SPY ON YOU.
WE FOUND NOTHING IN HIS LUGGAGE. BUT THAT DOESN'T MEAN HE ISN'T EQUIPPED SOMEHOW.
AFTER WHAT HAPPENED AT THE HOSPITAL, THEN AT HORNCHURCH TOWERS, AND EVERYTHING ELSE . . . I MADE INQUIRIES.
THE BIKE ACCIDENT WAS REALLY A BULLET WOUND? I DON'T—
WAIT, OF COURSE! THE PASSPORT BUSINESS IN NEW YORK!

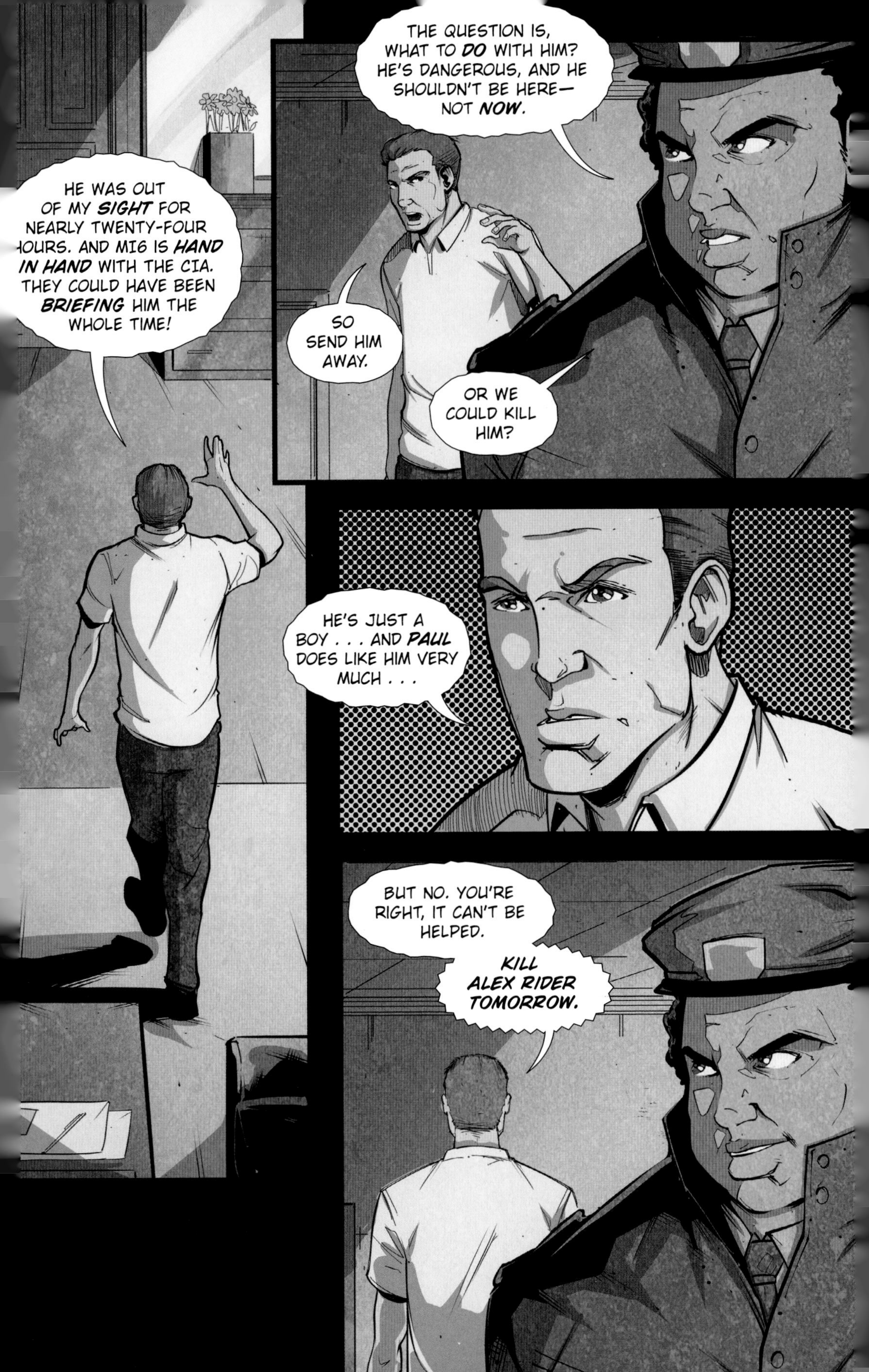
HE WAS OUT OF MY SIGHT FOR NEARLY TWENTY-FOUR HOURS. AND MI6 IS HAND IN HAND WITH THE CIA. THEY COULD HAVE BEEN BRIEFING HIM THE WHOLE TIME!
THE QUESTION IS, WHAT TO DO WITH HIM? HE'S DANGEROUS, AND HE SHOULDN'T BE HERE— NOT NOW.
SO SEND HIM AWAY.
OR WE COULD KILL HIM?
HE'S JUST A BOY . . . AND PAUL DOES LIKE HIM VERY MUCH . . .
BUT NO. YOU'RE RIGHT, IT CAN'T BE HELPED.
KILL ALEX RIDER TOMORROW.

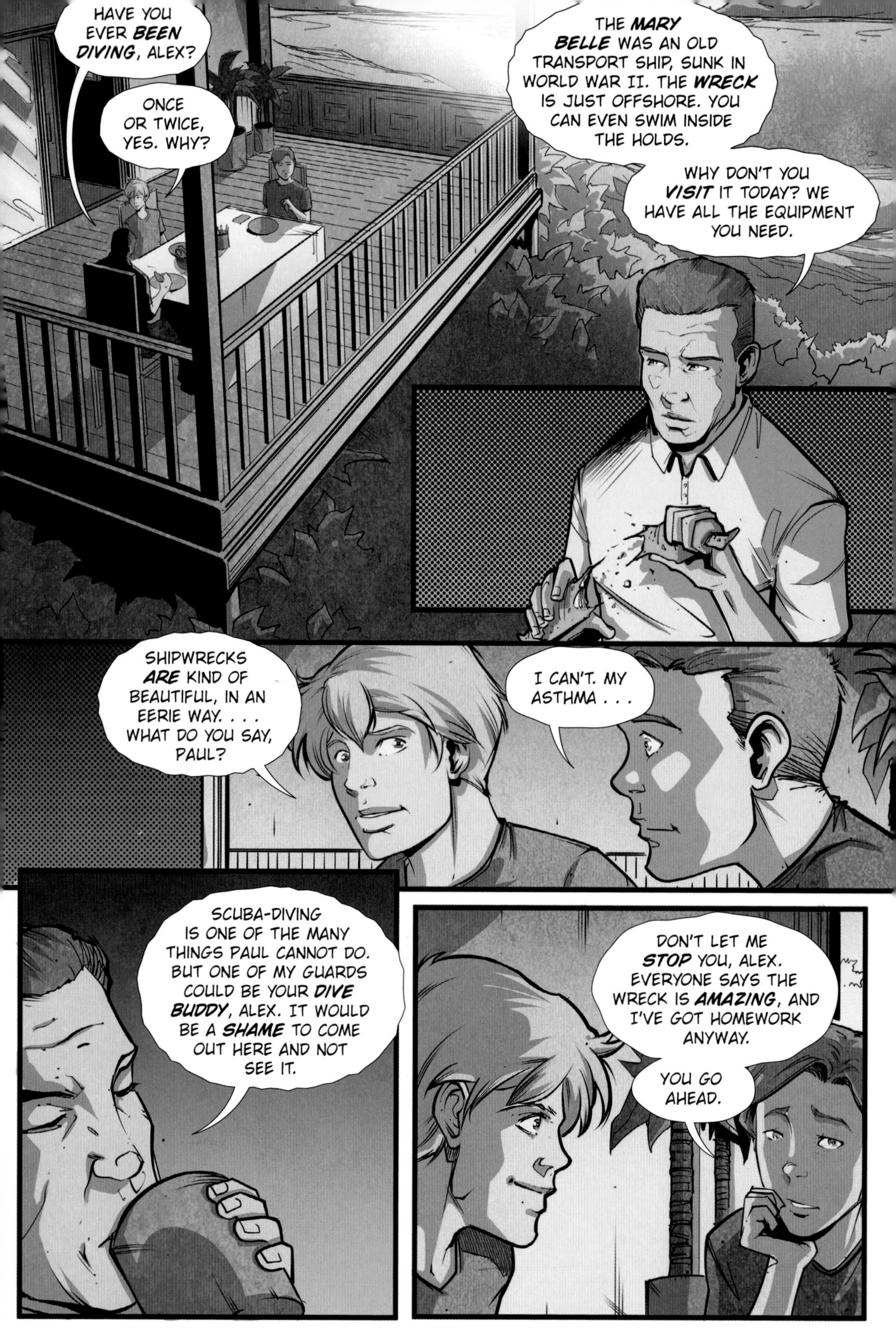
HAVE YOU EVER **BEEN DIVING**, ALEX?
ONCE OR TWICE, YES. WHY?
THE **MARY BELLE** WAS AN OLD TRANSPORT SHIP, SUNK IN WORLD WAR II. THE **WRECK** IS JUST OFFSHORE. YOU CAN EVEN SWIM INSIDE THE HOLDS.
WHY DON'T YOU **VISIT** IT TODAY? WE HAVE ALL THE EQUIPMENT YOU NEED.
SHIPWRECKS **ARE** KIND OF BEAUTIFUL, IN AN EERIE WAY. . . . WHAT DO YOU SAY, PAUL?
I CAN'T. MY ASTHMA . . .
SCUBA-DIVING IS ONE OF THE MANY THINGS PAUL CANNOT DO. BUT ONE OF MY GUARDS COULD BE YOUR **DIVE BUDDY**, ALEX. IT WOULD BE A **SHAME** TO COME OUT HERE AND NOT SEE IT.
DON'T LET ME **STOP** YOU, ALEX. EVERYONE SAYS THE WRECK IS **AMAZING**, AND I'VE GOT HOMEWORK ANYWAY.
YOU GO AHEAD.

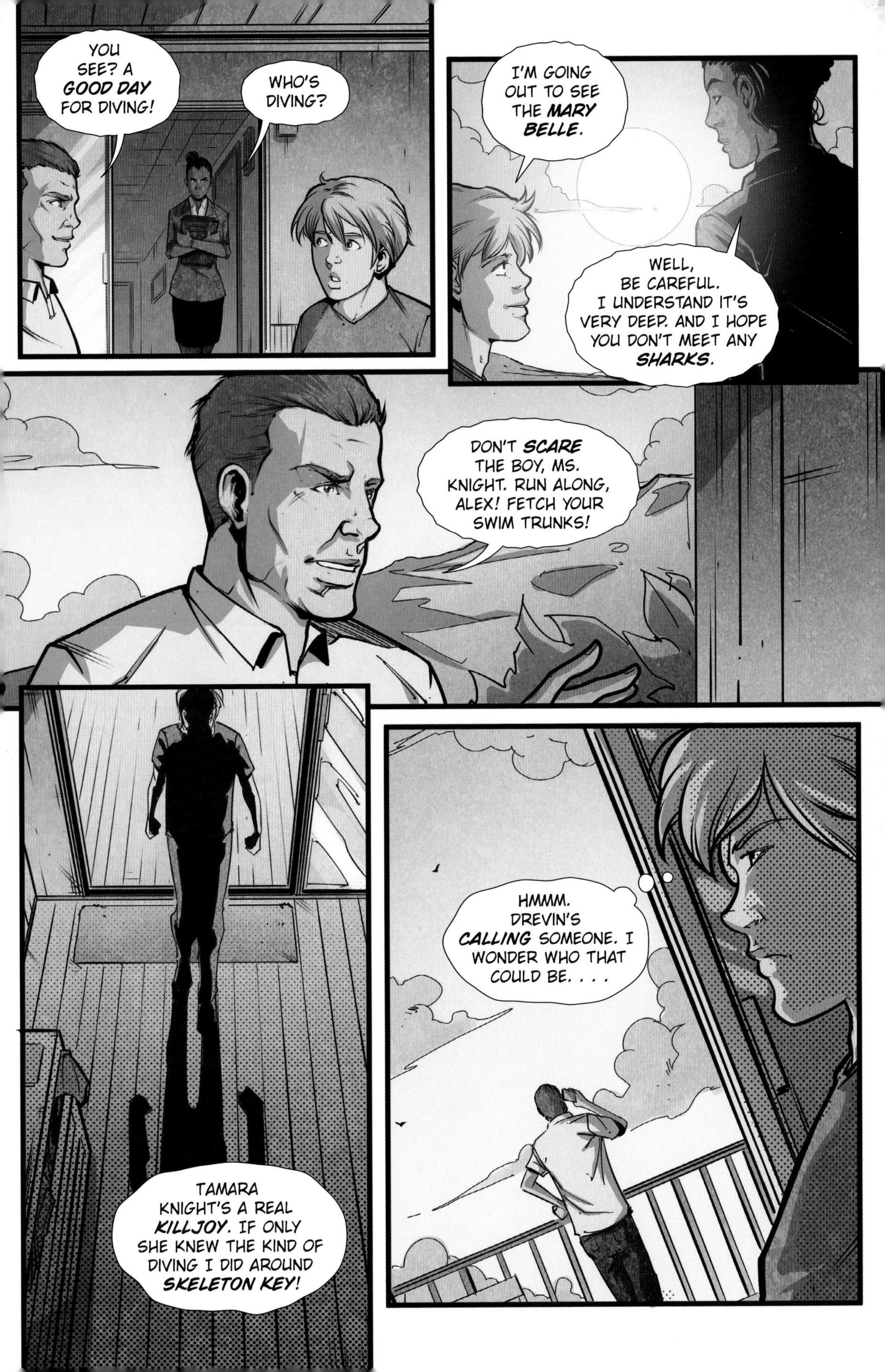
YOU SEE? A GOOD DAY FOR DIVING!
WHO'S DIVING?
I'M GOING OUT TO SEE THE MARY BELLE.
WELL, BE CAREFUL. I UNDERSTAND IT'S VERY DEEP. AND I HOPE YOU DON'T MEET ANY SHARKS.
DON'T SCARE THE BOY, MS. KNIGHT. RUN ALONG, ALEX! FETCH YOUR SWIM TRUNKS!
TAMARA KNIGHT'S A REAL KILLJOY. IF ONLY SHE KNEW THE KIND OF DIVING I DID AROUND SKELETON KEY!
HMMM. DREVIN'S CALLING SOMEONE. I WONDER WHO THAT COULD BE. . . .

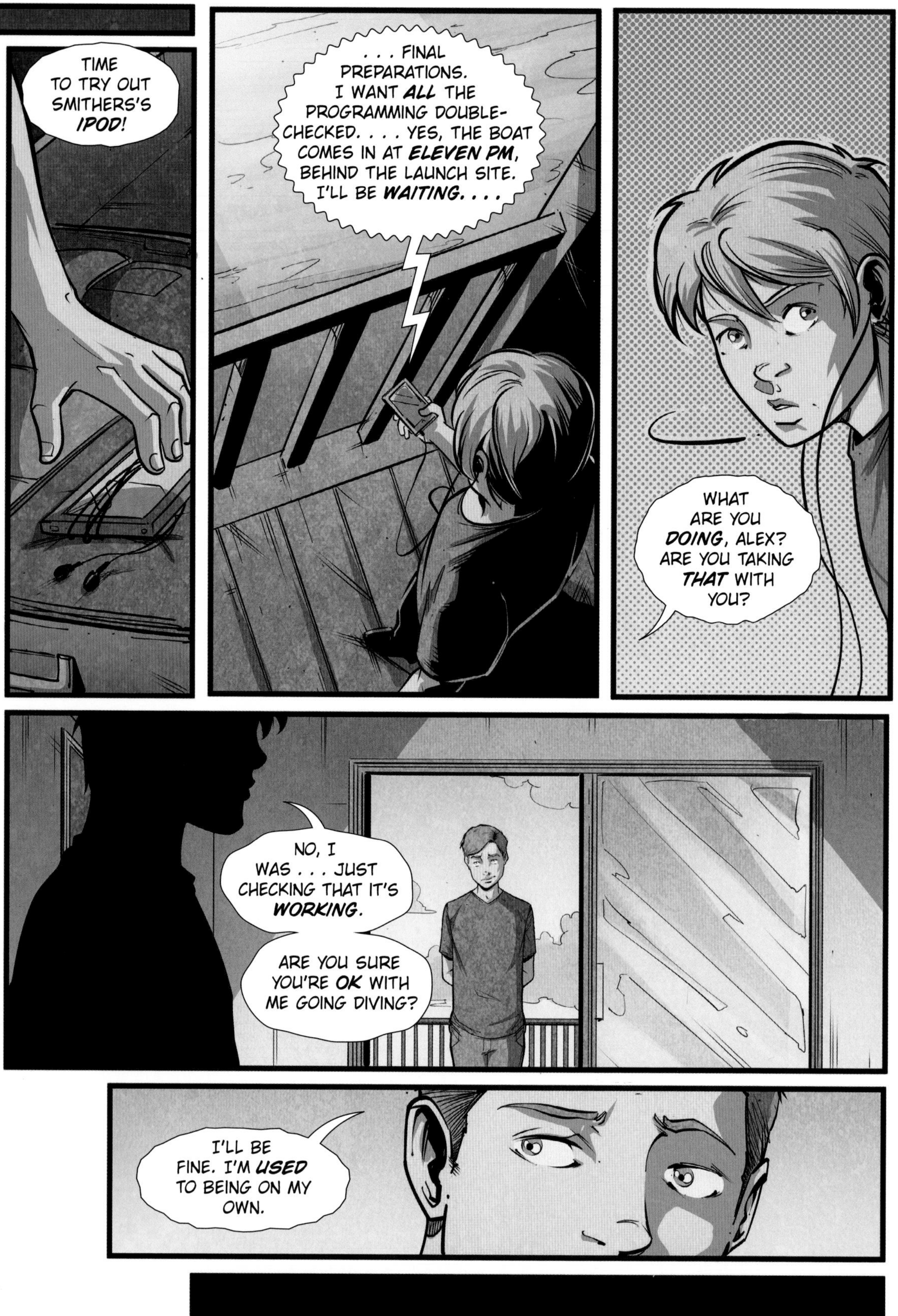
TIME TO TRY OUT SMITHERS'S *IPOD!*
. . . FINAL PREPARATIONS. I WANT ***ALL*** THE PROGRAMMING DOUBLE-CHECKED. . . . YES, THE BOAT COMES IN AT ***ELEVEN PM***, BEHIND THE LAUNCH SITE. I'LL BE ***WAITING. . . .***
WHAT ARE YOU ***DOING***, ALEX? ARE YOU TAKING ***THAT*** WITH YOU?
NO, I WAS . . . JUST CHECKING THAT IT'S ***WORKING***.
ARE YOU SURE YOU'RE ***OK*** WITH ME GOING DIVING?
I'LL BE FINE. I'M ***USED*** TO BEING ON MY OWN.

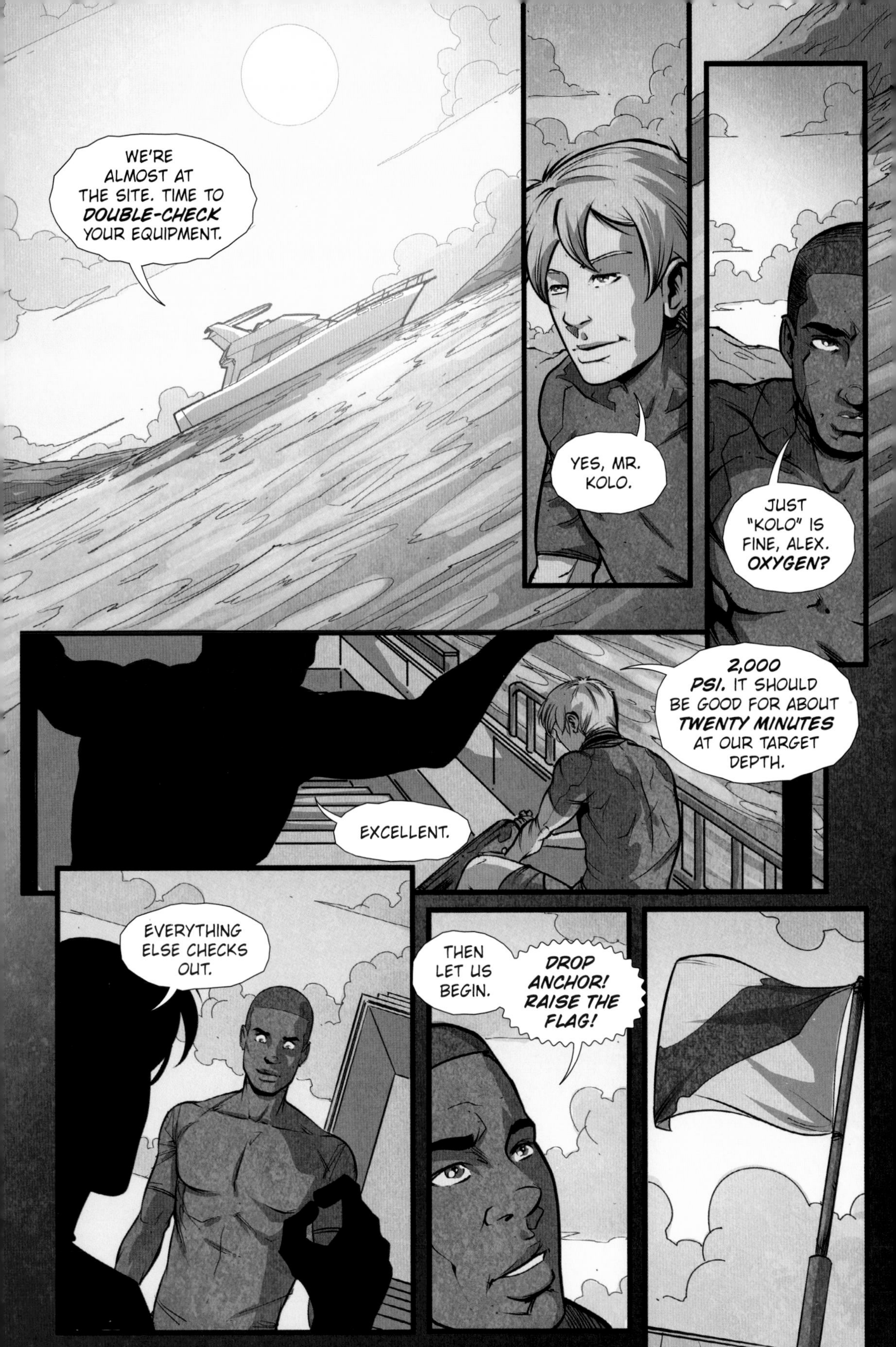
WE'RE ALMOST AT THE SITE. TIME TO DOUBLE-CHECK YOUR EQUIPMENT.
YES, MR. KOLO.
JUST "KOLO" IS FINE, ALEX. OXYGEN?
2,000 PSI. IT SHOULD BE GOOD FOR ABOUT TWENTY MINUTES AT OUR TARGET DEPTH.
EXCELLENT.
EVERYTHING ELSE CHECKS OUT.
THEN LET US BEGIN.
DROP ANCHOR! RAISE THE FLAG!

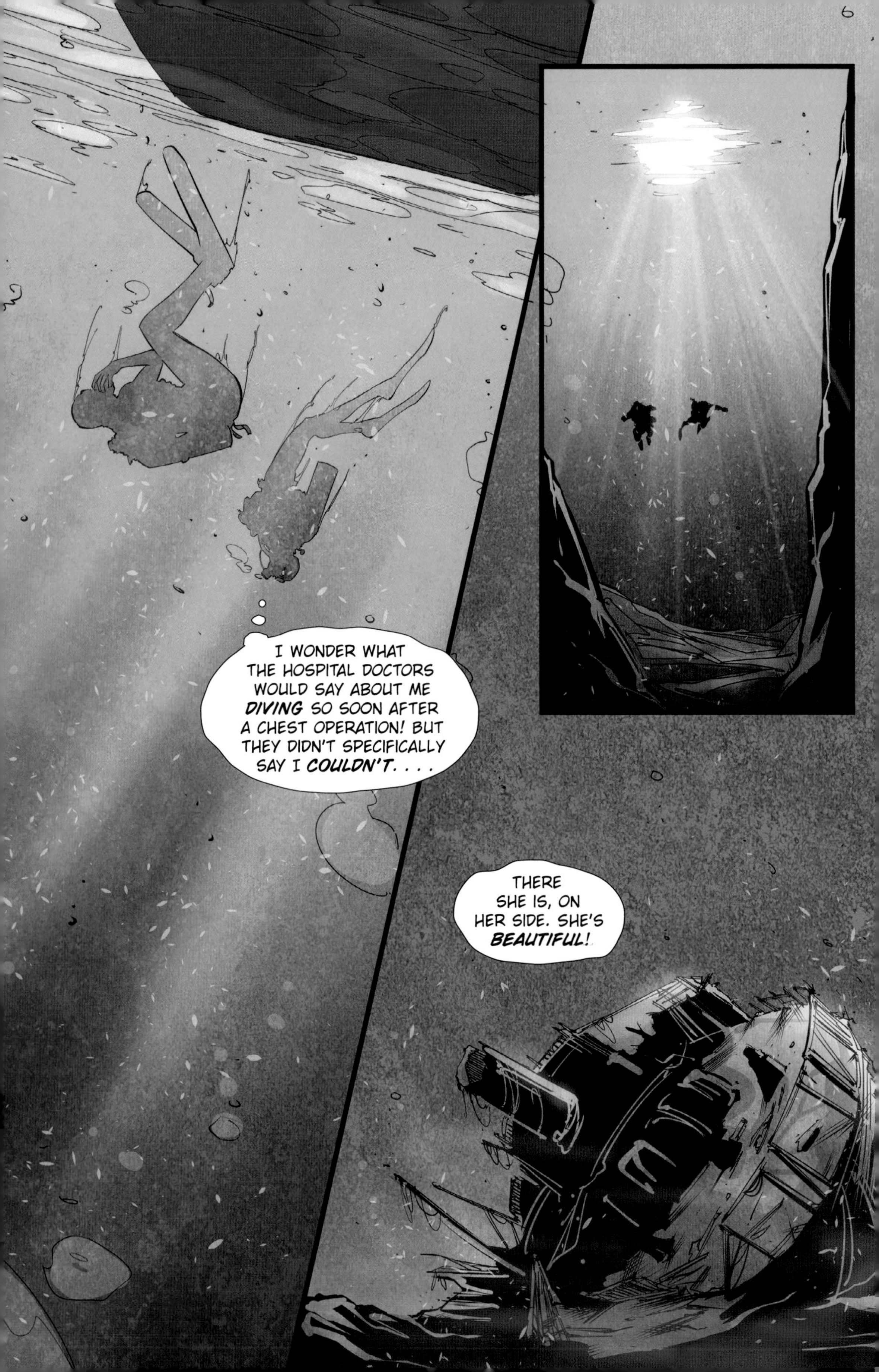
I WONDER WHAT THE HOSPITAL DOCTORS WOULD SAY ABOUT ME DIVING SO SOON AFTER A CHEST OPERATION! BUT THEY DIDN'T SPECIFICALLY SAY I COULDN'T. . . .
THERE SHE IS, ON HER SIDE. SHE'S BEAUTIFUL!

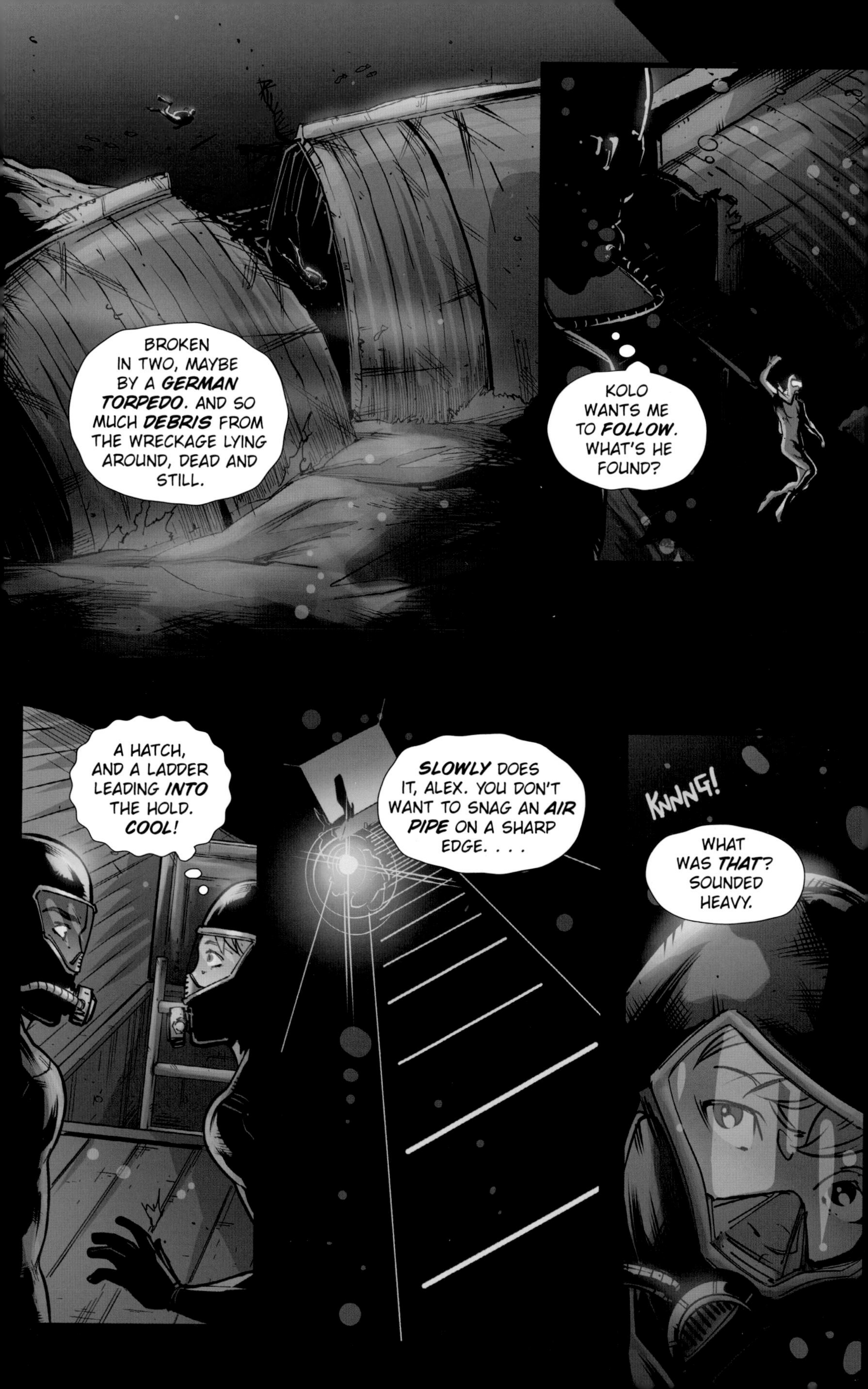
BROKEN IN TWO, MAYBE BY A GERMAN TORPEDO. AND SO MUCH DEBRIS FROM THE WRECKAGE LYING AROUND, DEAD AND STILL.
KOLO WANTS ME TO FOLLOW. WHAT'S HE FOUND?
A HATCH, AND A LADDER LEADING INTO THE HOLD. COOL!
SLOWLY DOES IT, ALEX. YOU DON'T WANT TO SNAG AN AIR PIPE ON A SHARP EDGE. . . .
KWNNG!
WHAT WAS THAT? SOUNDED HEAVY.

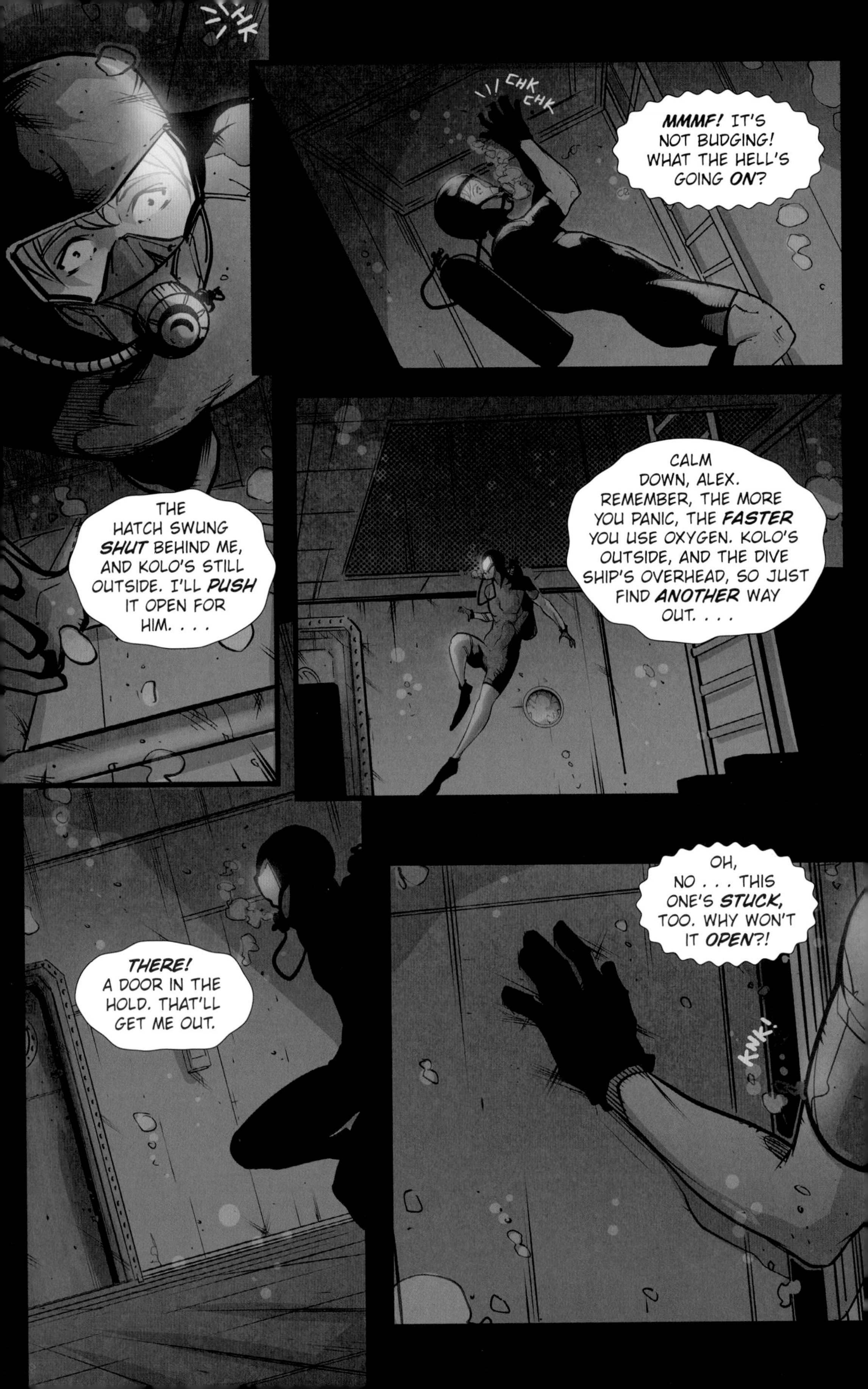
CHK
CHK CHK
MMMF! IT'S NOT BUDGING! WHAT THE HELL'S GOING ON?
THE HATCH SWUNG SHUT BEHIND ME, AND KOLO'S STILL OUTSIDE. I'LL PUSH IT OPEN FOR HIM. . . .
CALM DOWN, ALEX. REMEMBER, THE MORE YOU PANIC, THE FASTER YOU USE OXYGEN. KOLO'S OUTSIDE, AND THE DIVE SHIP'S OVERHEAD, SO JUST FIND ANOTHER WAY OUT. . . .
THERE! A DOOR IN THE HOLD. THAT'LL GET ME OUT.
OH, NO . . . THIS ONE'S STUCK, TOO. WHY WON'T IT OPEN?!
KNK!

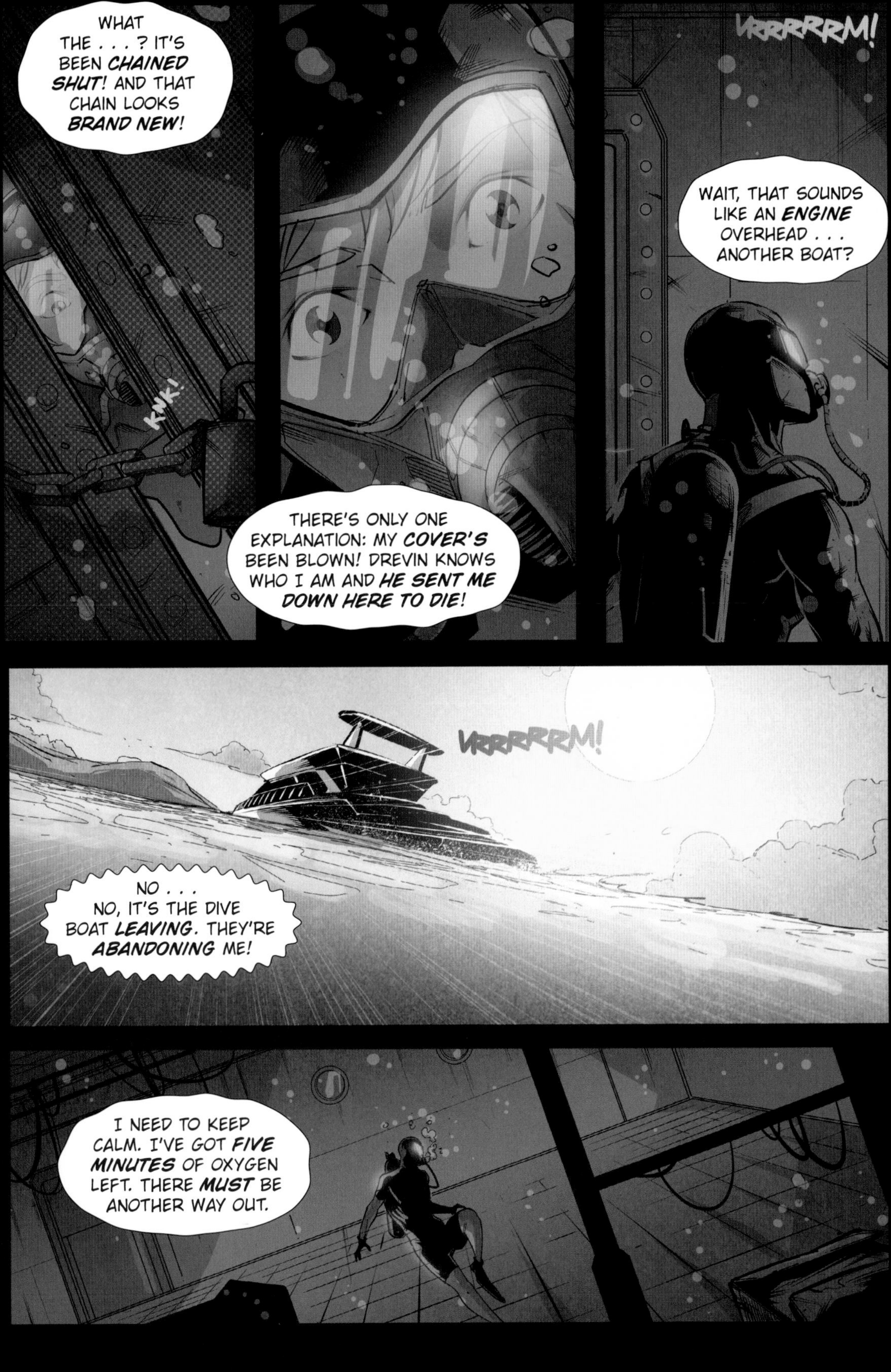
WHAT THE . . . ? IT'S BEEN CHAINED SHUT! AND THAT CHAIN LOOKS BRAND NEW!
KNK!
THERE'S ONLY ONE EXPLANATION: MY COVER'S BEEN BLOWN! DREVIN KNOWS WHO I AM AND HE SENT ME DOWN HERE TO DIE!
VRRRRRM!
WAIT, THAT SOUNDS LIKE AN ENGINE OVERHEAD . . . ANOTHER BOAT?
VRRRRRM!
NO . . . NO, IT'S THE DIVE BOAT LEAVING. THEY'RE ABANDONING ME!
I NEED TO KEEP CALM. I'VE GOT FIVE MINUTES OF OXYGEN LEFT. THERE MUST BE ANOTHER WAY OUT.

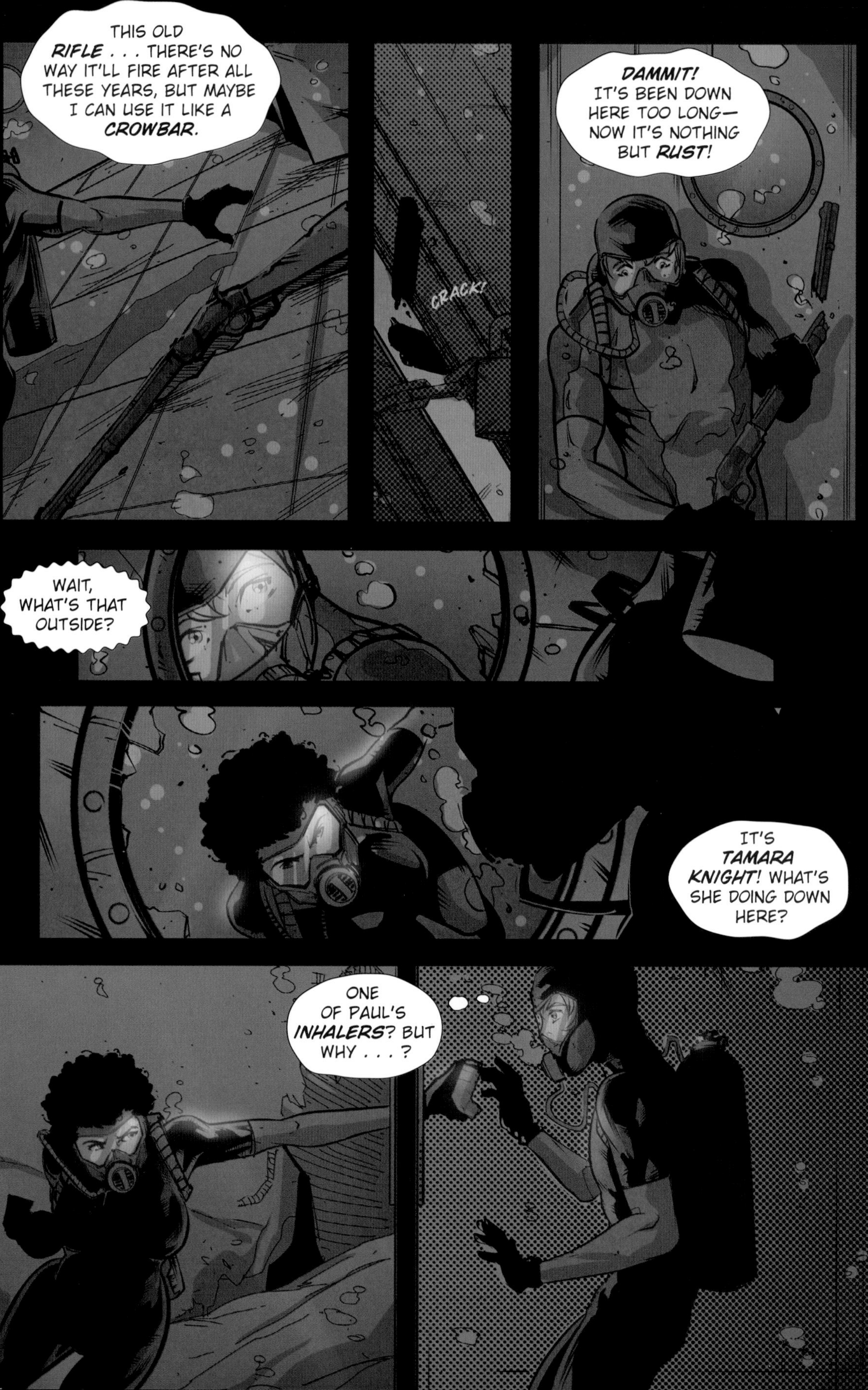
THIS OLD RIFLE . . . THERE'S NO WAY IT'LL FIRE AFTER ALL THESE YEARS, BUT MAYBE I CAN USE IT LIKE A CROWBAR.
CRACK!
DAMMIT! IT'S BEEN DOWN HERE TOO LONG— NOW IT'S NOTHING BUT RUST!
WAIT, WHAT'S THAT OUTSIDE?
IT'S TAMARA KNIGHT! WHAT'S SHE DOING DOWN HERE?
ONE OF PAUL'S INHALERS? BUT WHY . . . ?

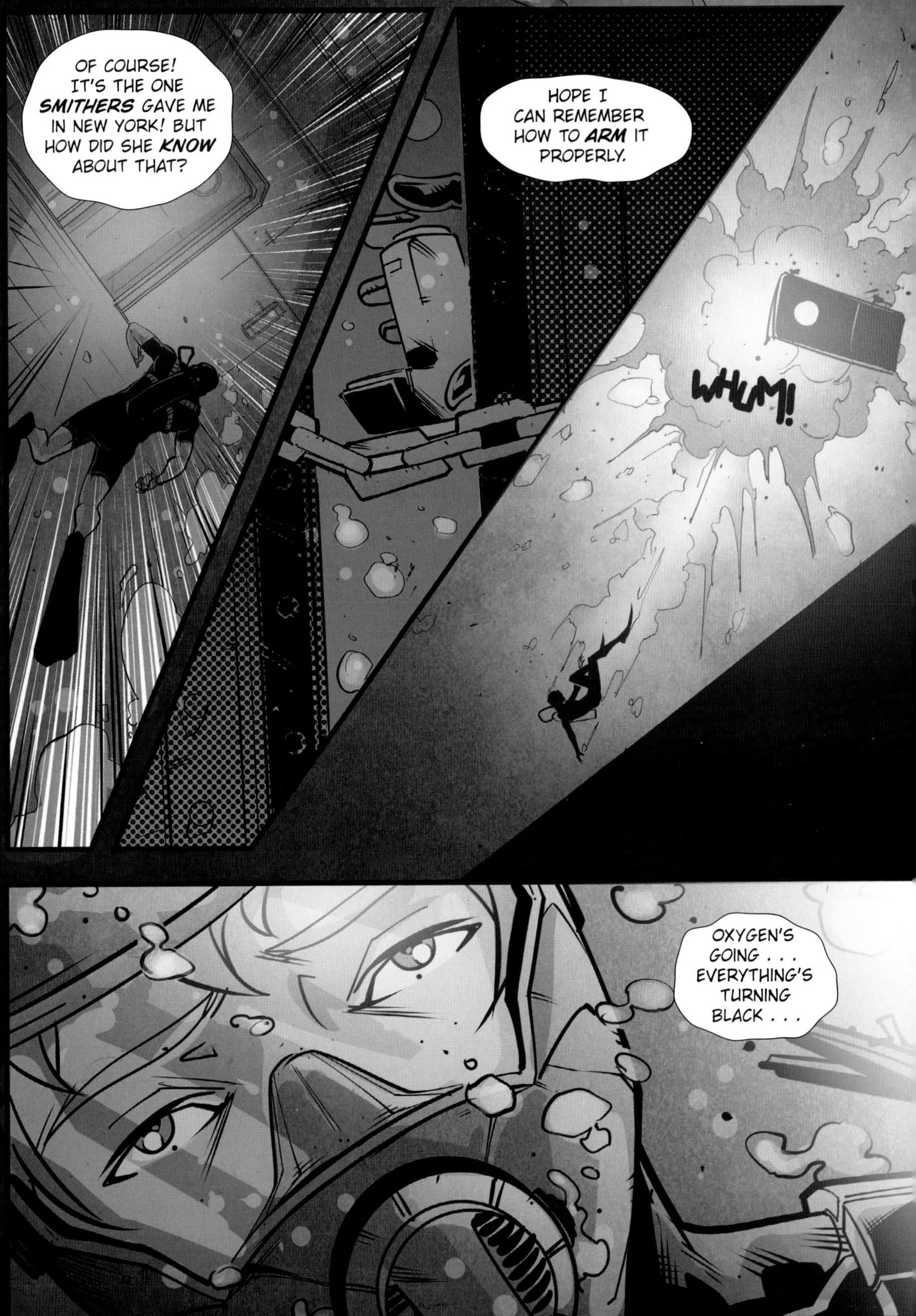
OF COURSE! IT'S THE ONE SMITHERS GAVE ME IN NEW YORK! BUT HOW DID SHE KNOW ABOUT THAT?
HOPE I CAN REMEMBER HOW TO ARM IT PROPERLY.
WHUM!
OXYGEN'S GOING . . . EVERYTHING'S TURNING BLACK . . .

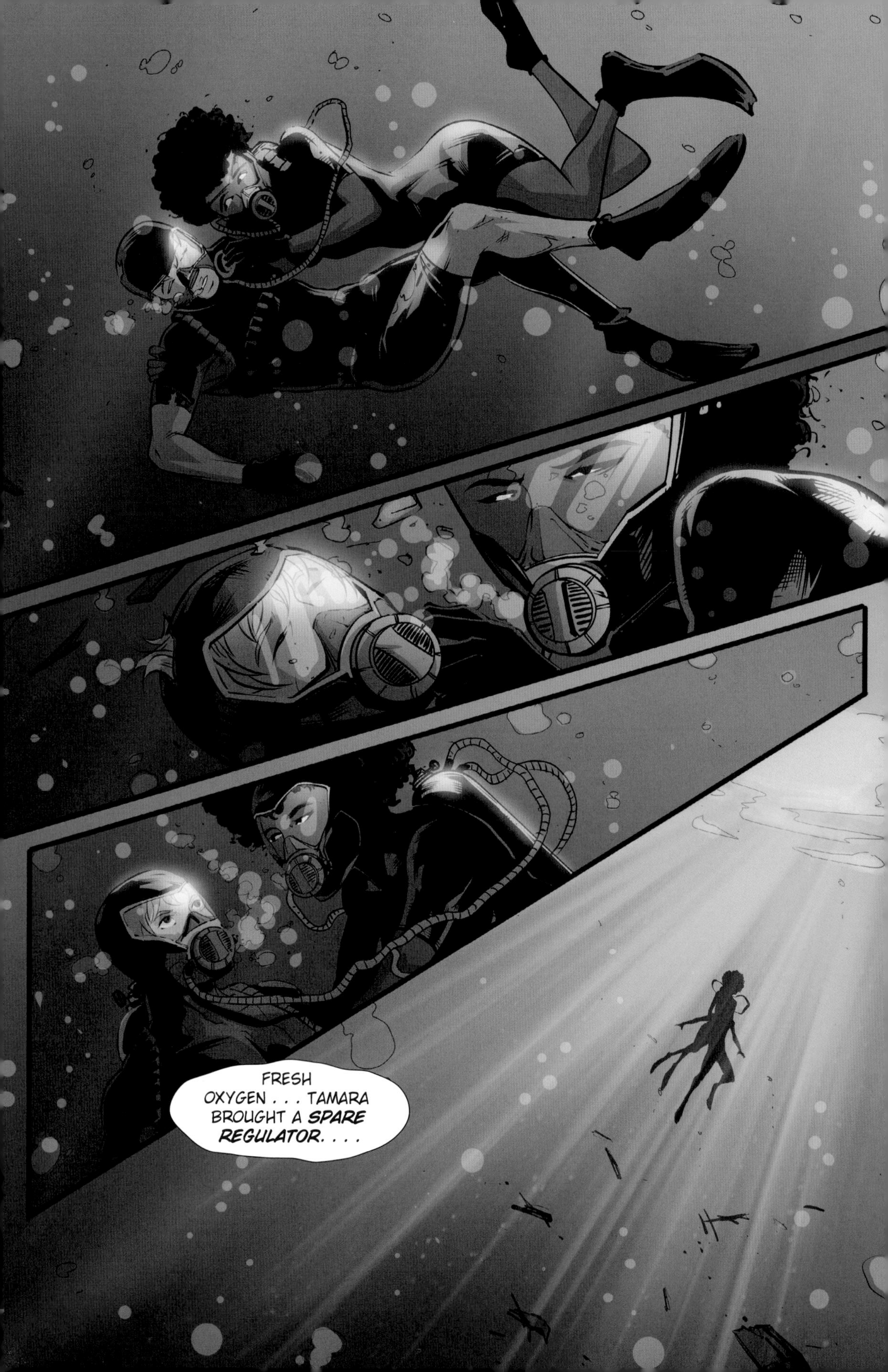
FRESH OXYGEN . . . TAMARA BROUGHT A *SPARE REGULATOR*. . . .

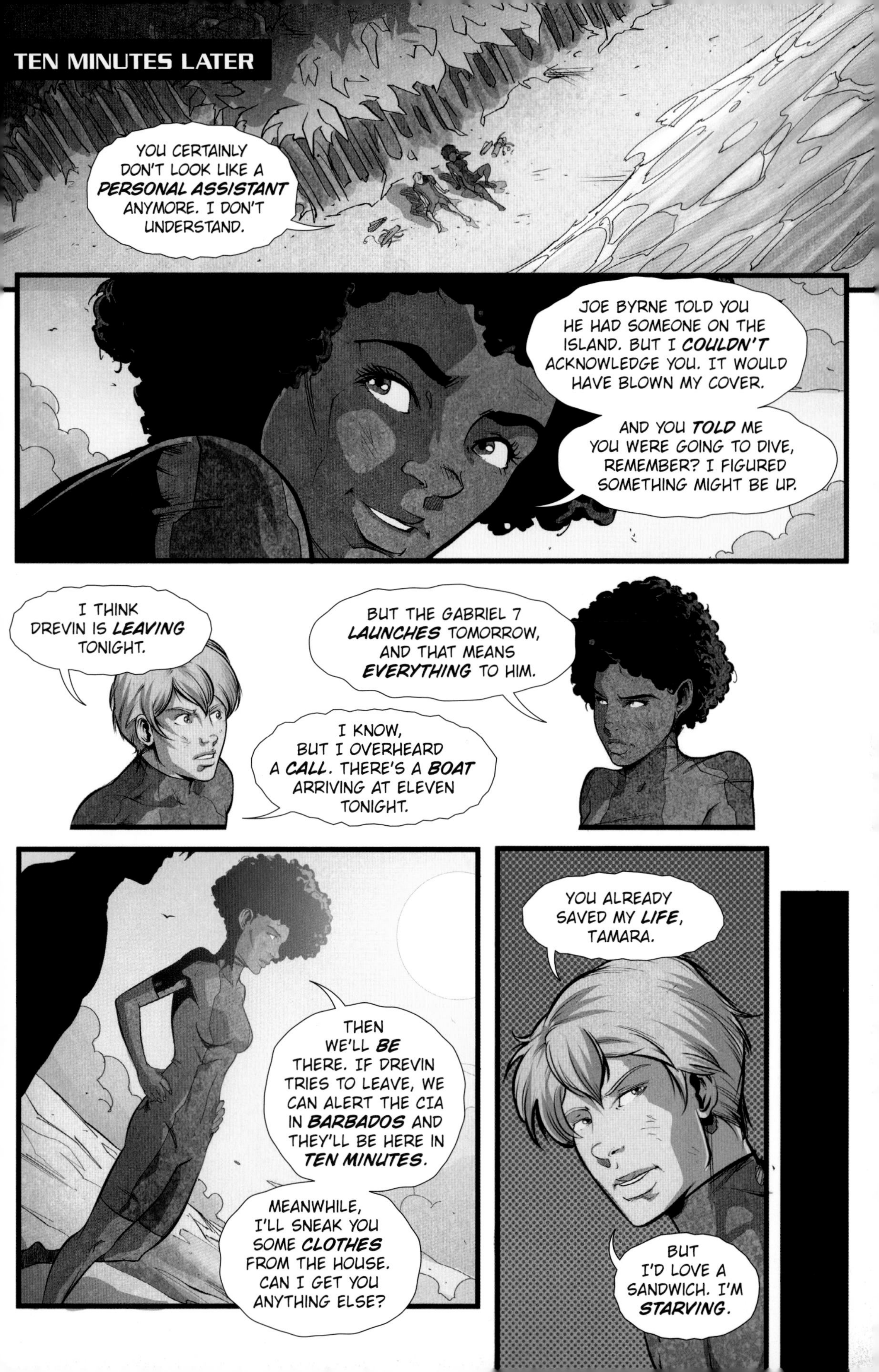
TEN MINUTES LATER
YOU CERTAINLY DON'T LOOK LIKE A PERSONAL ASSISTANT ANYMORE. I DON'T UNDERSTAND.
JOE BYRNE TOLD YOU HE HAD SOMEONE ON THE ISLAND. BUT I COULDN'T ACKNOWLEDGE YOU. IT WOULD HAVE BLOWN MY COVER.
AND YOU TOLD ME YOU WERE GOING TO DIVE, REMEMBER? I FIGURED SOMETHING MIGHT BE UP.
I THINK DREVIN IS LEAVING TONIGHT.
BUT THE GABRIEL 7 LAUNCHES TOMORROW, AND THAT MEANS EVERYTHING TO HIM.
I KNOW, BUT I OVERHEARD A CALL. THERE'S A BOAT ARRIVING AT ELEVEN TONIGHT.
THEN WE'LL BE THERE. IF DREVIN TRIES TO LEAVE, WE CAN ALERT THE CIA IN BARBADOS AND THEY'LL BE HERE IN TEN MINUTES.
MEANWHILE, I'LL SNEAK YOU SOME CLOTHES FROM THE HOUSE. CAN I GET YOU ANYTHING ELSE?
YOU ALREADY SAVED MY LIFE, TAMARA.
BUT I'D LOVE A SANDWICH. I'M STARVING.

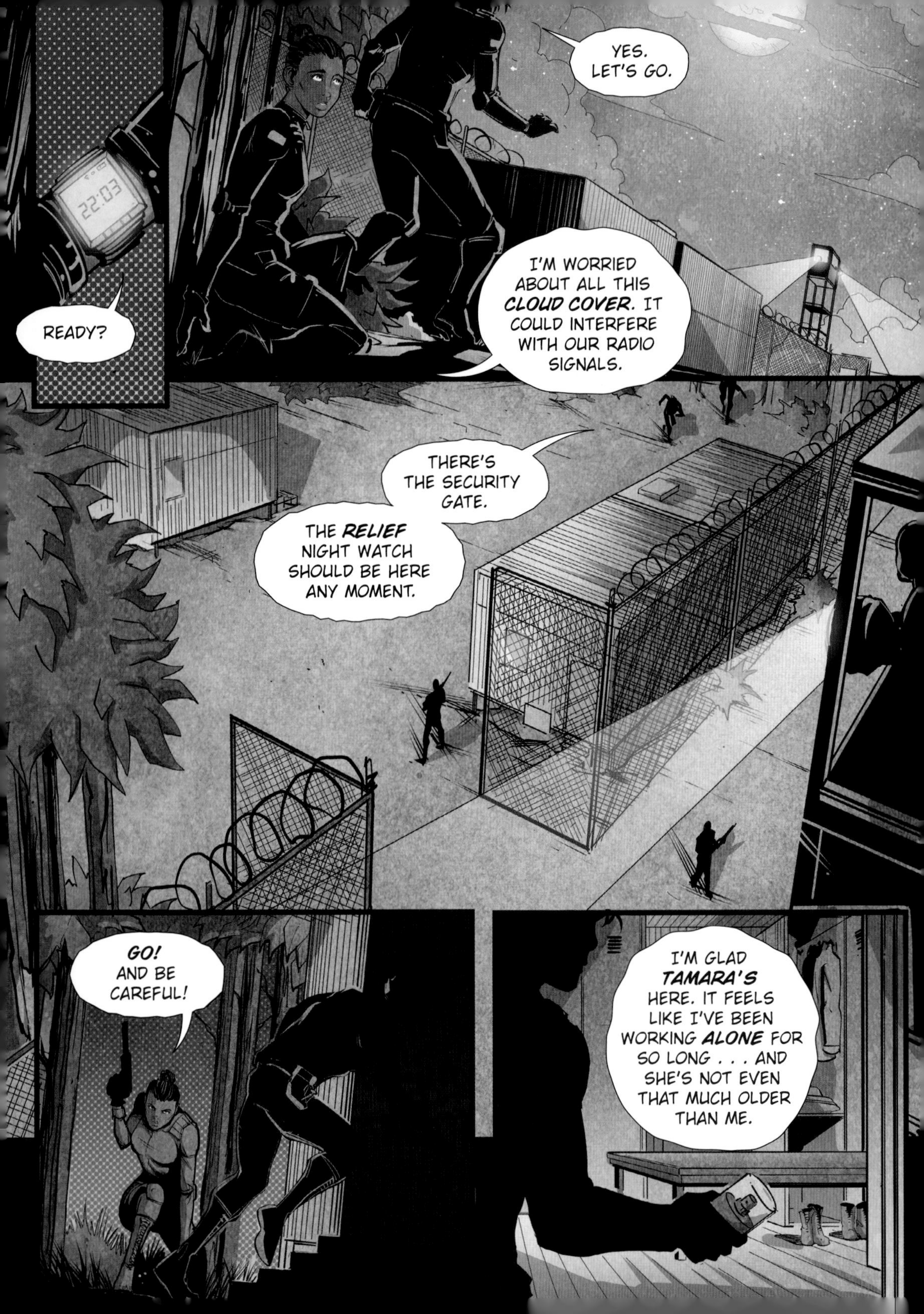
22:03
READY?
YES. LET'S GO.
I'M WORRIED ABOUT ALL THIS CLOUD COVER. IT COULD INTERFERE WITH OUR RADIO SIGNALS.
THERE'S THE SECURITY GATE.
THE RELIEF NIGHT WATCH SHOULD BE HERE ANY MOMENT.
GO! AND BE CAREFUL!
I'M GLAD TAMARA'S HERE. IT FEELS LIKE I'VE BEEN WORKING ALONE FOR SO LONG . . . AND SHE'S NOT EVEN THAT MUCH OLDER THAN ME.

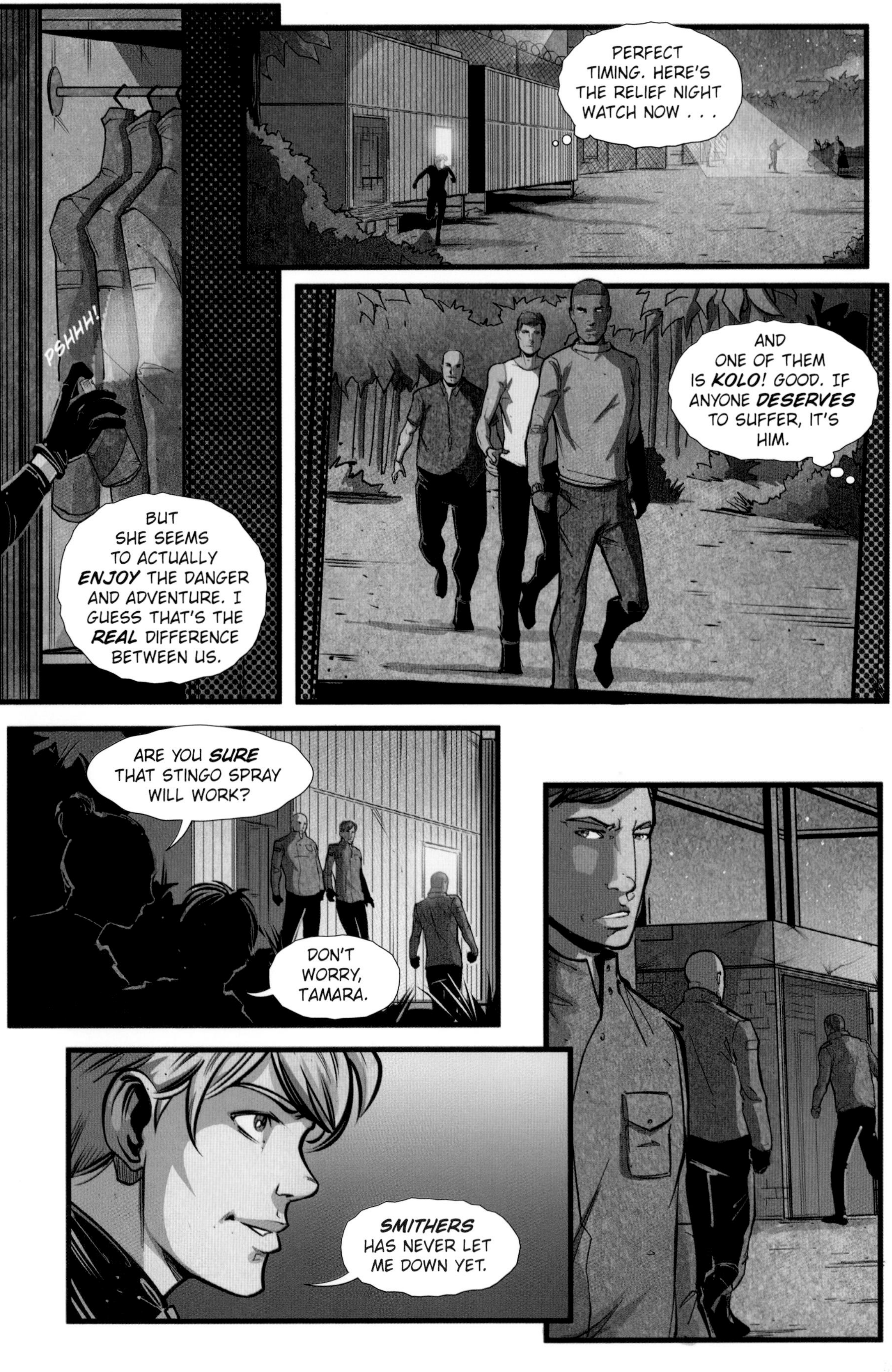
PSHHH!
BUT SHE SEEMS TO ACTUALLY ENJOY THE DANGER AND ADVENTURE. I GUESS THAT'S THE REAL DIFFERENCE BETWEEN US.
PERFECT TIMING. HERE'S THE RELIEF NIGHT WATCH NOW . . .
AND ONE OF THEM IS KOLO! GOOD. IF ANYONE DESERVES TO SUFFER, IT'S HIM.
ARE YOU SURE THAT STINGO SPRAY WILL WORK?
DON'T WORRY, TAMARA.
SMITHERS HAS NEVER LET ME DOWN YET.

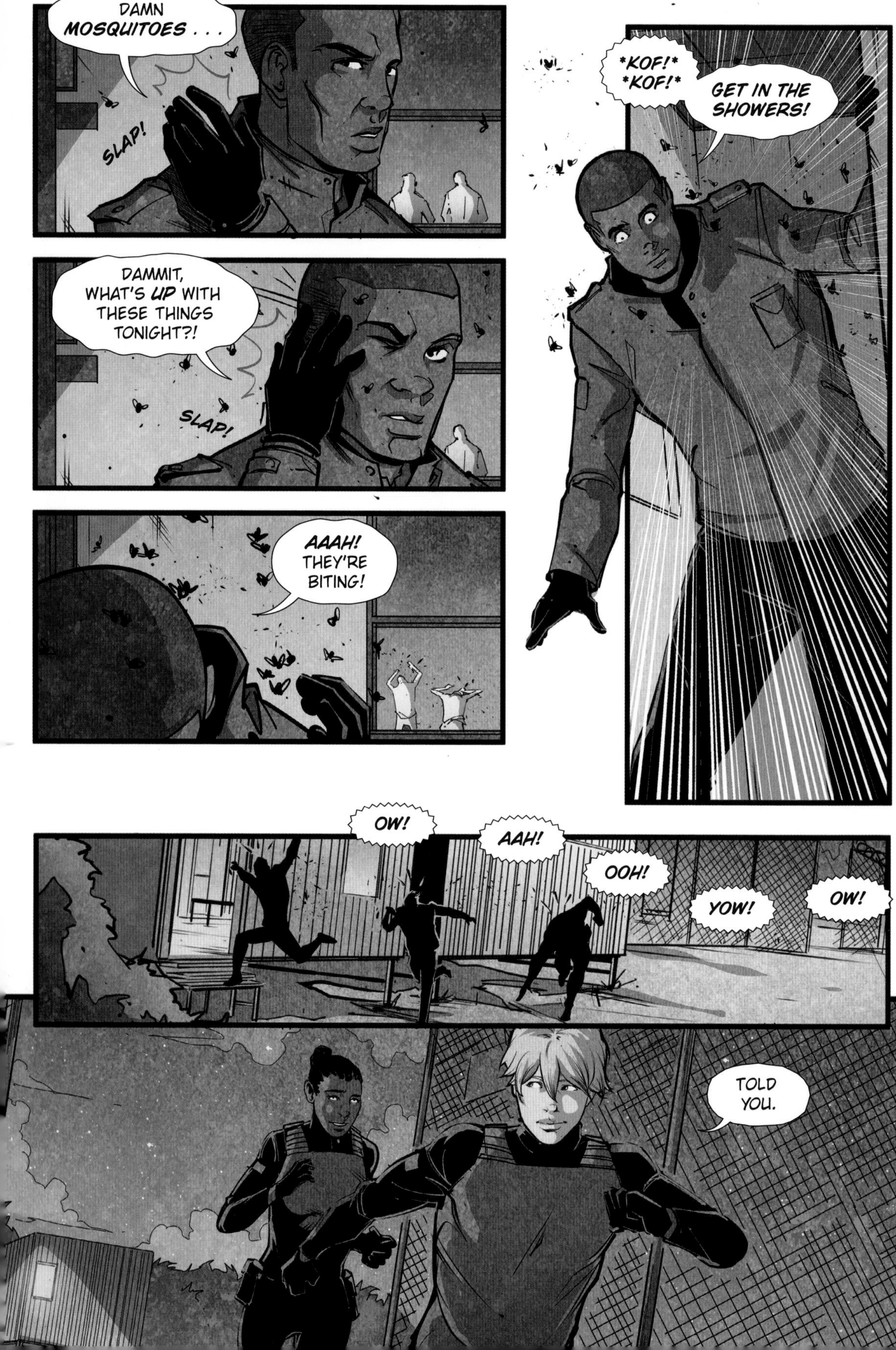
DAMN MOSQUITOES . . .
SLAP!
DAMMIT, WHAT'S UP WITH THESE THINGS TONIGHT?!
SLAP!
AAAH! THEY'RE BITING!
KOF! *KOF!*
GET IN THE SHOWERS!
OW!
AAH!
OOH!
YOW!
OW!
TOLD YOU.

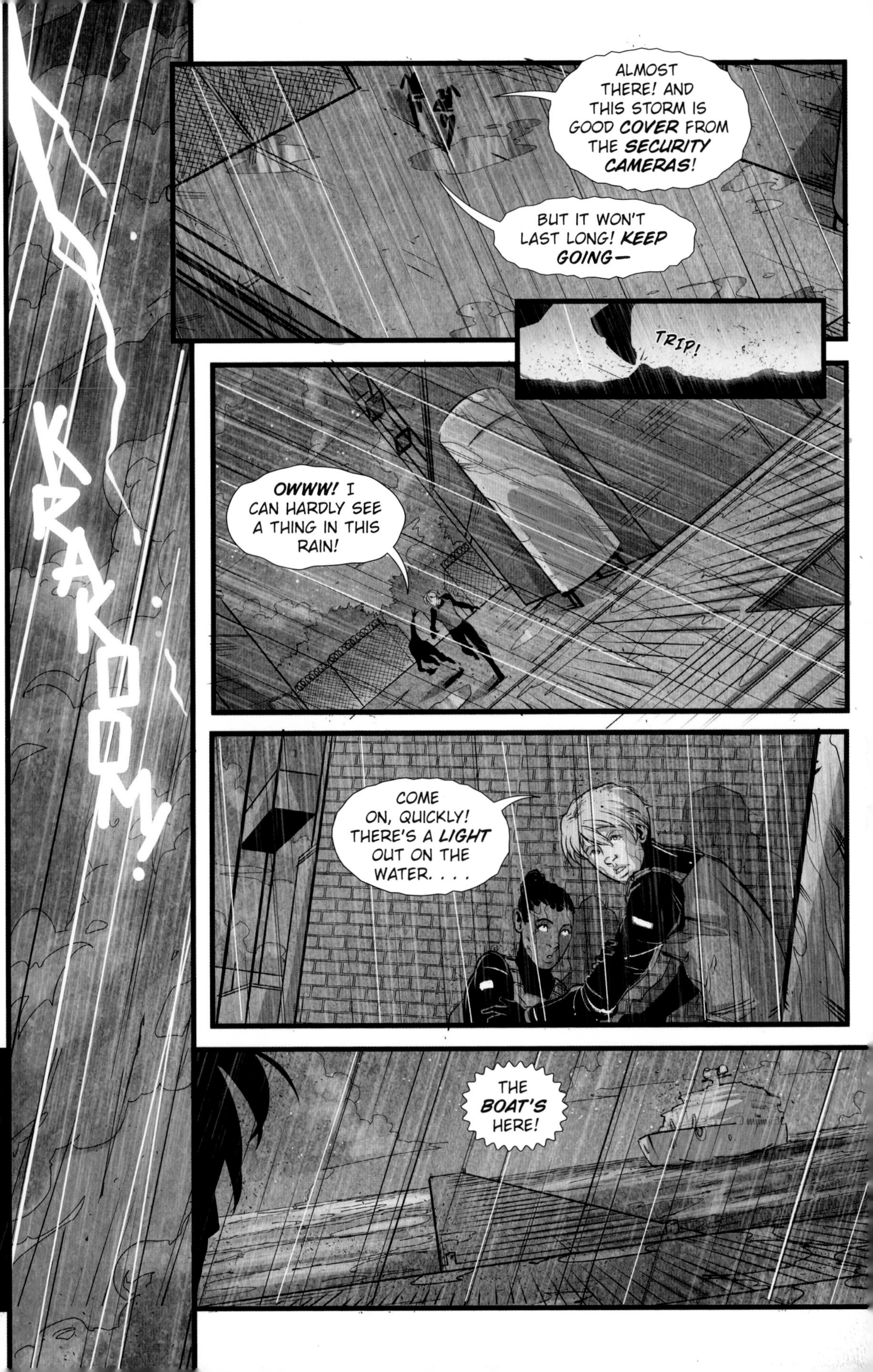
ALMOST THERE! AND THIS STORM IS GOOD COVER FROM THE SECURITY CAMERAS!
BUT IT WON'T LAST LONG! KEEP GOING—
TRIP!
OWWW! I CAN HARDLY SEE A THING IN THIS RAIN!
KRAKOOM!
COME ON, QUICKLY! THERE'S A LIGHT OUT ON THE WATER. . . .
THE BOAT'S HERE!

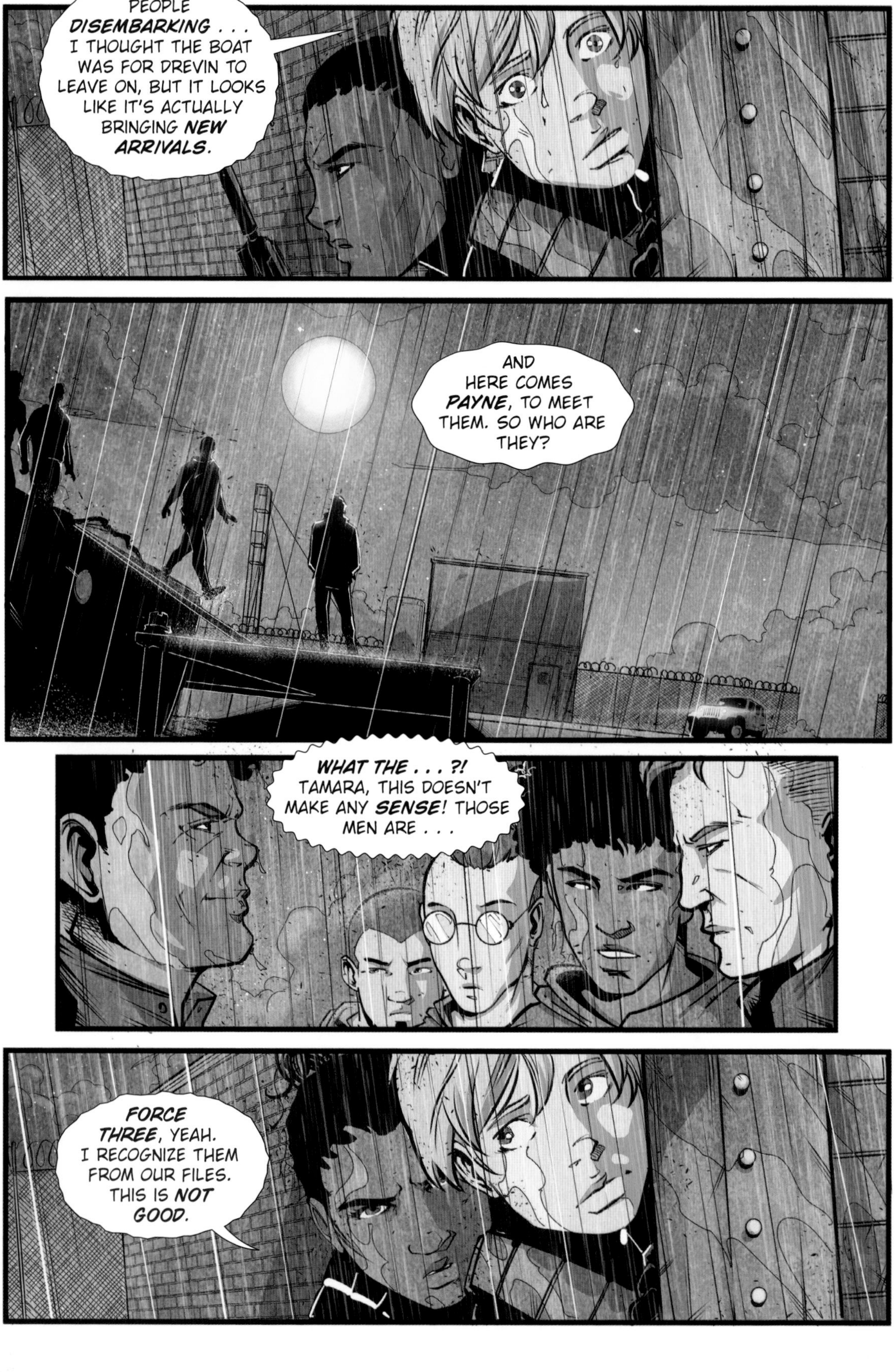
PEOPLE DISEMBARKING . . . I THOUGHT THE BOAT WAS FOR DREVIN TO LEAVE ON, BUT IT LOOKS LIKE IT'S ACTUALLY BRINGING NEW ARRIVALS.
AND HERE COMES PAYNE, TO MEET THEM. SO WHO ARE THEY?
WHAT THE . . . ?! TAMARA, THIS DOESN'T MAKE ANY SENSE! THOSE MEN ARE . . .
FORCE THREE, YEAH. I RECOGNIZE THEM FROM OUR FILES. THIS IS NOT GOOD.

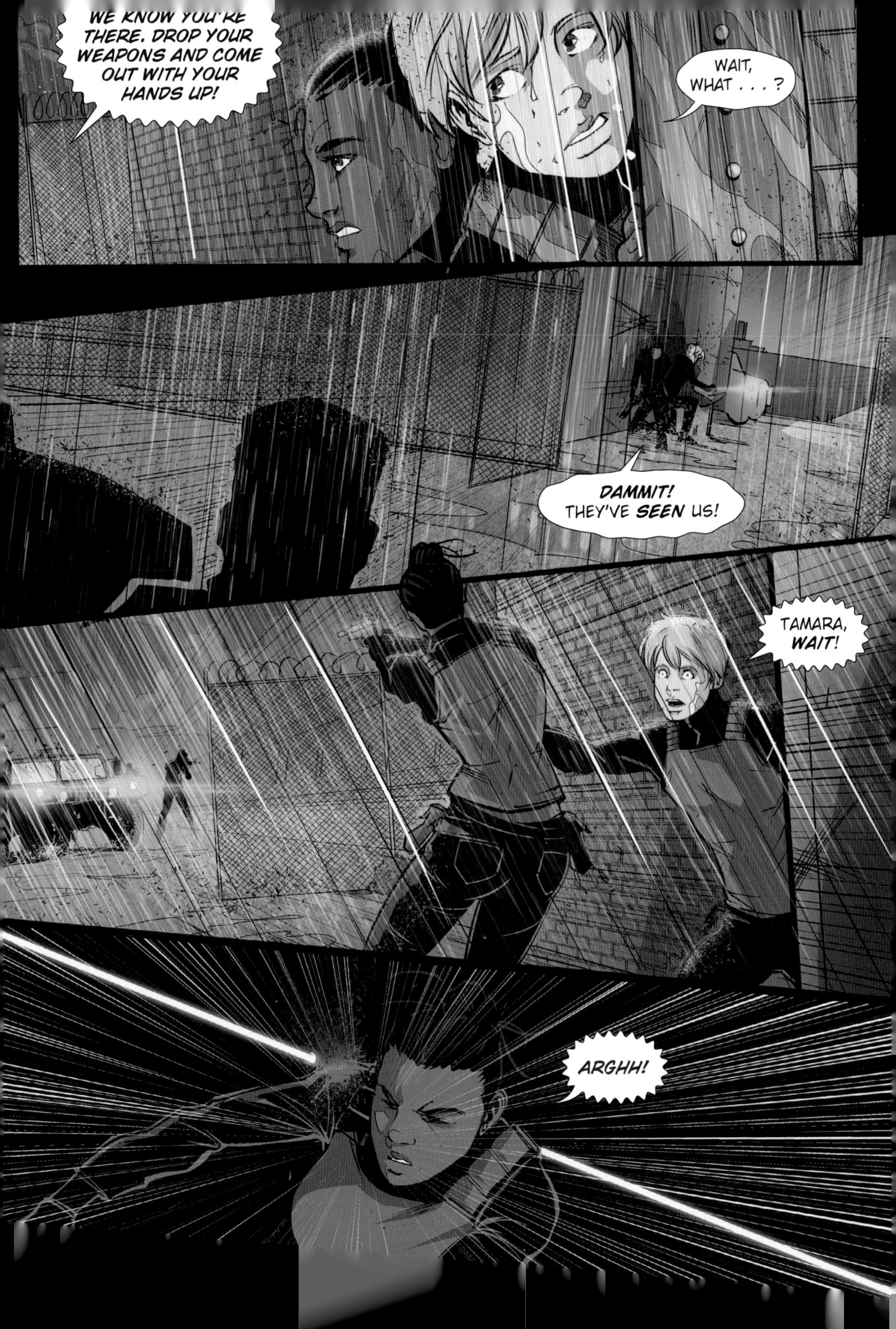
WE KNOW YOU'RE THERE. DROP YOUR WEAPONS AND COME OUT WITH YOUR HANDS UP!
WAIT, WHAT . . . ?
DAMMIT! THEY'VE SEEN US!
TAMARA, WAIT!
ARGHH!

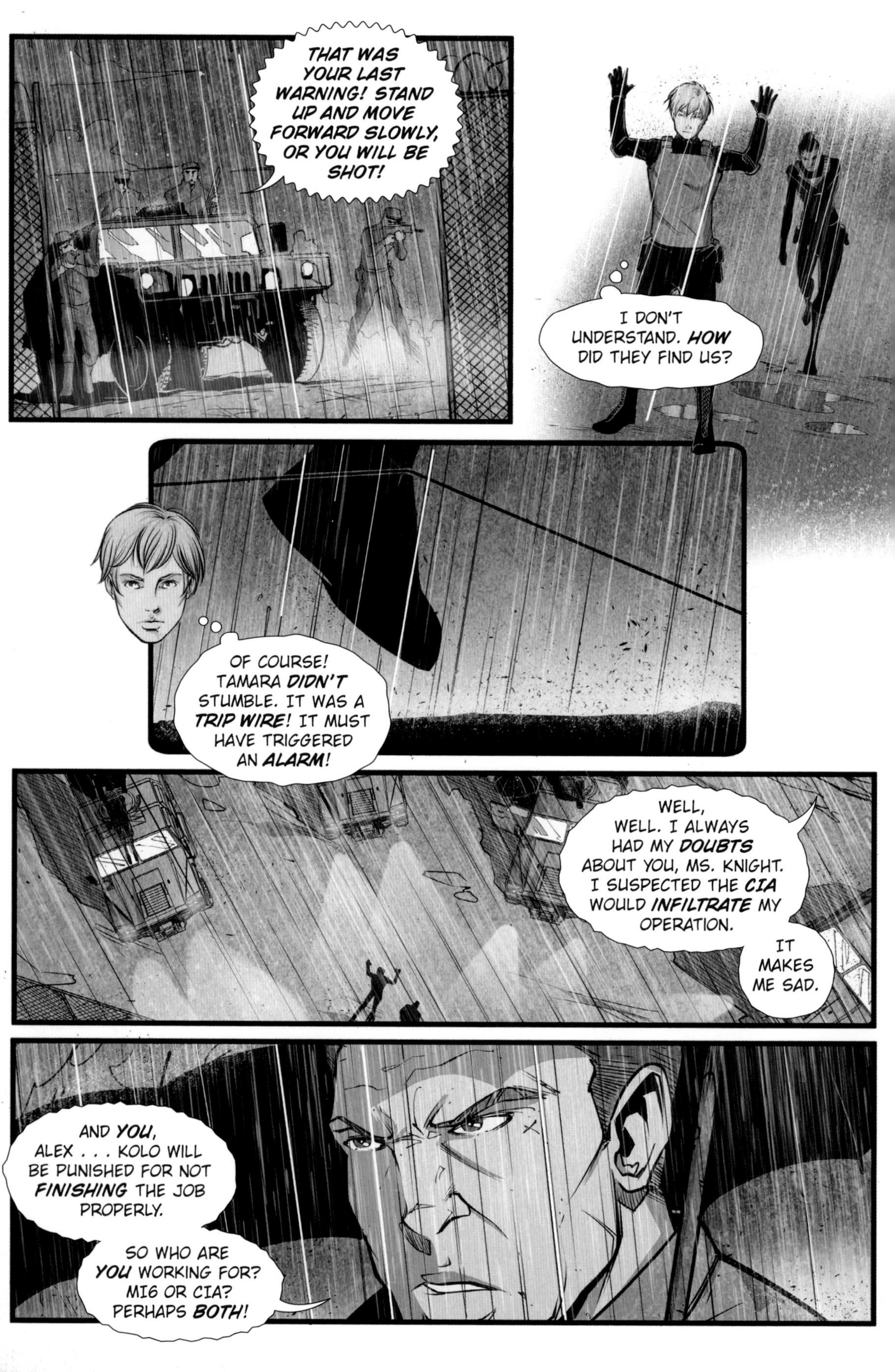
THAT WAS YOUR LAST WARNING! STAND UP AND MOVE FORWARD SLOWLY, OR YOU WILL BE SHOT!
I DON'T UNDERSTAND. HOW DID THEY FIND US?
OF COURSE! TAMARA DIDN'T STUMBLE. IT WAS A TRIP WIRE! IT MUST HAVE TRIGGERED AN ALARM!
WELL, WELL. I ALWAYS HAD MY DOUBTS ABOUT YOU, MS. KNIGHT. I SUSPECTED THE CIA WOULD INFILTRATE MY OPERATION.
IT MAKES ME SAD.
AND YOU, ALEX . . . KOLO WILL BE PUNISHED FOR NOT FINISHING THE JOB PROPERLY.
SO WHO ARE YOU WORKING FOR? MI6 OR CIA? PERHAPS BOTH!

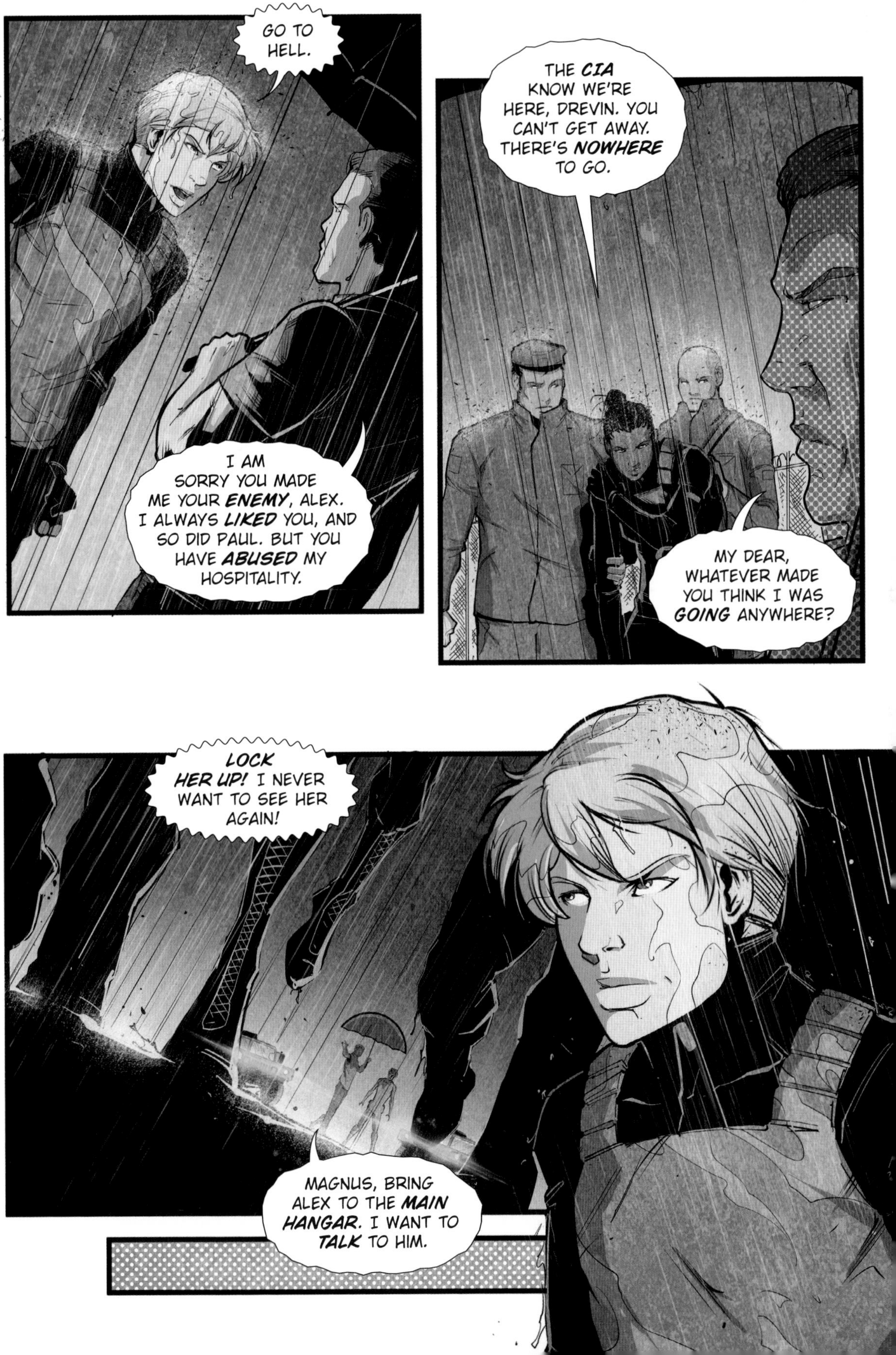
GO TO HELL.
I AM SORRY YOU MADE ME YOUR ENEMY, ALEX. I ALWAYS LIKED YOU, AND SO DID PAUL. BUT YOU HAVE ABUSED MY HOSPITALITY.
THE CIA KNOW WE'RE HERE, DREVIN. YOU CAN'T GET AWAY. THERE'S NOWHERE TO GO.
MY DEAR, WHATEVER MADE YOU THINK I WAS GOING ANYWHERE?
LOCK HER UP! I NEVER WANT TO SEE HER AGAIN!
MAGNUS, BRING ALEX TO THE MAIN HANGAR. I WANT TO TALK TO HIM.

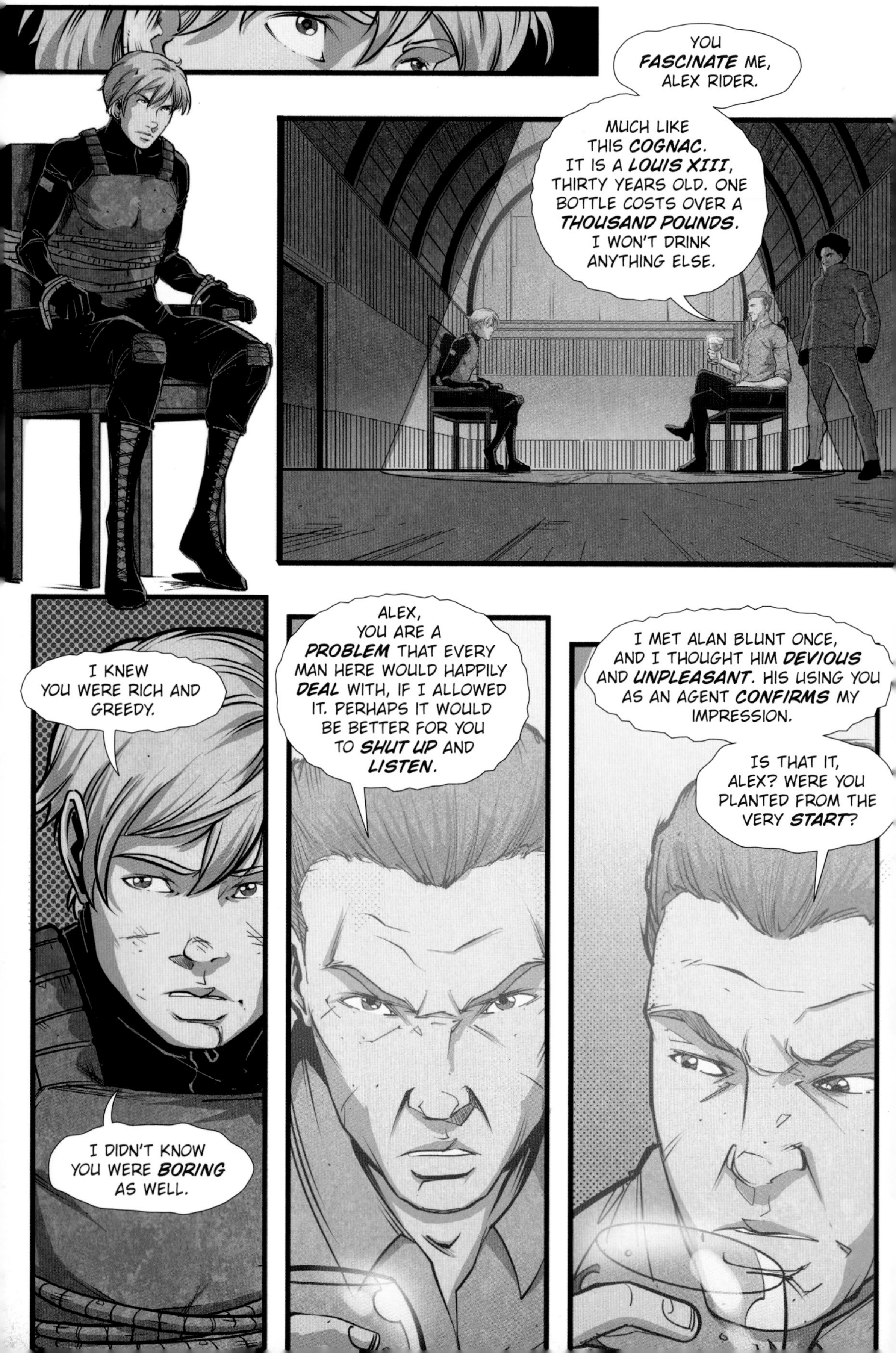
YOU FASCINATE ME, ALEX RIDER.
MUCH LIKE THIS COGNAC. IT IS A LOUIS XIII, THIRTY YEARS OLD. ONE BOTTLE COSTS OVER A THOUSAND POUNDS. I WON'T DRINK ANYTHING ELSE.
I KNEW YOU WERE RICH AND GREEDY.
I DIDN'T KNOW YOU WERE BORING AS WELL.
ALEX, YOU ARE A PROBLEM THAT EVERY MAN HERE WOULD HAPPILY DEAL WITH, IF I ALLOWED IT. PERHAPS IT WOULD BE BETTER FOR YOU TO SHUT UP AND LISTEN.
I MET ALAN BLUNT ONCE, AND I THOUGHT HIM DEVIOUS AND UNPLEASANT. HIS USING YOU AS AN AGENT CONFIRMS MY IMPRESSION.
IS THAT IT, ALEX? WERE YOU PLANTED FROM THE VERY START?

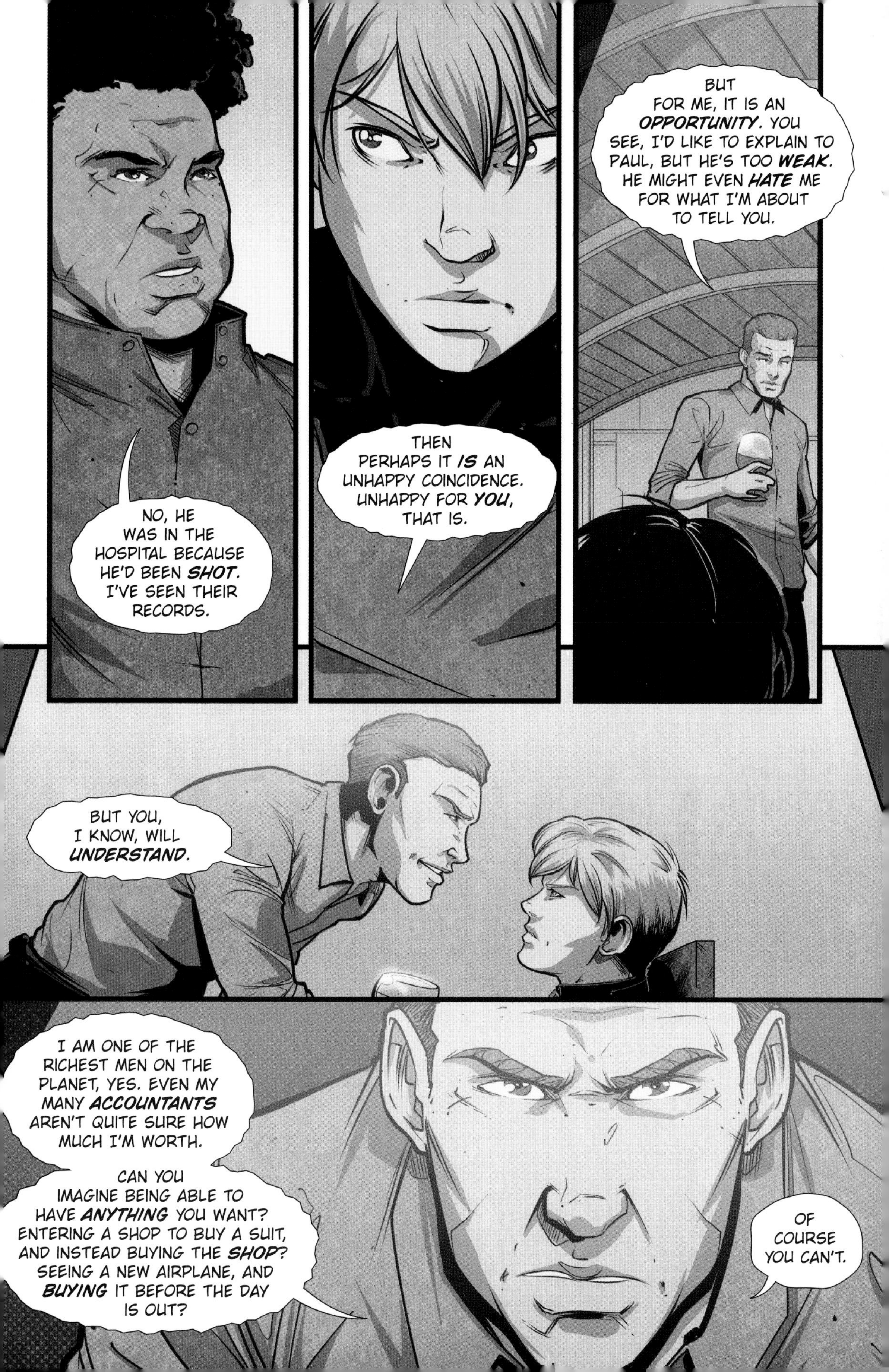
NO, HE WAS IN THE HOSPITAL BECAUSE HE'D BEEN **SHOT**. I'VE SEEN THEIR RECORDS.
THEN PERHAPS IT **IS** AN UNHAPPY COINCIDENCE. UNHAPPY FOR **YOU**, THAT IS.
BUT FOR ME, IT IS AN **OPPORTUNITY**. YOU SEE, I'D LIKE TO EXPLAIN TO PAUL, BUT HE'S TOO **WEAK**. HE MIGHT EVEN **HATE** ME FOR WHAT I'M ABOUT TO TELL YOU.
BUT YOU, I KNOW, WILL **UNDERSTAND**.
I AM ONE OF THE RICHEST MEN ON THE PLANET, YES. EVEN MY MANY **ACCOUNTANTS** AREN'T QUITE SURE HOW MUCH I'M WORTH.
CAN YOU IMAGINE BEING ABLE TO HAVE **ANYTHING** YOU WANT? ENTERING A SHOP TO BUY A SUIT, AND INSTEAD BUYING THE **SHOP**? SEEING A NEW AIRPLANE, AND **BUYING** IT BEFORE THE DAY IS OUT?
OF COURSE YOU CAN'T.

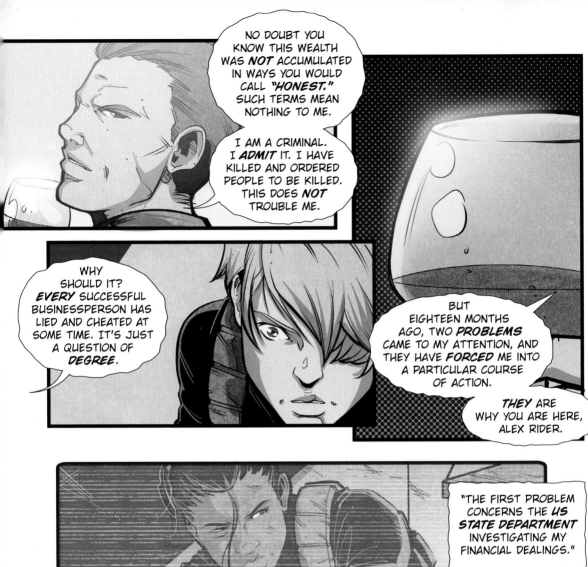

NO DOUBT YOU KNOW THIS WEALTH WAS *NOT* ACCUMULATED IN WAYS YOU WOULD CALL *"HONEST."* SUCH TERMS MEAN NOTHING TO ME.

I AM A CRIMINAL. I *ADMIT* IT. I HAVE KILLED AND ORDERED PEOPLE TO BE KILLED. THIS DOES *NOT* TROUBLE ME.

WHY SHOULD IT? *EVERY* SUCCESSFUL BUSINESSPERSON HAS LIED AND CHEATED AT SOME TIME. IT'S JUST A QUESTION OF *DEGREE*.

BUT EIGHTEEN MONTHS AGO, TWO *PROBLEMS* CAME TO MY ATTENTION, AND THEY HAVE *FORCED* ME INTO A PARTICULAR COURSE OF ACTION.

THEY ARE WHY YOU ARE HERE, ALEX RIDER.

"THE FIRST PROBLEM CONCERNS THE *US STATE DEPARTMENT* INVESTIGATING MY FINANCIAL DEALINGS."

OF COURSE, I HAVE ALWAYS *KNOWN* THEY WERE BUILDING A CASE AGAINST ME.

BUT I AM A CAREFUL MAN. I DO *NOT* LEAVE PAPER EVIDENCE, OR WITNESSES.

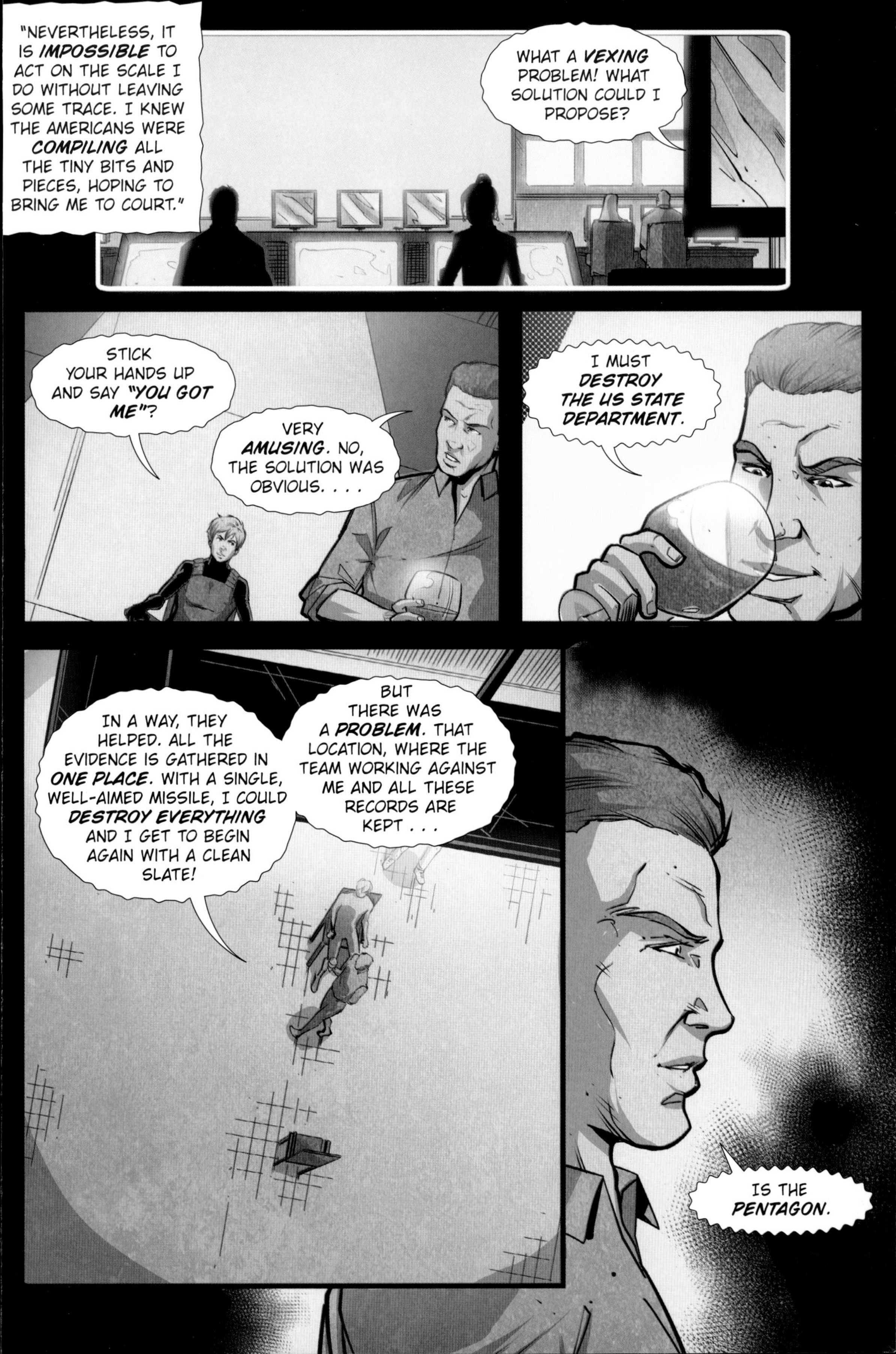
"NEVERTHELESS, IT IS IMPOSSIBLE TO ACT ON THE SCALE I DO WITHOUT LEAVING SOME TRACE. I KNEW THE AMERICANS WERE COMPILING ALL THE TINY BITS AND PIECES, HOPING TO BRING ME TO COURT."
WHAT A VEXING PROBLEM! WHAT SOLUTION COULD I PROPOSE?
STICK YOUR HANDS UP AND SAY "YOU GOT ME"?
VERY AMUSING. NO, THE SOLUTION WAS OBVIOUS. . . .
I MUST DESTROY THE US STATE DEPARTMENT.
IN A WAY, THEY HELPED. ALL THE EVIDENCE IS GATHERED IN ONE PLACE. WITH A SINGLE, WELL-AIMED MISSILE, I COULD DESTROY EVERYTHING AND I GET TO BEGIN AGAIN WITH A CLEAN SLATE!
BUT THERE WAS A PROBLEM. THAT LOCATION, WHERE THE TEAM WORKING AGAINST ME AND ALL THESE RECORDS ARE KEPT . . .
IS THE PENTAGON.

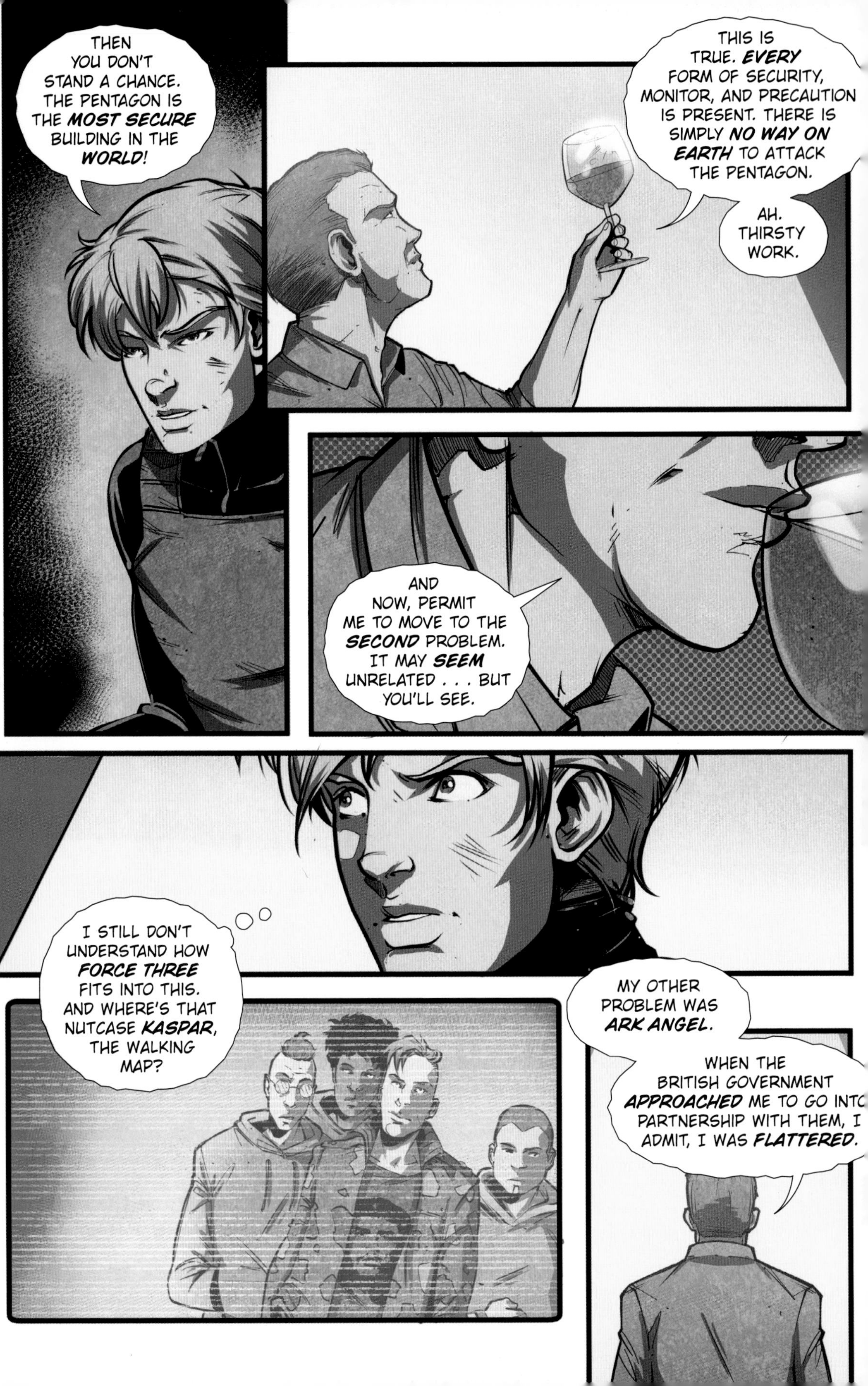
THEN YOU DON'T STAND A CHANCE. THE PENTAGON IS THE MOST SECURE BUILDING IN THE WORLD!
THIS IS TRUE. EVERY FORM OF SECURITY, MONITOR, AND PRECAUTION IS PRESENT. THERE IS SIMPLY NO WAY ON EARTH TO ATTACK THE PENTAGON.
AH. THIRSTY WORK.
AND NOW, PERMIT ME TO MOVE TO THE SECOND PROBLEM. IT MAY SEEM UNRELATED . . . BUT YOU'LL SEE.
I STILL DON'T UNDERSTAND HOW FORCE THREE FITS INTO THIS. AND WHERE'S THAT NUTCASE KASPAR, THE WALKING MAP?
MY OTHER PROBLEM WAS ARK ANGEL.
WHEN THE BRITISH GOVERNMENT APPROACHED ME TO GO INTO PARTNERSHIP WITH THEM, I ADMIT, I WAS FLATTERED.

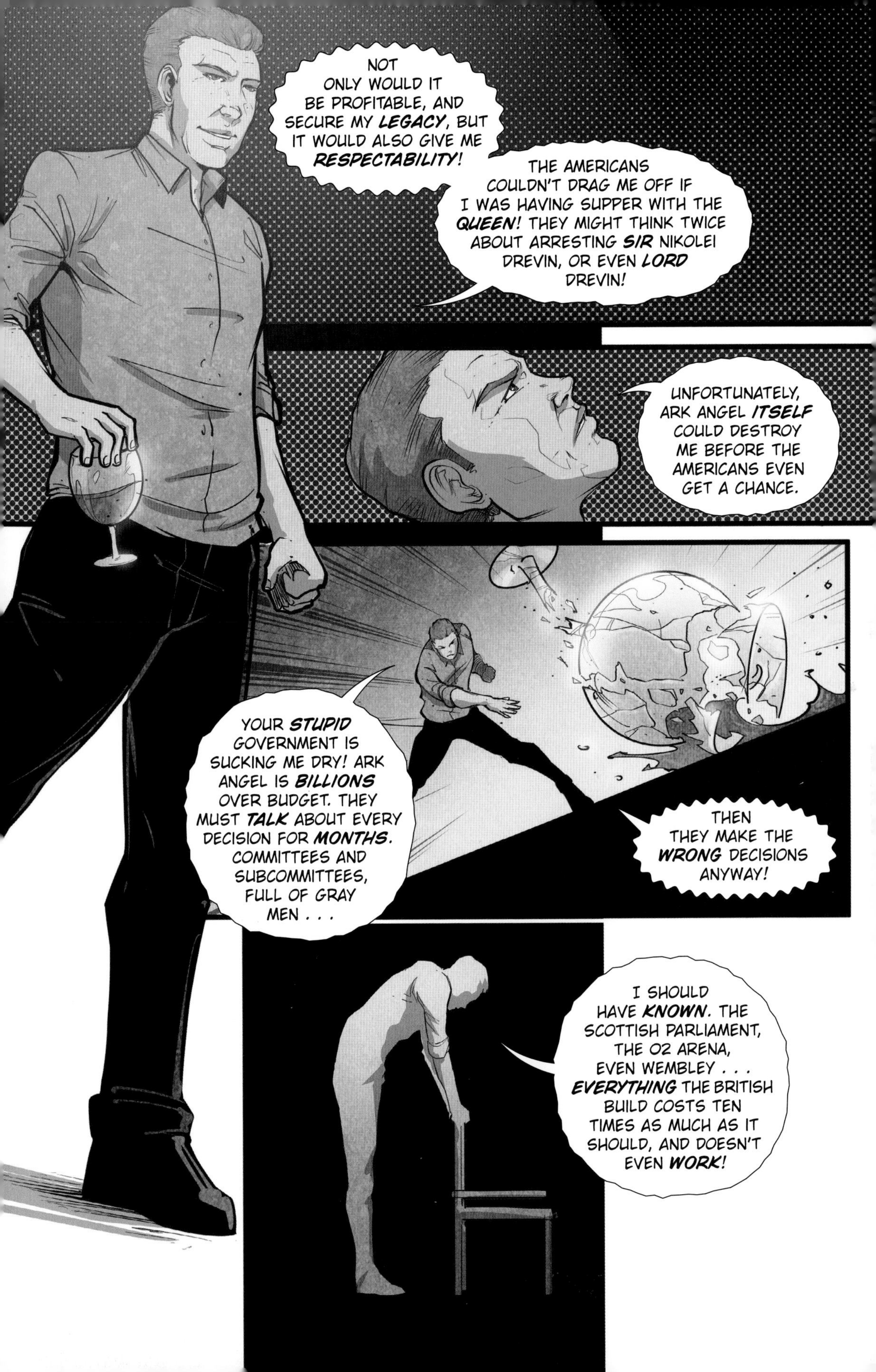
NOT ONLY WOULD IT BE PROFITABLE, AND SECURE MY LEGACY, BUT IT WOULD ALSO GIVE ME RESPECTABILITY!
THE AMERICANS COULDN'T DRAG ME OFF IF I WAS HAVING SUPPER WITH THE QUEEN! THEY MIGHT THINK TWICE ABOUT ARRESTING SIR NIKOLEI DREVIN, OR EVEN LORD DREVIN!
UNFORTUNATELY, ARK ANGEL ITSELF COULD DESTROY ME BEFORE THE AMERICANS EVEN GET A CHANCE.
YOUR STUPID GOVERNMENT IS SUCKING ME DRY! ARK ANGEL IS BILLIONS OVER BUDGET. THEY MUST TALK ABOUT EVERY DECISION FOR MONTHS. COMMITTEES AND SUBCOMMITTEES, FULL OF GRAY MEN . . .
THEN THEY MAKE THE WRONG DECISIONS ANYWAY!
I SHOULD HAVE KNOWN. THE SCOTTISH PARLIAMENT, THE O2 ARENA, EVEN WEMBLEY . . . EVERYTHING THE BRITISH BUILD COSTS TEN TIMES AS MUCH AS IT SHOULD, AND DOESN'T EVEN WORK!

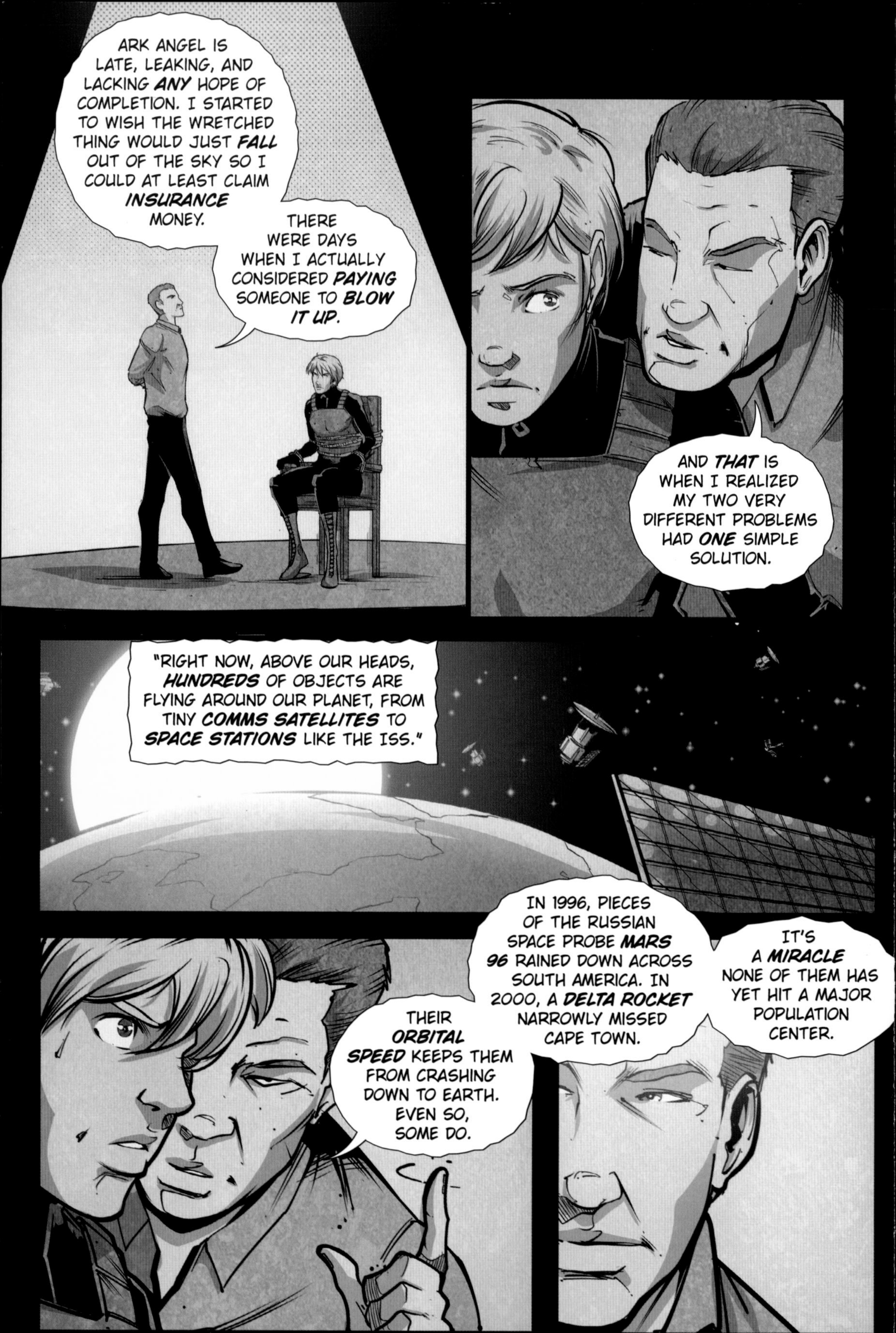
ARK ANGEL IS LATE, LEAKING, AND LACKING ANY HOPE OF COMPLETION. I STARTED TO WISH THE WRETCHED THING WOULD JUST FALL OUT OF THE SKY SO I COULD AT LEAST CLAIM INSURANCE MONEY.
THERE WERE DAYS WHEN I ACTUALLY CONSIDERED PAYING SOMEONE TO BLOW IT UP.
AND THAT IS WHEN I REALIZED MY TWO VERY DIFFERENT PROBLEMS HAD ONE SIMPLE SOLUTION.
"RIGHT NOW, ABOVE OUR HEADS, HUNDREDS OF OBJECTS ARE FLYING AROUND OUR PLANET, FROM TINY COMMS SATELLITES TO SPACE STATIONS LIKE THE ISS."
THEIR ORBITAL SPEED KEEPS THEM FROM CRASHING DOWN TO EARTH. EVEN SO, SOME DO.
IN 1996, PIECES OF THE RUSSIAN SPACE PROBE MARS 96 RAINED DOWN ACROSS SOUTH AMERICA. IN 2000, A DELTA ROCKET NARROWLY MISSED CAPE TOWN.
IT'S A MIRACLE NONE OF THEM HAS YET HIT A MAJOR POPULATION CENTER.

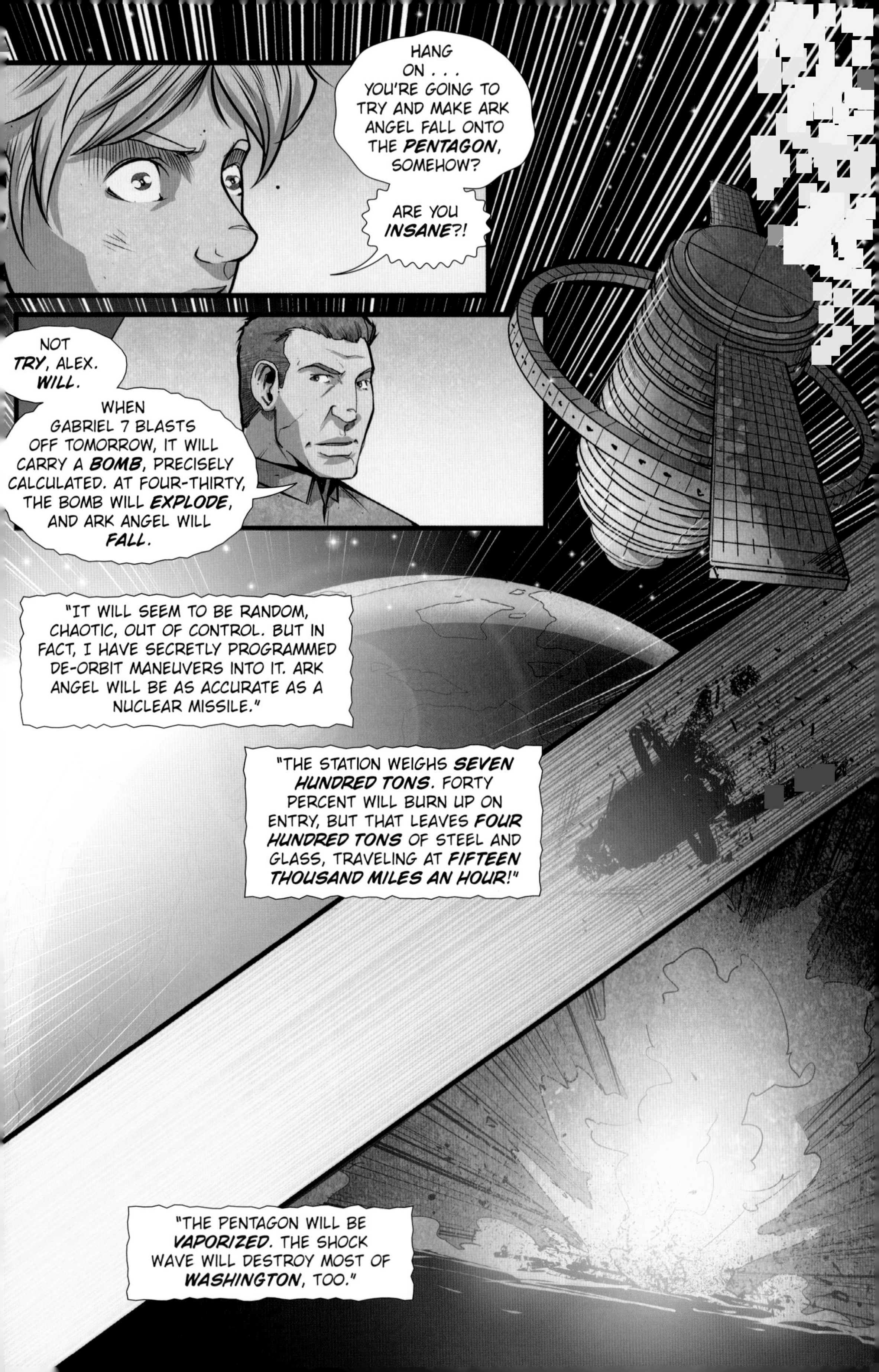
HANG ON . . . YOU'RE GOING TO TRY AND MAKE ARK ANGEL FALL ONTO THE PENTAGON, SOMEHOW?
ARE YOU INSANE?!
NOT TRY, ALEX. WILL.
WHEN GABRIEL 7 BLASTS OFF TOMORROW, IT WILL CARRY A BOMB, PRECISELY CALCULATED. AT FOUR-THIRTY, THE BOMB WILL EXPLODE, AND ARK ANGEL WILL FALL.
"IT WILL SEEM TO BE RANDOM, CHAOTIC, OUT OF CONTROL. BUT IN FACT, I HAVE SECRETLY PROGRAMMED DE-ORBIT MANEUVERS INTO IT. ARK ANGEL WILL BE AS ACCURATE AS A NUCLEAR MISSILE."
"THE STATION WEIGHS SEVEN HUNDRED TONS. FORTY PERCENT WILL BURN UP ON ENTRY, BUT THAT LEAVES FOUR HUNDRED TONS OF STEEL AND GLASS, TRAVELING AT FIFTEEN THOUSAND MILES AN HOUR!"
"THE PENTAGON WILL BE VAPORIZED. THE SHOCK WAVE WILL DESTROY MOST OF WASHINGTON, TOO."

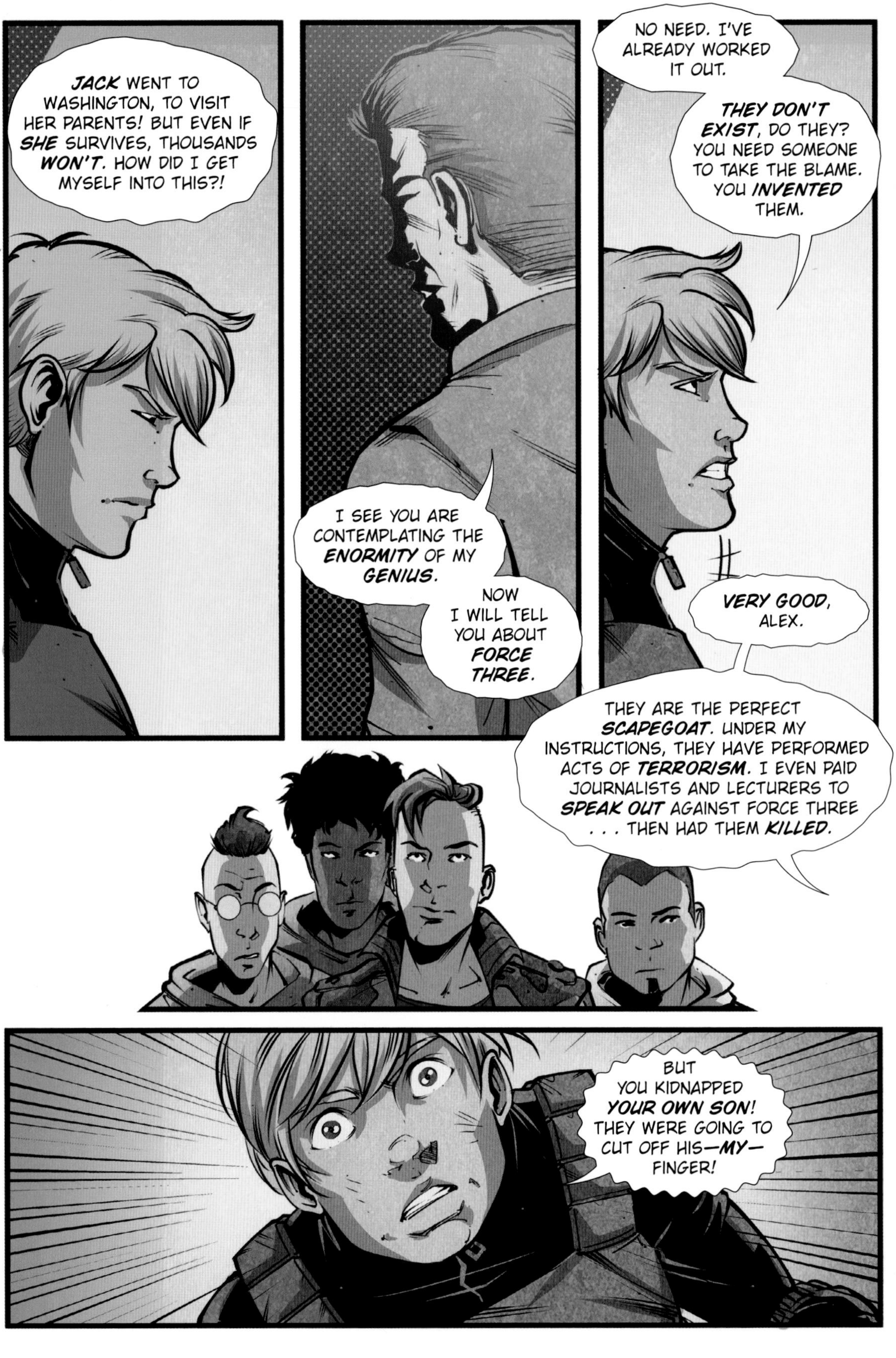
JACK WENT TO WASHINGTON, TO VISIT HER PARENTS! BUT EVEN IF SHE SURVIVES, THOUSANDS WON'T. HOW DID I GET MYSELF INTO THIS?!
I SEE YOU ARE CONTEMPLATING THE ENORMITY OF MY GENIUS.
NOW I WILL TELL YOU ABOUT FORCE THREE.
NO NEED. I'VE ALREADY WORKED IT OUT.
THEY DON'T EXIST, DO THEY? YOU NEED SOMEONE TO TAKE THE BLAME. YOU INVENTED THEM.
VERY GOOD, ALEX.
THEY ARE THE PERFECT SCAPEGOAT. UNDER MY INSTRUCTIONS, THEY HAVE PERFORMED ACTS OF TERRORISM. I EVEN PAID JOURNALISTS AND LECTURERS TO SPEAK OUT AGAINST FORCE THREE . . . THEN HAD THEM KILLED.
BUT YOU KIDNAPPED YOUR OWN SON! THEY WERE GOING TO CUT OFF HIS—MY—FINGER!

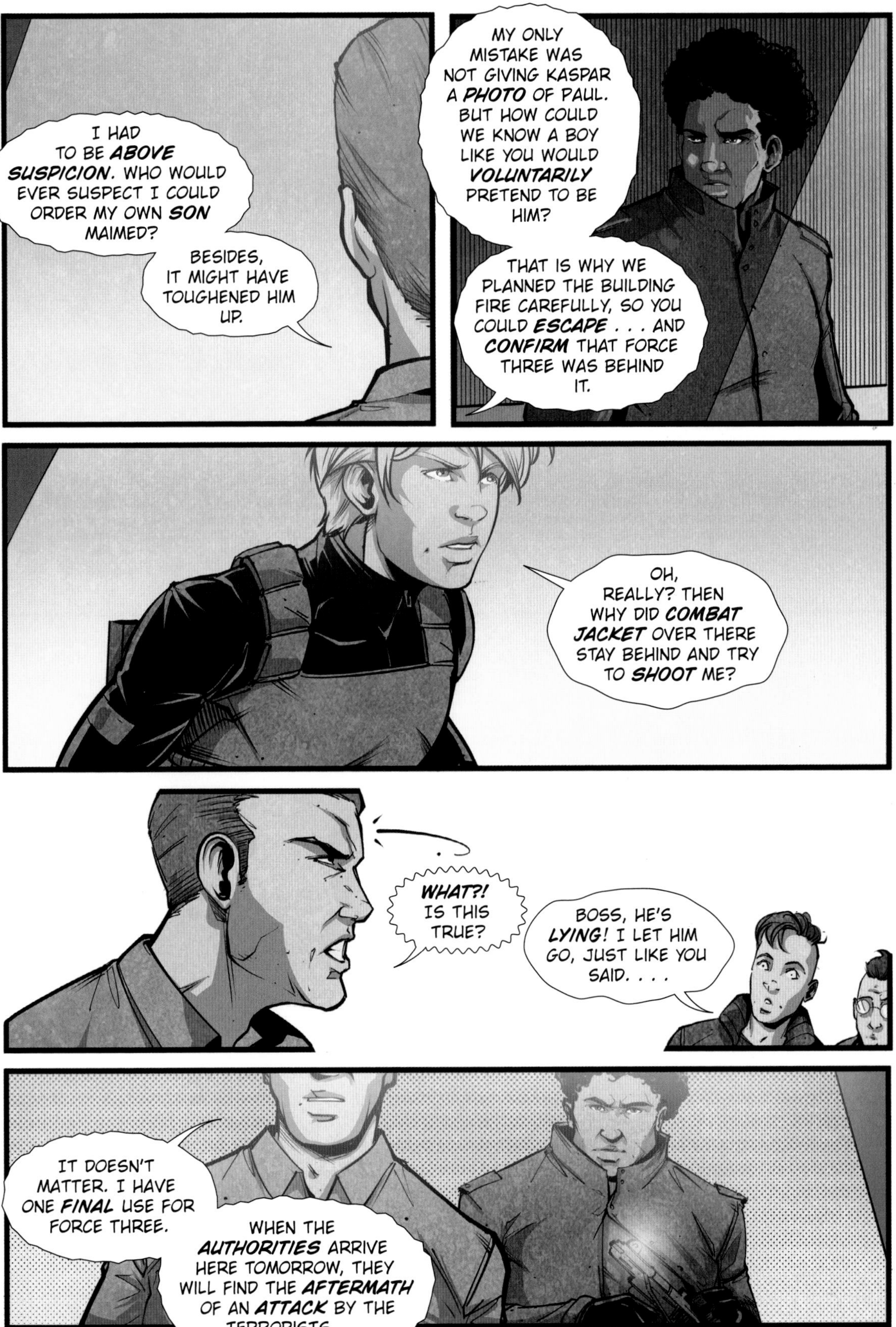
I HAD TO BE ABOVE SUSPICION. WHO WOULD EVER SUSPECT I COULD ORDER MY OWN SON MAIMED?
BESIDES, IT MIGHT HAVE TOUGHENED HIM UP.
MY ONLY MISTAKE WAS NOT GIVING KASPAR A PHOTO OF PAUL. BUT HOW COULD WE KNOW A BOY LIKE YOU WOULD VOLUNTARILY PRETEND TO BE HIM?
THAT IS WHY WE PLANNED THE BUILDING FIRE CAREFULLY, SO YOU COULD ESCAPE . . . AND CONFIRM THAT FORCE THREE WAS BEHIND IT.
OH, REALLY? THEN WHY DID COMBAT JACKET OVER THERE STAY BEHIND AND TRY TO SHOOT ME?
WHAT?! IS THIS TRUE?
BOSS, HE'S LYING! I LET HIM GO, JUST LIKE YOU SAID. . . .
IT DOESN'T MATTER. I HAVE ONE FINAL USE FOR FORCE THREE.
WHEN THE AUTHORITIES ARRIVE HERE TOMORROW, THEY WILL FIND THE AFTERMATH OF AN ATTACK BY THE TERRORISTS . . .

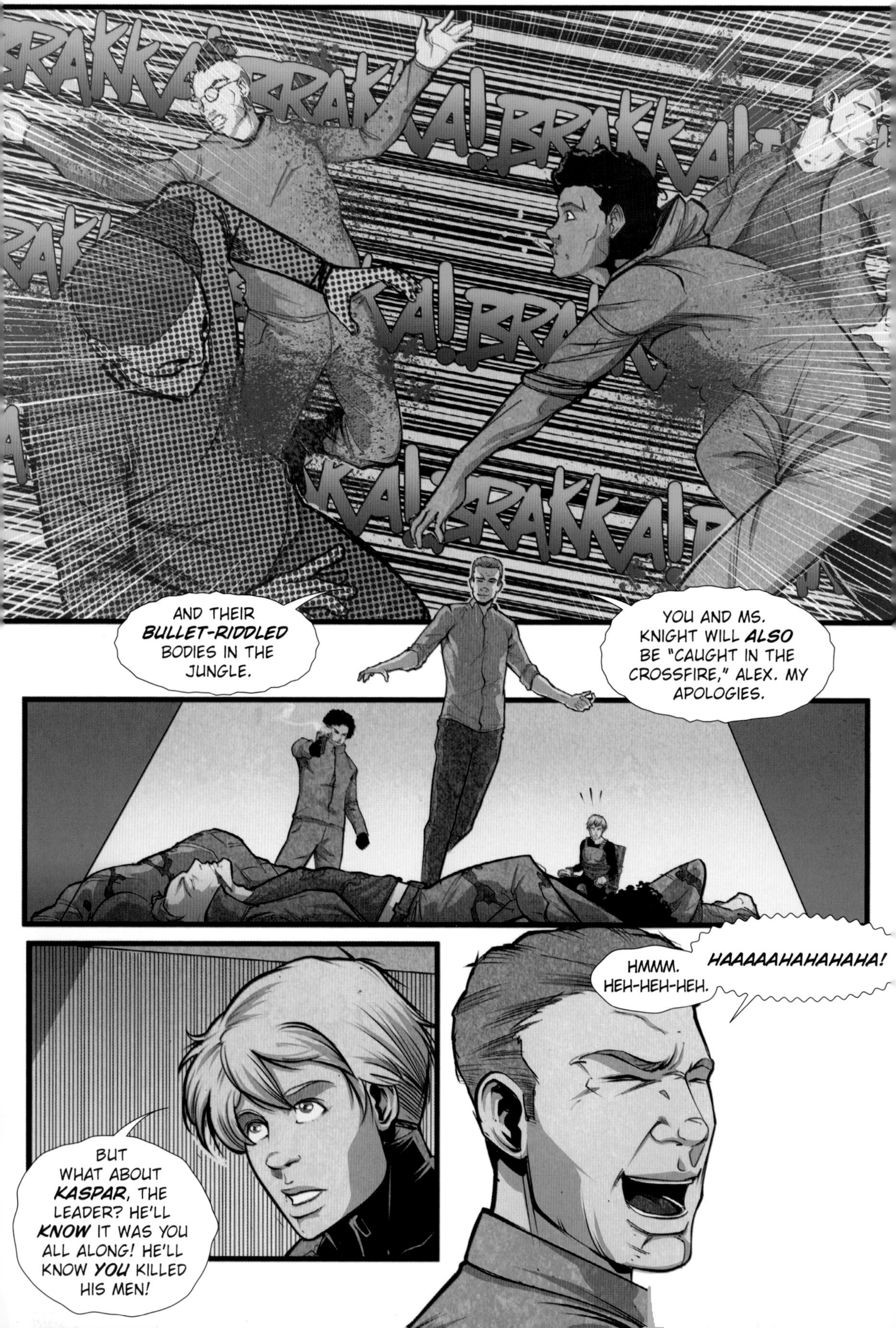
BRAKKA! BRAKKA! BRAKKA!
AND THEIR BULLET-RIDDLED BODIES IN THE JUNGLE.
YOU AND MS. KNIGHT WILL ALSO BE "CAUGHT IN THE CROSSFIRE," ALEX. MY APOLOGIES.
BUT WHAT ABOUT KASPAR, THE LEADER? HE'LL KNOW IT WAS YOU ALL ALONG! HE'LL KNOW YOU KILLED HIS MEN!
HMMM. HEH-HEH-HEH.
HAAAAAHAHAHAHA!

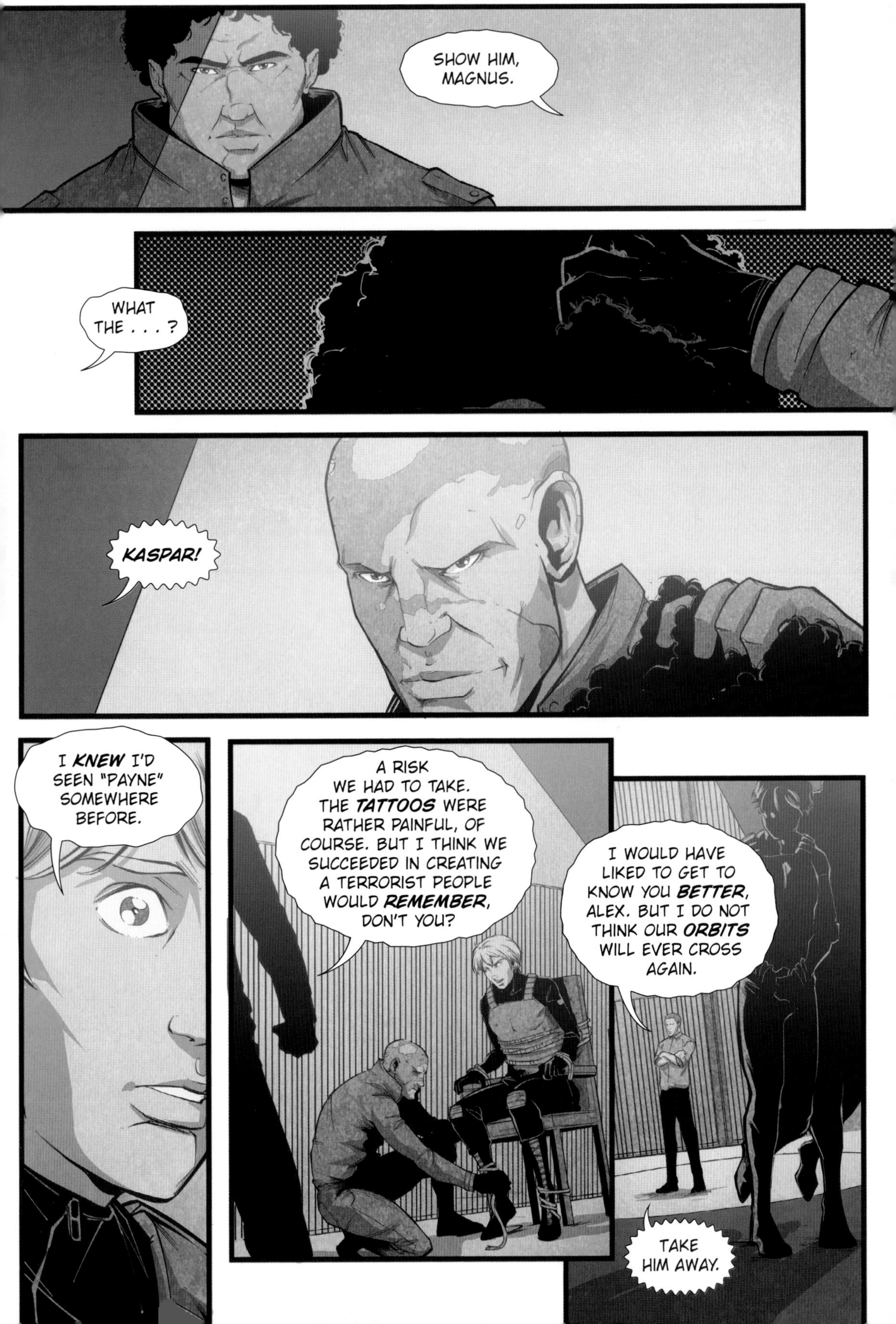
SHOW HIM, MAGNUS.
WHAT THE . . . ?
KASPAR!
I KNEW I'D SEEN "PAYNE" SOMEWHERE BEFORE.
A RISK WE HAD TO TAKE. THE TATTOOS WERE RATHER PAINFUL, OF COURSE. BUT I THINK WE SUCCEEDED IN CREATING A TERRORIST PEOPLE WOULD REMEMBER, DON'T YOU?
I WOULD HAVE LIKED TO GET TO KNOW YOU BETTER, ALEX. BUT I DO NOT THINK OUR ORBITS WILL EVER CROSS AGAIN.
TAKE HIM AWAY.

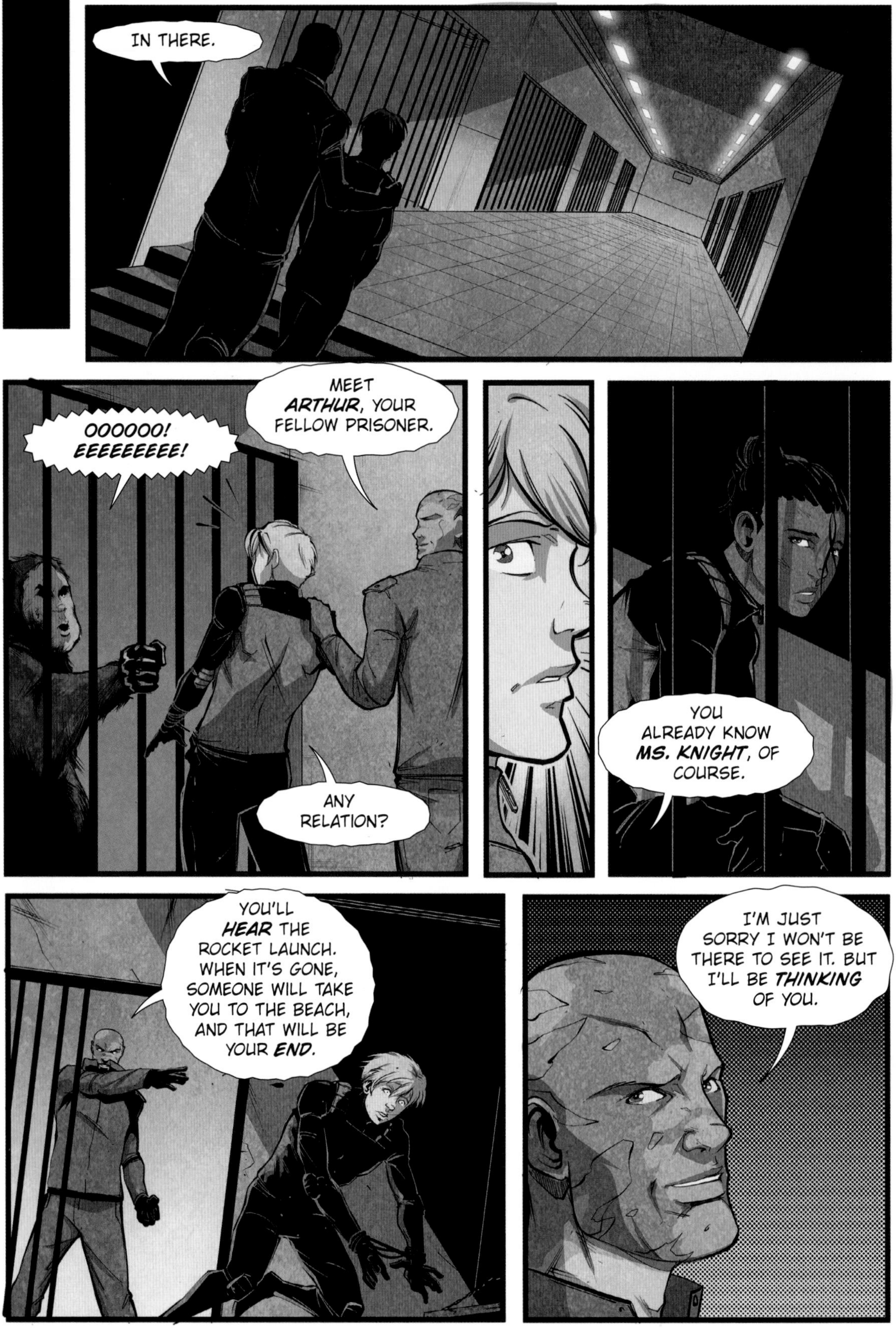
IN THERE.
OOOOOO! EEEEEEEEE!
MEET ARTHUR, YOUR FELLOW PRISONER.
ANY RELATION?
YOU ALREADY KNOW MS. KNIGHT, OF COURSE.
YOU'LL HEAR THE ROCKET LAUNCH. WHEN IT'S GONE, SOMEONE WILL TAKE YOU TO THE BEACH, AND THAT WILL BE YOUR END.
I'M JUST SORRY I WON'T BE THERE TO SEE IT. BUT I'LL BE THINKING OF YOU.

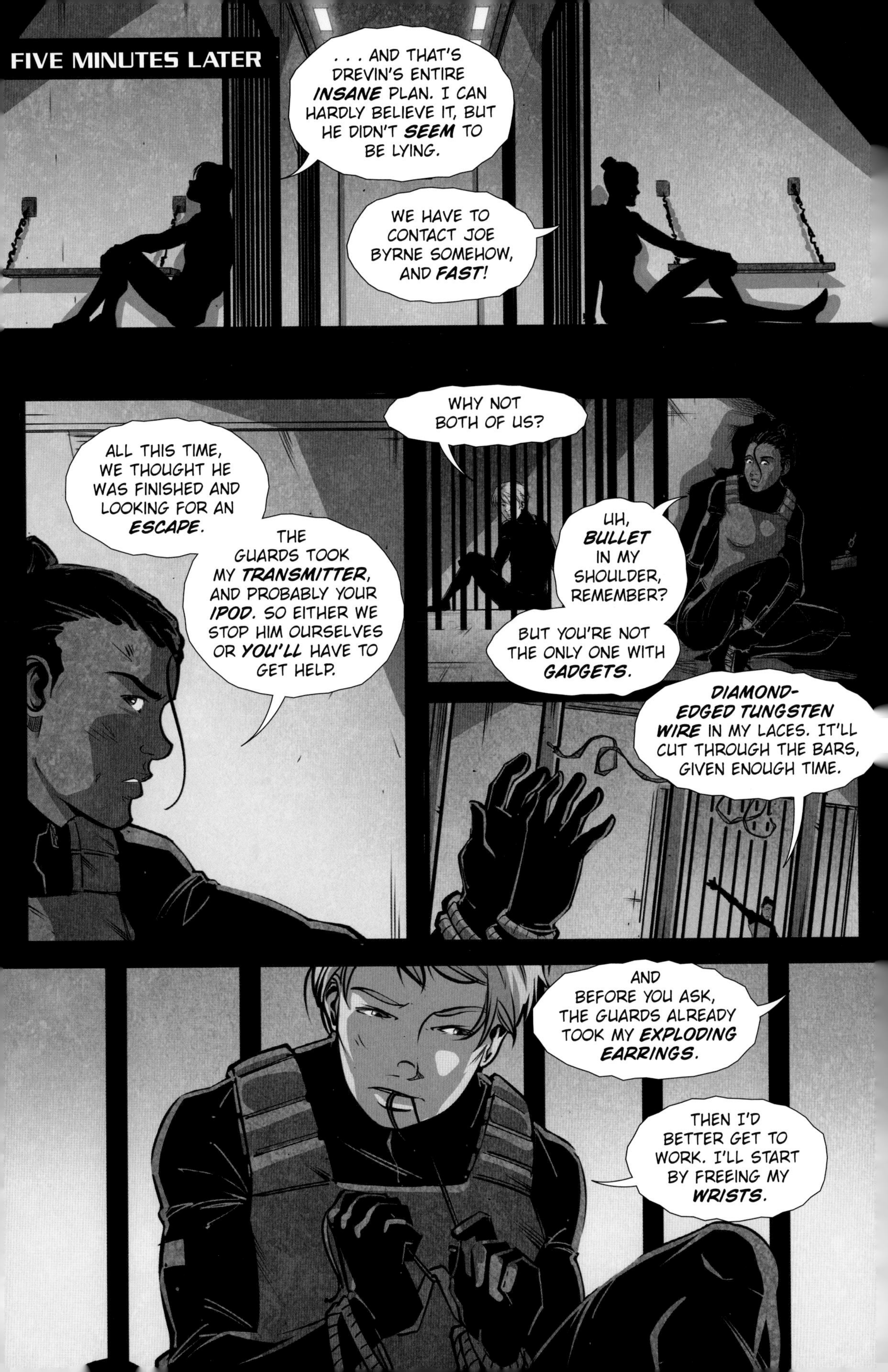
FIVE MINUTES LATER
. . . AND THAT'S DREVIN'S ENTIRE INSANE PLAN. I CAN HARDLY BELIEVE IT, BUT HE DIDN'T SEEM TO BE LYING.
WE HAVE TO CONTACT JOE BYRNE SOMEHOW, AND FAST!
ALL THIS TIME, WE THOUGHT HE WAS FINISHED AND LOOKING FOR AN ESCAPE.
THE GUARDS TOOK MY TRANSMITTER, AND PROBABLY YOUR IPOD. SO EITHER WE STOP HIM OURSELVES OR YOU'LL HAVE TO GET HELP.
WHY NOT BOTH OF US?
UH, BULLET IN MY SHOULDER, REMEMBER?
BUT YOU'RE NOT THE ONLY ONE WITH GADGETS.
DIAMOND-EDGED TUNGSTEN WIRE IN MY LACES. IT'LL CUT THROUGH THE BARS, GIVEN ENOUGH TIME.
AND BEFORE YOU ASK, THE GUARDS ALREADY TOOK MY EXPLODING EARRINGS.
THEN I'D BETTER GET TO WORK. I'LL START BY FREEING MY WRISTS.

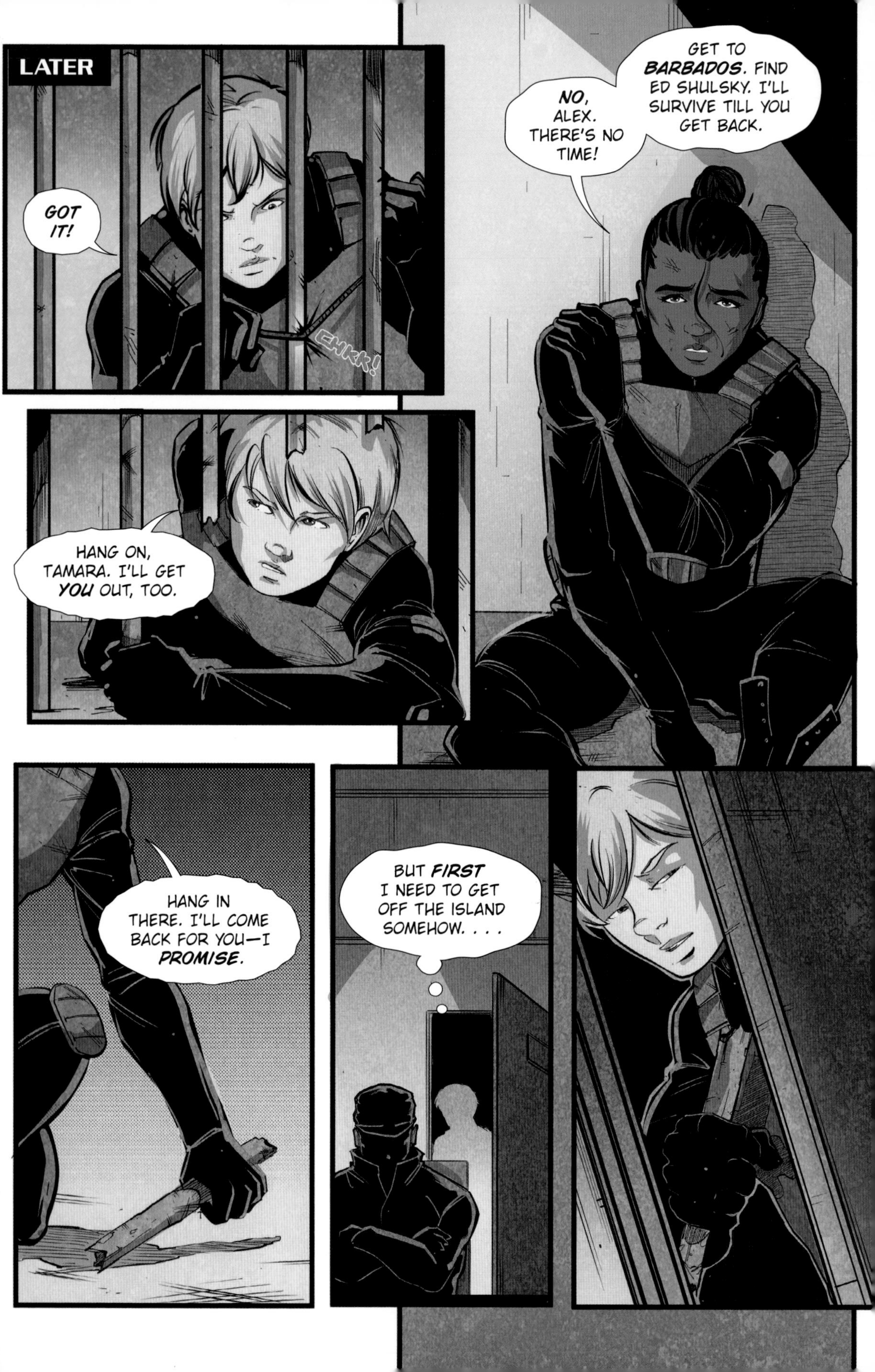
LATER
GOT IT!
CHKK!
NO, ALEX. THERE'S NO TIME!
GET TO BARBADOS. FIND ED SHULSKY. I'LL SURVIVE TILL YOU GET BACK.
HANG ON, TAMARA. I'LL GET YOU OUT, TOO.
HANG IN THERE. I'LL COME BACK FOR YOU—I PROMISE.
BUT FIRST I NEED TO GET OFF THE ISLAND SOMEHOW. . . .

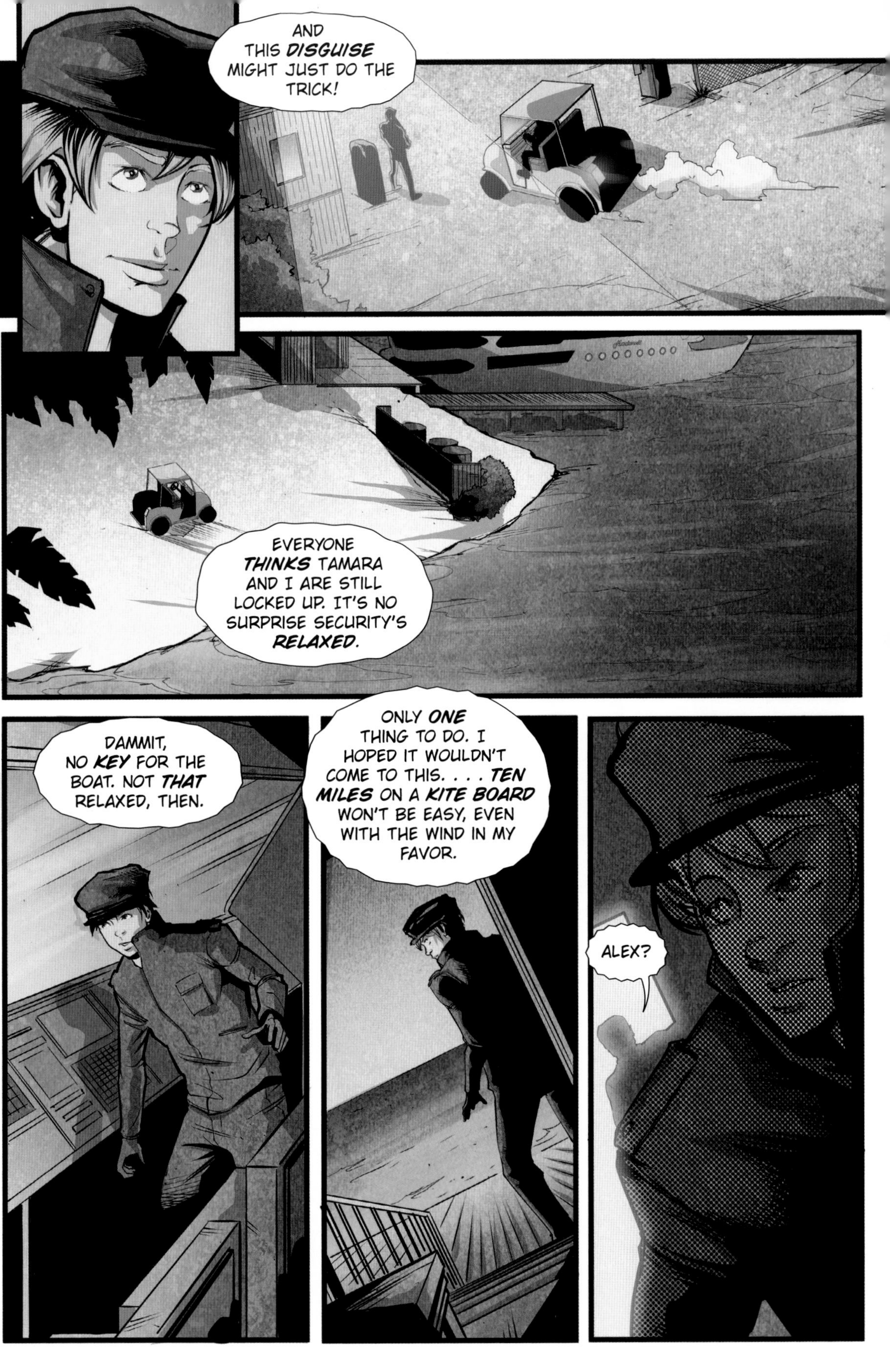
AND THIS DISGUISE MIGHT JUST DO THE TRICK!
EVERYONE THINKS TAMARA AND I ARE STILL LOCKED UP. IT'S NO SURPRISE SECURITY'S RELAXED.
DAMMIT, NO KEY FOR THE BOAT. NOT THAT RELAXED, THEN.
ONLY ONE THING TO DO. I HOPED IT WOULDN'T COME TO THIS. . . . TEN MILES ON A KITE BOARD WON'T BE EASY, EVEN WITH THE WIND IN MY FAVOR.
ALEX?

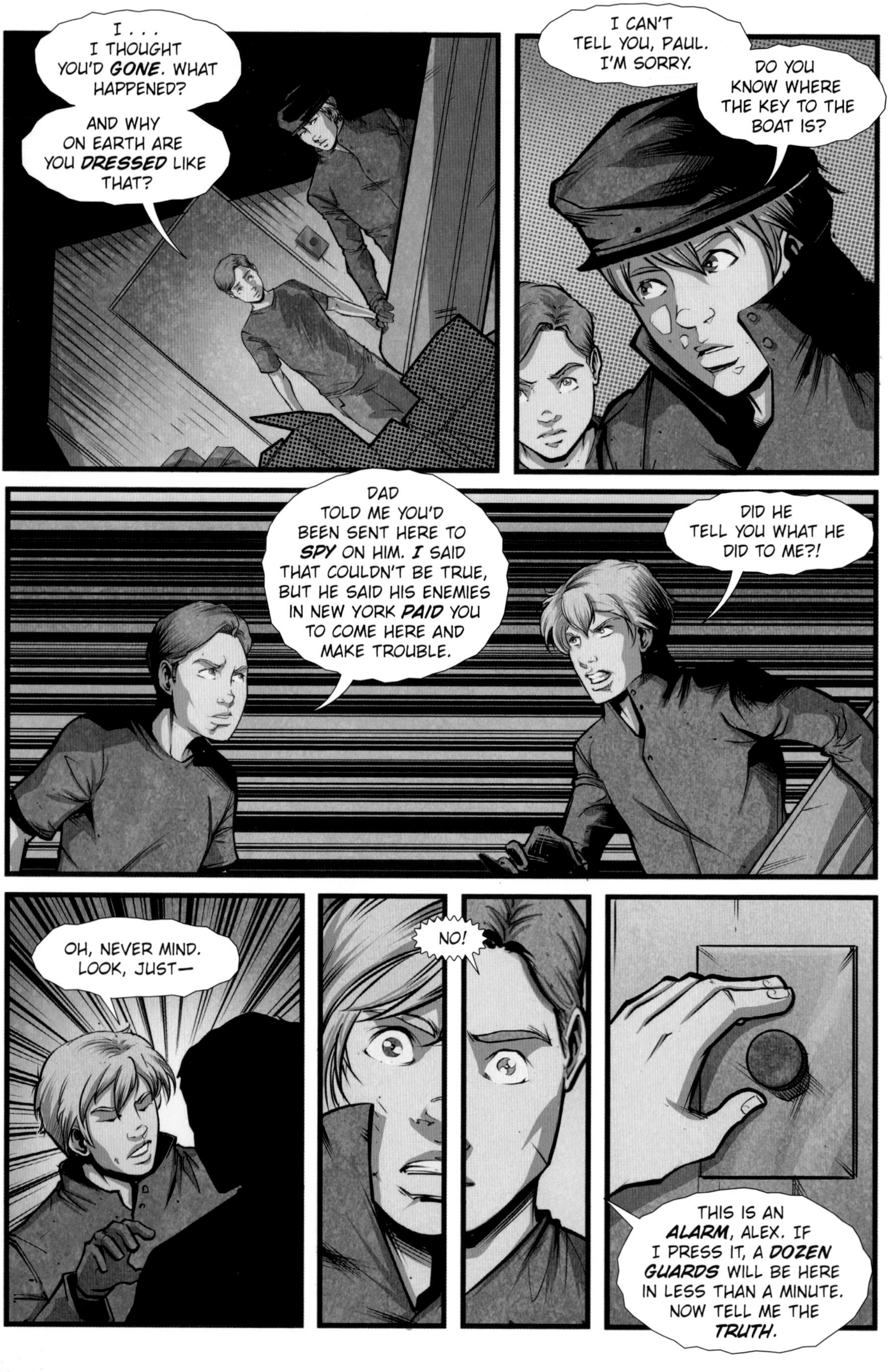
I . . . I THOUGHT YOU'D **GONE**. WHAT HAPPENED?
AND WHY ON EARTH ARE YOU **DRESSED** LIKE THAT?
I CAN'T TELL YOU, PAUL. I'M SORRY.
DO YOU KNOW WHERE THE KEY TO THE BOAT IS?
DAD TOLD ME YOU'D BEEN SENT HERE TO **SPY** ON HIM. **I** SAID THAT COULDN'T BE TRUE, BUT HE SAID HIS ENEMIES IN NEW YORK **PAID** YOU TO COME HERE AND MAKE TROUBLE.
DID HE TELL YOU WHAT HE DID TO ME?!
OH, NEVER MIND. LOOK, JUST—
NO!
THIS IS AN **ALARM**, ALEX. IF I PRESS IT, A **DOZEN GUARDS** WILL BE HERE IN LESS THAN A MINUTE. NOW TELL ME THE **TRUTH**.

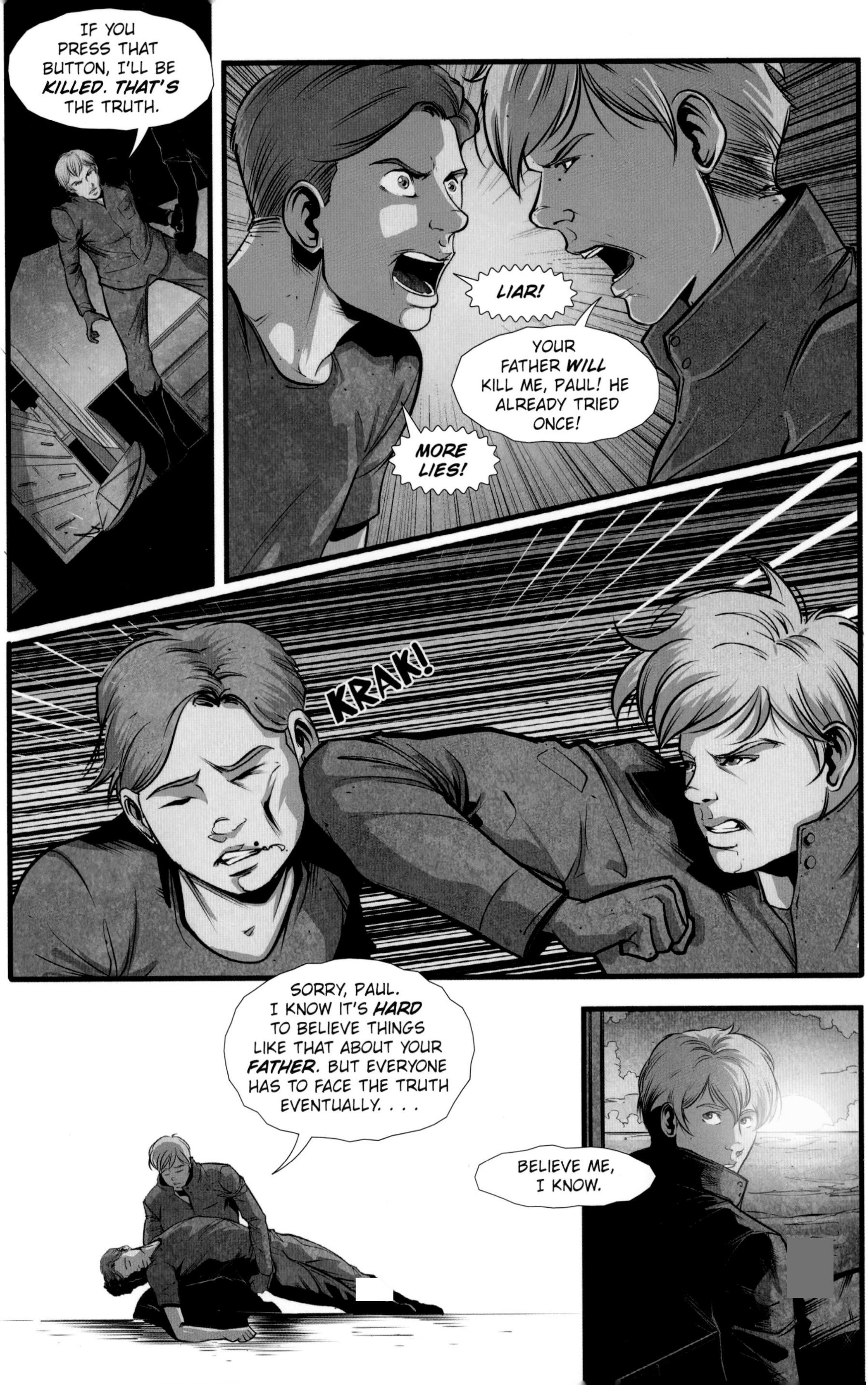
IF YOU PRESS THAT BUTTON, I'LL BE KILLED. THAT'S THE TRUTH.
LIAR!
YOUR FATHER WILL KILL ME, PAUL! HE ALREADY TRIED ONCE!
MORE LIES!
KRAK!
SORRY, PAUL. I KNOW IT'S HARD TO BELIEVE THINGS LIKE THAT ABOUT YOUR FATHER. BUT EVERYONE HAS TO FACE THE TRUTH EVENTUALLY. . . .
BELIEVE ME, I KNOW.

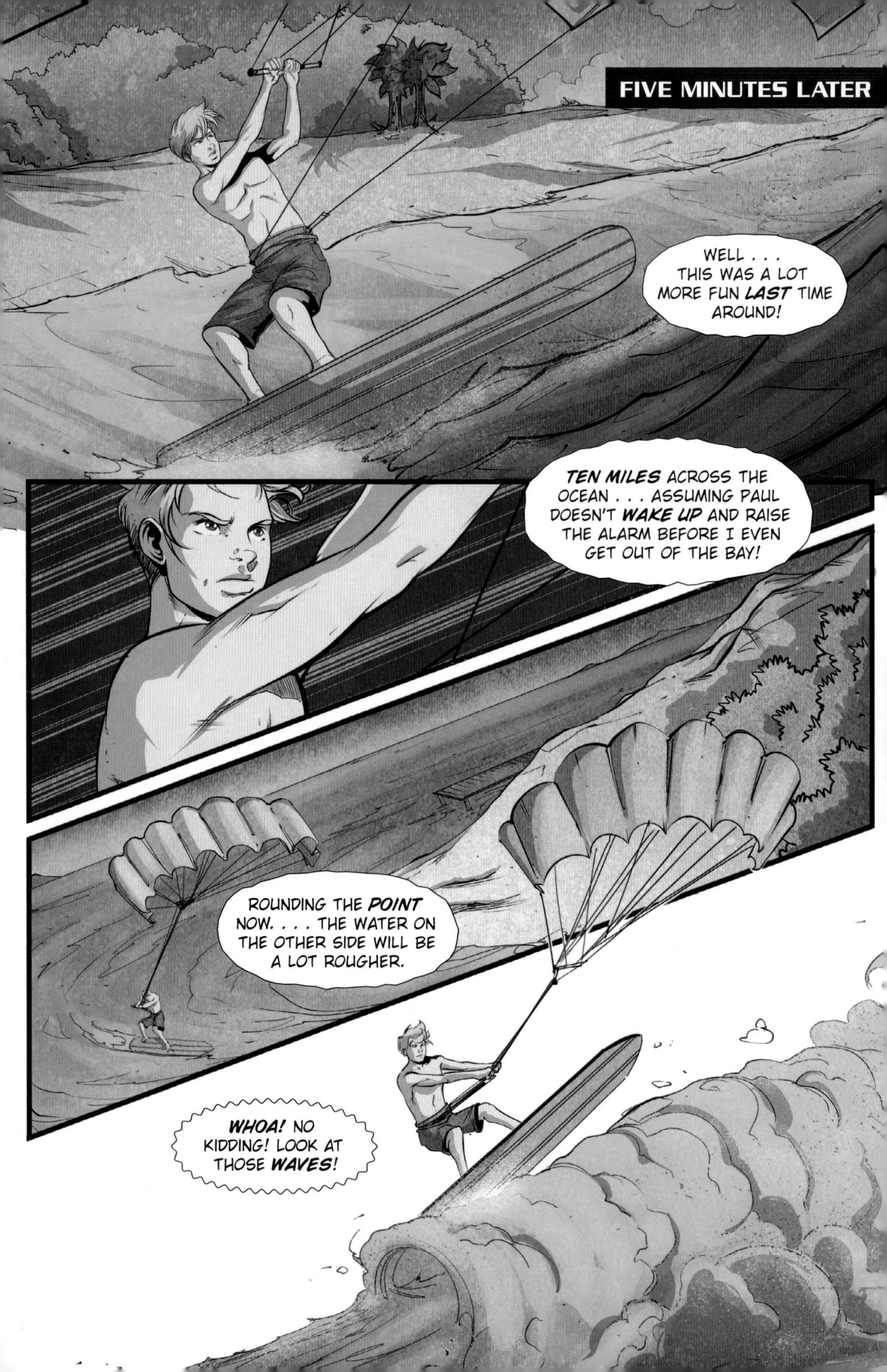
FIVE MINUTES LATER
WELL . . . THIS WAS A LOT MORE FUN LAST TIME AROUND!
TEN MILES ACROSS THE OCEAN . . . ASSUMING PAUL DOESN'T WAKE UP AND RAISE THE ALARM BEFORE I EVEN GET OUT OF THE BAY!
ROUNDING THE POINT NOW. . . . THE WATER ON THE OTHER SIDE WILL BE A LOT ROUGHER.
WHOA! NO KIDDING! LOOK AT THOSE WAVES!

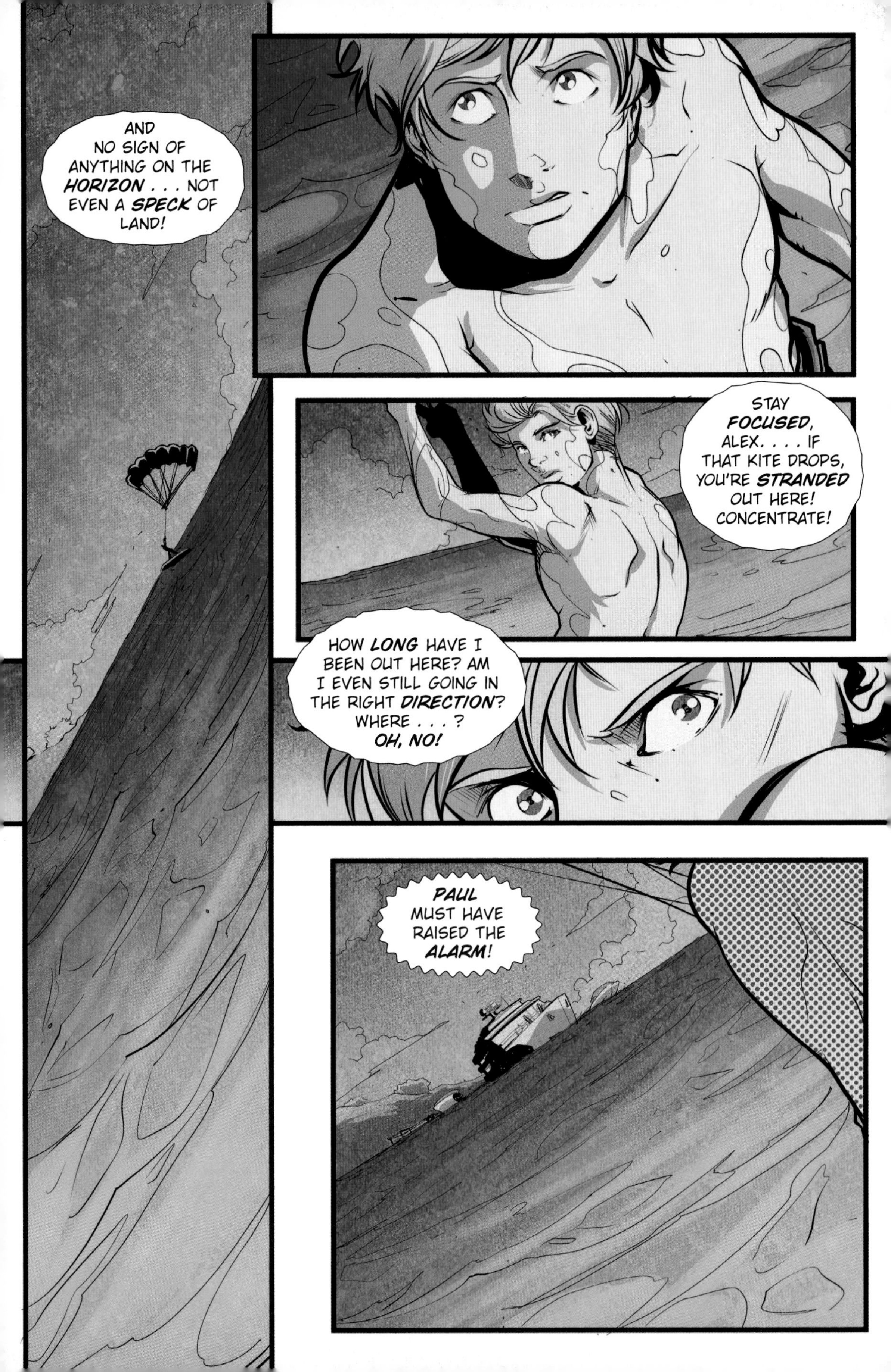
AND NO SIGN OF ANYTHING ON THE HORIZON . . . NOT EVEN A SPECK OF LAND!
STAY FOCUSED, ALEX. . . . IF THAT KITE DROPS, YOU'RE STRANDED OUT HERE! CONCENTRATE!
HOW LONG HAVE I BEEN OUT HERE? AM I EVEN STILL GOING IN THE RIGHT DIRECTION? WHERE . . . ? OH, NO!
PAUL MUST HAVE RAISED THE ALARM!

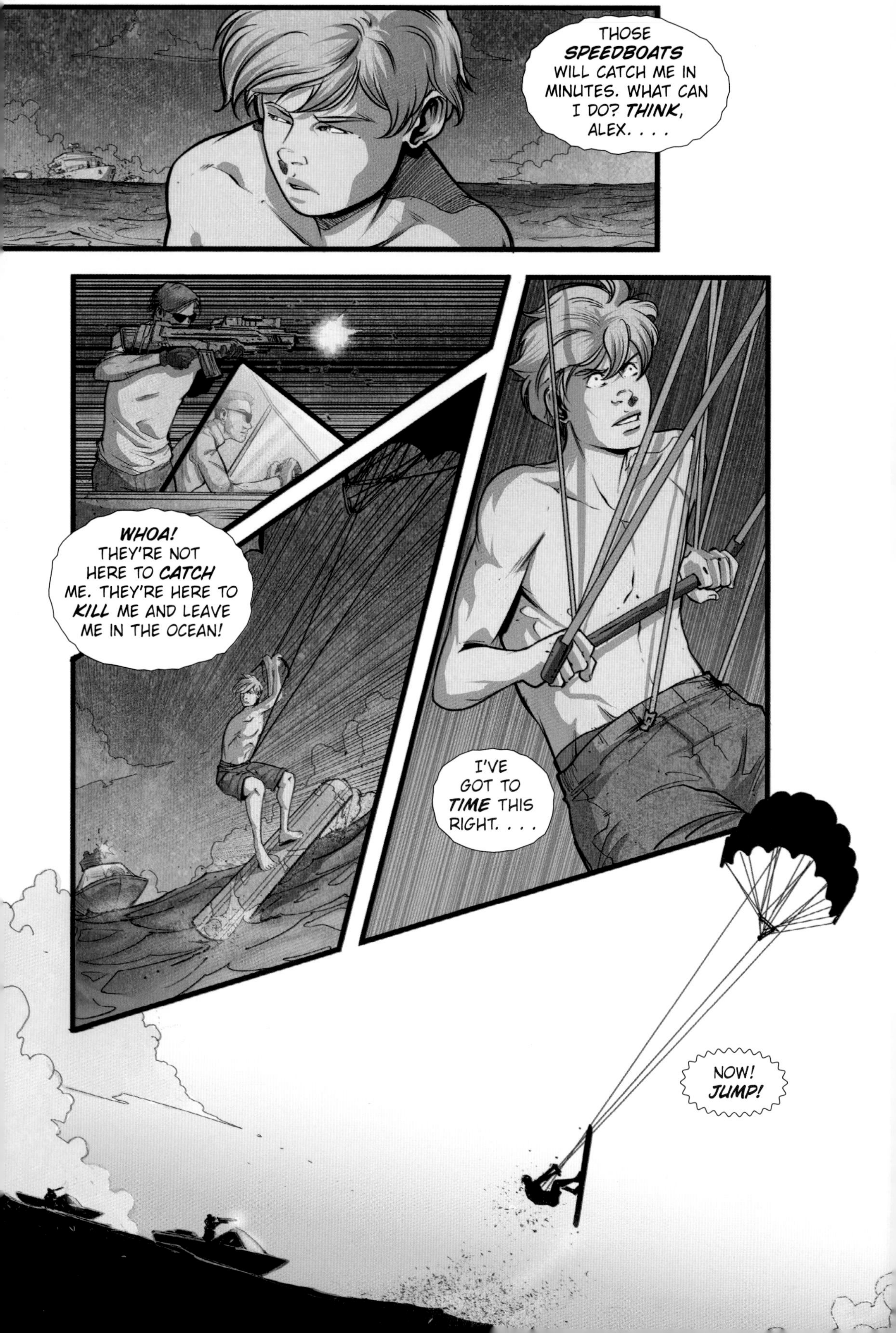
THOSE SPEEDBOATS WILL CATCH ME IN MINUTES. WHAT CAN I DO? THINK, ALEX. . . .
WHOA! THEY'RE NOT HERE TO CATCH ME. THEY'RE HERE TO KILL ME AND LEAVE ME IN THE OCEAN!
I'VE GOT TO TIME THIS RIGHT. . . .
NOW! JUMP!

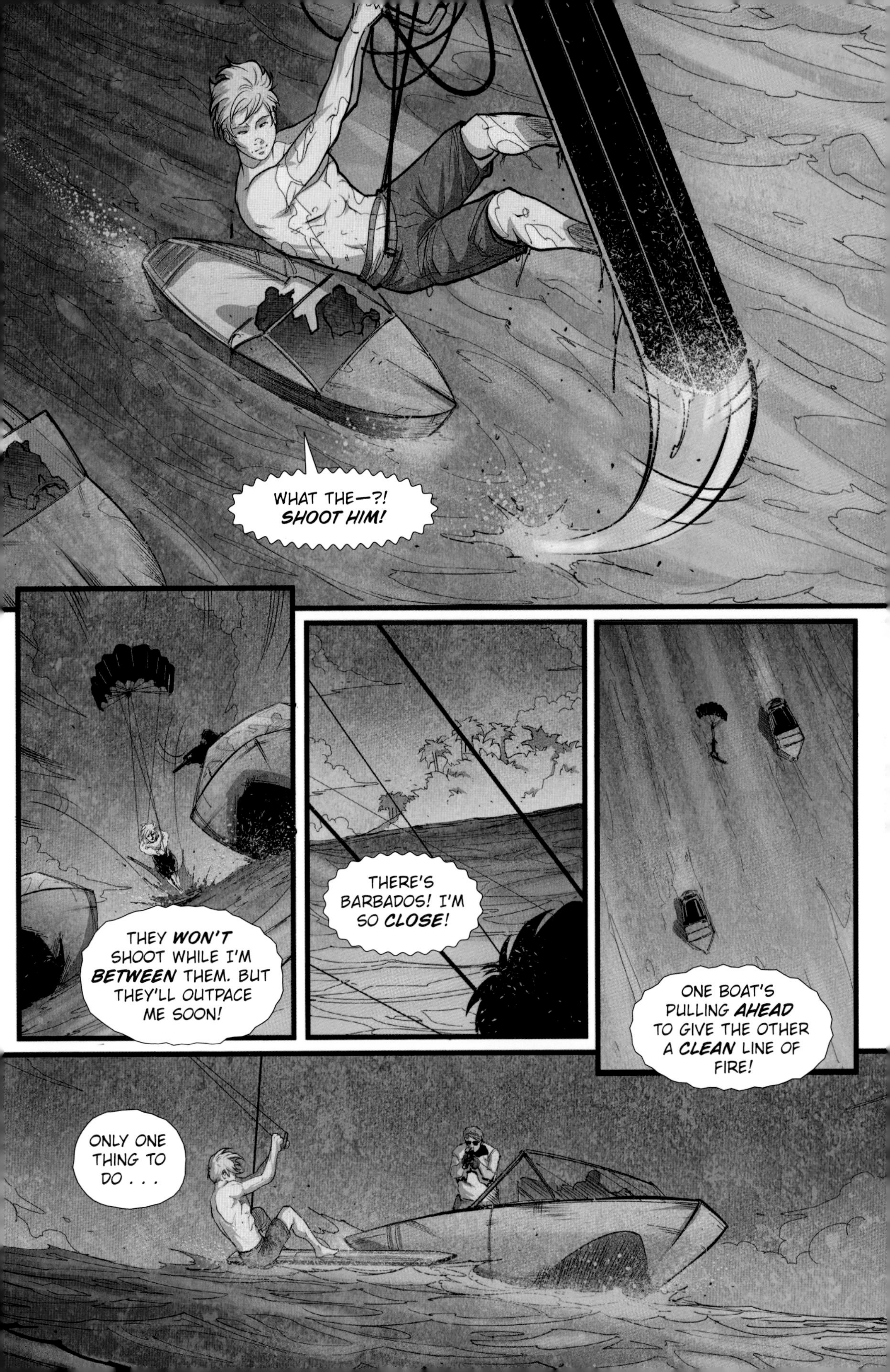
WHAT THE—?! SHOOT HIM!
THEY WON'T SHOOT WHILE I'M BETWEEN THEM. BUT THEY'LL OUTPACE ME SOON!
THERE'S BARBADOS! I'M SO CLOSE!
ONE BOAT'S PULLING AHEAD TO GIVE THE OTHER A CLEAN LINE OF FIRE!
ONLY ONE THING TO DO . . .

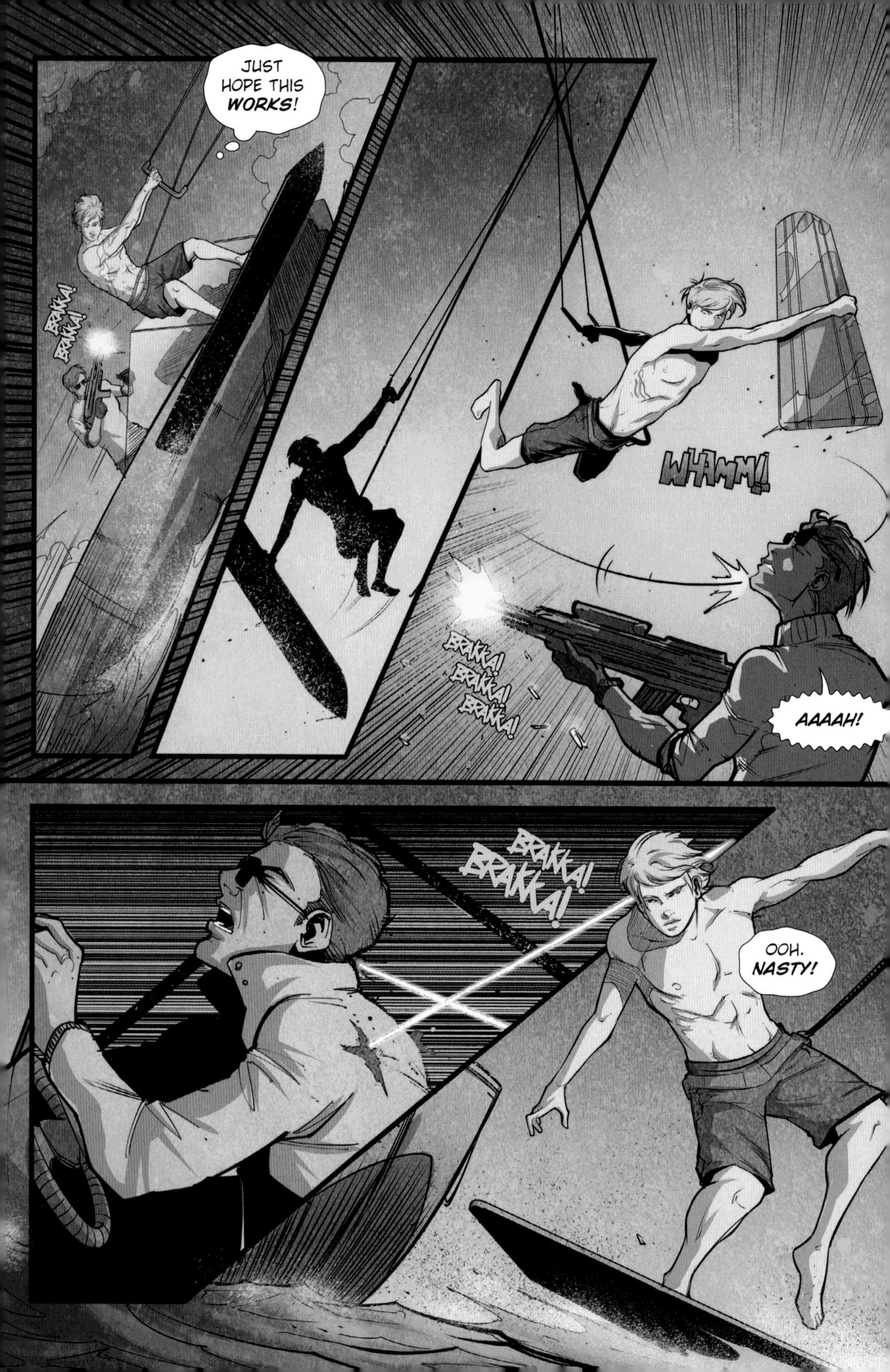
JUST HOPE THIS WORKS!
BRAKKA! BRAKKA!
WHAMM!!
BRAKKA! BRAKKA! BRAKKA!
AAAAH!
BRAKKA! BRAKKA!
OOH. NASTY!

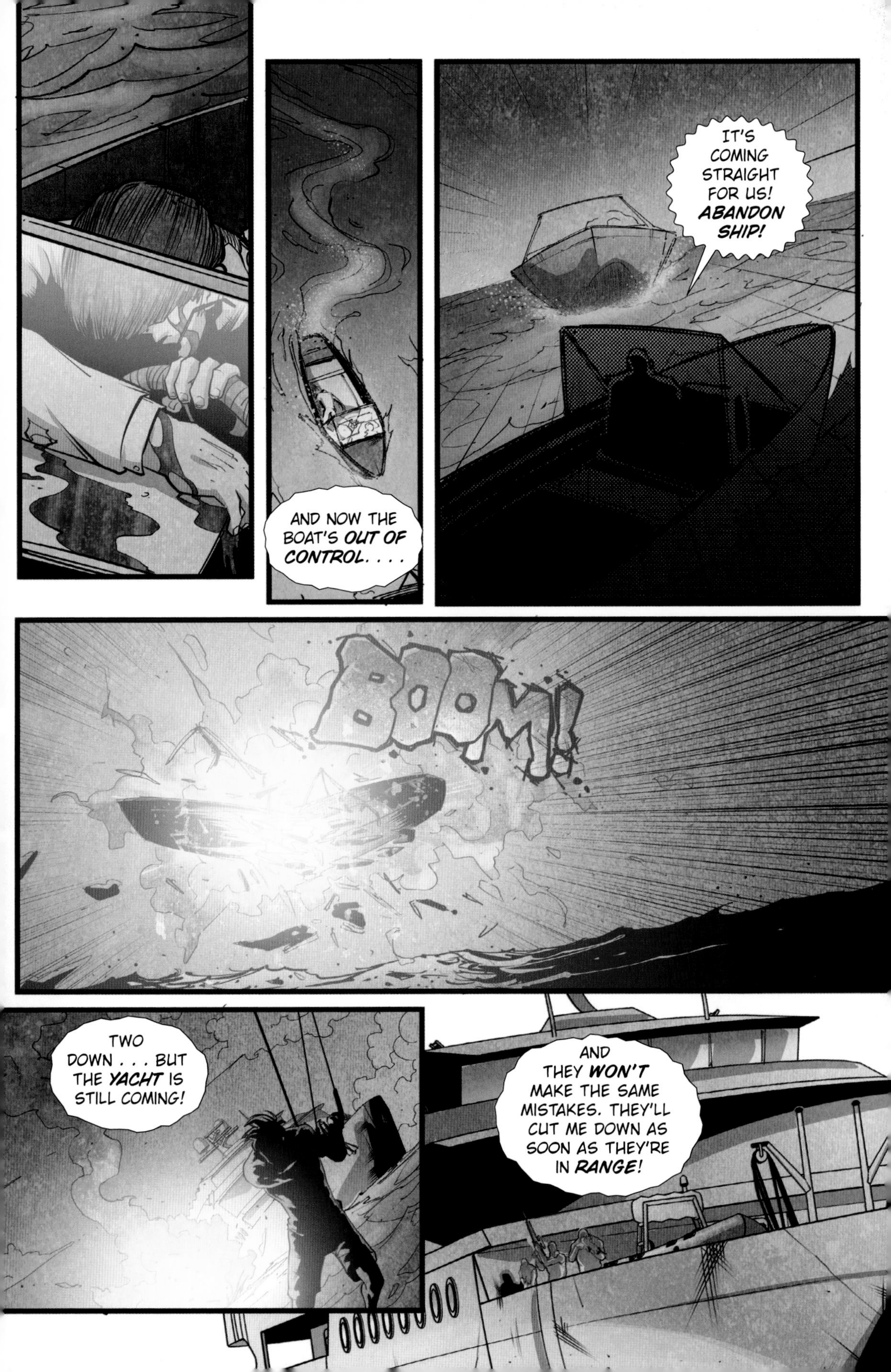
AND NOW THE BOAT'S OUT OF CONTROL. . . .
IT'S COMING STRAIGHT FOR US! ABANDON SHIP!
BOOM!
TWO DOWN . . . BUT THE YACHT IS STILL COMING!
AND THEY WON'T MAKE THE SAME MISTAKES. THEY'LL CUT ME DOWN AS SOON AS THEY'RE IN RANGE!

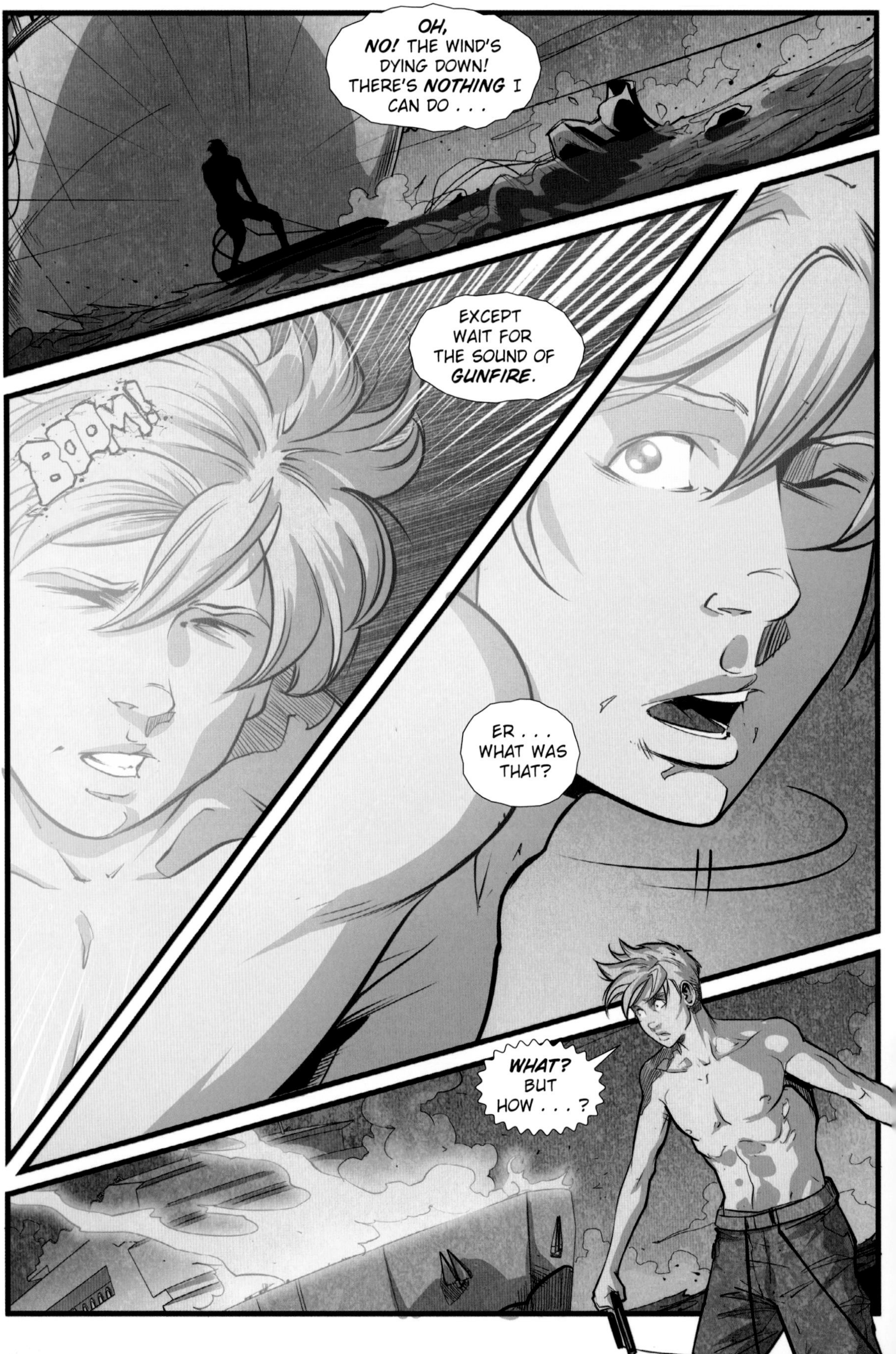
OH, NO! THE WIND'S DYING DOWN! THERE'S NOTHING I CAN DO . . .
EXCEPT WAIT FOR THE SOUND OF GUNFIRE.
BOOM!
ER . . . WHAT WAS THAT?
WHAT? BUT HOW . . . ?

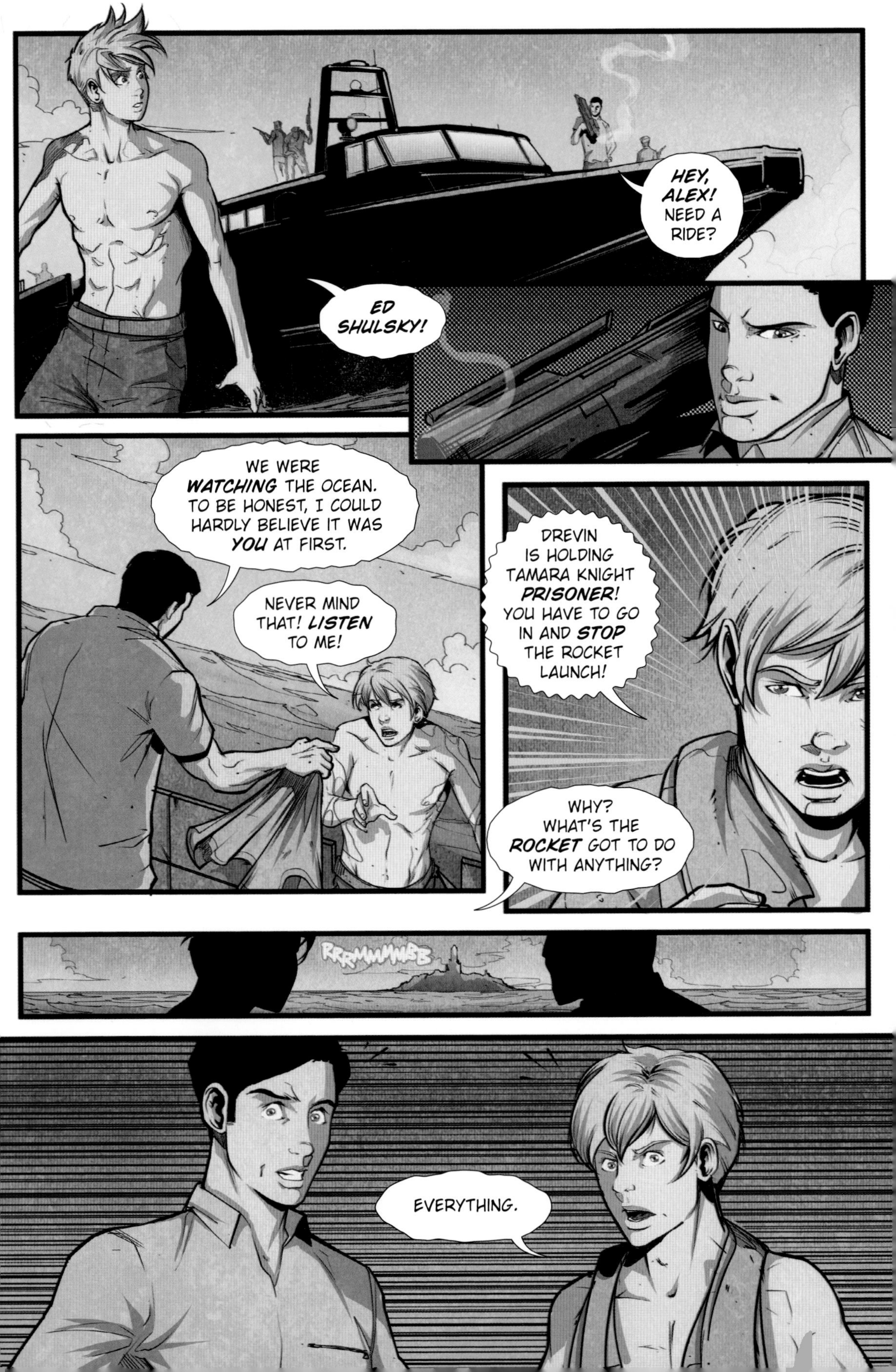
HEY, ALEX! NEED A RIDE?
ED SHULSKY!
WE WERE WATCHING THE OCEAN. TO BE HONEST, I COULD HARDLY BELIEVE IT WAS YOU AT FIRST.
NEVER MIND THAT! LISTEN TO ME!
DREVIN IS HOLDING TAMARA KNIGHT PRISONER! YOU HAVE TO GO IN AND STOP THE ROCKET LAUNCH!
WHY? WHAT'S THE ROCKET GOT TO DO WITH ANYTHING?
RRRMMMMBB
EVERYTHING.

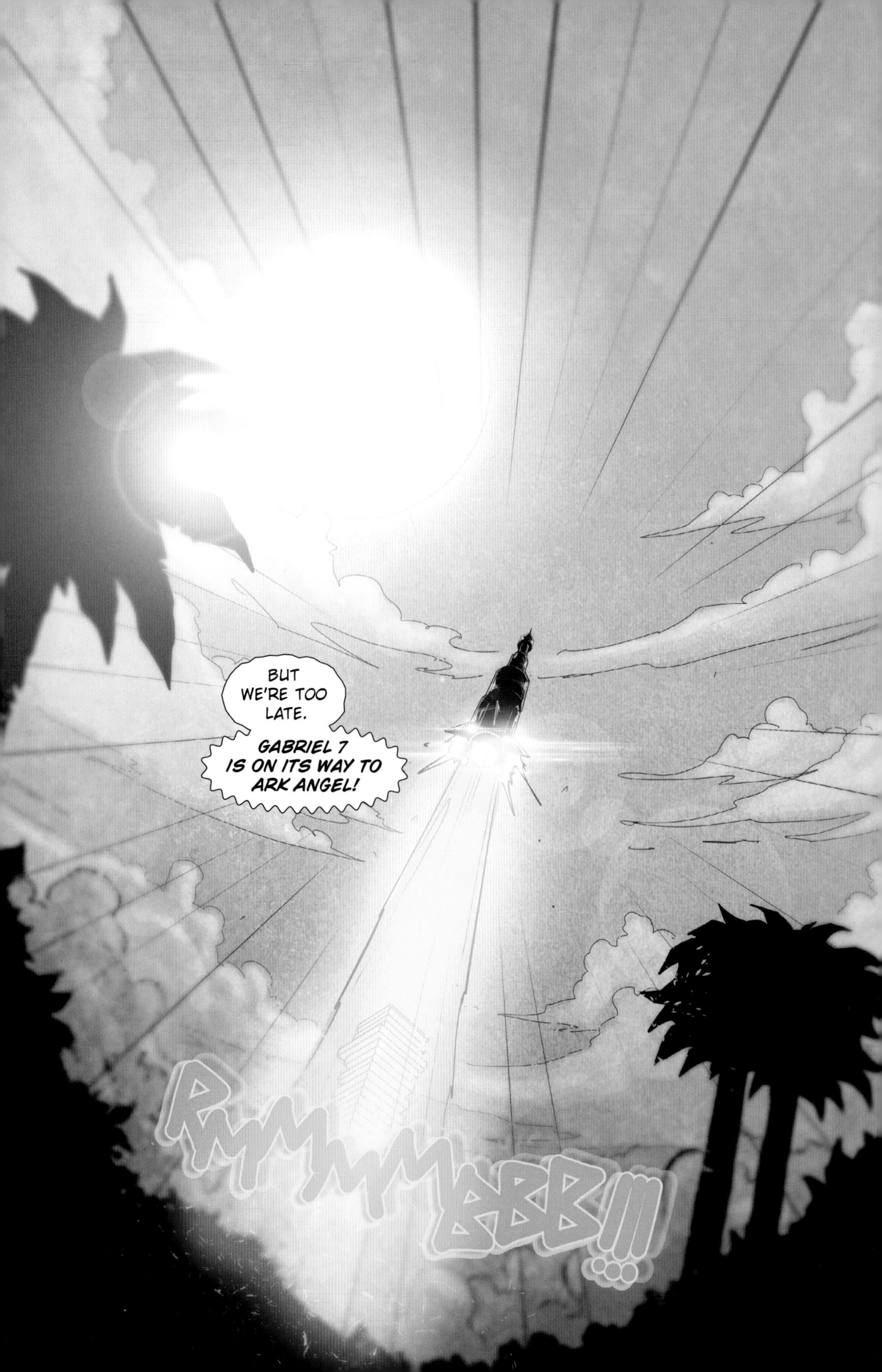
BUT WE'RE TOO LATE.
GABRIEL 7 IS ON ITS WAY TO ARK ANGEL!
RMMMMBBB!!!

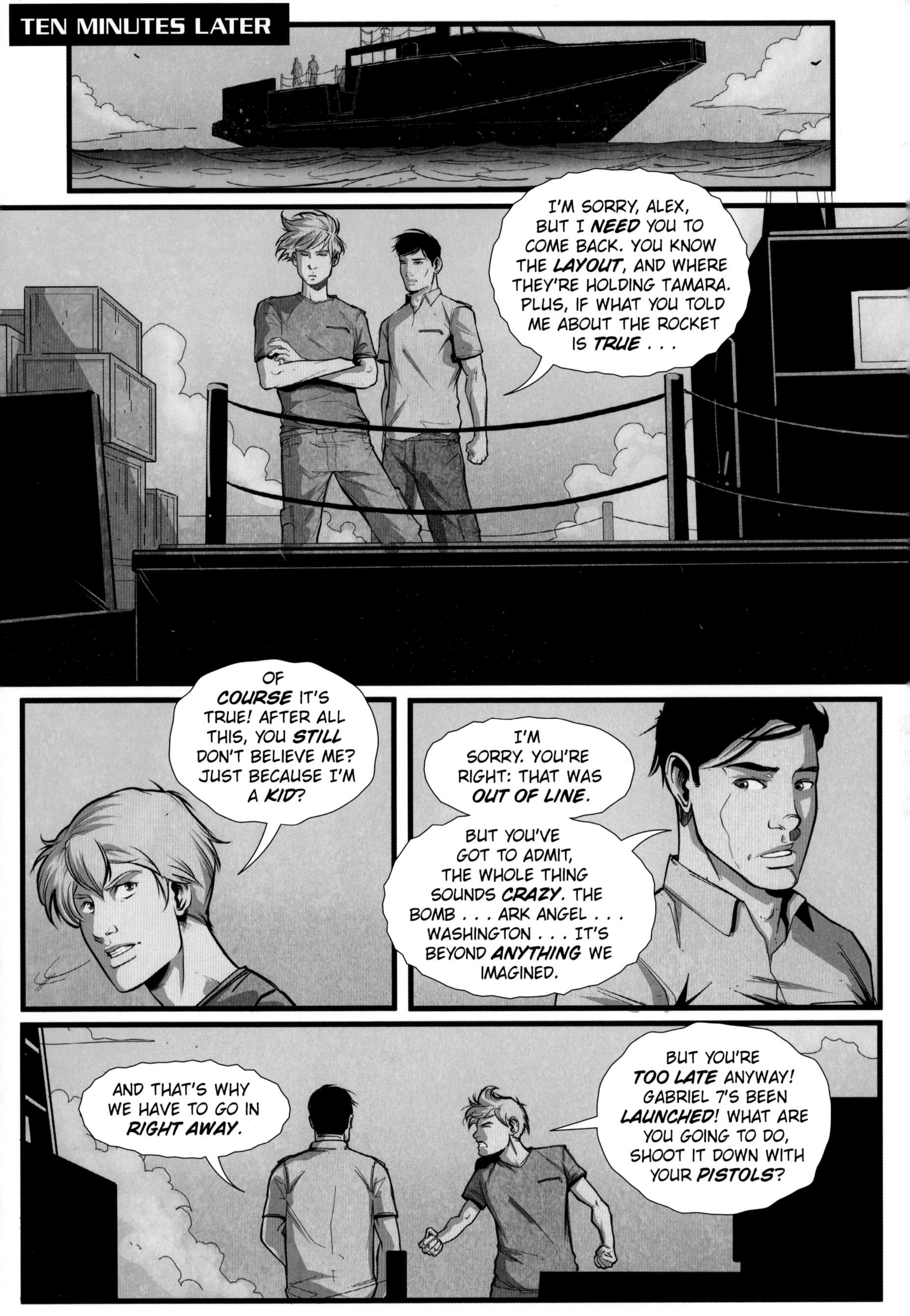
TEN MINUTES LATER
I'M SORRY, ALEX, BUT I NEED YOU TO COME BACK. YOU KNOW THE LAYOUT, AND WHERE THEY'RE HOLDING TAMARA. PLUS, IF WHAT YOU TOLD ME ABOUT THE ROCKET IS TRUE . . .
OF COURSE IT'S TRUE! AFTER ALL THIS, YOU STILL DON'T BELIEVE ME? JUST BECAUSE I'M A KID?
I'M SORRY. YOU'RE RIGHT: THAT WAS OUT OF LINE.
BUT YOU'VE GOT TO ADMIT, THE WHOLE THING SOUNDS CRAZY. THE BOMB . . . ARK ANGEL . . . WASHINGTON . . . IT'S BEYOND ANYTHING WE IMAGINED.
AND THAT'S WHY WE HAVE TO GO IN RIGHT AWAY.
BUT YOU'RE TOO LATE ANYWAY! GABRIEL 7'S BEEN LAUNCHED! WHAT ARE YOU GOING TO DO, SHOOT IT DOWN WITH YOUR PISTOLS?

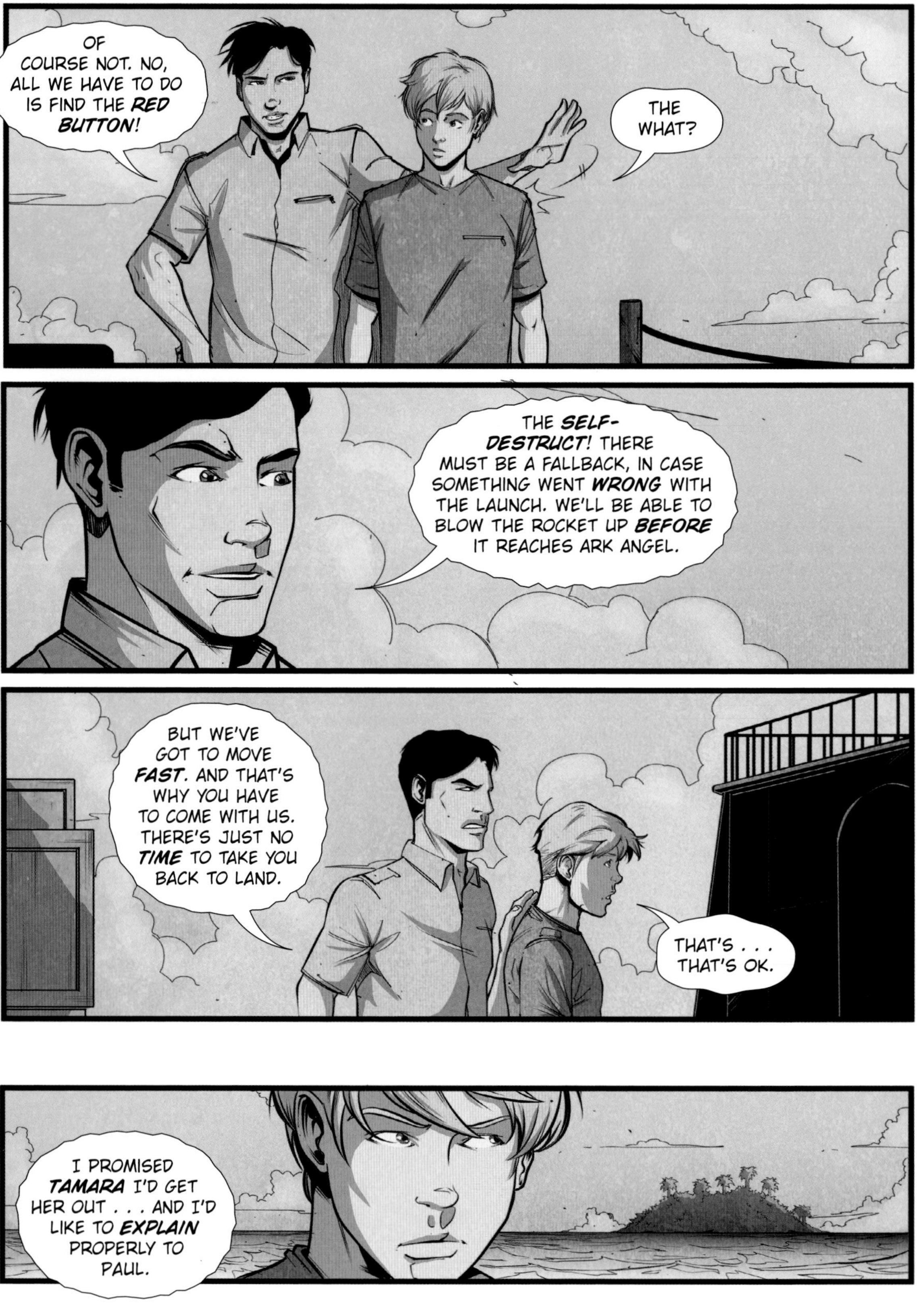
OF COURSE NOT. NO, ALL WE HAVE TO DO IS FIND THE *RED BUTTON*!
THE WHAT?
THE *SELF-DESTRUCT*! THERE MUST BE A FALLBACK, IN CASE SOMETHING WENT *WRONG* WITH THE LAUNCH. WE'LL BE ABLE TO BLOW THE ROCKET UP *BEFORE* IT REACHES ARK ANGEL.
BUT WE'VE GOT TO MOVE *FAST*. AND THAT'S WHY YOU HAVE TO COME WITH US. THERE'S JUST NO *TIME* TO TAKE YOU BACK TO LAND.
THAT'S . . . THAT'S OK.
I PROMISED *TAMARA* I'D GET HER OUT . . . AND I'D LIKE TO *EXPLAIN* PROPERLY TO PAUL.

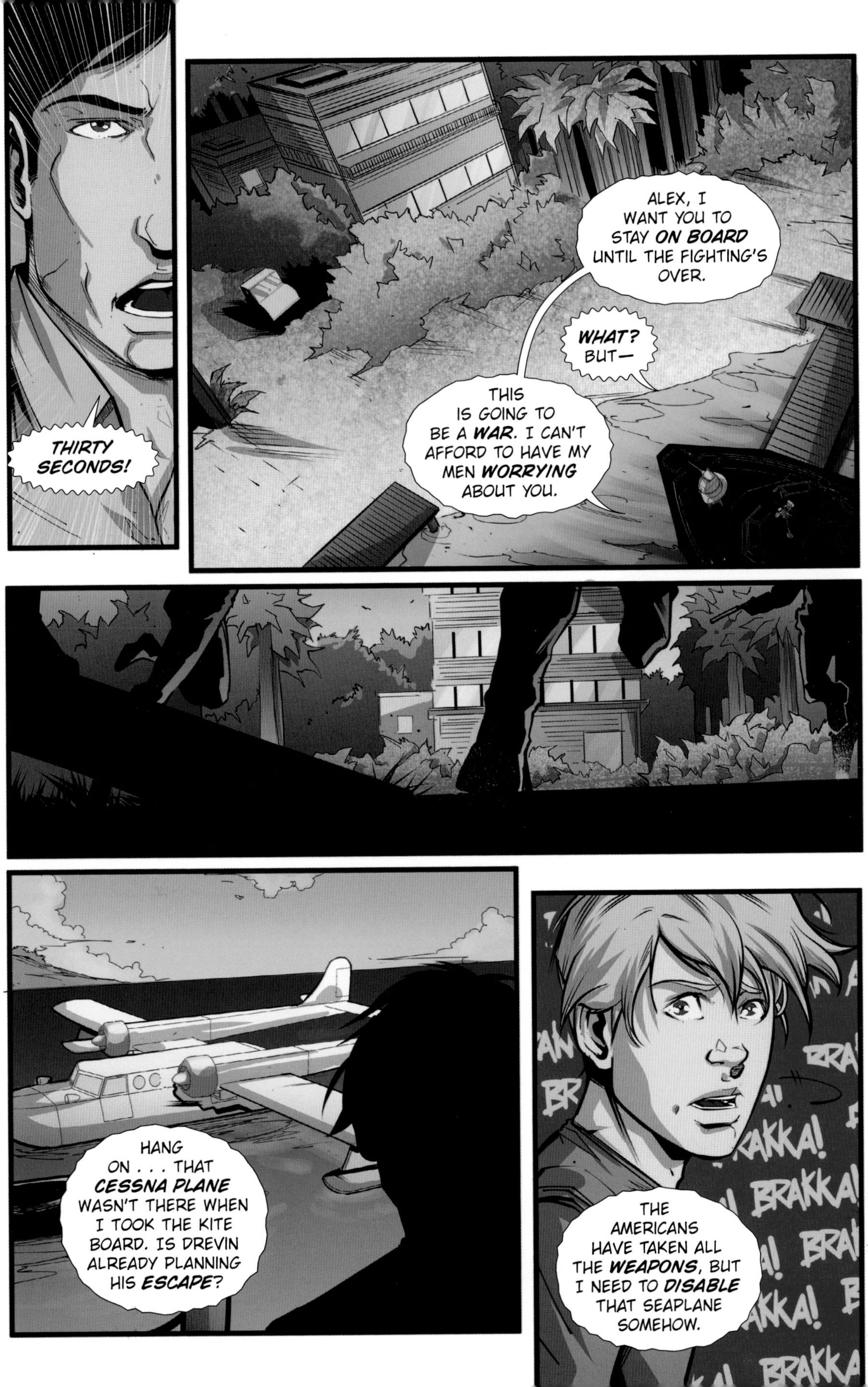
THIRTY SECONDS!
ALEX, I WANT YOU TO STAY ON BOARD UNTIL THE FIGHTING'S OVER.
WHAT? BUT—
THIS IS GOING TO BE A WAR. I CAN'T AFFORD TO HAVE MY MEN WORRYING ABOUT YOU.
HANG ON . . . THAT CESSNA PLANE WASN'T THERE WHEN I TOOK THE KITE BOARD. IS DREVIN ALREADY PLANNING HIS ESCAPE?
BRAKKA! BRAKKA!
THE AMERICANS HAVE TAKEN ALL THE WEAPONS, BUT I NEED TO DISABLE THAT SEAPLANE SOMEHOW.

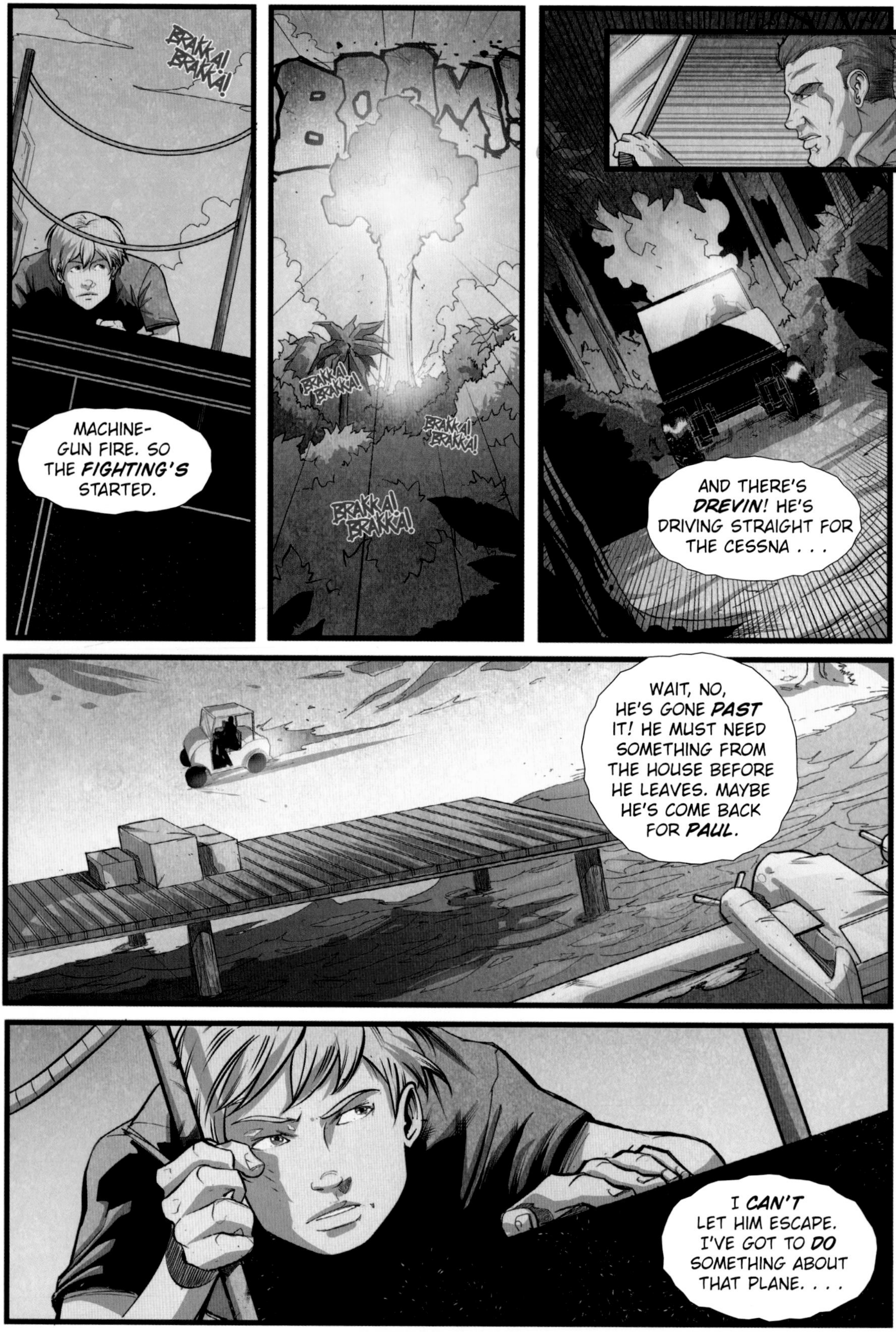
BRAKKA! BRAKKA!
MACHINE-GUN FIRE. SO THE *FIGHTING'S* STARTED.
BOOM!
BRAKKA! BRAKKA!
BRAKKA! BRAKKA!
BRAKKA! BRAKKA!
AND THERE'S *DREVIN*! HE'S DRIVING STRAIGHT FOR THE CESSNA . . .
WAIT, NO, HE'S GONE *PAST* IT! HE MUST NEED SOMETHING FROM THE HOUSE BEFORE HE LEAVES. MAYBE HE'S COME BACK FOR *PAUL*.
I *CAN'T* LET HIM ESCAPE. I'VE GOT TO *DO* SOMETHING ABOUT THAT PLANE. . . .

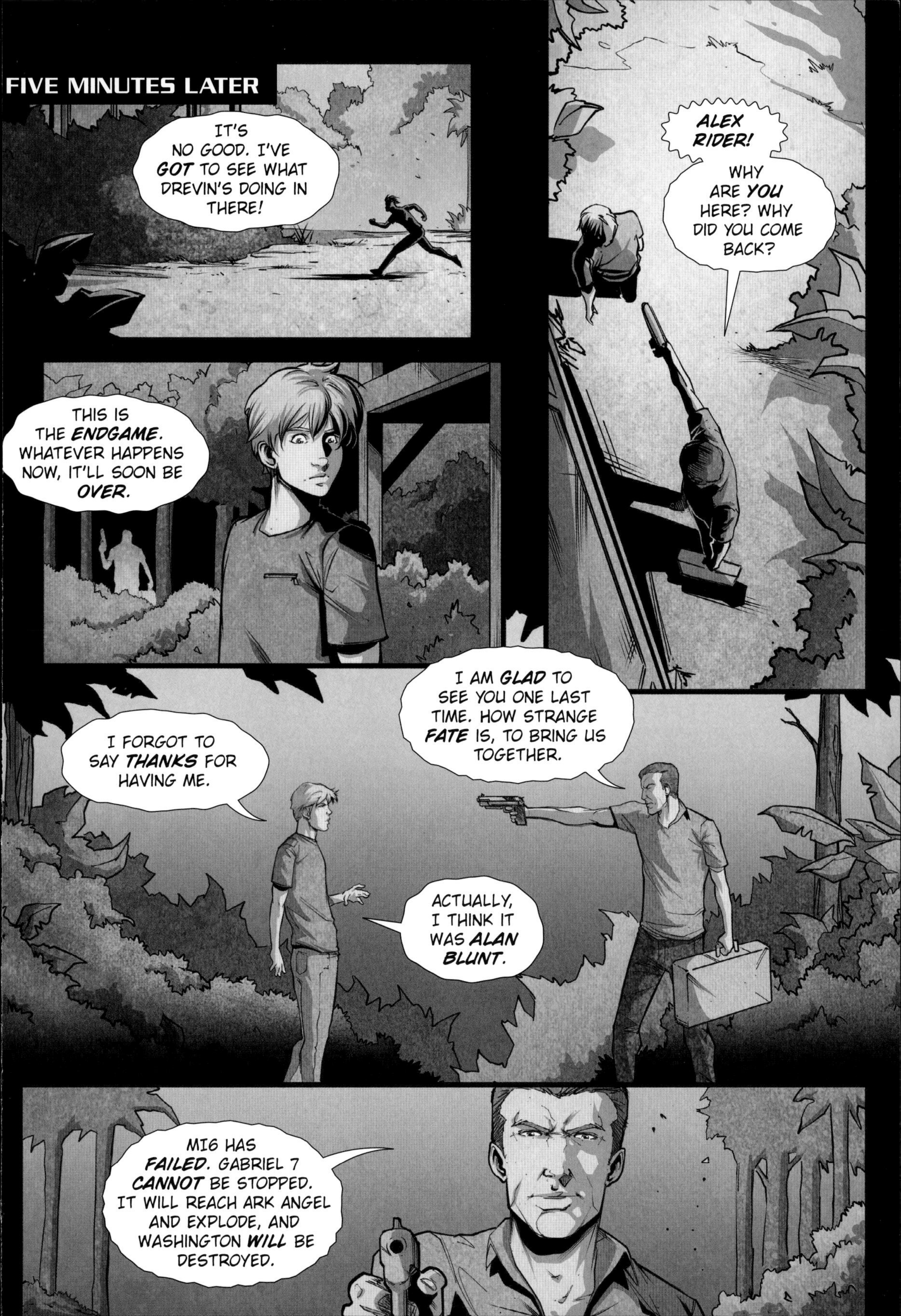
FIVE MINUTES LATER
IT'S NO GOOD. I'VE GOT TO SEE WHAT DREVIN'S DOING IN THERE!
ALEX RIDER!
WHY ARE YOU HERE? WHY DID YOU COME BACK?
THIS IS THE ENDGAME. WHATEVER HAPPENS NOW, IT'LL SOON BE OVER.
I FORGOT TO SAY THANKS FOR HAVING ME.
I AM GLAD TO SEE YOU ONE LAST TIME. HOW STRANGE FATE IS, TO BRING US TOGETHER.
ACTUALLY, I THINK IT WAS ALAN BLUNT.
MI6 HAS FAILED. GABRIEL 7 CANNOT BE STOPPED. IT WILL REACH ARK ANGEL AND EXPLODE, AND WASHINGTON WILL BE DESTROYED.

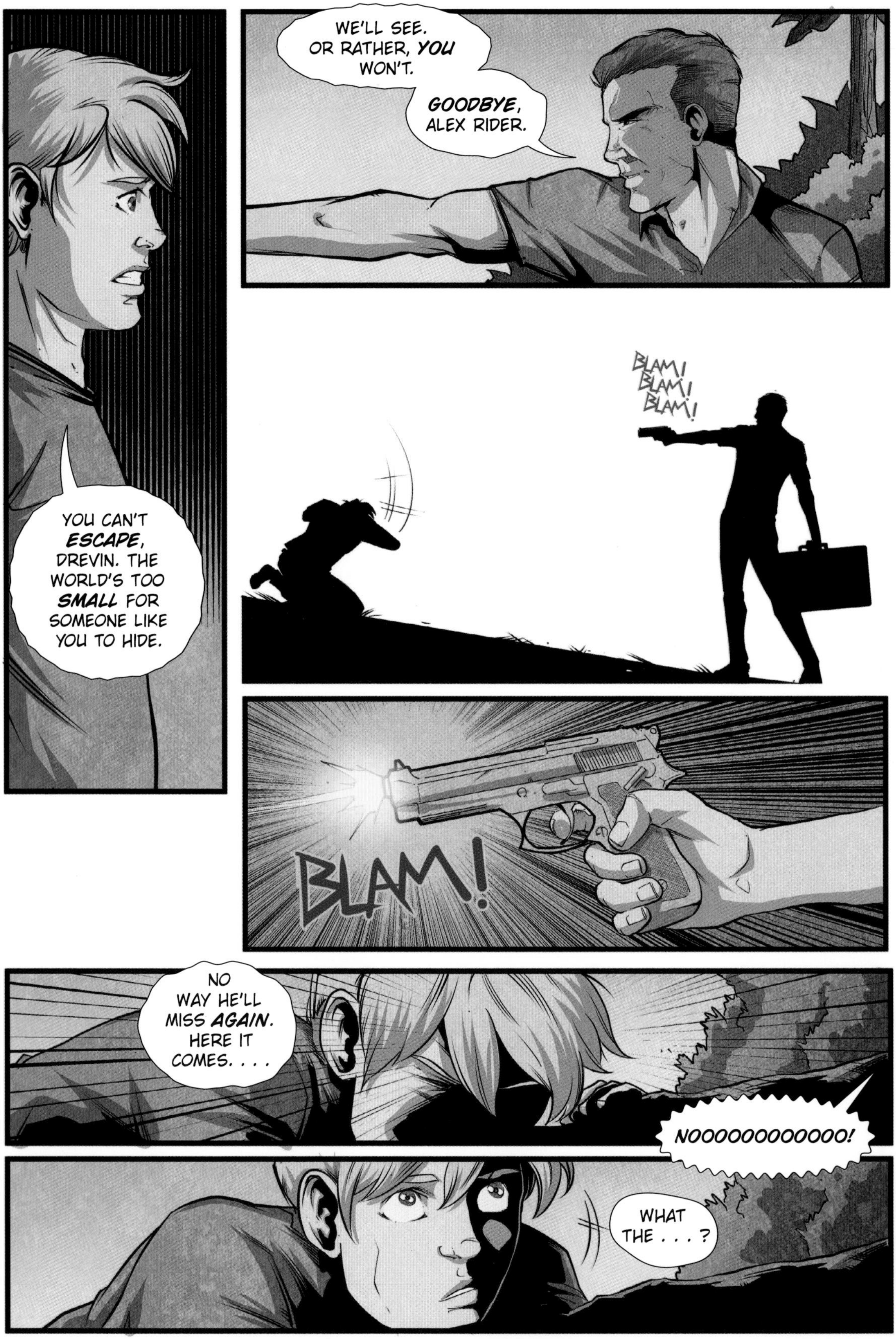
WE'LL SEE. OR RATHER, YOU WON'T.
GOODBYE, ALEX RIDER.
YOU CAN'T ESCAPE, DREVIN. THE WORLD'S TOO SMALL FOR SOMEONE LIKE YOU TO HIDE.
BLAM! BLAM! BLAM!
BLAM!
NO WAY HE'LL MISS AGAIN. HERE IT COMES. . . .
NOOOOOOOOOOOO!
WHAT THE . . . ?

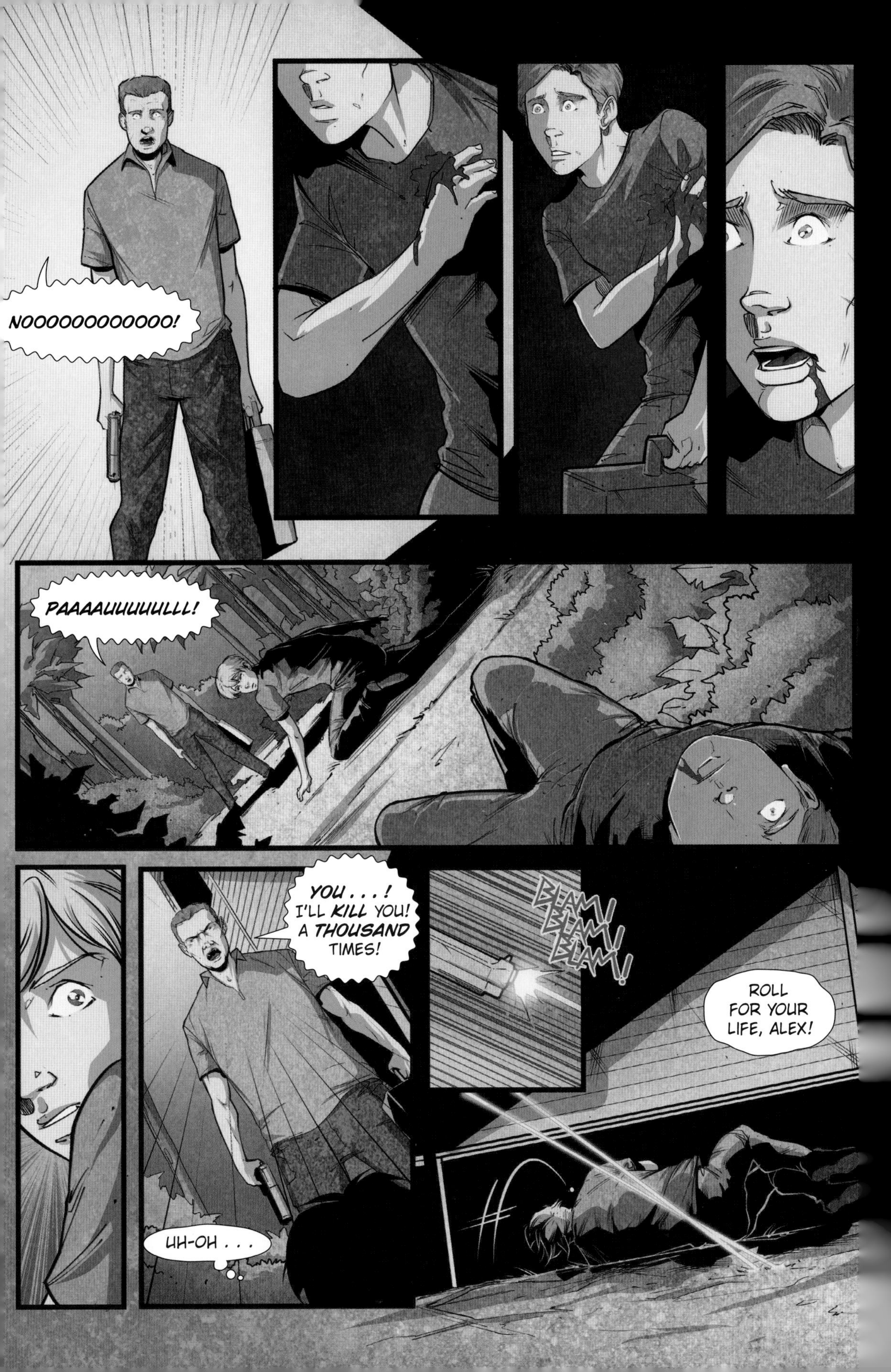
NOOOOOOOOOOOO!
PAAAAUUUUULLL!
YOU . . . ! I'LL KILL YOU! A THOUSAND TIMES!
UH-OH . . .
BLAM! BLAM! BLAM!
ROLL FOR YOUR LIFE, ALEX!

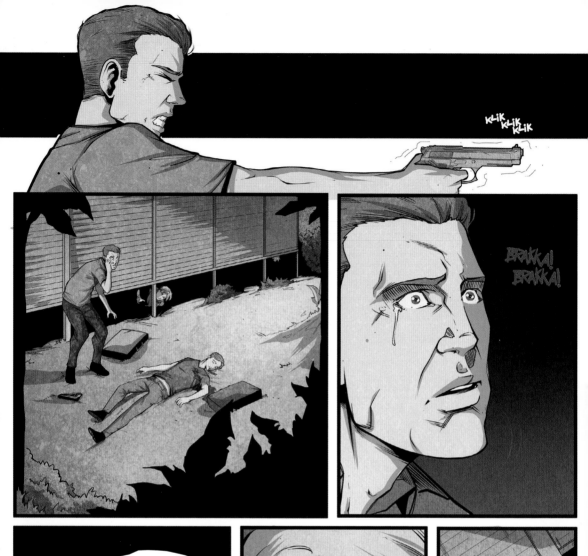

KLIK KLIK KLIK

BRAKKA! BRAKKA!

THE CIA MUST BE *CLOSE*. BUT THEY'LL NEVER CATCH DREVIN *BEFORE* HE REACHES THAT PLANE.

ALEX . . .

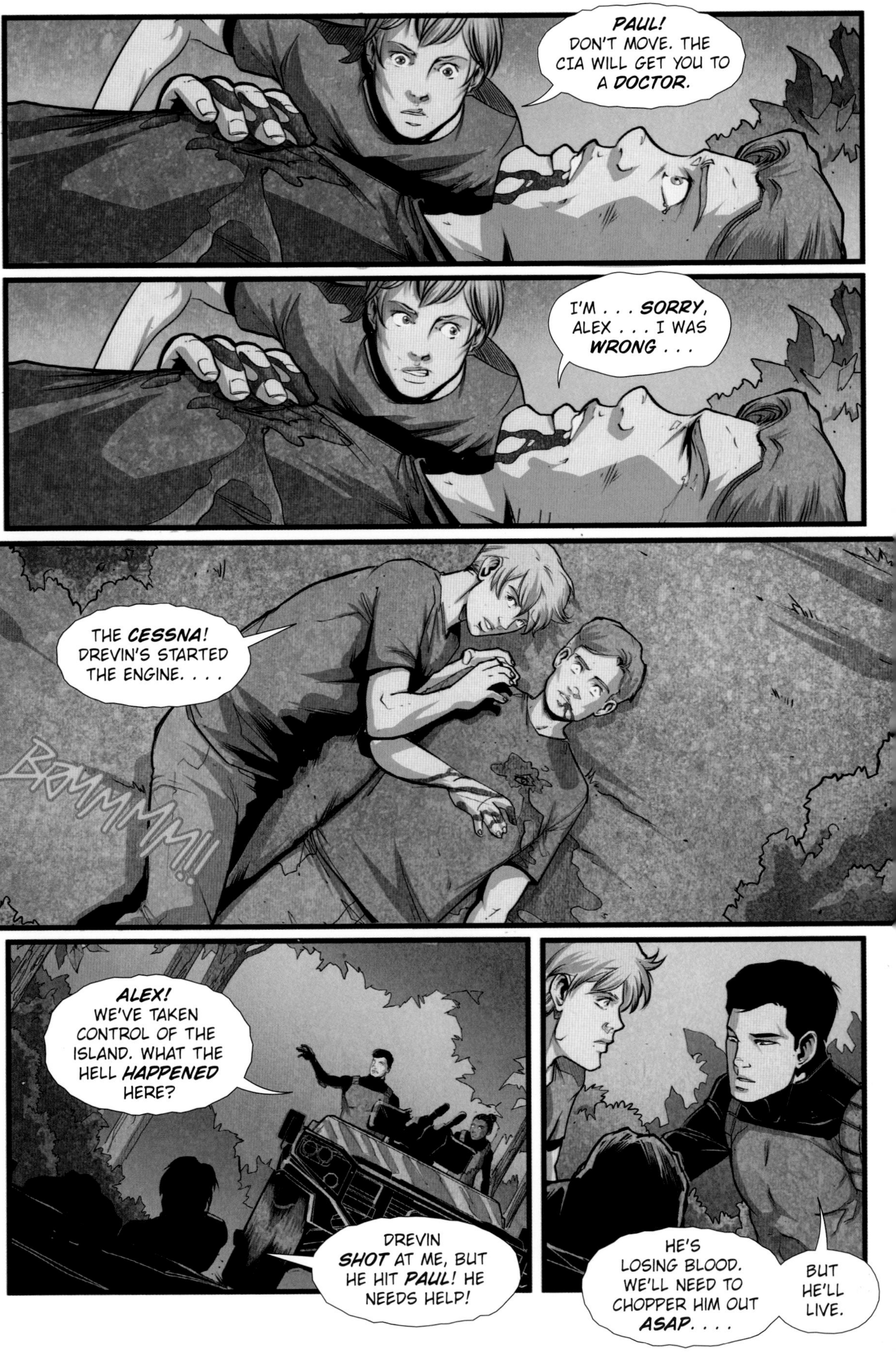
PAUL! DON'T MOVE. THE CIA WILL GET YOU TO A DOCTOR.
I'M . . . SORRY, ALEX . . . I WAS WRONG . . .
THE CESSNA! DREVIN'S STARTED THE ENGINE. . . .
BRMMM!!
ALEX! WE'VE TAKEN CONTROL OF THE ISLAND. WHAT THE HELL HAPPENED HERE?
DREVIN SHOT AT ME, BUT HE HIT PAUL! HE NEEDS HELP!
HE'S LOSING BLOOD. WE'LL NEED TO CHOPPER HIM OUT ASAP. . . .
BUT HE'LL LIVE.

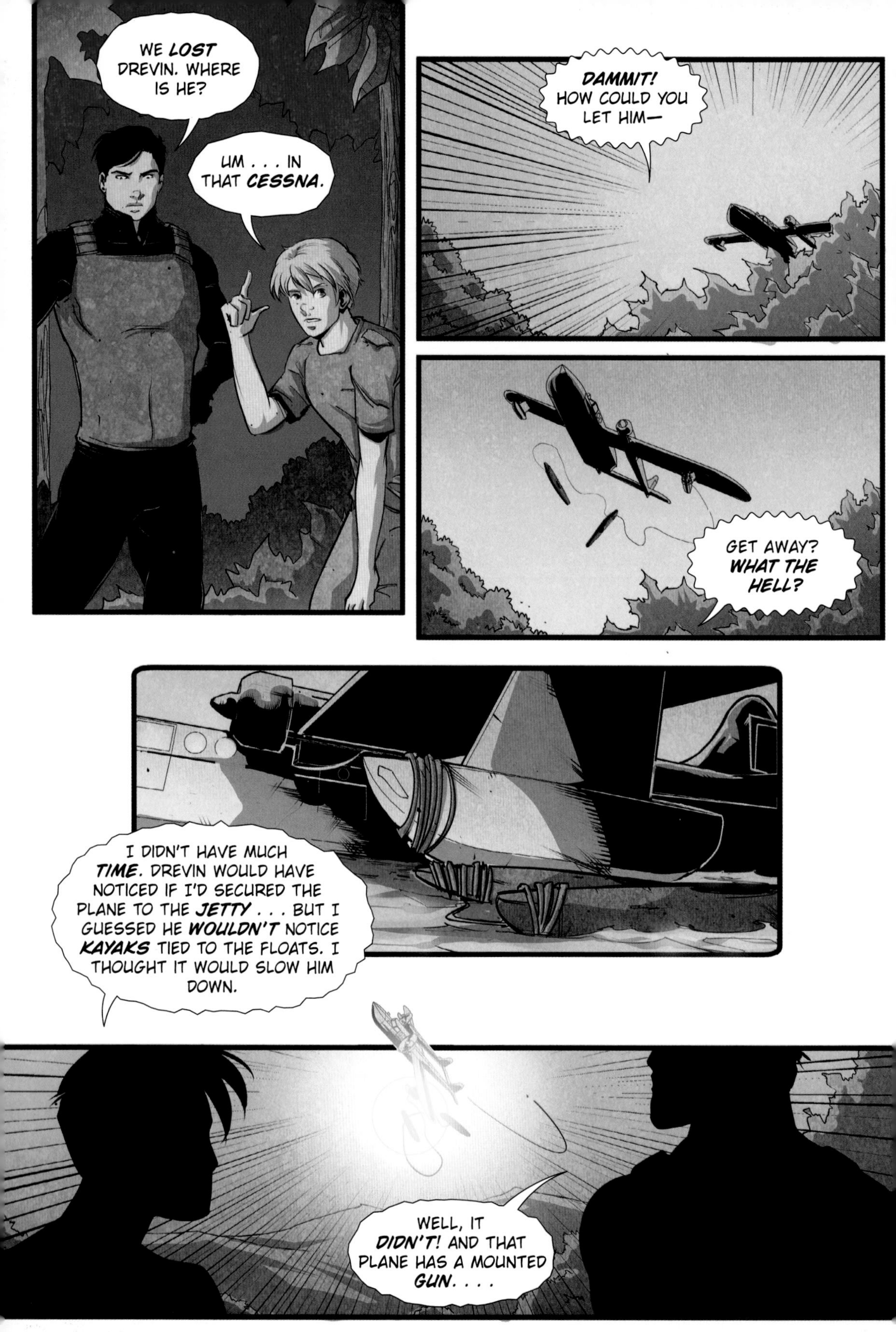
WE LOST DREVIN. WHERE IS HE?
UM . . . IN THAT CESSNA.
DAMMIT! HOW COULD YOU LET HIM—
GET AWAY? WHAT THE HELL?
I DIDN'T HAVE MUCH TIME. DREVIN WOULD HAVE NOTICED IF I'D SECURED THE PLANE TO THE JETTY . . . BUT I GUESSED HE WOULDN'T NOTICE KAYAKS TIED TO THE FLOATS. I THOUGHT IT WOULD SLOW HIM DOWN.
WELL, IT DIDN'T! AND THAT PLANE HAS A MOUNTED GUN. . . .

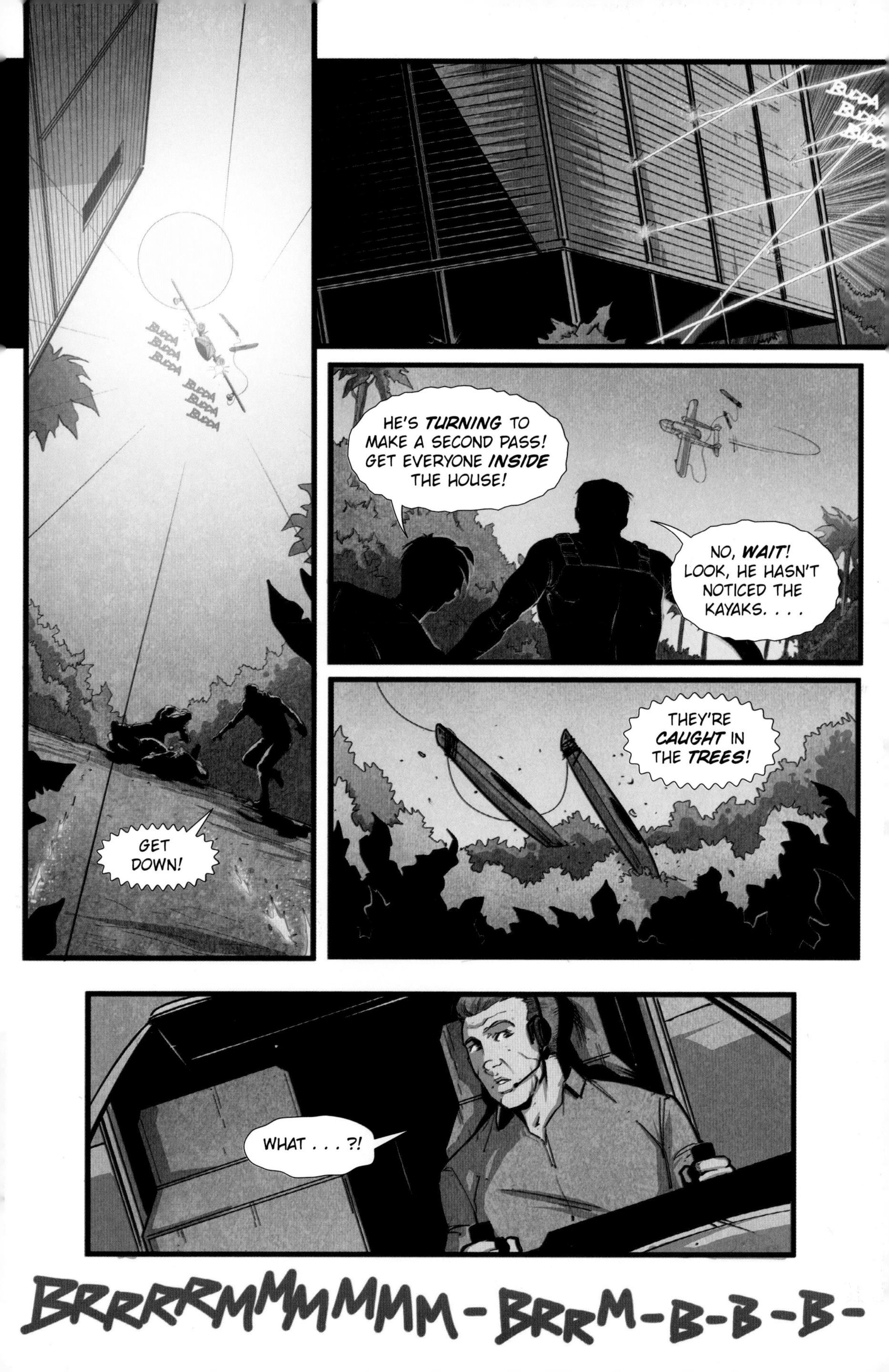
BUDDA
BUDDA
BUDDA
BUDDA
BUDDA
BUDDA
BUDDA
BUDDA
BUDDA
GET DOWN!
HE'S TURNING TO MAKE A SECOND PASS! GET EVERYONE INSIDE THE HOUSE!
NO, WAIT! LOOK, HE HASN'T NOTICED THE KAYAKS. . . .
THEY'RE CAUGHT IN THE TREES!
WHAT . . . ?!
BRRRRMMMMMMM-BRRM-B-B-B-

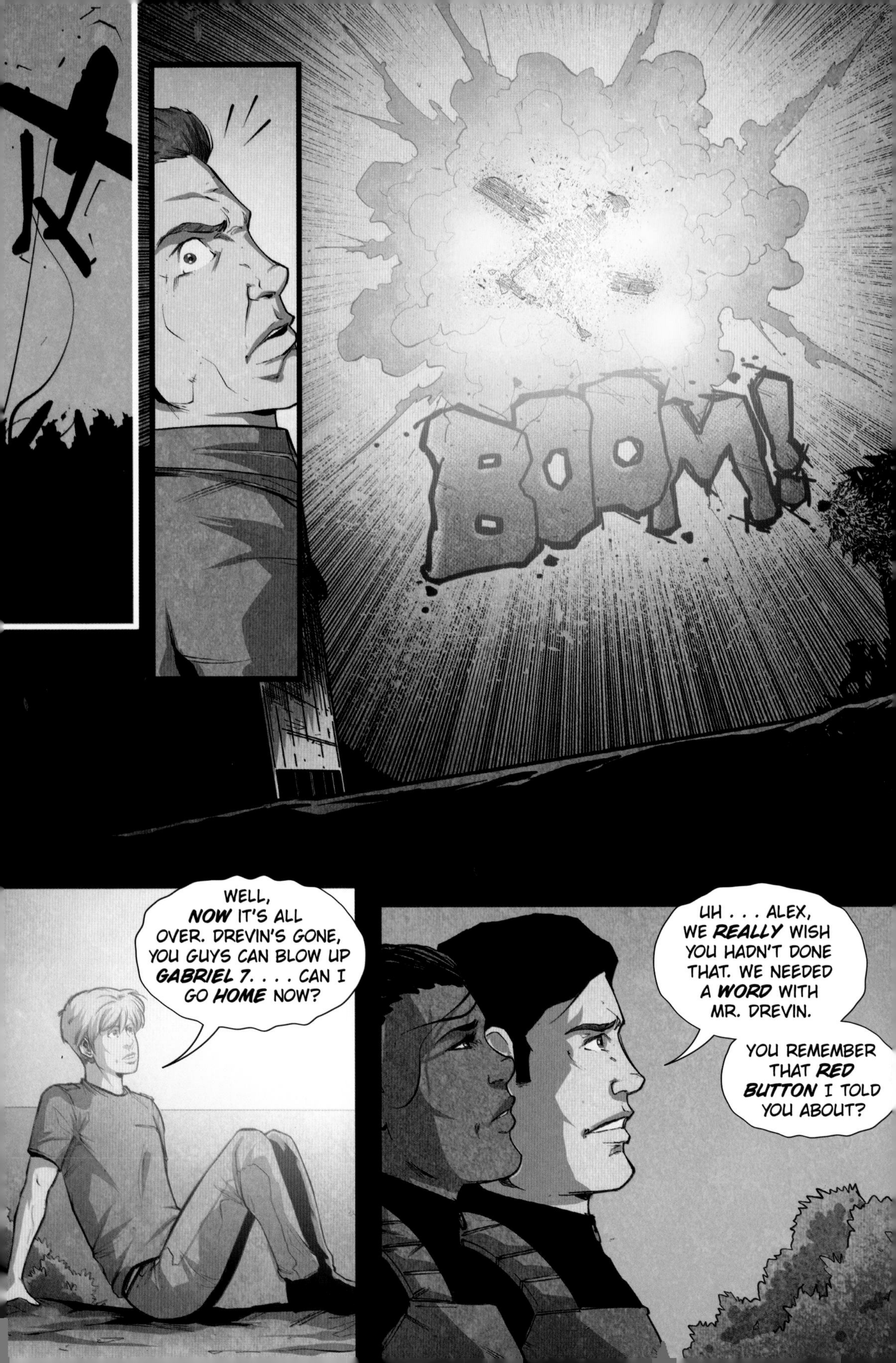
BOOM!
WELL, NOW IT'S ALL OVER. DREVIN'S GONE, YOU GUYS CAN BLOW UP GABRIEL 7. . . . CAN I GO HOME NOW?
UH . . . ALEX, WE REALLY WISH YOU HADN'T DONE THAT. WE NEEDED A WORD WITH MR. DREVIN.
YOU REMEMBER THAT RED BUTTON I TOLD YOU ABOUT?

WELL, UH . . . THERE *ISN'T* ONE.

YOU SAID YOU WERE *IN CONTROL* OF THE ISLAND!

DREVIN WAS THE *ONLY ONE* WITH THE CODES. WE CAN'T *COMMUNICATE* WITH GABRIEL 7, AND THAT MEANS WE *CAN'T* BRING IT BACK OR DIVERT IT.

IN LESS THAN THREE HOURS, GABRIEL 7 WILL *DOCK* WITH ARK ANGEL. THE BOMB IS ON A *TIMER*. IT'S ALL GOING TO HAPPEN EXACTLY AS DREVIN PLANNED.

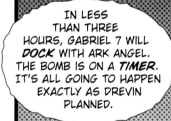

UNLESS, THAT IS . . .

UNLESS WHAT?

ALEX, I'M REALLY SORRY . . .

BUT WE NEED YOUR *HELP* AGAIN.

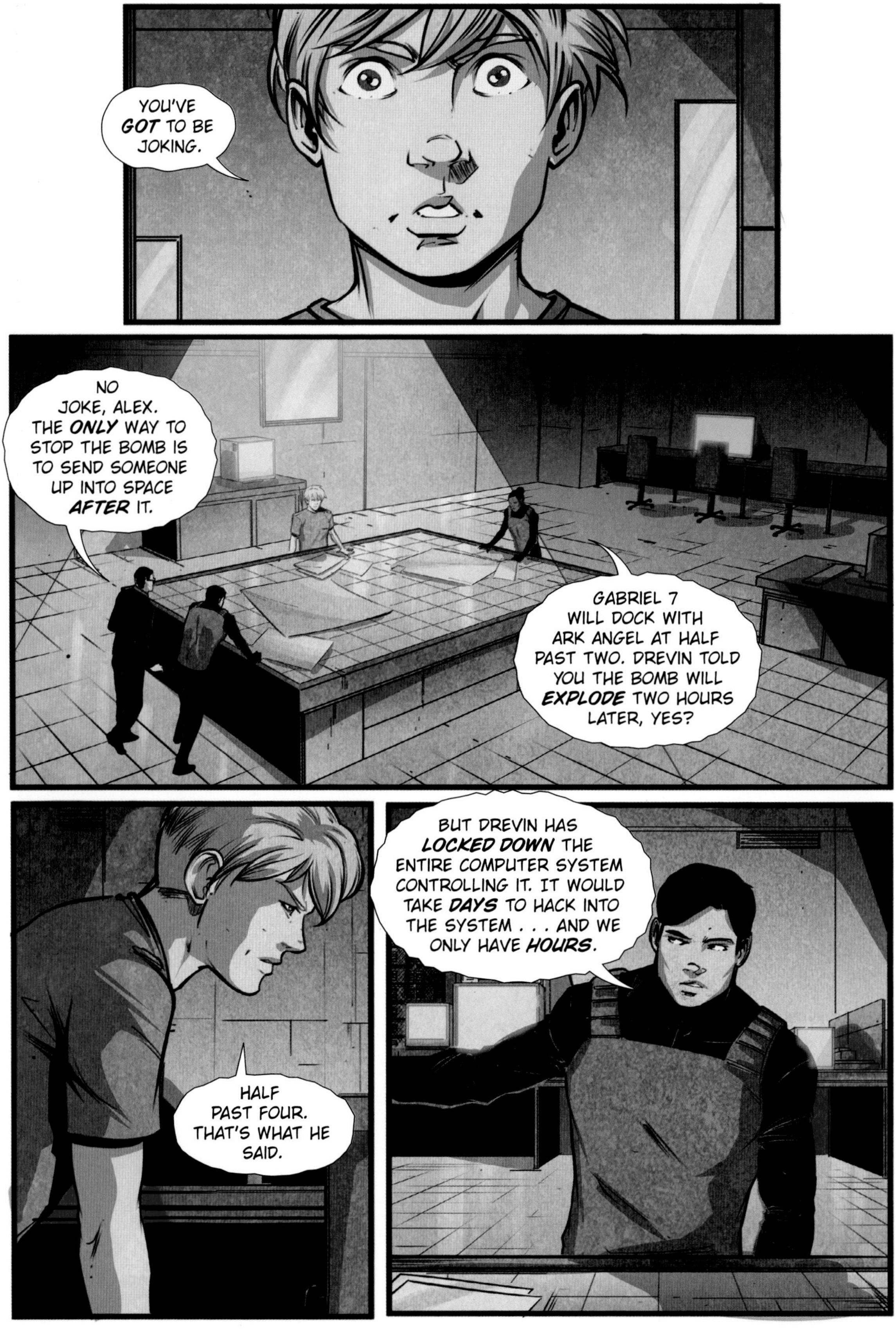
YOU'VE GOT TO BE JOKING.
NO JOKE, ALEX. THE ONLY WAY TO STOP THE BOMB IS TO SEND SOMEONE UP INTO SPACE AFTER IT.
GABRIEL 7 WILL DOCK WITH ARK ANGEL AT HALF PAST TWO. DREVIN TOLD YOU THE BOMB WILL EXPLODE TWO HOURS LATER, YES?
HALF PAST FOUR. THAT'S WHAT HE SAID.
BUT DREVIN HAS LOCKED DOWN THE ENTIRE COMPUTER SYSTEM CONTROLLING IT. IT WOULD TAKE DAYS TO HACK INTO THE SYSTEM . . . AND WE ONLY HAVE HOURS.

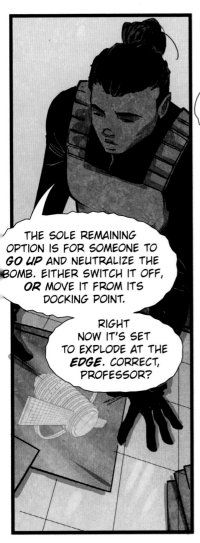

THE SOLE REMAINING OPTION IS FOR SOMEONE TO *GO UP* AND NEUTRALIZE THE BOMB. EITHER SWITCH IT OFF, *OR* MOVE IT FROM ITS DOCKING POINT.

RIGHT NOW IT'S SET TO EXPLODE AT THE *EDGE*. CORRECT, PROFESSOR?

YES! THE VERY EDGE! THAT'S WHAT MR. DREVIN INSISTED.

AN EXPLOSION THERE WILL LEAVE MOST OF ARK ANGEL *INTACT* BUT SEND THE REST *SPINNING* OUT OF ORBIT . . . AND DOWN ON WASHINGTON.

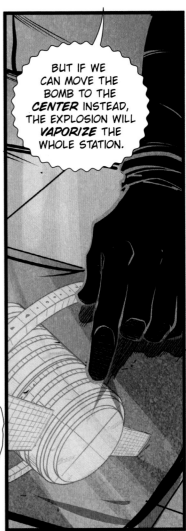

BUT IF WE CAN MOVE THE BOMB TO THE *CENTER* INSTEAD, THE EXPLOSION WILL *VAPORIZE* THE WHOLE STATION.

YOU KEEP SAYING *"WE."* BUT ACTUALLY, YOU MEAN *ME*.

I'M SORRY, ALEX, BUT YOU'RE THE *ONLY* PERSON HERE WHO CAN RIDE THE *SOYUZ-FREGAT* UP TO THE STATION.

IT'S TRUE! WE PLANNED TO PUT **ARTHUR**, THE APE, INTO SPACE. I MADE ALL THE CALCULATIONS **PERSONALLY**.

THOSE CALCULATIONS RELY ON HIS **HEIGHT** AND **WEIGHT**.

YOU'RE **ABOUT** THE SAME SIZE AS ARTHUR—CLOSE ENOUGH TO BE WITHIN THE MARGIN OF ERROR.

THE REST OF US ARE JUST **TOO BIG.**

THIS WHOLE IDEA IS **INSANE.** BUT THERE'S SOMETHING ELSE, SOMETHING ABOUT THE **PROFESSOR**, THAT'S BUGGING ME. HE CLAIMS HE **DIDN'T KNOW** ABOUT THE PLANS . . .

ALEX, **PAY ATTENTION!** THIS IS IMPORTANT STUFF THAT YOU **NEED** TO KNOW!

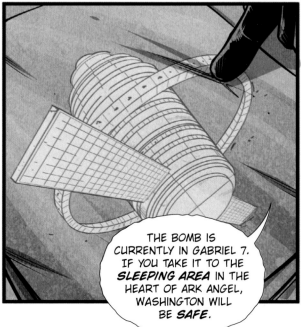

THE BOMB IS CURRENTLY IN GABRIEL 7. IF YOU TAKE IT TO THE **SLEEPING AREA** IN THE HEART OF ARK ANGEL, WASHINGTON WILL BE **SAFE.**

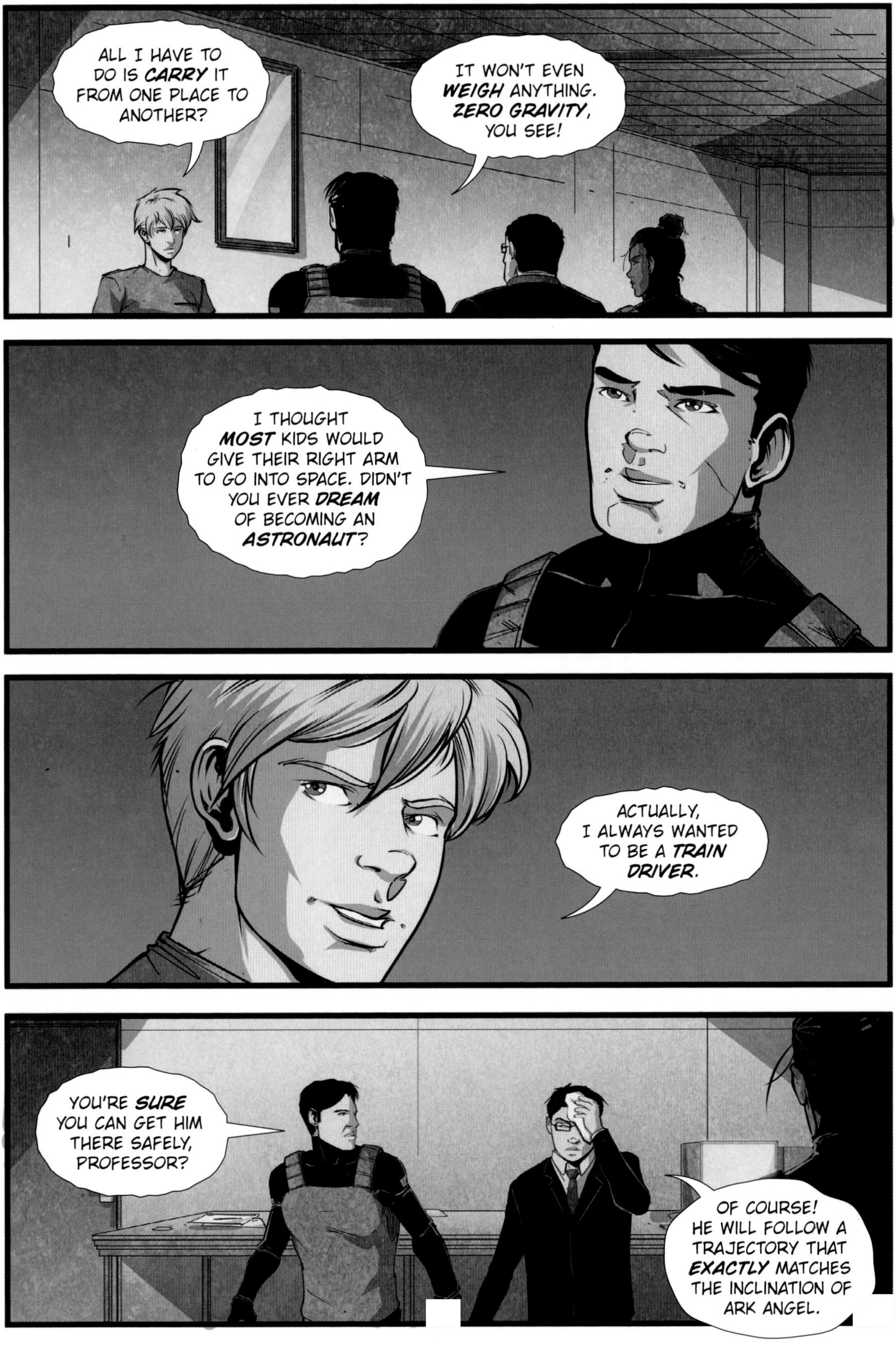
ALL I HAVE TO DO IS CARRY IT FROM ONE PLACE TO ANOTHER?
IT WON'T EVEN WEIGH ANYTHING. ZERO GRAVITY, YOU SEE!
I THOUGHT MOST KIDS WOULD GIVE THEIR RIGHT ARM TO GO INTO SPACE. DIDN'T YOU EVER DREAM OF BECOMING AN ASTRONAUT?
ACTUALLY, I ALWAYS WANTED TO BE A TRAIN DRIVER.
YOU'RE SURE YOU CAN GET HIM THERE SAFELY, PROFESSOR?
OF COURSE! HE WILL FOLLOW A TRAJECTORY THAT EXACTLY MATCHES THE INCLINATION OF ARK ANGEL.

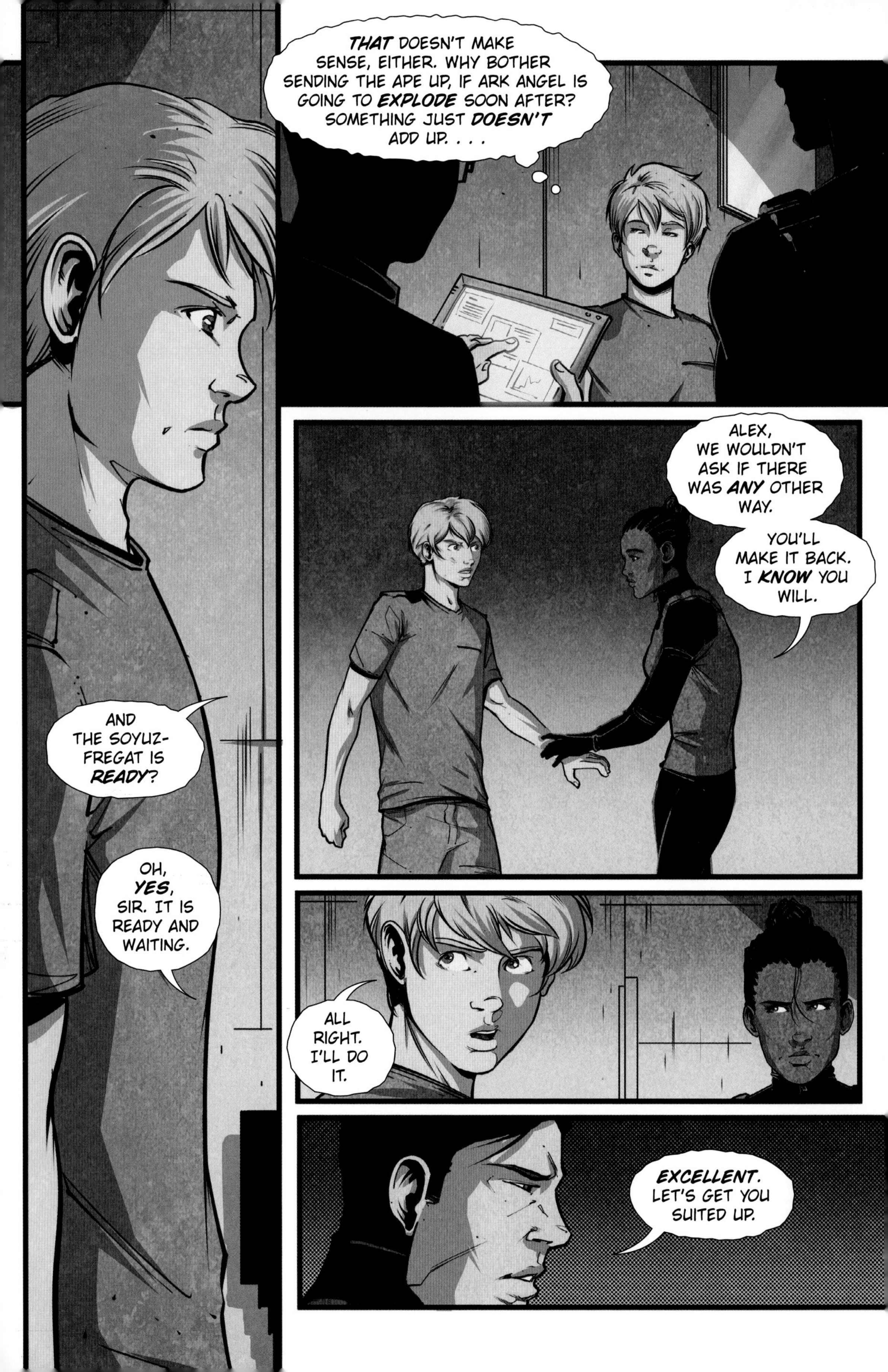
THAT DOESN'T MAKE SENSE, EITHER. WHY BOTHER SENDING THE APE UP, IF ARK ANGEL IS GOING TO EXPLODE SOON AFTER? SOMETHING JUST DOESN'T ADD UP. . . .
AND THE SOYUZ-FREGAT IS READY?
OH, YES, SIR. IT IS READY AND WAITING.
ALEX, WE WOULDN'T ASK IF THERE WAS ANY OTHER WAY.
YOU'LL MAKE IT BACK. I KNOW YOU WILL.
ALL RIGHT. I'LL DO IT.
EXCELLENT. LET'S GET YOU SUITED UP.

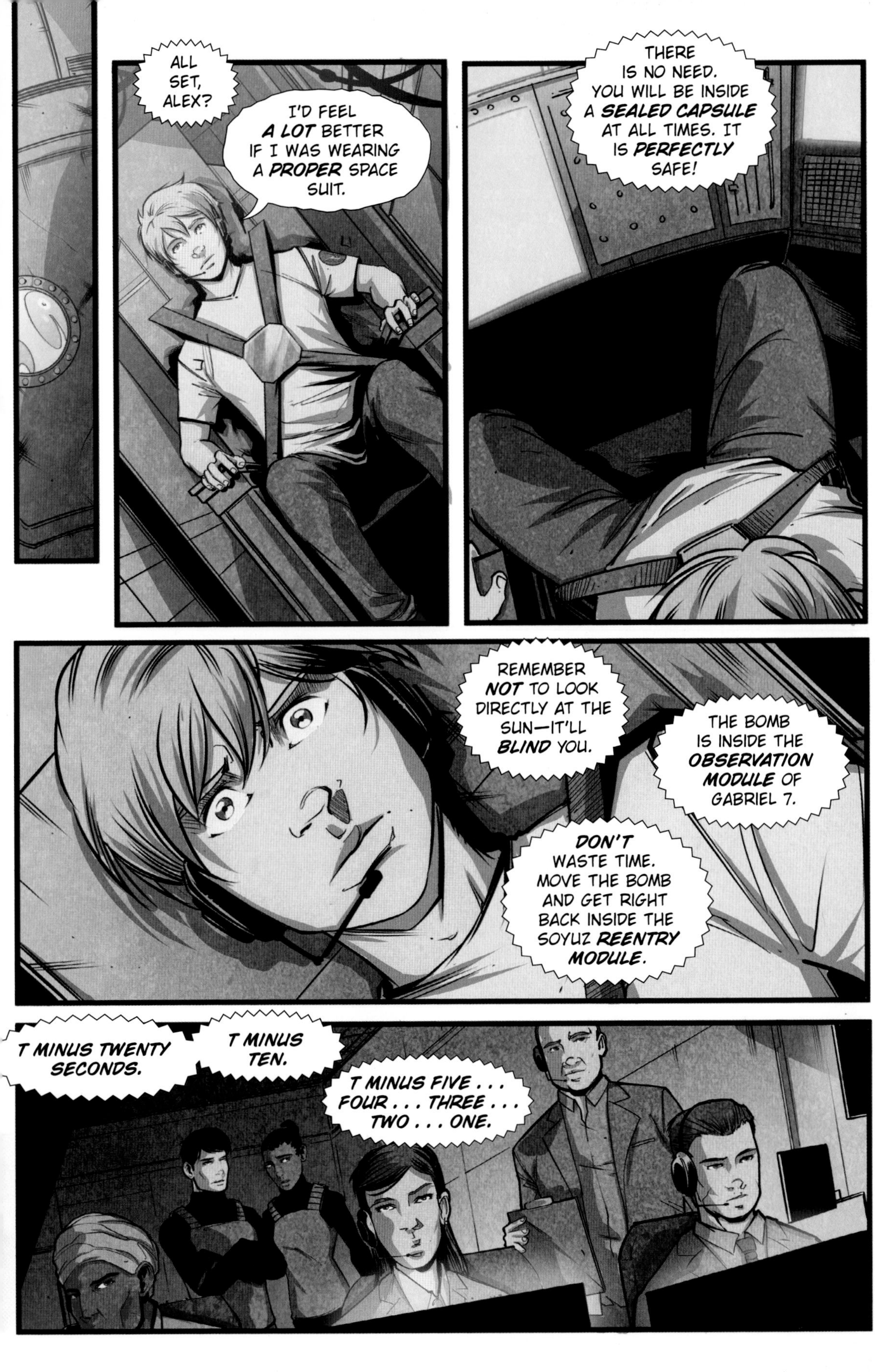
ALL SET, ALEX?
I'D FEEL A LOT BETTER IF I WAS WEARING A PROPER SPACE SUIT.
THERE IS NO NEED. YOU WILL BE INSIDE A SEALED CAPSULE AT ALL TIMES. IT IS PERFECTLY SAFE!
REMEMBER NOT TO LOOK DIRECTLY AT THE SUN—IT'LL BLIND YOU.
THE BOMB IS INSIDE THE OBSERVATION MODULE OF GABRIEL 7.
DON'T WASTE TIME. MOVE THE BOMB AND GET RIGHT BACK INSIDE THE SOYUZ REENTRY MODULE.
T MINUS TWENTY SECONDS.
T MINUS TEN.
T MINUS FIVE . . . FOUR . . . THREE . . . TWO . . . ONE.

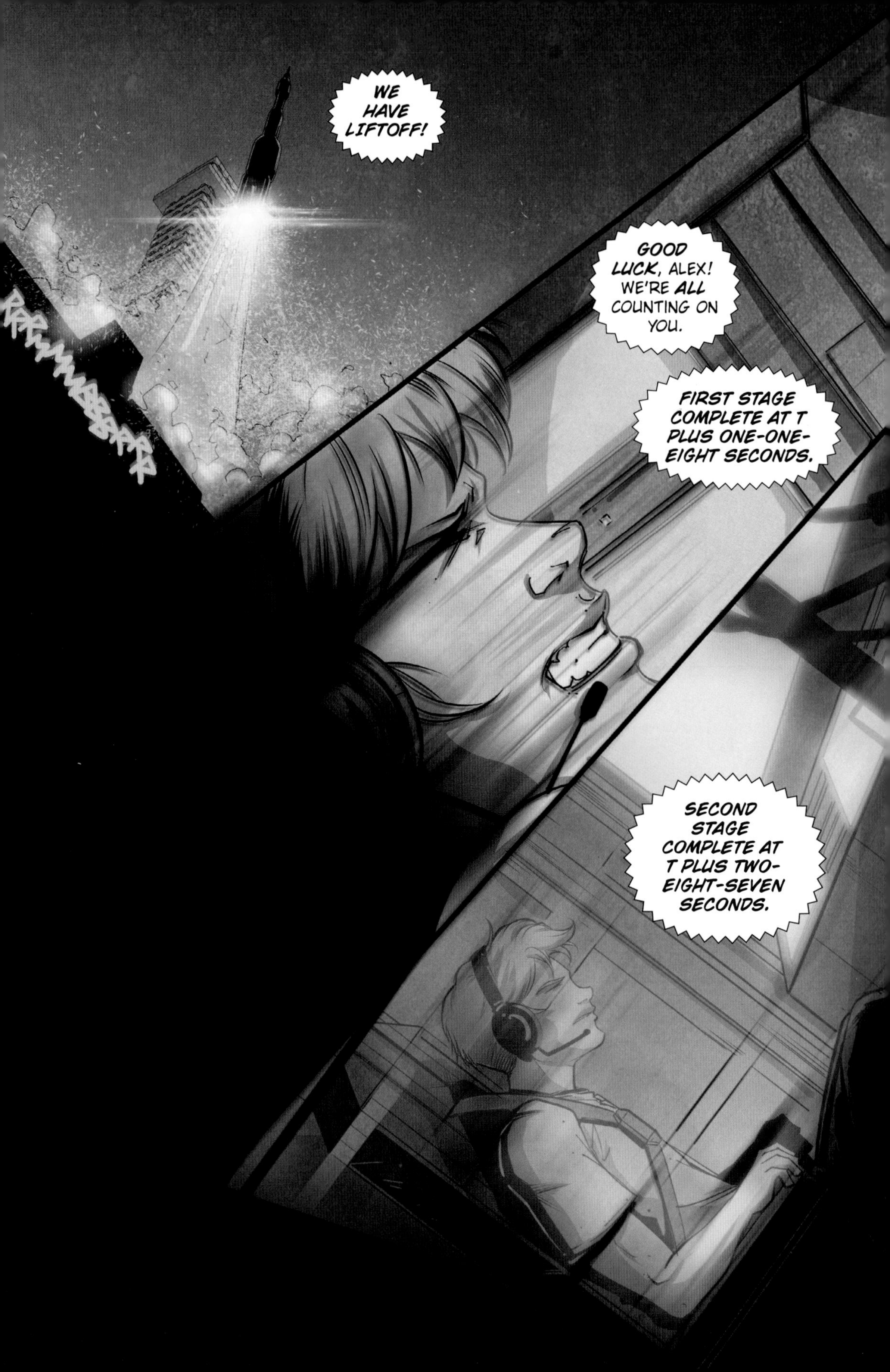
RRRMMBBRRR
WE HAVE LIFTOFF!
GOOD LUCK, ALEX! WE'RE ALL COUNTING ON YOU.
FIRST STAGE COMPLETE AT T PLUS ONE-ONE-EIGHT SECONDS.
SECOND STAGE COMPLETE AT T PLUS TWO-EIGHT-SEVEN SECONDS.

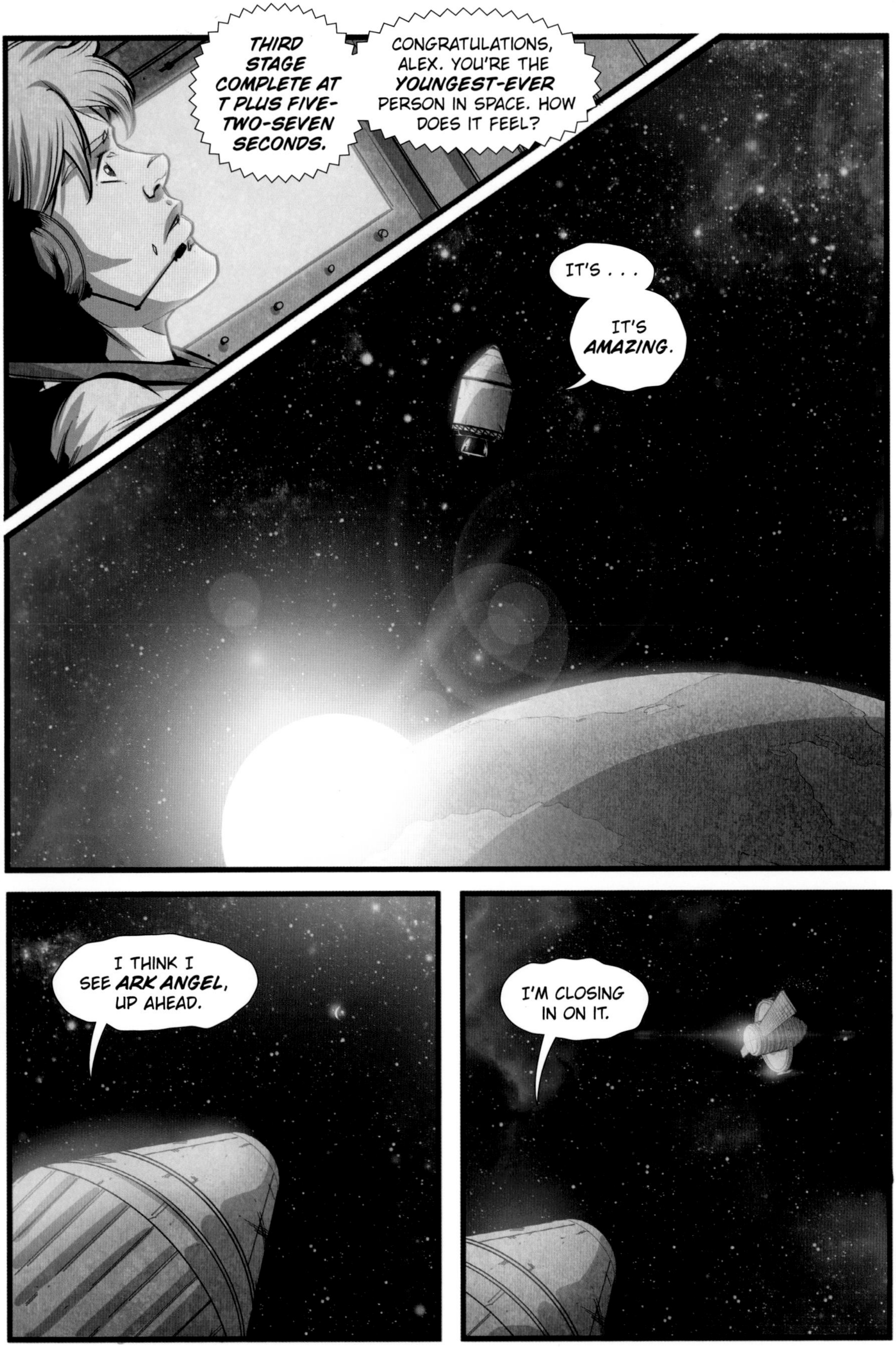
THIRD STAGE COMPLETE AT T PLUS FIVE-TWO-SEVEN SECONDS.
CONGRATULATIONS, ALEX. YOU'RE THE YOUNGEST-EVER PERSON IN SPACE. HOW DOES IT FEEL?
IT'S . . .
IT'S AMAZING.
I THINK I SEE ARK ANGEL, UP AHEAD.
I'M CLOSING IN ON IT.

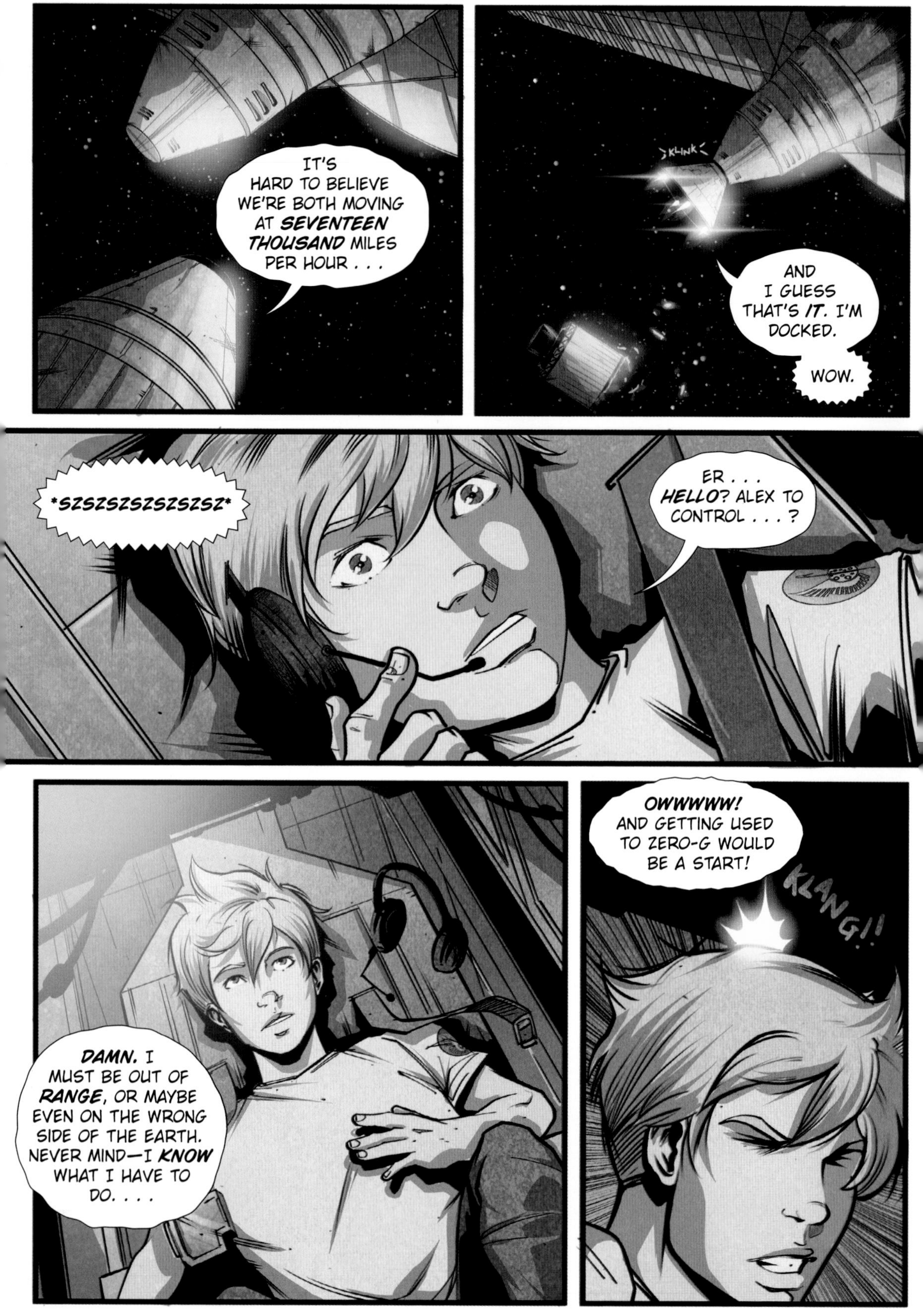
IT'S HARD TO BELIEVE WE'RE BOTH MOVING AT **SEVENTEEN THOUSAND** MILES PER HOUR . . .
KLINK
AND I GUESS THAT'S *IT*. I'M DOCKED.
WOW.
SZSZSZSZSZSZSZ
ER . . . ***HELLO***? ALEX TO CONTROL . . . ?
DAMN. I MUST BE OUT OF **RANGE**, OR MAYBE EVEN ON THE WRONG SIDE OF THE EARTH. NEVER MIND—I ***KNOW*** WHAT I HAVE TO DO. . . .
OWWWWW! AND GETTING USED TO ZERO-G WOULD BE A START!
KLANG!!

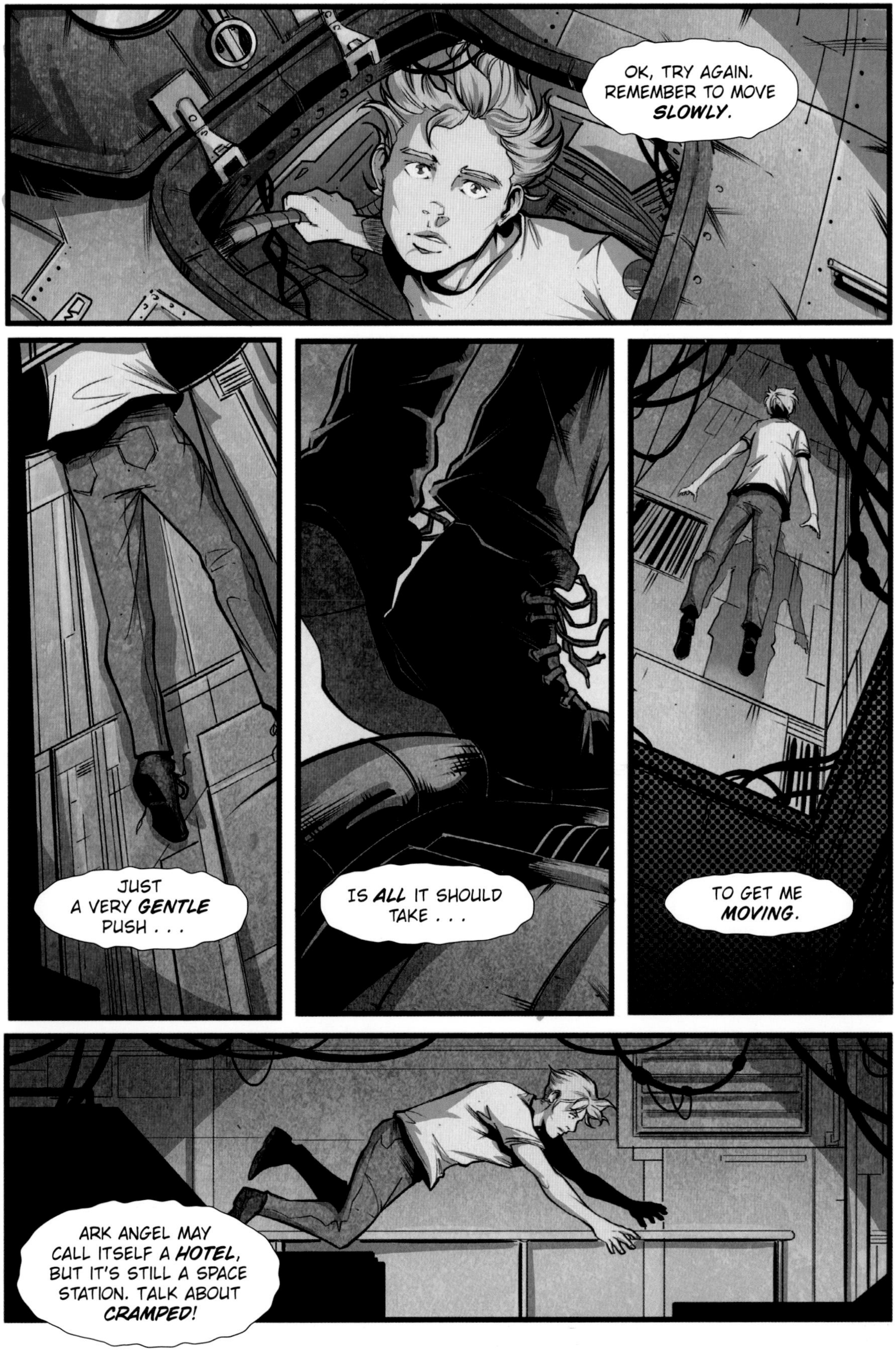
OK, TRY AGAIN. REMEMBER TO MOVE SLOWLY.
JUST A VERY GENTLE PUSH . . .
IS ALL IT SHOULD TAKE . . .
TO GET ME MOVING.
ARK ANGEL MAY CALL ITSELF A HOTEL, BUT IT'S STILL A SPACE STATION. TALK ABOUT CRAMPED!

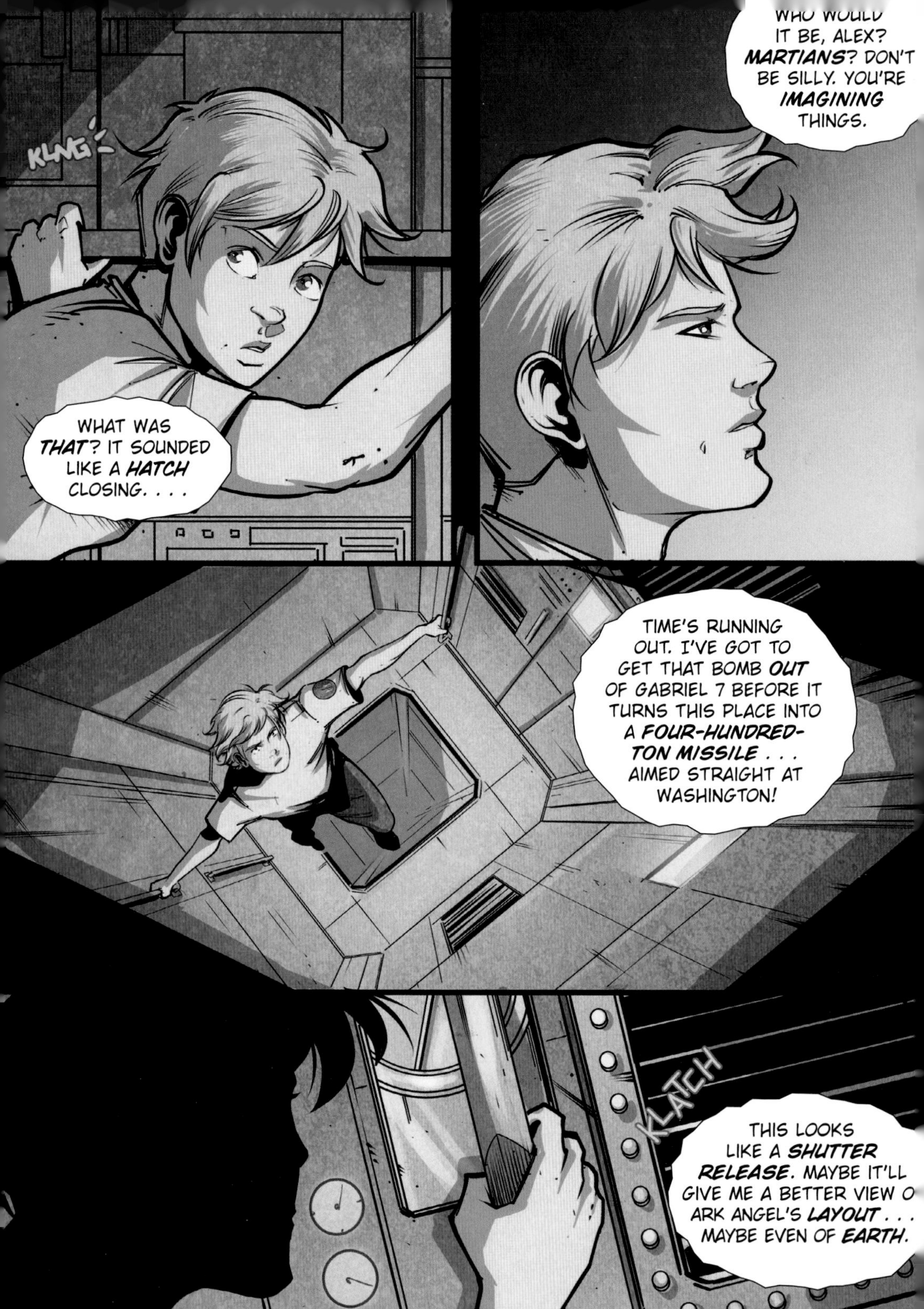
KLNG
WHAT WAS THAT? IT SOUNDED LIKE A HATCH CLOSING. . . .
WHO WOULD IT BE, ALEX? MARTIANS? DON'T BE SILLY. YOU'RE IMAGINING THINGS.
TIME'S RUNNING OUT. I'VE GOT TO GET THAT BOMB OUT OF GABRIEL 7 BEFORE IT TURNS THIS PLACE INTO A FOUR-HUNDRED-TON MISSILE . . . AIMED STRAIGHT AT WASHINGTON!
KLATCH
THIS LOOKS LIKE A SHUTTER RELEASE. MAYBE IT'LL GIVE ME A BETTER VIEW O ARK ANGEL'S LAYOUT . . . MAYBE EVEN OF EARTH.

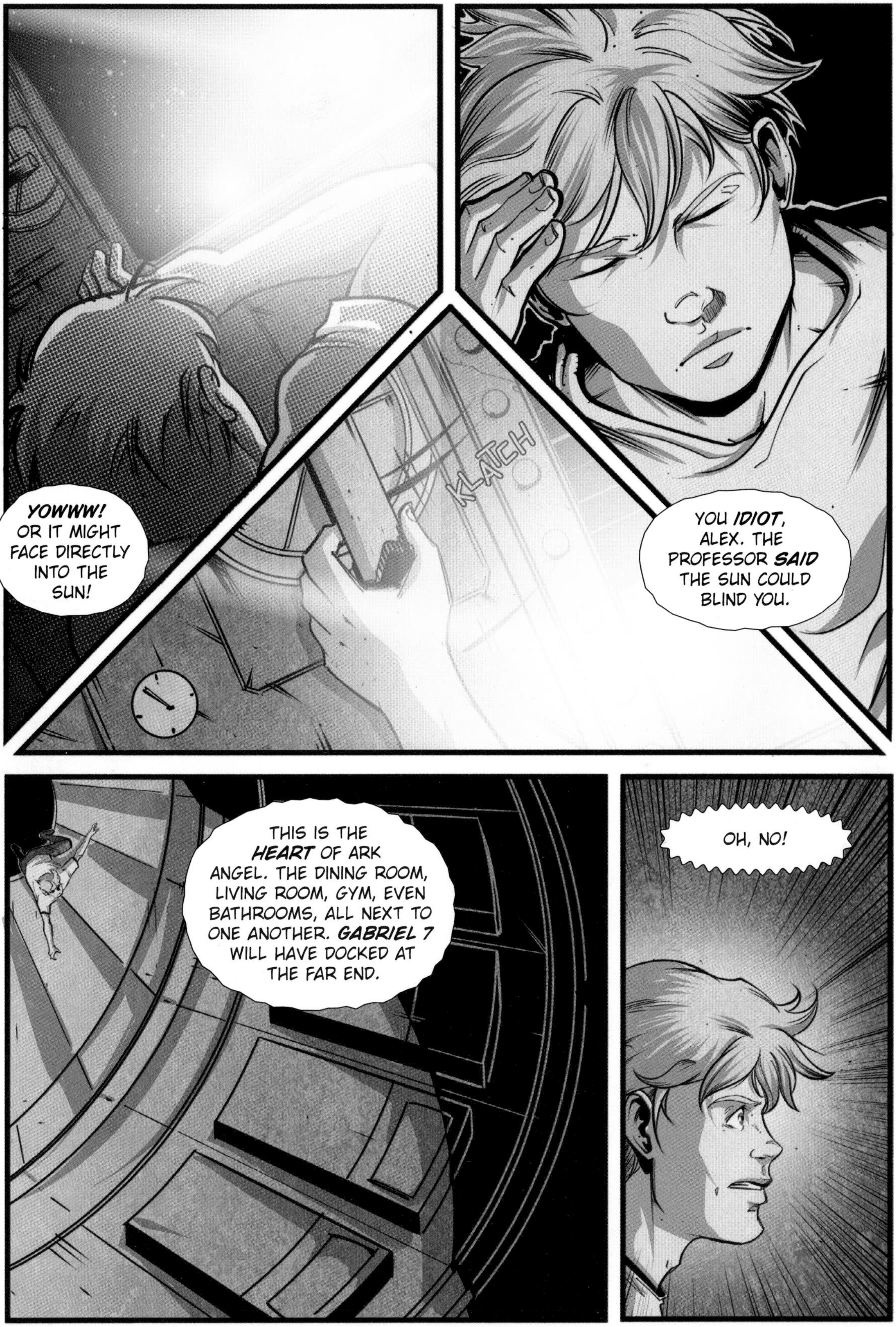
YOWWW! OR IT MIGHT FACE DIRECTLY INTO THE SUN!
KLATCH
YOU IDIOT, ALEX. THE PROFESSOR SAID THE SUN COULD BLIND YOU.
THIS IS THE HEART OF ARK ANGEL. THE DINING ROOM, LIVING ROOM, GYM, EVEN BATHROOMS, ALL NEXT TO ONE ANOTHER. GABRIEL 7 WILL HAVE DOCKED AT THE FAR END.
OH, NO!

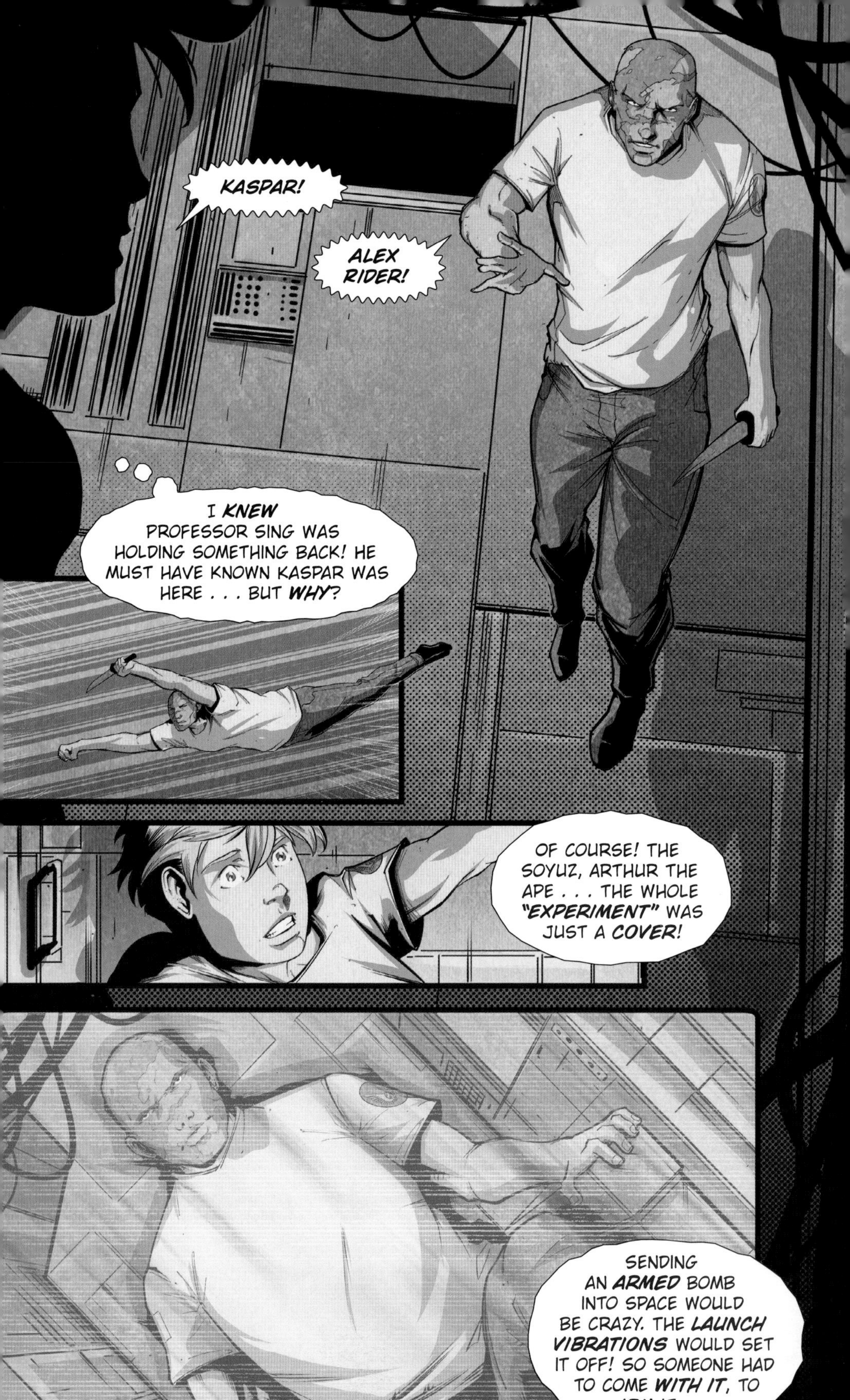
KASPAR!
ALEX RIDER!
I KNEW PROFESSOR SING WAS HOLDING SOMETHING BACK! HE MUST HAVE KNOWN KASPAR WAS HERE . . . BUT WHY?
OF COURSE! THE SOYUZ, ARTHUR THE APE . . . THE WHOLE "EXPERIMENT" WAS JUST A COVER!
SENDING AN ARMED BOMB INTO SPACE WOULD BE CRAZY. THE LAUNCH VIBRATIONS WOULD SET IT OFF! SO SOMEONE HAD TO COME WITH IT, TO

AND THEN PROFESSOR SING WOULD SEND THE SOYUZ UP TO **COLLECT** HIM. NO WONDER SING LOOKED **NERVOUS**! I BET THERE WERE ORDERS TO **KILL** HIM IF HE DIDN'T SEND THE ROCKET.

BUT NOW THERE ARE **TWO** OF US, AND ONLY ONE SEAT BACK DOWN. IT'S ME OR HIM . . . AND KASPAR LOOKS A **LOT** MORE COMFORTABLE IN ZERO-G THAN ME!

ONLY **ONE** CHANCE TO GET THIS MOVE RIGHT!

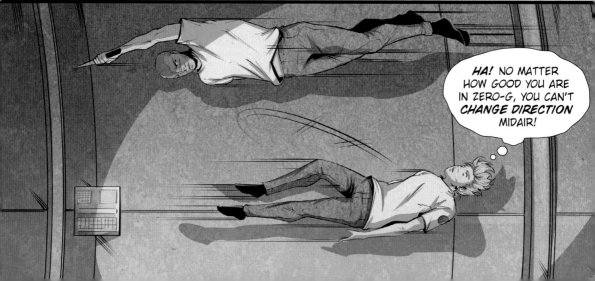

HA! NO MATTER HOW GOOD YOU ARE IN ZERO-G, YOU CAN'T **CHANGE DIRECTION** MIDAIR!

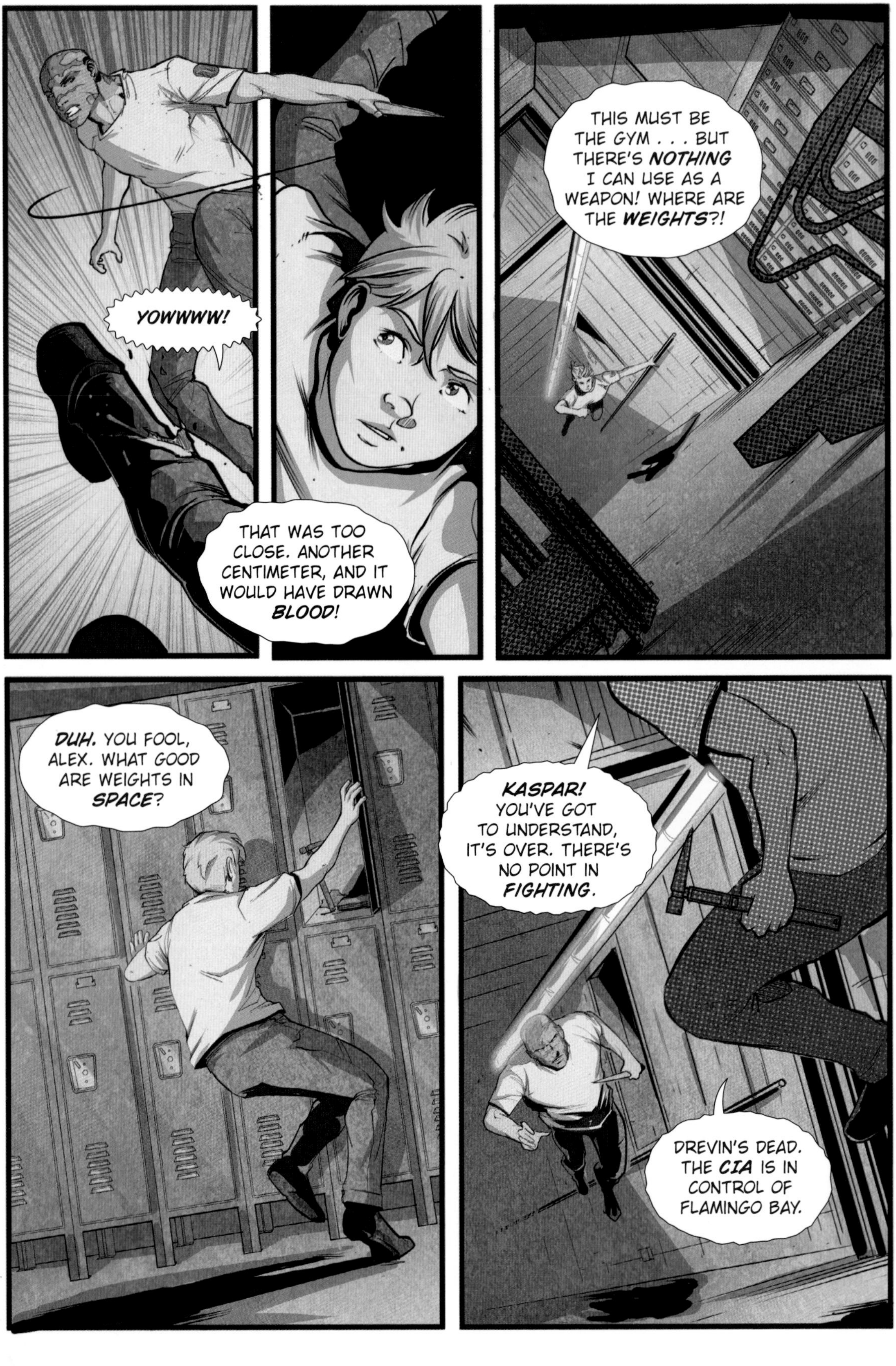
YOWWWW!
THAT WAS TOO CLOSE. ANOTHER CENTIMETER, AND IT WOULD HAVE DRAWN BLOOD!
THIS MUST BE THE GYM . . . BUT THERE'S NOTHING I CAN USE AS A WEAPON! WHERE ARE THE WEIGHTS?!
DUH. YOU FOOL, ALEX. WHAT GOOD ARE WEIGHTS IN SPACE?
KASPAR! YOU'VE GOT TO UNDERSTAND, IT'S OVER. THERE'S NO POINT IN FIGHTING.
DREVIN'S DEAD. THE CIA IS IN CONTROL OF FLAMINGO BAY.

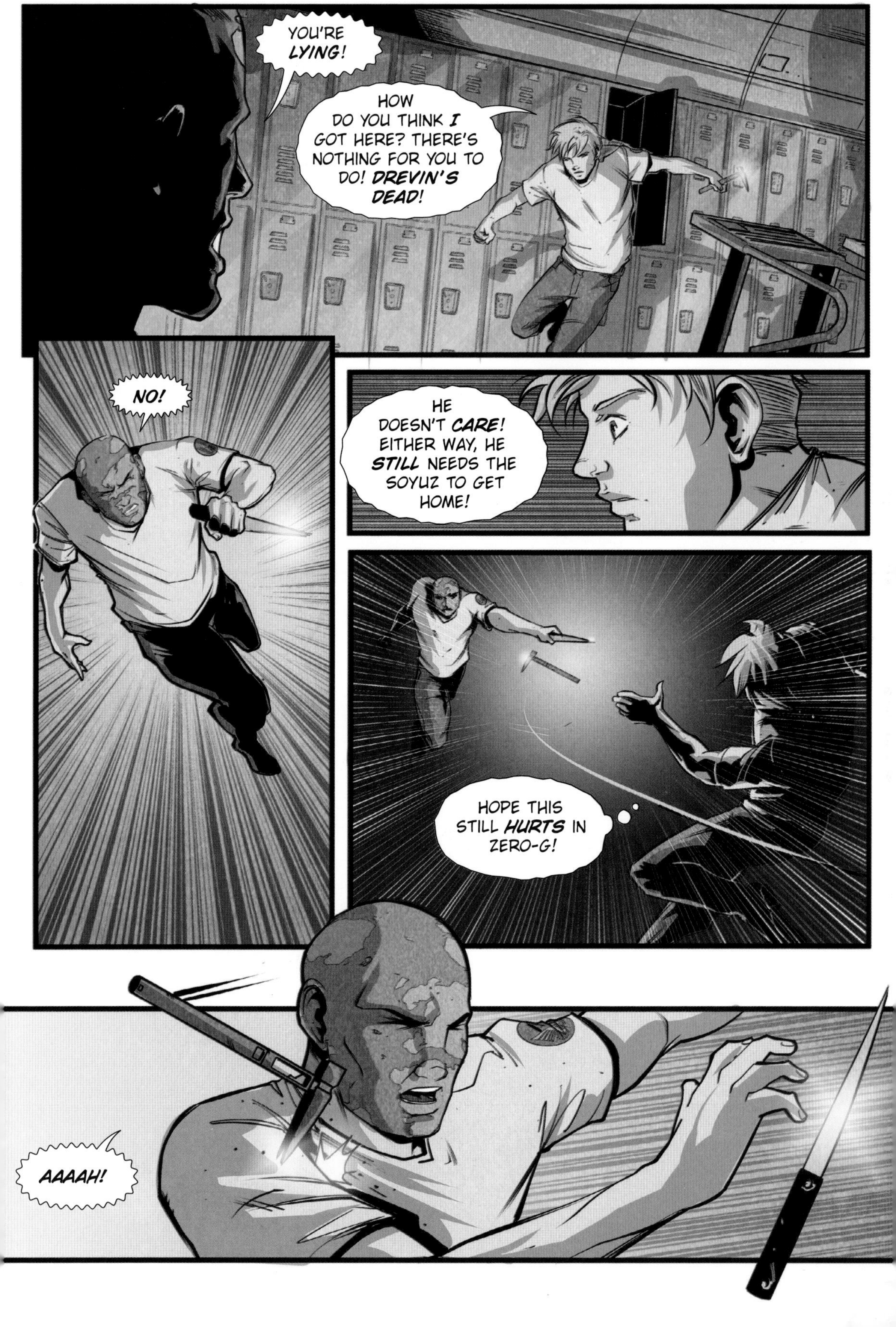
YOU'RE LYING!
HOW DO YOU THINK I GOT HERE? THERE'S NOTHING FOR YOU TO DO! DREVIN'S DEAD!
NO!
HE DOESN'T CARE! EITHER WAY, HE STILL NEEDS THE SOYUZ TO GET HOME!
HOPE THIS STILL HURTS IN ZERO-G!
AAAAH!

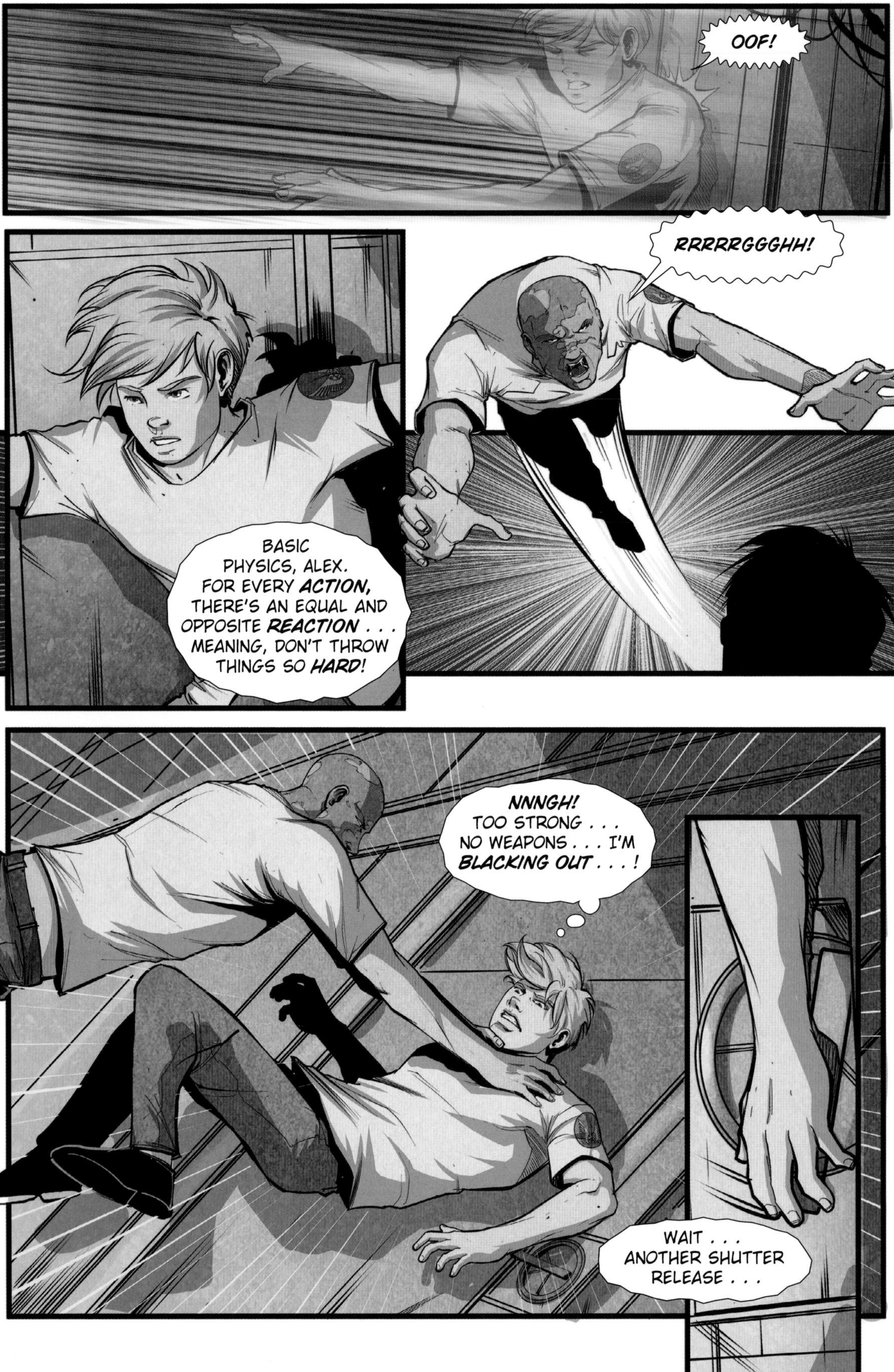
OOF!
RRRRRGGGHH!
BASIC PHYSICS, ALEX. FOR EVERY ACTION, THERE'S AN EQUAL AND OPPOSITE REACTION . . . MEANING, DON'T THROW THINGS SO HARD!
NNNGH! TOO STRONG . . . NO WEAPONS . . . I'M BLACKING OUT . . . !
WAIT . . . ANOTHER SHUTTER RELEASE . . .

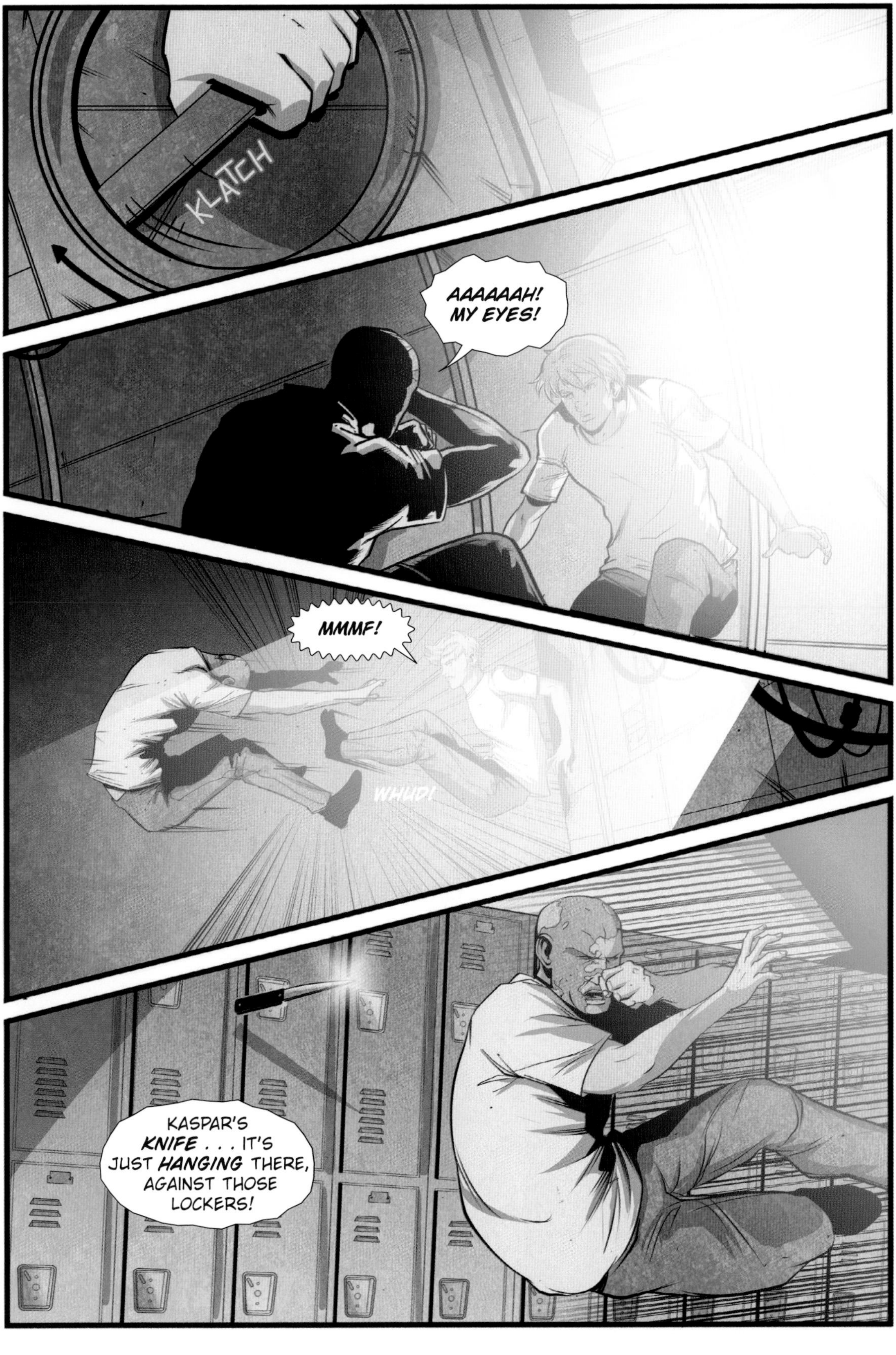
KLATCH
AAAAAAH! MY EYES!
MMMF!
WHUD!
KASPAR'S KNIFE . . . IT'S JUST HANGING THERE, AGAINST THOSE LOCKERS!

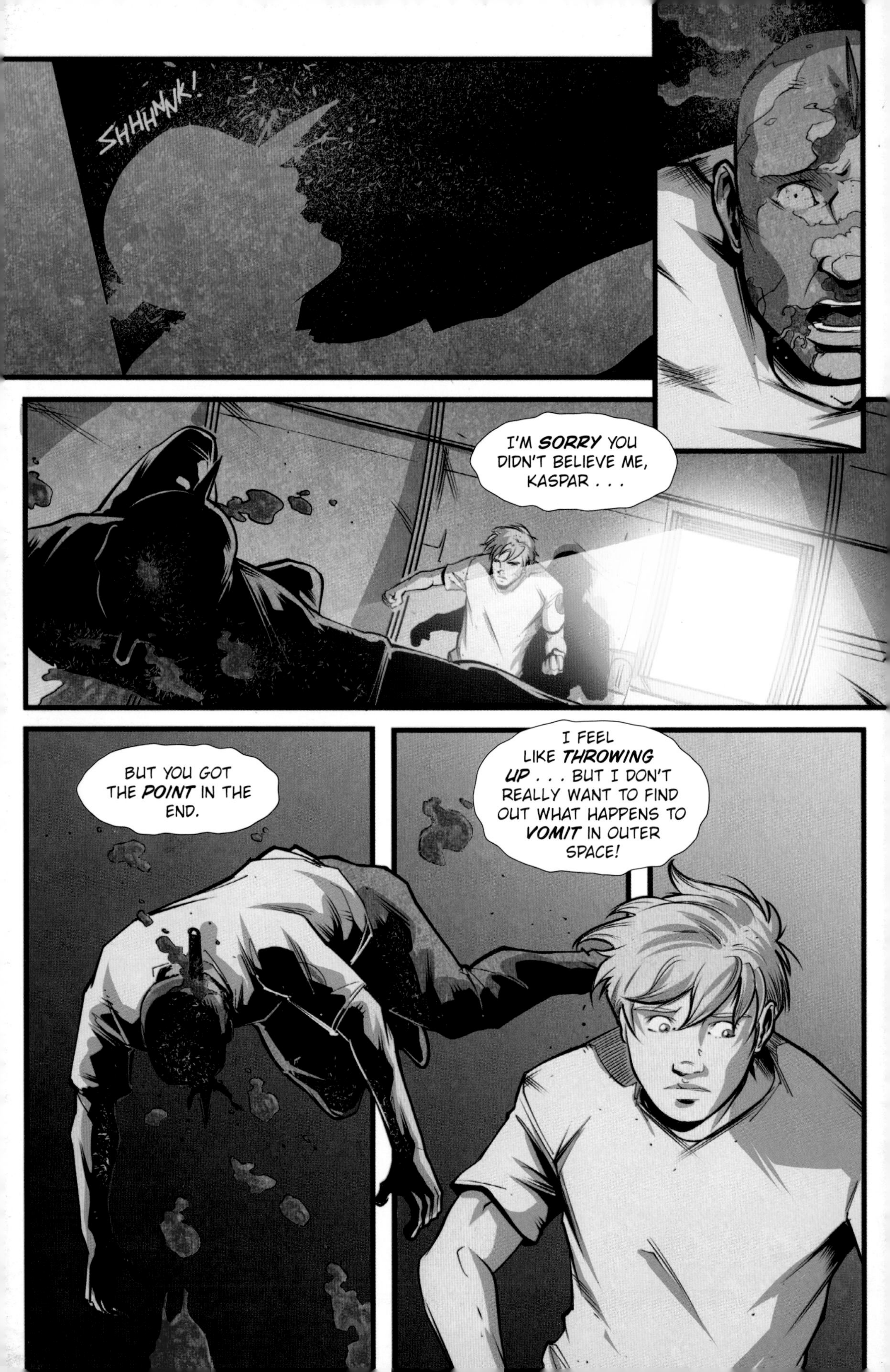
SHHHNNK!
I'M SORRY YOU DIDN'T BELIEVE ME, KASPAR . . .
BUT YOU GOT THE POINT IN THE END.
I FEEL LIKE THROWING UP . . . BUT I DON'T REALLY WANT TO FIND OUT WHAT HAPPENS TO VOMIT IN OUTER SPACE!

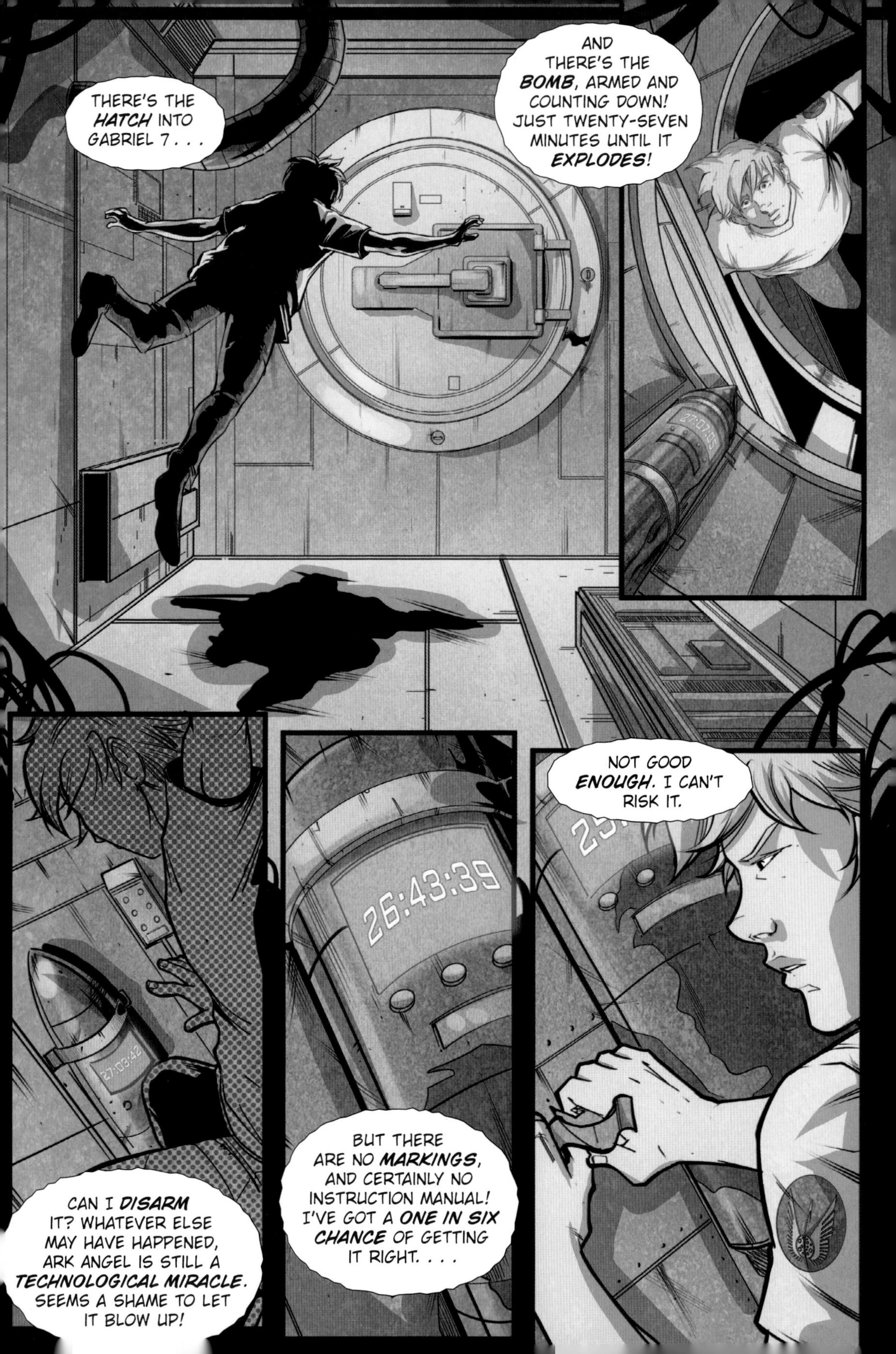
THERE'S THE HATCH INTO GABRIEL 7 . . .
AND THERE'S THE BOMB, ARMED AND COUNTING DOWN! JUST TWENTY-SEVEN MINUTES UNTIL IT EXPLODES!
CAN I DISARM IT? WHATEVER ELSE MAY HAVE HAPPENED, ARK ANGEL IS STILL A TECHNOLOGICAL MIRACLE. SEEMS A SHAME TO LET IT BLOW UP!
26:43:39
BUT THERE ARE NO MARKINGS, AND CERTAINLY NO INSTRUCTION MANUAL! I'VE GOT A ONE IN SIX CHANCE OF GETTING IT RIGHT. . . .
NOT GOOD ENOUGH. I CAN'T RISK IT.

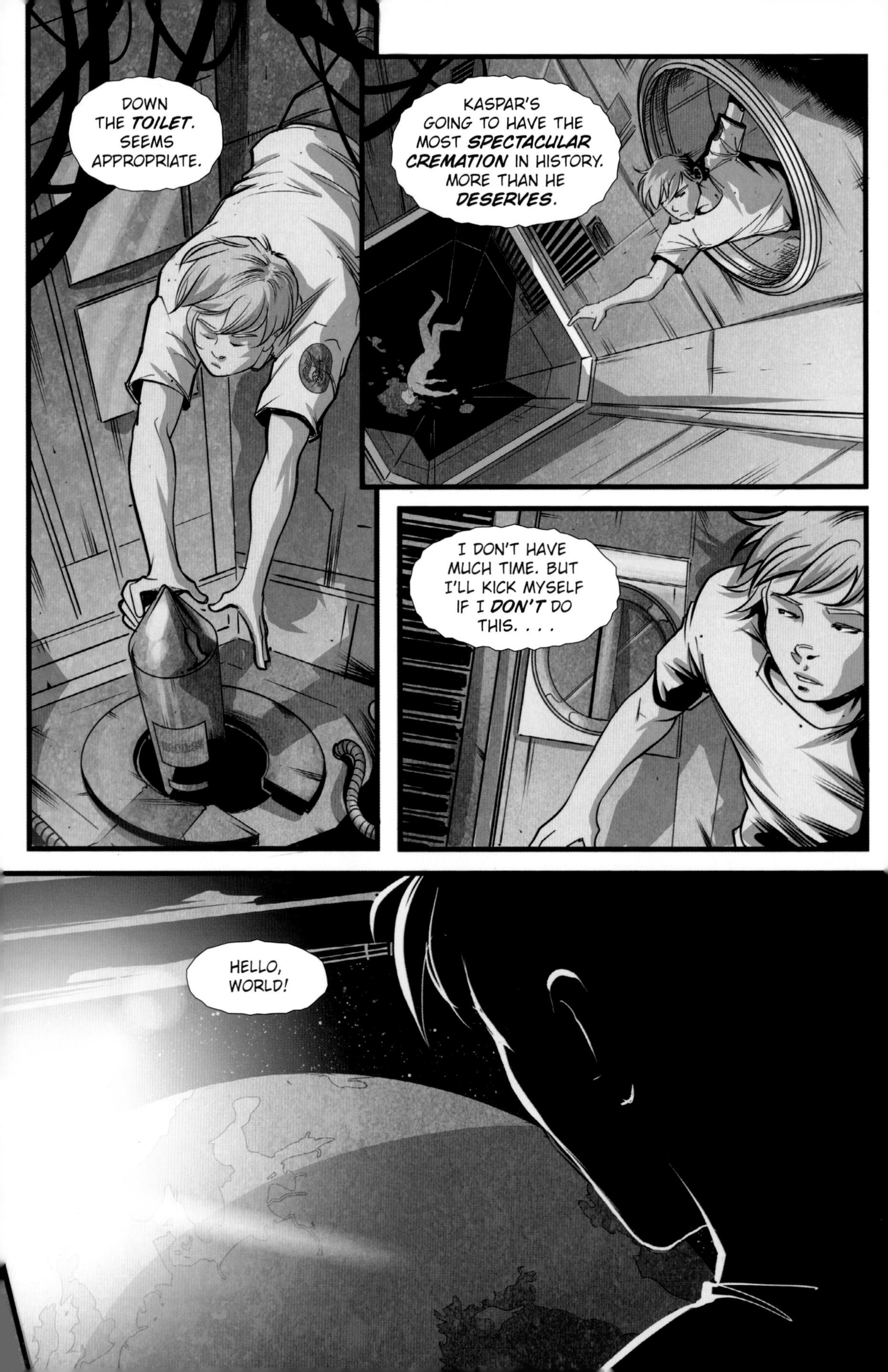
DOWN THE *TOILET*. SEEMS APPROPRIATE.
KASPAR'S GOING TO HAVE THE MOST ***SPECTACULAR CREMATION*** IN HISTORY. MORE THAN HE ***DESERVES***.
I DON'T HAVE MUCH TIME. BUT I'LL KICK MYSELF IF I ***DON'T*** DO THIS. . . .
HELLO, WORLD!

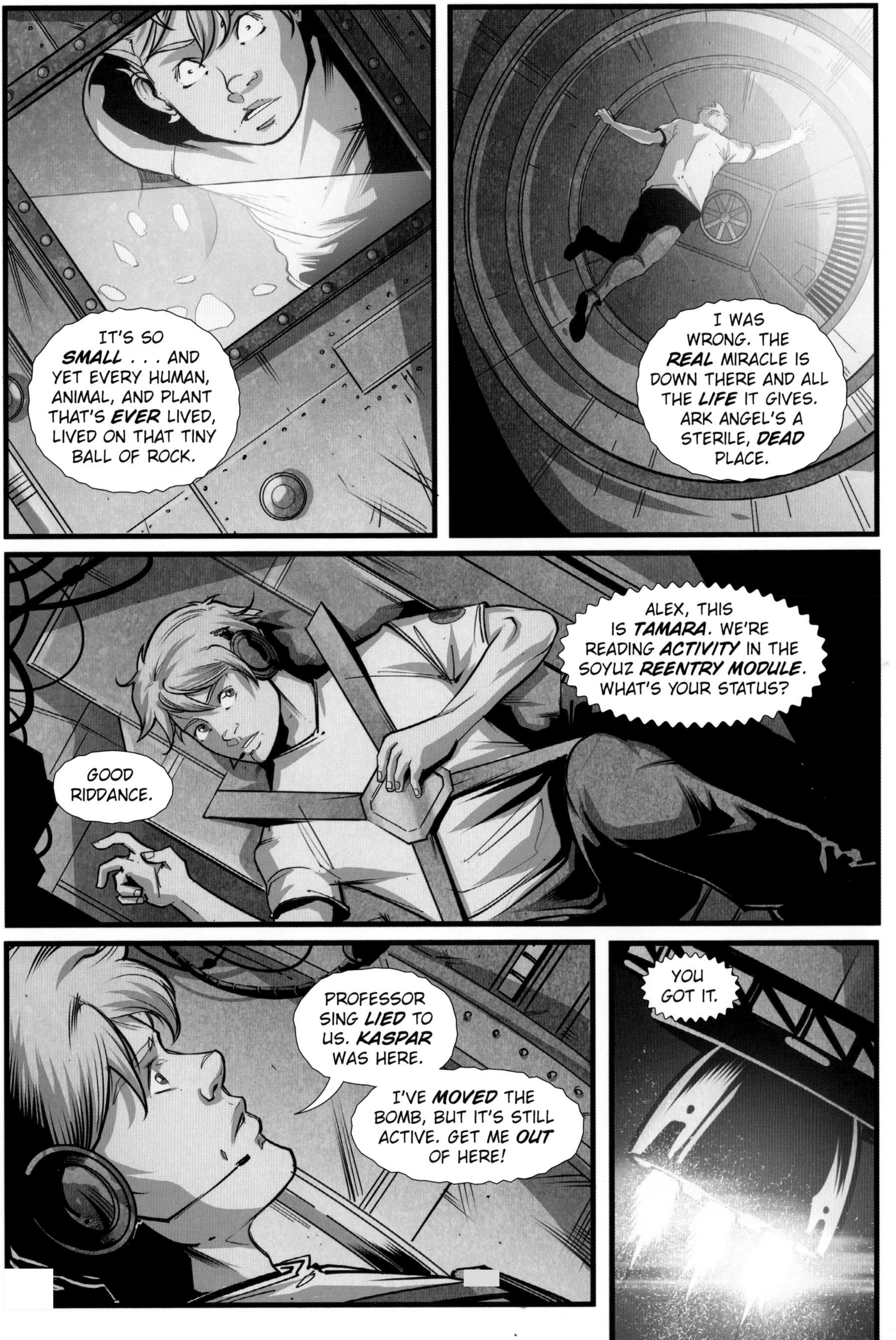
IT'S SO SMALL . . . AND YET EVERY HUMAN, ANIMAL, AND PLANT THAT'S EVER LIVED, LIVED ON THAT TINY BALL OF ROCK.
I WAS WRONG. THE REAL MIRACLE IS DOWN THERE AND ALL THE LIFE IT GIVES. ARK ANGEL'S A STERILE, DEAD PLACE.
ALEX, THIS IS TAMARA. WE'RE READING ACTIVITY IN THE SOYUZ REENTRY MODULE. WHAT'S YOUR STATUS?
GOOD RIDDANCE.
PROFESSOR SING LIED TO US. KASPAR WAS HERE.
I'VE MOVED THE BOMB, BUT IT'S STILL ACTIVE. GET ME OUT OF HERE!
YOU GOT IT.

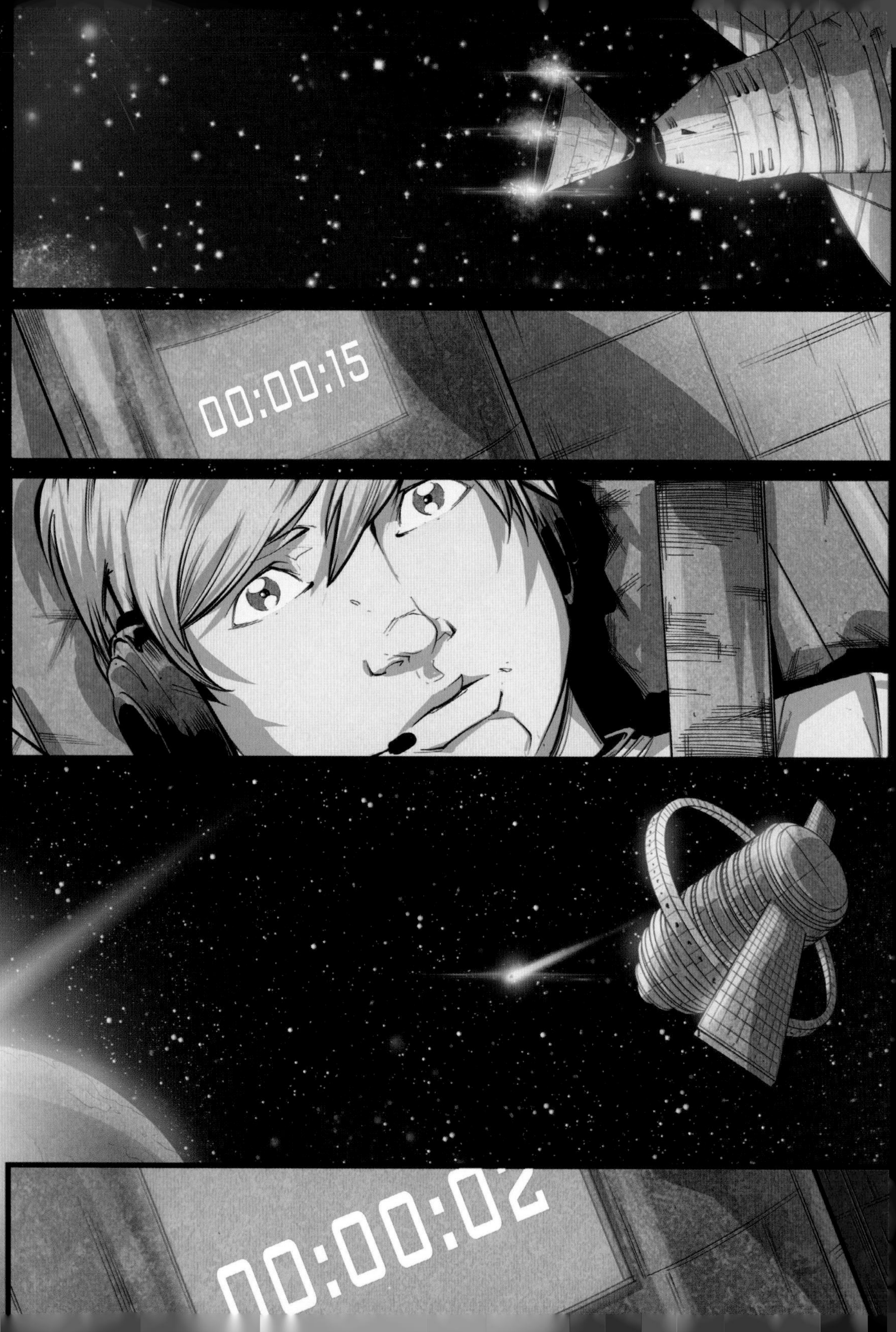

00:00:15
00:00:02

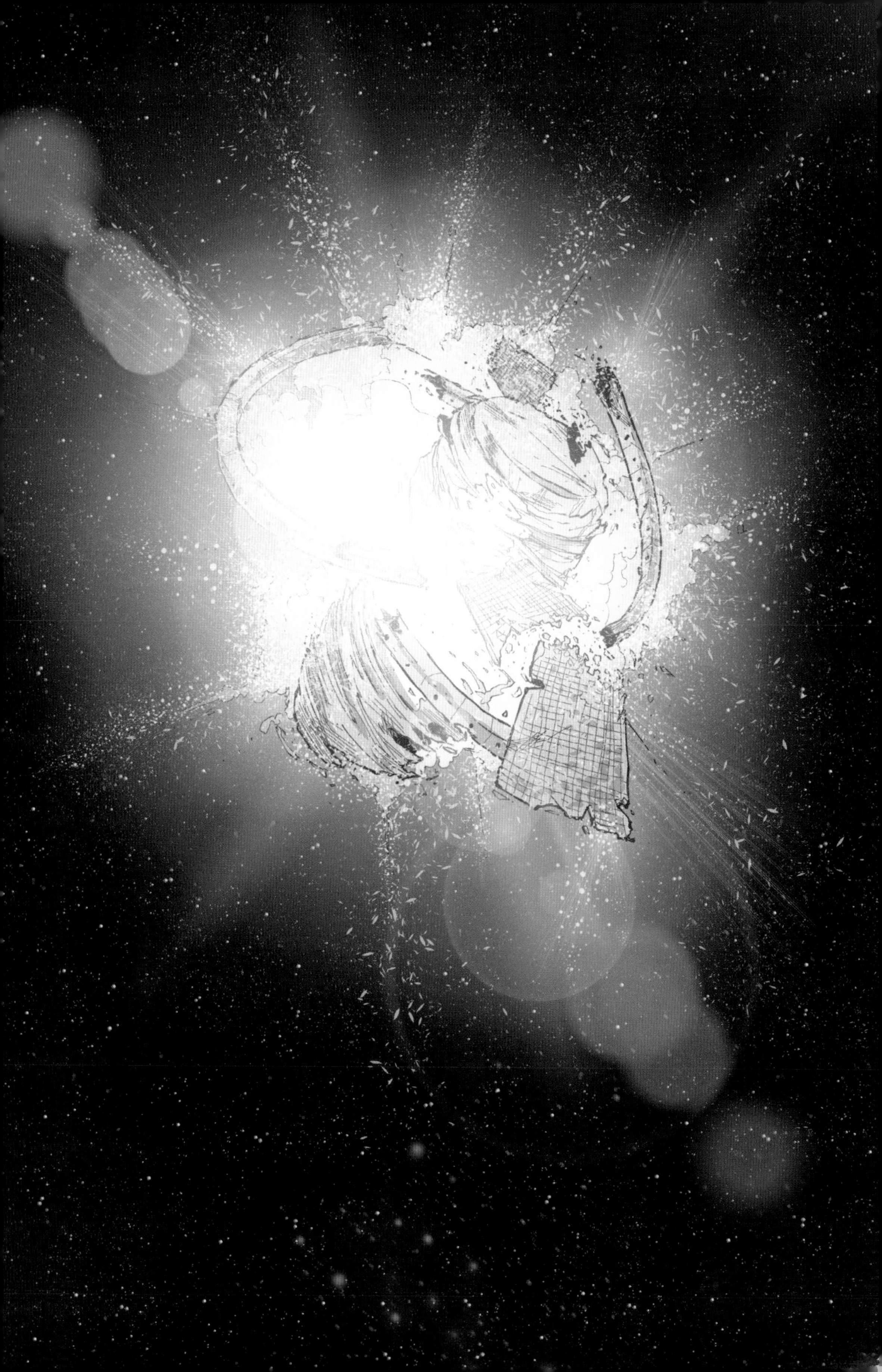

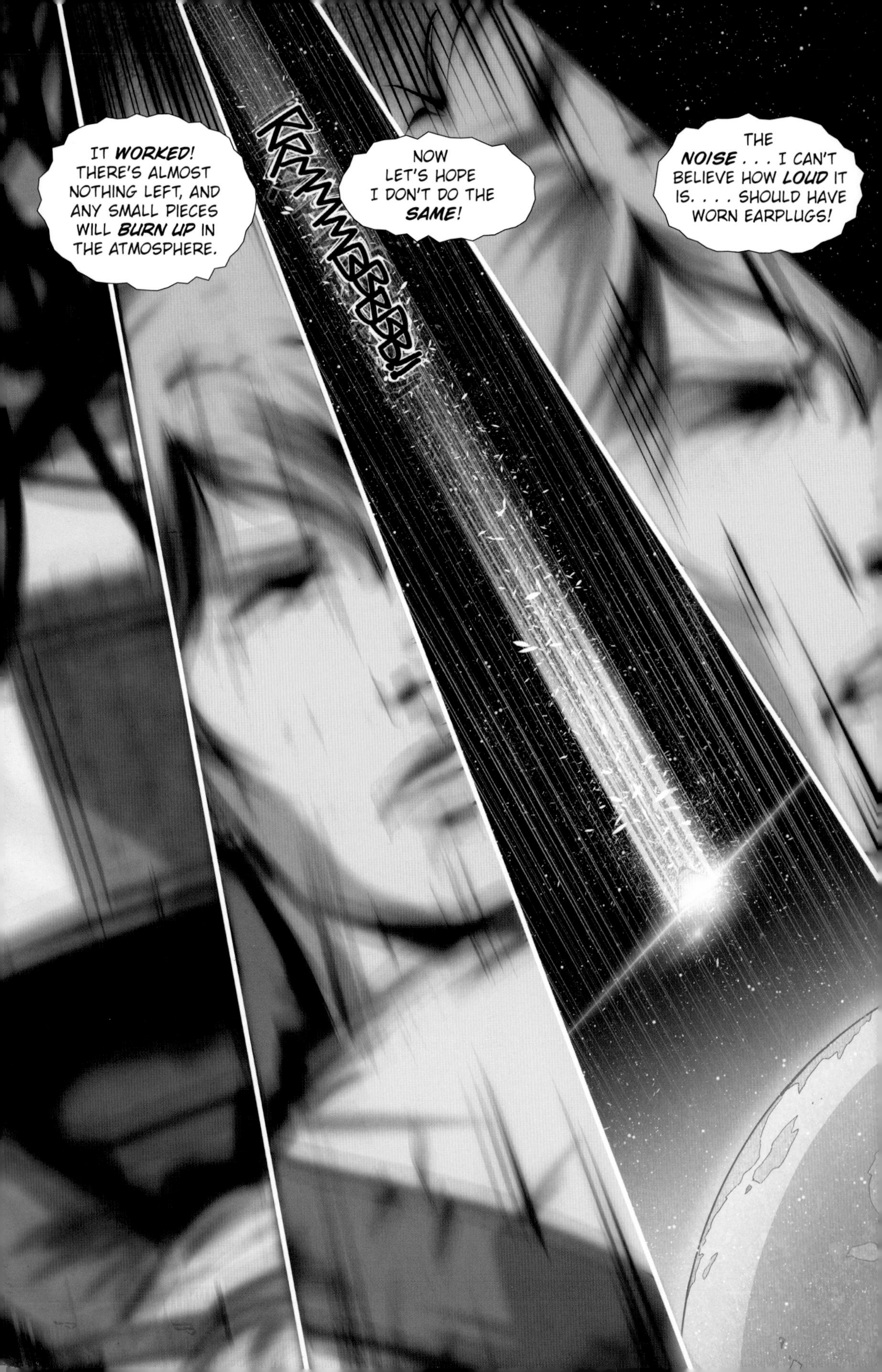
IT WORKED! THERE'S ALMOST NOTHING LEFT, AND ANY SMALL PIECES WILL BURN UP IN THE ATMOSPHERE.
KRMMMBBBB!
NOW LET'S HOPE I DON'T DO THE SAME!
THE NOISE . . . I CAN'T BELIEVE HOW LOUD IT IS. . . . SHOULD HAVE WORN EARPLUGS!

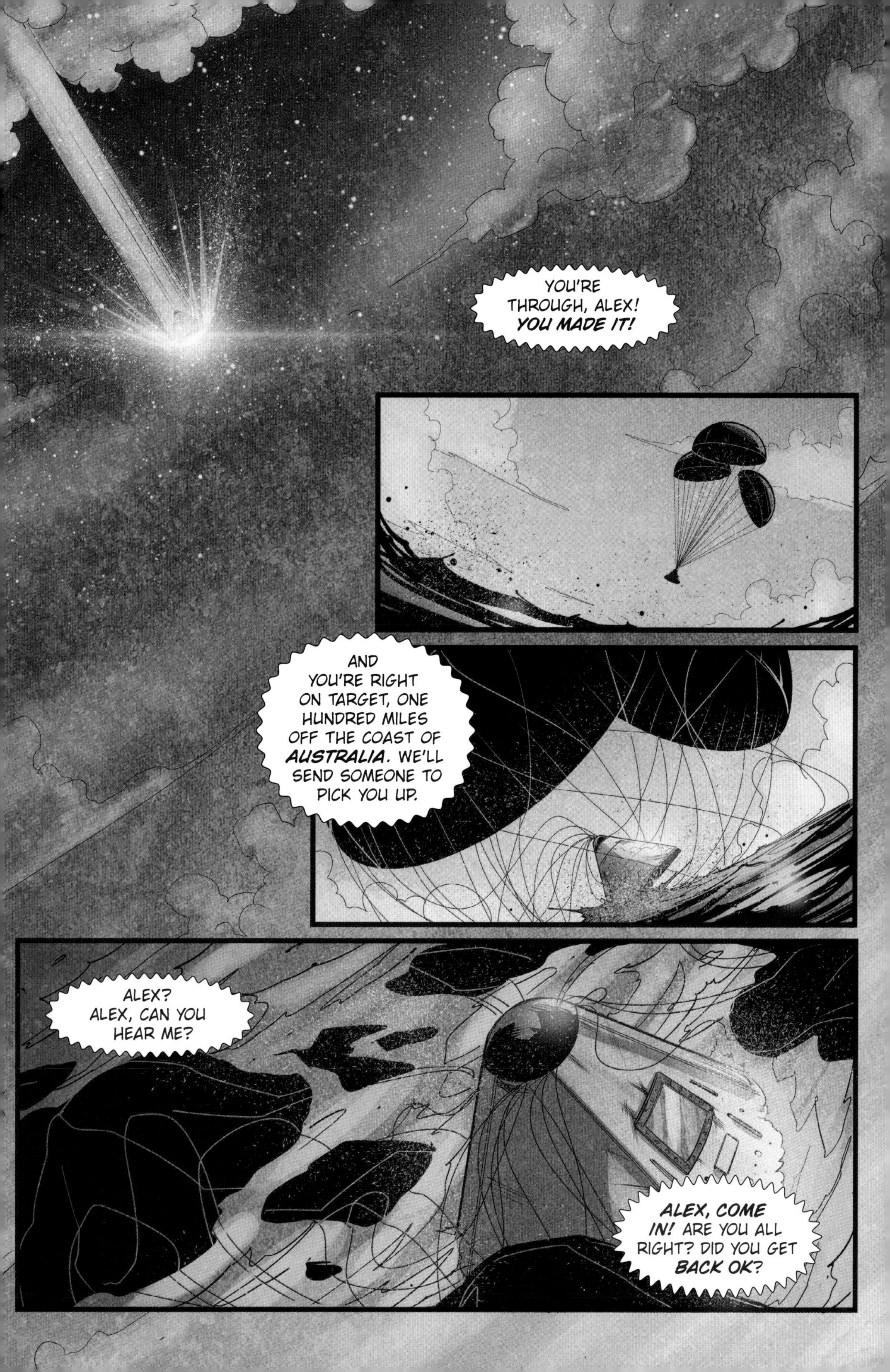
YOU'RE THROUGH, ALEX! ***YOU MADE IT!***
AND YOU'RE RIGHT ON TARGET, ONE HUNDRED MILES OFF THE COAST OF ***AUSTRALIA***. WE'LL SEND SOMEONE TO PICK YOU UP.
ALEX? ALEX, CAN YOU HEAR ME?
ALEX, COME IN! ARE YOU ALL RIGHT? DID YOU GET ***BACK OK***?

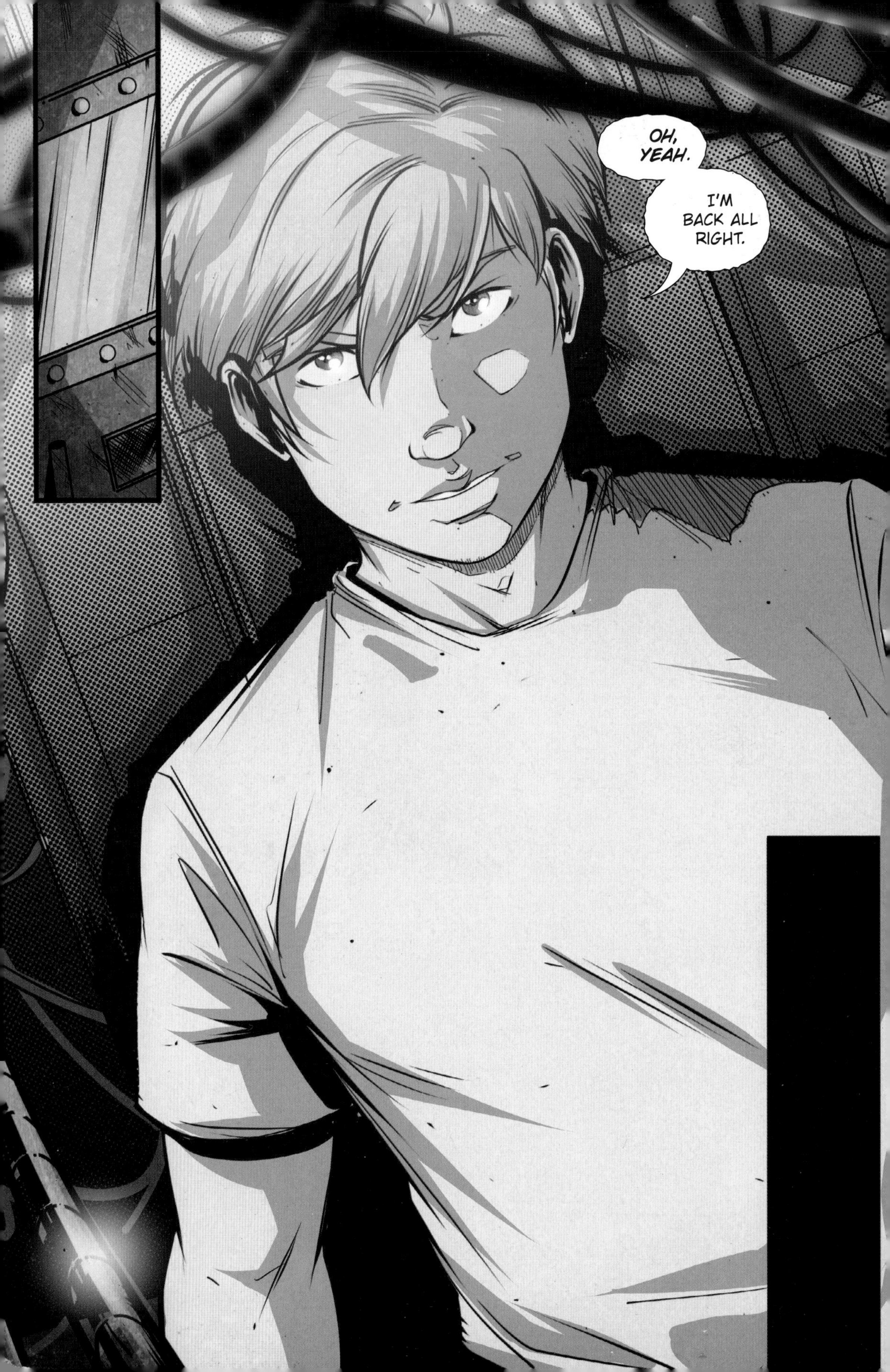
OH, YEAH.
I'M BACK ALL RIGHT.